ADRIFT

DOMINICA MALCOLM

SOLARWYRM PRESS

2013

Max Fuentes and Sean McCoy were created by Jeremiah Murphy, used with permission.
Read more about them at http://www.jrmhmurphy.com

Find Jaclyn Rousseau on Facebook:
http://www.facebook.com/JaclynRousseau

For more about the author see
http://dominica.malcolm.id.au

Cover photography:
Jaclyn on the beach, front © 2013 Jeremy Malcolm
New York skyline, front © 2009 Dominica Malcolm
Jaclyn on the beach, back © 2013 Jeremy Malcolm
Cover design by Dominica Malcolm,
with thanks to Lisa Emmanuel
Typeset in LyX by Dominica Malcolm

Published and produced by
Solarwyrm Press
http://www.solarwyrm.com

ISBN: 978-0-9805084-2-0

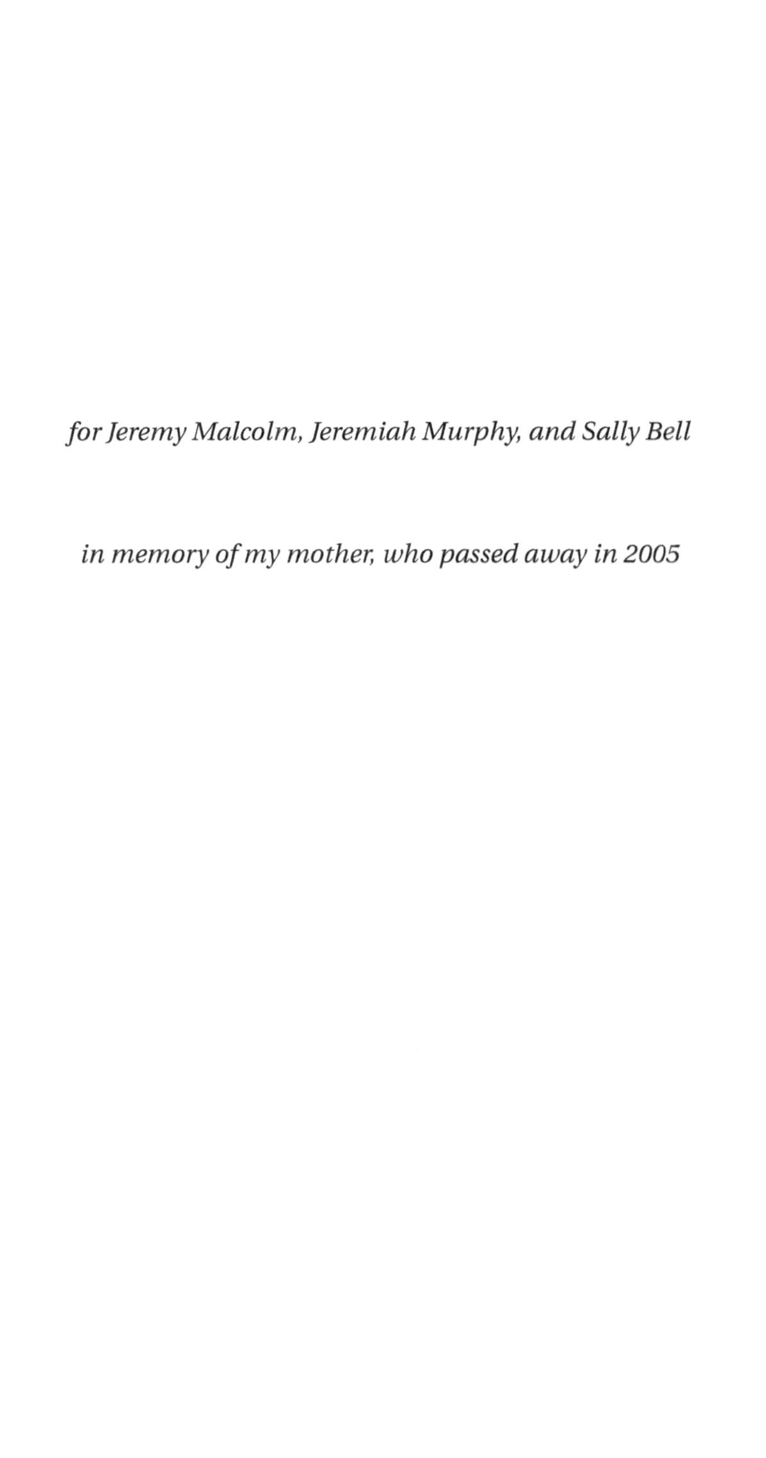

for Jeremy Malcolm, Jeremiah Murphy, and Sally Bell

in memory of my mother, who passed away in 2005

ONE

Alone in a stairwell, a young woman climbs the steps two at a time. Sweat drips down her chest, beneath the purple corset that adorns it. The fluorescent light causes her gold hoop earrings to shine. Adrenaline coursing through her veins, her eyes are focused upward. With a quick glance backwards, her brown hair and the ends of the scarf she wears around her head bounce over her shoulder and back again.

Reaching the top, the woman kicks a boot at the door to push her way through, and slams it shut behind her.

Now she finds herself in an open hallway lined with more doors, though these ones are numbered. She moves quickly to the closest one and pulls out a narrow item wrapped in a cloth from somewhere beneath her corset. Unwrapping it reveals a metal implement, which she uses to slip into the cracks between the door and its frame. After trying for a couple of minutes with no success, she slaps the door with her right hand, then turns her back to it and slumps to the floor.

Just minutes before, from the other side of the door, a man

yells, "I don't care how you do it, just get it done! I want it dealt with before I'm back on Monday."

He slams the phone down on the receiver and starts pacing his hotel room until he finds himself punching a pillow on the bed. Then he moves over to the window and looks out at the stunning blend of greens and blues that make up Carlisle Bay. A heavy sigh escapes his mouth when his gaze is drawn down to his tie, his business shirt, and slacks, then another escapes when his attention turns to the briefcase open on the desk.

That's when the man hears a noise coming from outside his room. Suspicious, he walks over and looks out the eye piece. He can't see anything at first, until he looks down and sees a woman slapping the wood. Pulling away, the man contemplates what to do. Did she just forget what room she was in? Deciding to help, he opens the door. The woman falls backwards into the room and looks up to see him looking down at her.

That's when the man gets his first good look at her, and her outfit. Cringing, he says, "Please don't tell me Jason hired me a stripper, or a hooker, or something."

As the woman stands and gives him a death stare, he clenches his teeth, realising his words hadn't just been inside his own head. Caught up in his own embarrassment, he barely notices when the woman walks in and closes the door. She doesn't acknowledge him any further, and instead crosses the room to the window to shut the curtains before turning around.

Frozen in place, the man is left to watch her take in her surroundings. He is unable to determine where her mind is at.

"What are you doing?" the man asks, hoping her answer will tell him whether or not he should be calling hotel security.

Ignoring his question, she peeks through the curtains, and finally asks. "What is this place?"

He looks at the woman strangely, not quite understanding the question. When he doesn't reply, she looks at him and raises her eyebrows at him to prompt an answer.

"A… hotel?" he says, wondering how she could even be in a hotel and not know where she is. The woman appears unfamiliar with this word, so he adds, "Somewhere people stay when they're from out of town," thinking that English must not be her first language. She does speak with an accent unfamiliar to him, though he'd guess it sounds similar to a mix of British and something European. That could also explain her funny clothes.

"Ahh, like an inn," the woman replies. "Yes, this is just what I need."

"You're from out of town?" he asks stupidly, and mentally kicks himself for saying so. Of course she is. Her accent isn't Barbadian.

"You could say that," she replies, not looking at him. Instead she looks out at the ocean again. When she turns her attention back to the man, finally giving him a once over, in particular noting his clothes, she adds, "My sincerest apologies. I am being uncouth. My name is Jaclyn, and you are?"

"Dick," he says automatically, still looking at her strangely. Jaclyn's bizarre choice of words gives him the courage to consider her harmless and add, "You know, you can get your own room here. This isn't really somewhere you can just… squat. I paid for this room.”

“I respect that. You have my gratitude,” Jaclyn says before moving over to the bed and laying down on it. “May I inquire as to what your profession is?”

“Are you seriously going to lay there and make idle chitchat with me?” Dick asks, walking toward her. When he reaches the end of the bed, he folds his arms and adds, “I should’ve left here half an hour ago and you’re holding me up.”

Jaclyn looks at Dick and raises an eyebrow.

“Okay, niceties it is,” he says, realising conforming to her requests is probably the easiest way to get rid of her and get on with his life. “And I have a feeling you’re going to prefer I describe my job than give you the title of my position because it isn’t particularly descriptive. Mostly I do high stress office work. Sometimes I go away on business, like now.”

Jaclyn is looking up at the ceiling when she asks, “Do you mean that you are an officer on a ship?”

Unfolding his arms to rest his hands on the edge of the bed, Dick leans in closer to Jaclyn. “Where are you from?”

The woman changes position, sitting on the side of the bed that faces the door. “Where I am from does not look at all like this.”

“Well, Barbados is a bit of a tourist hot spot,” Dick says. “I don’t think very many people live in a place like this.”

“Barbados?” Jaclyn asks, and idly moves a hand to rest atop her right thigh.

“Yeah?” Dick replies, feeling even more confused now. Maybe he could forgive her not knowing she’s in a hotel, but how could she not know what country she’s in?

That's when Dick notices something next to her hand. A gun, stashed in the sash wrapped around her waist. Though not a gun aficionado, Dick is still able to determine that it doesn't look anything like the ones in the movies he's seen. If nothing else, the handle is carved out of wood and looks like it has a skull fashioned into the bottom. He swallows hard as he considers the possibility of it being a functional weapon. Suddenly Jaclyn does not seem so harmless, but he's not in any position to call for hotel security.

Jaclyn interrupts Dick's thoughts by asking, "I believe the question you should be asking me is *when* am I from?"

"Huh?"

"What year is this?"

"Two-thousand and eleven," Dick says automatically, before realising the absurdity of the question.

Jaclyn bolts upright and runs out the door into the open hallway to look down at the street. Thinking this might be the best opportunity to lock her out of the room, Dick quickly follows her.

Unfortunately he doesn't reach the door in time, and Jaclyn barges past him again, asking herself, "Three hundred and fifty years?"

Jaclyn is back at the window before Dick can say, "Eh?"

There's a long silence before Jaclyn looks at Dick again. "When I awoke this morning, it was sixteen sixty-one."

"Wait a minute," Dick says, observing her with a skeptical eye, "let me get this straight... you're saying you're a time-traveller?"

"I am not sure what you mean by that," Jaclyn says. "All I know is what I was doing in Bridgetown this morning, before finding myself here."

"Are you having me on?" Dick asks. "Like, are you some actor who is out here for some fan convention and you're... what's the word? Method acting?"

"Preposterous! I have never heard of women actors. That is absurd."

"And travelling through time *isn't*?" Dick asks.

"Yes, I concede you may have a point there. Well, you could simply decide that I am insane... but what if I am not?"

"If you're telling the truth, then how exactly did you get here? A crack in time? Time machine?" He scoffs at the absurdity.

Jaclyn glances down. "I cannot tell you how I came to be here," she says, "but perhaps I have some other proof."

Her right hand moves toward her waist, reminding Dick of her gun. He hopes that isn't the proof she's talking about. Thankfully her hand reaches inside a pocket in her breeches instead of for the weapon. She pulls something out and walks over to Dick.

Holding the object up in the palm of her hand, Jaclyn asks, "Does this jewellery look like anything from your time?"

It's a necklace. The featured ornament is an Indian elephant carved out of black onyx, and covered with gold and diamonds. It looks relatively new, but the design doesn't look particularly modern. To Dick's mind, that doesn't mean anything. The fashion industry is always stealing ideas from different time periods.

"You must think I'm pretty thick," Dick says finally. "I don't know why you're trying to con me this way, but it's pretty obvious you stole that."

When Jaclyn glares at Dick, he bites his tongue, hating his ability to run off at the mouth around some women. And why did he forget that she could just shoot him in the head for making such an accusation?

Jaclyn returns the necklace to her pocket while keeping her eyes pinned on Dick's. "You should watch your mouth," she says. "I am not some common thief."

"No, I can tell that from your outfit," Dick replies, cursing himself again.

"My what?" she asks, and looks down. She pulls her pistol from her sash and waves it around the air. "Do you mean this?"

Dick quickly assesses his chances of escaping out the door before she can shoot him. If he were the violent type, his size alone would allow him to tackle her to the floor, but he doesn't seem to be able to muster the emotional strength to attempt that. He finds he can't even gather the strength to run away.

"Are you gonna kill me?"

"With my flintlock?" Jaclyn asks, moving the pistol point blank to his chest.

"Ye–Yes," Dick says with a gulp.

"I hardly think that would be necessary," she responds, returning the weapon to its place. "And it would be an impossible feat as I am out of gunpowder."

He's not sure he believes her, but tries to change tack. "Then why are you still here? What do you want from me?"

Jaclyn turns and heads back to the window, contemplating Dick's questions. Does she need him? Could she survive in this world on her own? If Dick is unwilling, could she find someone else?

"I am unfamiliar with your time," she finally says, gazing at him with her best innocent look. "I need a guide."

There is an awkward silence between them before Dick shakes his head. Not desiring to find someone else to repeat this process with, Jaclyn cocks her head to the side, and looks at him with disappointment. Her fingers take a lock of hair that falls over her corset, drawing his gaze to her chest. After all, it was a trick that worked well with the men from her own time.

"Grant me your day," she says. "That is all I desire; all I need in order to learn to survive here on my own. I will not ask for more."

Dick shakes himself out of the daze Jaclyn pulled him into, stands up, and walks over to the window beside her. Peeking through the curtains himself, Dick looks out at the water again. This woman has already kept him from his job for, he checks his watch, at least fifteen minutes. How much longer can he really get away with trying to humour her before they miss him at the office?

A melody announces itself on Dick's mobile, and he figures that answers that question. He pulls the phone from his pants pocket to answer it.

"Yeah?" Dick asks into the phone, distractedly since he's watching the curiosity build on Jaclyn's face.

"Where are you, Dick?" asks the voice on the other end.

This would be the point of decision, Dick supposes. He starts to wonder what would be the harm in taking just a day off from work just to see where this takes him. Her accent is appealing, and despite the strange clothes, she's not exactly bad on his eyes. Perhaps it is time for him to take a short break from his drab life.

"Dick?" the voice asks again, snapping Dick out of his thoughts.

Dick coughs into the phone, "I'm sorry, I think I'm coming down with something."

A day is all she wants. By the end of it, he should be able to figure out what's going on with this woman. She clearly needs help, even if it's just someone to take her to a mental institution. And when was the last time he took a sick day anyway?

"I'm gonna rest up. Can we postpone that meeting until tomorrow?" Dick adds.

"Can't promise anything," the voice says, "but I'll see what I can do."

Dick hangs up his phone and returns it to his pocket.

As soon as he looks up again, Jaclyn says, "And you think I might be insane. You talk to a little box that plays music."

Dick wonders if it's conceivable that there are any European countries that don't use mobile phones, still hanging onto the hope that that's the reason for some of her lack of understanding some of his vocabulary.

"You never told me where you were from," Dick says, ignoring her last remark. "And I mean originally. I don't care what century you say you're from. You're clearly not from Barbados."

"England," she says.

"You don't have an English accent."

"Neither do you."

"I wasn't the one claiming to be English."

"Will you help me despite my accent?" Jaclyn asks, changing the subject back to the the topic they were on prior to the phone interruption.

For a moment Dick wonders if he doesn't just need a mental health day to recover from this experience with Jaclyn after he manages to kick her out of his room.

Then Dick asks, "So you think I'm going to help you just because you're hot?"

She seems flustered. "It is true I am hot. What else would you expect when someone has had to run in this heat? Yet I do not see what that has to do with you helping me."

Dick shakes his head, thinking the theory that English isn't Jaclyn's first language still rings true. Surely a modern day English speaking lunatic would still understand what he intended.

Then suddenly he's asking himself, well, what if she isn't lying?

"I don't even get to enjoy the scenery when I travel for business," Dick says to himself, accidentally aloud. "I don't take time off work, let alone use it for some crazy far-fetched adventure."

"Please," Jaclyn says. "Perhaps I could also teach you a little of my time?"

Her insistence causes him to wonder whether it would be that bad of an idea to play along with this game for a little while. A day of make-believe adventure could be fun; it's not like he has any kids to play pretend with, and maybe this will help inspire him at work.

Dick turns his attention back to the attractive woman in a corset. The strange woman who does not quite understand him but wants him to spend time with her anyway. His eyes focus on Jaclyn's full lips. Without warning, he finds himself subconsciously removing his tie from around his neck and drops it to the ground.

"Okay," Dick says with a nod, pushing down the niggling fear. "I think… I want to do this."

Jaclyn moves in between Dick and the window, brushing her back against his body. He swallows nervously, wondering if she's suggesting she might offer more than a history lesson.

Though there's a height difference of about a foot, Dick gets a waft of her scent. It's not pretty, but if he's playing pretend, he can excuse it as a sign that she's not faking the time travel.

Presuming from the evidence presented to him that Jaclyn is most likely meant to be a pirate, he ponders the idea that pirates probably didn't wear perfume. Deodorant wouldn't have been invented yet and, heck, she had been running and worked up a fair amount of sweat.

Logically, Dick's mind reminds him that she's probably just some hippy who doesn't shower. Thinking about how attractive he finds her allows Dick to ignore the smell.

"Could I first ask a favour?" Jaclyn asks as she looks out at the ocean.

"What?" Dick asks back.

"Show me the beach? I need to feel the sand between my toes to be sure this is not a dream."

As Dick takes in her question, and her scent again, he decides that the saltwater would definitely be an improvement.

"Of course," Dick says, and leads Jaclyn to the door.

Throwing himself into her reality entirely, Dick opens the door, thinking that despite Jaclyn's profession, she is probably more accustomed to such chivalrous behaviour in her time, what with the whole feminist movement not having happened yet.

This really is not stereotypical Dick behaviour, but for some reason, Jaclyn fascinates him, and he wants to impress her. Jaclyn passes through the door without acknowledgement, and starts to casually walk back toward the stairwell. She's acting calmer now that it seems like no one has been following her.

"Wait," Dick says, just as Jaclyn puts her hand on the door to the stairwell. "We're on the sixth floor. Why would you use the stairs?"

Jaclyn is unsure how to respond, as this seems like such a nonsense question to her. "I may be fit, but I would break my bones if I jumped over that wall to get to the ground. What kind of person do you think I am?"

Dick chuckles to himself. "Well," he says, "you do seem adventurous, but I didn't think you were that skilled. I realise this three hundred and fifty year difference is probably going to take a while for us to get used to..." Dick pauses, not quite believing those words escaped his lips, and looks down the open hall in the opposite direction. "See those metal doors down there?" he asks Jaclyn.

She walks back to his side and looks in the same direction. "What odd looking doors," she says.

"Those doors open into a small, uh, I guess sort of a room, which can then move up and down to take you to different floors in a building," Dick explains. "It's called a lift, or an elevator, depending on what part of the world you're in."

"Which word do you use?" Jaclyn asks.

"It varies, but habitually, I use lift." Dick says, and begins to head in the direction of the lift doors.

"Why not elevator?" Jaclyn asks, following him.

"My mother is Australian. Lift is the word I heard most when I was a kid."

Dick presses the down button, and watching the red light come on around the button distracts Jaclyn from the conversation.

"Is this magic?" Jaclyn asks, running her finger over the light. "How does the light work without fire?"

The lift bell dings and the doors open. "Electricity," Dick says. "Probably a concept we should save for another time," he adds, stepping inside the lift.

Jaclyn joins Dick inside the lift. "Could I try?" she asks, watching his fingers move toward the buttons, just before he has the chance to press one.

"Uh, sure," he says. After a brief hesitation, he takes Jaclyn's right hand in his and guides it towards the button for the ground floor, then adds, "Press this one."

Dick lets go of Jaclyn's hand and she uses her index finger to press the button. She smiles to herself as she watches the 'G' light up, then turns her head around to look at him.

"It may not be magic, but it feels like it is," she says.

Dick smiles back at Jaclyn. He's still unsure what to make of the woman. For someone who looks like a pirate, she comes across as pretty innocent, a little curious, and just full of awe about the twenty-first century.

"Magic isn't real, though," says Dick.

"Perhaps you should believe in the unreal," Jaclyn suggests. "After all, had you not met me, would you have believed in meeting a person who was born centuries before you?"

Dick ponders this thought as the lift doors open in front of them.

"No, I suppose not," he says, not admitting to her that he still doesn't really believe her. He exits the lift behind Jaclyn and adds, "Even if I had thought it was possible, I'd certainly not have dreamed of meeting a *pirate*."

"I never said I was a pirate," Jaclyn says, turning on her heel. "It is a wonder you even believe it possible of a woman." She then raises an eyebrow at Dick and asks, "Why would you assume such a thing?"

"What else would you be, dressed like that, and carrying a flintlock?"

"So a woman cannot carry a pistol to defend herself? She must be a violent criminal?"

"You're just going to keep making me feel stupid about everything I say in front of you, aren't you?"

At this, Jaclyn cannot help but let a laugh escape. "My apologies," she says. "But why would you be willing to help me if you considered me a pirate?"

"Good question." Dick doesn't know how to answer it. Fear that she'd kill him if he didn't? That didn't seem to be it. "I don't know."

"I intrigue you," she answers for him, and brushes a hand across his cheek. "Do not be shy. I intrigue many men. It is why I must be able to defend myself."

"So you're not a pirate?"

Her only response is to smile at him, which doesn't answer his question at all.

"Fine, don't tell the person helping you anything about who you are."

"All in good time. I need to know I can trust you first. Now, the beach."

Dick lowers his head in a nod, then inches it to his left, toward the sea. "This way," he says.

Since Dick's hotel is right on the beach, it is only a matter of seconds before they hit the sand. Jaclyn immediately removes her boots and stockings, drops them, and plants her feet in the white sand, wiggling her toes in a way that allows the sand to trickle up between them.

Still not quite satisfied, Jaclyn runs into the sea, deep enough that the bottom of her breeches hit the water. Dick follows Jaclyn, albeit at a slower pace, refusing to remove his business shoes and not wanting to get them *too* dirty. After all, he'll be going back to work tomorrow. He stops walking when he reaches the wet sand, but far enough from the tide so his shoes don't get wet. Jaclyn, however, has another plan for Dick. She reaches down to the water, cupping it with both hands, and before Dick realises what she's doing, Jaclyn splashes the water into Dick's face.

Jaclyn cracks a smile when Dick scrunches up his face and wipes the water out of his eyes.

"Happy now?" Dick asks, slightly bothered but trying not to show it.

"Yes; you have my gratitude. I am not dreaming. This," Jaclyn indicates her surroundings, "and you are certainly real."

She leaves the water, and as she passes Dick, his brain returns to the theory that she's escaped from some mental institution and genuinely believes she's a woman from the seventeenth century. Or maybe she's a habitual sleepwalker and this is the sort of thing she dreams about—being someone who travels through time, only now her dreams have become a fake reality. Still, as Dick turns around and watches Jaclyn collect her boots and stockings, then move further up the shore, he can't help being intrigued and wanting to know more, the real truth.

As Jaclyn watches the sea, Dick follows her path and sits down beside her.

"I am going to have to teach you a lot about my world," Dick says, continuing to play along.

Jaclyn doesn't respond. She's too busy looking at a tanned woman walking past them, wearing a bikini. Her gaze follows the woman down the beach until she is well out of earshot.

"Women in your time do not wear much, do they?" Jaclyn asks.

Dick shakes his head with a smile, but he's not really paying attention to the woman in the bikini. His focus has returned to Jaclyn's full lips. Those distracting lips that somehow, for some reason that Dick is unable to determine, make Dick want to believe her. Jaclyn's still too busy staring at the woman in the bikini to notice Dick staring at her.

"So do you think you would be able to get back to your own time?" Dick asks, figuring he should make some conversation.

Jaclyn sighs as she turns her attention back to Dick. "This is the unfortunate part," she says. "If there was a door I passed through to be here, I do not know where it is. I did not notice when things began to look unfamiliar.”

“Why not?” Dick asks, wondering if he should continue to poke holes in the ridiculous notion of cracks in time.

“How much do you notice of your surroundings when you are trying to escape?”

Dick ponders the question, thinking back to the last time he ever had to worry about something like that. He was a senior in high school and had just toilet papered the quarterback, Randy’s entire front garden on the same day Randy started seeing Dick’s best friend at the time, Julie. She was the girl he’d been interested in since Freshman year and never had the guts to ask out on a date. Just as Dick had finished covering the final rose bush with toilet paper, Randy pulled into the drive in his pick-up, saw Dick, and reversed back out again. Dick had to leg it and to this day, he still has no idea how he managed to get home whilst being tailed by a douchebag in a car. The only positive thing that came out of that night was the heart to heart talk he had with his mother about feeling like he had missed his chance with Julie.

At this memory, Dick acknowledges to himself that Jaclyn does make a good point. So he changes tack, and somewhat sarcastically asks, “Okay, so, what next? Are you going to expect me to take you back to New York with me?”

“New York?” Jaclyn asks. “Where is that?”

Dick says, “Let me think what you might be familiar with… it’s near New England.”

“And you travel to *Barbados* for business?” Jaclyn asks in disbelief. “For how long do you stay here? Months?”

Dick shakes his head, “No. Usually just anywhere between a couple of days to about a week.”

Jaclyn raises her eyebrows at Dick, her disbelief obviously increasing, and says, "I would never have imagined men travelling for weeks across the sea simply for a couple of days of business, unless they are a sailor. Yet you did not suggest you were a ship's officer."

A laugh accidentally escapes Dick's lips when he opens his mouth to reply, but he quickly conceals it and says, "Actually, I fly."

Jaclyn giggles to herself at the thought, then lies back in the sand and closes her eyes. Speaking to herself, but loud enough for Dick to hear her, she says, "Never in my life have I imagined people flying." Then, in the straightest expression possible, she turns to Dick and asks, "Where are your wings? Did you copulate with faeries?"

Dick wonders if Jaclyn has finally blown her cover. He might be able to barely buy the time travel thing, but there's no way he could believe faeries actually existed. He stares directly into Jaclyn's eyes to determine how serious she is, until she cracks a smile.

"I jest," she says. "You do not have to worry about my sanity. I do not believe in faeries." She pauses to ponder Dick's words further, and then adds, "Were you being truthful with regards to flying?"

Dick nods. "Early last century, the Wright brothers invented a machine we now call a plane. Aircraft... er, they're vessels that can carry a lot of passengers through the air, travel long distances in a short period of time."

"You have certainly piqued my curiosity," Jaclyn says. "Flying may indeed be fascinating for me."

Dick isn't really sure what to make of this plan. Is he going to have to adopt her? He still doesn't even know if he can trust her. And how difficult would it be to get her a passport if he did choose to go along with it? Those things aren't exactly easy to forge. Then he wonders why he's even contemplating such ridiculous things. He'll leave the woman in Barbados when he leaves unless she already has a passport. He doesn't want to have to deal with that process. In the meantime, he at least needs to get to know her well enough to trust that she's not a wanted fugitive in the present, just looking for a way to skip out of Barbados.

Lying back in the sand next to Jaclyn, Dick looks up at the clear blue sky with her, and says, "Can I ask you something?"

"You may," Jaclyn responds.

"What will you miss most about where you're from, if you have to stay here?"

Her answer is immediate. "Nothing."

"Nothing?"

"Nothing."

"Care to elaborate?"

Silence falls between them as Jaclyn contemplates her answer. "I lost everything that meant anything to me." She rolls onto her side to face him and changes the subject by asking, "So when are you going to fly me to this 'New York'?" The confidence she exudes with the presumption means Dick can't tell whether she's asking because she genuinely believes he'll take her there, or if she just wants to avoid explaining things further.

"I thought you only needed me for the day?"

"That was before you told me people fly now. Do you think I can discover how to do that on my own?"

"The thing is," Dick says, "there's a lot of security

measures in place that you have to pass before you can fly. The most important of these is getting you a passport—passenger identification. It includes your picture, date of birth, place of birth... that sort of thing. I just don't know how to organise that for you."

"Why ever not? You must have a passport of your own."

"Sure, I know how to get a legitimate one, but I don't think we can go that route for you. They're not going to accept a passport that says you were born in sixteen thirty-one."

"Please. Sixteen thirty-four. Do not overestimate my year of birth. It causes me offence."

Dick smirks a little, and says to himself, "Some things never change." Then, louder and to Jaclyn, he says, "I'm sorry. Sixteen thirty-four. In any case, they're not easy to forge."

Jaclyn shakes her head. "You are speaking with one resourceful woman. Help me with the picture, and leave the rest to me. I shall find someone who can forge me a passport."

Whether Dick believes Jaclyn is actually capable of this or not, he doesn't let his thoughts show on his face. Instead, his mind is drawn to the idea of photographing her, capturing the image of this strange woman, and the possibilities of what he might do with the results.

"I can do that," Dick says. He stands back up in the sand and reaches down to Jaclyn, taking both of her hands in his and pulling her up, too. Then he adds, "But we need to go back to my room."

Inside the hotel room, Dick digs out a camera bag from his

suitcase. When he looks back up, he finds Jaclyn sitting comfortably with her legs crossed on the bed. Dick's eyes are again drawn to Jaclyn's lips, but he shakes his head out of the momentary trance so he can put the bag on the bed and remove a DSLR from it.

As Dick fiddles with some of the buttons on the camera, Jaclyn asks, "That thing can take an instant portrait of me?"

"Yeah," replies Dick, not looking up.

"This will be my first portrait. Not even once has an artist painted a picture of me," Jaclyn says with an air of sadness.

This draws Dick's attention away from the camera and back up to Jaclyn's face. He examines the way her hair falls over her bare shoulders, despite the scarf that is wrapped around her head. Her strong jawline, and the cute freckles that sprinkle the bridge of her nose. Then there's a hint of something in her blue eyes that overpowers him to pull in his gaze. He can't figure out what she is thinking, but he wishes he could.

Dick has to pry his eyes away from them to scan the rest of her body, and the way her clothes fit her form so perfectly without being tramp-like. He admires her hips and her shape, acknowledging to himself the appeal of a woman who isn't model-thin. After his eyes work their way down Jaclyn's thighs, knees, and the top of her calves where her breeches meet her skin, he notices the light hair that covers it. Jaclyn's still bare feet look tight and weather-worn, suggesting that she rarely wears shoes.

Realising he is taking a long time to respond, Dick is unable to meet Jaclyn's eyes again. Instead he focuses his attention back on the camera and replies, "An attractive woman like you deserves to be shown off. Why wouldn't someone paint you?"

"I am not royalty," Jaclyn smirks. "Perhaps if I were the captain of a ship," she adds, more seriously, "or had not departed London for a life in the West Indies, though it is hard to say if that might have helped."

At this point, Dick feels like his lack of historical knowledge is showing and thus, despite his wanting to ask her to explain further, he decides to change the topic back to something he is actually familiar with.

"You know, I always bring this camera with me on these trips, but I never use it," he says. Then, so as not to seem like he's changing the topic entirely, he adds, "But… even if I didn't need to do this for your passport, I would want to photograph you."

Jaclyn shifts her body so that she's kneeling now, and looks directly at Dick to ask, "Would you?"

Without missing a beat, but still focused on his camera, Dick says, "I would."

Crawling on her knees, Jaclyn moves toward Dick at the end of the bed. "No," she says, using an index finger to raise his chin so that his eyes meet hers. "I mean, will you?" She searches his eyes and considers that it might help to be a little more polite. "Please?"

The small gap between their faces flusters Dick. He blinks a couple of times, and swallows hard, before asking for clarification. "Take other photos?"

Jaclyn nods. He takes Jaclyn's wrist, moving her finger away from his chin and letting it drop to her side. It's just photos, Dick reminds himself; it's not like she's propositioning him. Why is he acting like this? He swallows again, trying not to think about how many years it's been since he even dated a woman, let alone slept with one. Is she flirting with him? He can't tell. Women don't flirt with him as far as he knows. Why would Jaclyn? Well… what if she is? Dick looks around the room, realising that—hey—they're essentially in a *bedroom*. What if the photography could lead to *sex*?

After swallowing again, Dick asks, "Here? Now?"

A shrug from Jaclyn causes Dick to think she's pretty casual about life and—well, maybe he's not wrong about that sex thing. Even if women in the past were more conservative in their private lives, that doesn't mean Jaclyn is.

He smiles at this train of thought until Jaclyn gets back off the bed and says, "I am rather famished right now. Could we find some food first?"

Dick shakes himself out of his fantasy. The mention of food causes his stomach to grumble so he promptly agrees.

He puts his camera down and finds the room service menu since this is the first time he's stayed in The Sky Hotel. Usually he ends up at the Frigatebird Towers. When he sees the prices, his eyes sort of bulge a bit. "If only room service was also covered by work," he says to himself.

Then Dick looks at Jaclyn and ponders whether she can get away with looking like that in public. The beach wasn't a big deal, but the street? A restaurant? And what will people think of him if he's with her? Surely they'll assume she's a hooker, too. Or maybe a gypsy. If only he had a crystal ball on him, he could bring that with them and pretend she's telling him his fortune.

In the end, Dick decides he doesn't care. "Put your boots back on," he says. "We're going out to eat."

When the pair reach the street, it's the first time Jaclyn truly notices her surroundings. She looks at the asphalt and comments, "The street is so… smooth. And black." Then she notices the cars driving past. "What is that?" she asks, pointing to a red sedan.

"Am I going to have to explain everything that has been invented since the seventeenth century to you?" Dick asks, a little frustrated. "Because you're starting to sound a little bit like *The Little Mermaid.*"

Jaclyn shifts her weight a little awkwardly. "Little mermaid?" she asks. "I thought you did not believe in such fantasy?"

"I don't. It's a story." Dick says, and adds with a bit of an eye-roll, "Which I, unfortunately, know more about than I'd like because I work for a toy manufacturer. Researching our competitors' products and so forth." When he realises that much of what he has just said has gone completely over Jaclyn's head, he adds, "Maybe I'll have to explain consumerism to you sometime, too."

They begin crossing over a bridge.

"If you do not wish to teach me the way of your world, I am more than willing to find someone who is," Jaclyn says, and for the first time Dick feels like she's genuinely giving him the chance to walk away from this bizarre situation she's landed him in. As he starts to process the idea of having an out, she adds, "I am sure I would also be able to find another photographer if I am not worth any more of your time."

Dick thinks back to the camera he never uses and the sex he never gets and how sticking around at least a little longer could solve at least one, maybe both of those problems. "Okay," he agrees, "but can you at least pretend that everything looks normal for now and ask me what things are in private?"

"I shall attempt your request," she replies, and adds a slow blink of her eyes, furthering her confirmation.

They only walk a few hundred metres along the wharf on the other side of the bridge before Jaclyn stops outside a store selling swimwear. She focuses immediately on a floral patterned bikini, picks it up off the rack, holds it to her body and looks at Dick with a giant smile on her face.

"What do you think?" she asks. "Should I not wear something that helps me look as others do when I leave the inn?"

Dick feels like his mouth has dropped so far, he must be a cartoon character. He just doesn't know what to say.

"And would it not be an appropriate consideration to look like a twenty-first century woman for your photos?" Jaclyn continues. Dick is still speechless, so Jaclyn prompts him further, "Well?"

"Sorry. Pinch me. I think I'm the one who's dreaming now," Dick manages to mumble.

Despite his request, he doesn't actually expect Jaclyn to follow through. And yet she does, with a hard pinch to his cheek—so hard that he wouldn't be surprised if it drew blood. He can't avoid letting out a high-pitched yelp. Dick rubs his cheek and then checks his hand for any sign of bleeding, but thankfully there is none.

"Okay, I'm not dreaming," Dick concludes. Then he kind of wishes that he wasn't the kind of man who has to be honest and admit, "I would love to photograph you in that, but I should probably mention that outfit is beachwear. You'll stand out less in what you're wearing now in most public places."

Jaclyn looks at the bikini in her hand, a somewhat defeated expression crosses her face. A disappointed "Oh" is all that escapes her lips. Then she looks up at Dick, and if he hadn't seen it for himself, he probably never would have believed that someone from the seventeenth century would have known how to attempt the "sad puppy dog" look, let alone perfect it. It reminds him a lot of the face his ex, Georgia, used to pull a few times when he tried to tell her no.

"Would you be ever so kind as to purchase it for me, despite the limited functionality?" Jaclyn asks, helping Dick to brush aside any further thoughts of Georgia. Quickly, Dick ticks the puppy dog look off as another point in favour of Jaclyn not being honest about the time travel.

As Dick considers Jaclyn's request, he is torn. On one hand, it occurs to him that the only woman who has shown any sort of interest in him in the last few years, is doing nothing more than trying to manipulate him. On the other hand, he loves the idea of seeing her in a bikini, and specifically her breasts having more of an impact than where they are, hidden beneath her corset.

He starts to wonder if this is the kind of scenario that would be so much easier to handle if he were a woman. Surely a woman would be much more decisive? Or would a woman feel just as charmed? A slight smirk crosses his face as he imagines Jaclyn charming a woman into bed with her. Then he shakes his head, wiping the image from his mind. It's enough of a fantasy to have *one* woman interested in him. He doesn't need to think about an unlikely threesome scenario. There's no way a strong-willed woman like Jaclyn would go for anything like that.

His mind focuses back on the image of Jaclyn in the bikini, and his imagination scans down her body. When it reaches her legs, his mind reminds him of the difference between women he's used to in the twenty-first century, and this one... "Yikes," he thinks, feeling a little grossed out at the thought of the hair on her thighs. This could be a sign that he should run from her manipulative eyes. He tries to think of the best way to avoid actually purchasing the bikini.

"Will you use them aside from for the photos?" Dick asks, amused that he sounds so much like his father did when he was ten. Especially considering he never wanted children. He never even knew he could lay on the condescending tone so thick.

There's a long pause while he hopes Jaclyn will walk away from him and leave him alone because there's no way she could possibly put up with being spoken to like a child. Yet, she doesn't walk, nor does she answer. Is this some other form of manipulation to get Dick to say something nicer? Because if so, it works.

He switches his tone to say something that sounds like he's not actually condescending, and just clarifying, like, "Would you like to go for a swim as well? I don't have any swimming trunks myself, but I could buy some at the same time so I can join you."

"Swimming trunks?" Jaclyn asks.

The curiosity causes Dick to wonder if Jaclyn is imagining an elephant, so he quickly scans the store and finds some board shorts. He speeds over to them and takes a pair off their rack, and holds them up to himself.

"That is what men wear in the sea?" Jaclyn asks, joining Dick at his side, still holding the bikini she wants.

"Well, it's that," Dick pulls some speedos off the rack above the shorts and holds them at his front, and adds with a slight smirk, "or these."

Jaclyn shudders, recoiling into herself. "I can swim alone," she says.

At this point, Dick wonders how Jaclyn managed to flip the tables on him. Wasn't he the one trying to avoid buying stuff? Wasn't he the one not wanting to see her hairy legs? So why is he the one feeling a little defeated?

After a moment's thought, it occurs to him that if this woman isn't interested in seeing him in swimwear, then chances are, she doesn't want to see him naked, either. Which means no sex. Well, it's not like his hand isn't used to that idea. Yet he wonders if that possibility is still salvageable. And what better way to a woman's heart than by buying her something?

At the very least, Dick thinks, if he can get her into a bikini, perhaps he can get her to have a bath, or a shower, and teach her how women of his century groom themselves. Any way to get rid of her stench. Plus, the bikini would make it less awkward than asking a woman who probably doesn't want to expose herself to strip naked for him to show her the way of the world.

Dick takes the bikini from Jaclyn's hands and says, "Wait outside."

As Jaclyn walks back to the front of the store, Dick takes the bikini, board shorts and speedos to the counter to pay for them. He doesn't want to risk being naked for the lesson either.

It's only a couple more blocks until Dick and Jaclyn reach the nearest food outlet—a KFC. As they enter the establishment, Dick begins to really notice everyone's eyes staring at Jaclyn.

"Go find somewhere to sit," Dick tells her, "I'll order us something."

Jaclyn raises an eyebrow, suggesting that this is not how she would expect things should be done, but as she had promised not to ask any questions to avoid drawing attention to herself, she does as she's told. Dick watches her walk with much confidence to a booth, clearly ignoring or not even noticing the way people are watching her.

"Going to a fancy dress party?" the cashier kid asks Dick when he reaches the counter.

"Something like that," Dick responds, primarily because it's easier than trying to offer any other explanation.

Once his order is served to him, Dick joins Jaclyn in the booth, sitting opposite her.

Jaclyn looks cautiously at the wrapped chicken burgers and fries, then takes a fry to examine it more closely.

"This is food?" she asks.

Dick frowns. It may not have been the closest or cheapest restaurant to his hotel, but he had chosen KFC for a specific reason.

"I wanted to get you something I damn well knew you couldn't have tried before," he says.

Then Dick unwraps a Zinger burger and uses both his hands to pass it to Jaclyn. She takes the burger tentatively.

With her first bite, she tries to pretend to enjoy the taste and texture, despite the strained expression on her face.

After Jaclyn swallows, she places the burger back down on the wrapper and says, "I think not that I can eat any more."

Too busy eating to notice Jaclyn's distaste, Dick responds, "Wow… I didn't expect one bite to fill you up. Don't you eat much?"

Jaclyn analyses Dick's face in an effort to determine his sanity, but doesn't reply.

While Dick continues to eat, Jaclyn asks, "What is the name of this establishment?" primarily because she wants to remember to avoid it in the future, should she be staying in Barbados long.

"KFC," Dick says, "It's a fast food chain. They're all over the world."

This knowledge informs Jaclyn that her question was even more pertinent, but she doesn't comment on that.

"If they had a McDonald's here, I'd have preferred to take you there."

Jaclyn reflects, "I had a captain by the name of McDonald for much of my time in the West Indies."

"Captain, you say?"

A slip of the tongue, Jaclyn realises. She hadn't meant to say anything that helped confirm Dick's piracy assumption. "Aye," she says, thinking she may as well answer in a way a sailor would.

"On what kind of ship?"

Jaclyn smirks at the obvious lack of a sailor's tongue. "It was not a ship," she says. "Captain McDonald's vessel was a brig."

"That's not what I meant," Dick says. "Women didn't

work much in your time, did they? So what were you doing with a captain?"

Side-stepping the truth no longer seems like an option, and Jaclyn refuses to lie to hide it. "Your assumption about me was correct. I was a pirate."

Dick puts his food down and furrows his brow. "Was, but not any more?"

"It is a little difficult to engage in piracy without a crew, is it not? Do you see me here with anyone else?"

Crossing his arms, Dick leans backwards, analysing Jaclyn again. "Would it kill you to give me a straight answer for once? That doesn't tell me if you were still engaging in piracy this morning, before you got here."

"Answering that is a little more complicated than you might think." It would require Jaclyn asking herself what makes a pirate.

Does she still consider herself one? Can someone really stop being a pirate? She has heard of some being given letters of marque, their charges dropped in favour of working for the Crown. Yet, there is little difference between their actions beyond a legal document.

Not having been issued such letters herself, she cannot make that claim. It is true that she no longer has a crew with which she sailed, even that morning, but after her years in the West Indies, piracy is in her blood now. She questions if it's even possible to run from that life. Could 350 years make that difference?

"I'll make it easier for you," Dick says, interrupting her thoughts. "If you hadn't travelled in time, would you still be part of a pirate crew?"

"No," she says simply.

"Then by your own admission, you're no longer a pirate." He picks up his burger and starts eating again.

Figuring that answer will make it easier for Dick to keep her around, she chooses not to argue with him. Whether she's a pirate or not should be up to her own mind, anyway, not someone she's just met.

Jaclyn decides to abruptly change their activity by asking, "Would it be possible for you to make those pictures of me now?"

Dick slowly wobbles his head from side to side, then nods tentatively. Jaclyn can sense nervousness, but she's not sure why.

He takes another couple of bites of his burger before depositing it on the table. Standing up to leave, Jaclyn doesn't even think to comment on Dick's lack of discarding the leftover food. They are both too distracted by thoughts of photography.

Back at the hotel, Dick retrieves the bikini he bought for Jaclyn from a plastic shopping bag. Before handing it to her, he says, "I'll give you some privacy while you change into this, but let me know if you need any help, okay?"

"Where?" Jaclyn asks, taking the bikini.

"Oh!" Dick laughs to himself for a moment, then shows her to the bathroom. "I suppose I should explain these things, too, huh?" he says, looking again at the astonishment on Jaclyn's face. "We have something called indoor plumbing now. Which means water is freely accessible in any building."

Dick turns on the tap for the sink to demonstrate, and takes Jaclyn's hand, placing it under the running water.

"I'm afraid I'm a little embarrassed about this, but, I should probably explain modern hygiene to you, too," Dick confesses, switching off the tap. "This water is for washing your hands after you use the toilet," he says, indicating the toilet. "Which is, uh, where we... how do I put this in terms I think you'll understand? I don't even know what you would've used back in your time."

He contemplates his phrasing while Jaclyn moves over to the toilet and lifts the lid to look inside.

"What is the water for?" she asks.

"Uh," he says, trying to speed himself up. "Well, it's where we do our business, you know, discard our human waste... urine, faeces... the water helps carry the waste out of the building."

"That is so much more convenient than a chamber pot," Jaclyn says. "How do you make it do that?"

Dick presses the flush button on the top of the cistern, and Jaclyn watches the old water disappear before new water refills the bowl.

"You have my gratitude," Jaclyn says. "Is that all?"

"Well, no," says Dick, "but I'm going to give you some privacy to change first before I say anything else."

Dick returns to the bedroom part of his room, closing the door behind him, and notices a light flashing on the room phone. He picks up the receiver and dials the number to listen to the messages he received while he was out with Jaclyn. Hearing the toilet flush distracts him from actually listening to the second message, though, and he chuckles to himself at the thought of Jaclyn's amazement when properly using the toilet for the first time.

He doesn't get to replay the message because Jaclyn

exits the bathroom, wearing the bikini bottoms just fine, but holding the top part to her chest. He looks lower, then, at her naked stomach, and notices a couple of scars that look like they could have come from sword fights. Then there's another that looks to be from a bullet wound. Nothing that looks terribly recent, though. The scars are the first real visible sign that allow him to really open his mind to the idea of Jaclyn being a legitimate time travelling pirate.

"This is more complicated than I might have expected," Jaclyn says. "And I wear corsets."

Dick returns the phone to the receiver and walks over to Jaclyn to help tie the strings behind her back and neck.

"It's been a long time since I've done anything like this," he says. Jaclyn doesn't respond, so he continues, "My ex-fiancée, Georgia, used to have me tie her bikini for her because she said it helped her feel close to me. It's a kind of intimacy I haven't had for about six years."

Jaclyn struggles with Dick's vocabulary. "What is an 'ex-fiancée'?" she asks.

"Ah," says Dick, "That just means I used to be engaged to marry her."

"So she was your betrothed?" Jaclyn turns around and asks him, "What became of her?"

"Long story short, she wanted children and I didn't, so I broke off the engagement."

Jaclyn looks interested in knowing more detail, but Dick is not remotely interested in sharing it right now. He doesn't think he should have to offer much about his life if she is not willing to do the same.

"Now," he says, injecting himself with a boost of confidence, "I'm going to teach you something else women do these days. It's something I think it important that we do before I take photos of you."

Back in the bathroom, Dick starts filling the tub, emptying the entire contents of the hotel supplied bath gel in the bottom, figuring more bubbles are better.

"Perhaps I should mention that I do know how to bathe," Jaclyn says as she watches the tub fill.

"How often do you?" Dick asks, curiously. He might be slowly becoming accustomed to her stench, but he still notices it.

"I confess, not as often as I might like to. It is not so easy when you live a life of piracy," Jaclyn admits.

"Well, anyway, that's not what I wanted to teach you," Dick adds. "You just have to promise to trust me, okay? I'm not going to try anything inappropriate. That's why I wanted you wearing that when we do this."

Jaclyn nods in agreement, and then she sits down on the lid of the toilet, watching the water flow from the tap. Meanwhile, Dick exits the bathroom to change into his board shorts for the occasion. When he returns, he switches off the tap, satisfied with the water level. He indicates with his hand for Jaclyn to step into the tub.

"Mmm," Jaclyn mumbles, delighted at the temperature of the water as she steps in, closing her eyes to enjoy it further as she lowers herself to sit.

Dick reaches into his toiletries bag and pulls out a disposable shaver. It's one marketed for men, but it's the only one he's got and he figures it's essentially the same thing. He then joins her in the bath on the opposite end, facing her and kneeling.

There are a few nerves before Dick starts, butterflies

in his stomach, but his shakes them out by stretching his arms. Then he reaches for Jaclyn's right leg with his hands, and she flinches, pulling it back.

"Please just trust me," Dick says. "I know what I'm doing. I used to do this for Georgia." Yet Dick still senses some apprehension on her part, so he changes tack. "Look, if I do anything you're not happy with, you can take my camera, sell it to a pawn broker… you'll probably get at least five hundred dollars for it."

Dick wonders if the fact inflation has developed at a rate of knots since Jaclyn's time makes it sound like his camera is worth a fortune. He doesn't think too hard about it, though, because Jaclyn then stretches her leg out for him again, placing it in his left hand.

With a deep breath, Dick rinses his shaver in the bathwater, and starts running it down the length of her thigh. Jaclyn watches each stroke intently as her hair begins to disappear.

"This is a common activity?" Jaclyn asks.

Dick nods, continuing the process of removing her hair. "Yeah, especially for models of swimwear. People tend to consider women unattractive if they go around unshaven."

"I have seen far more unsightly things than hair on women's legs."

"Such as?" he asks, noticing another sword scar on the outside of her thigh as he shaves over it, wondering if that's what she might be referring to.

"Pock scars covering one's face."

Dick laughs a little at the thought. "Yeah, that does sound pretty bad. At least you don't have those."

"There are things in life of more importance than

beauty," Jaclyn offers, clearly thinking of something in particular.

"Oh, sure there are, but much of the world today is obsessed with just that. Sometimes it seems like every second product marketed at women is meant to make them look or feel better about themselves." Dick finishes up Jaclyn's right leg and moves onto the left. "It's a load of horse shit, of course, but that's advertising."

"I am not sure I understand."

Dick pauses from the shaving while he figures out the best way to discuss this topic.

"Okay," he says. "Let me try to explain using the field I'm most familiar with..." Dick goes back to the shaving as he speaks. "I mentioned earlier that I work for a toy manufacturer. I'm not sure whether children had toys in your time, but what that essentially means is the company I work for makes things for children to play with, for mass consumption. We try to sell our toys to as many parents of children around the world as possible, and to do that, we employ advertising agencies.

"Now, while we try to come up with really good products, sometimes we just pull ideas out of our own asses and let the advertising make consumers think even the poor products are something they have to have.

"I can give you a specific example, too. About eight years ago, a colleague of mine came up with an idea to make a toy that was essentially badly scented play-dough that looked like a pile of poo, on the back of a remote control hermit crab. I have no idea how this ended up passing production approval, but it did. The product was atrocious, but it became a year-long fad because the advertising convinced kids that all their friends had one, and having one was the only way to be popular."

Dick finishes his explanation just as he finishes shaving. He looks up at Jaclyn, hoping she understands, since he can't think of any simpler way to explain such advertising.

There is a long pause while Jaclyn processes all of this information.

"So," Jaclyn says, "if I am to understand this correctly... advertising has convinced the world that only shaved women are attractive?"

Dick blinks a couple of times in disbelief. Not only has she understood, but has applied it to their present activity in a way he hadn't previously thought about it himself. He starts thinking about the morality of that, and how he has possibly been brainwashed his whole life about what constitutes beauty. Then he decides he doesn't really like that thought, and pushes it from his mind.

"Well," Dick says, "not all advertising is evil. I happen to agree with that one." He pauses to take hold of one of Jaclyn's hands then adds, "Here's why."

Dick places Jaclyn's hand on her leg and runs it down from the top of her thigh to her ankle.

"Smooth as silk," Jaclyn concedes.

"And besides, the toy designs I come up with are worth marketing. I'm not an idiot like the crab guy."

When Jaclyn doesn't respond, Dick figures she's heard enough about that. He watches her continue to feel her own legs for a few moments before saying anything else.

"So..." Dick says, "there's still one more thing to shave."

This time Dick exits the bath, being careful to hide the

erection that has formed beneath his shorts, and scoots Jaclyn forward so he can get in behind her. She jumps a little at the touch of his naked chest on her bare back. At least Dick hopes that's what she feels, because he's trying to be careful to avoid letting anything lower than his chest touch her.

Dick's cheek brushes past her hair and he notes how dry it feels. He raises his right hand to feel it better and notices how tangled and full of salt it is, even though he hadn't noticed that when she had been wearing the scarf over her head. Quickly glancing around the bathroom, Dick finds the hotel supplied shampoo and conditioner so he can do something about that, too.

"Do you still trust me?" Dick asks, talking in almost a whisper. It's not intended to sound sexy so much as it is his nerves getting the better of him.

Jaclyn clasps Dick's left fingers in hers and wraps his arm around her stomach. She closes her eyes and breathes in calmly. Dick is so moved by this gesture that he thinks she's melting in his arms as she breathes out.

"Yes," she says.

Dick uses his free hand to grab the bar of soap, wets it, and runs it up Jaclyn's right side until he reaches her armpit. Then he continues it up her arm, making sure she keeps it in the air. He notices a few more scars covering her arms, and quietly wonders to himself if the shirtless sleeves she was wearing earlier are worn primarily to hide the scars.

After lathering the soap further into her armpit, Dick gently runs the shaver over her hair. Jaclyn relaxes deeper into Dick's arms with each stroke.

"I have not been cared for like this for some time," Jaclyn confesses.

"No, I'd guess not," says Dick, "What with you being a pirate. Can't have much love out there on the seas."

"You may be surprised," Jaclyn replies.

Dick wants to ask her more, but he senses that it is too personal to question right now. He may have gained her physical trust, but emotionally, he knows she is still very closed off. Instead, he makes a mental note to inquire further when the time is right.

When Dick is silent too long, Jaclyn moves to compliment him, "I admire your gentleness."

"Thank you," says Dick. He may not be the best at relating to women, but he at least knows how to receive a compliment.

"You may guess that it is not what I am accustomed to from men."

"Mmm," Dick says with a nod, half-wondering if that grants points in his favour, but still thinking he doesn't really have a chance.

When Dick switches arms, Jaclyn automatically raises her left one for him.

"Not all men in this century are as chivalrous as this, either," Dick says softly, hoping to gain more favour.

"Then I have been fortunate to meet you before them."

They finish up the rest of the shaving in silence.

"Wait here," Dick says, quickly exiting the tub to grab the required hair products, and a mug, also provided by the hotel for the free tea and coffee service, before returning to his position behind Jaclyn. "I'm going to fix your hair, too," he adds.

"Now this is something I know I need," Jaclyn says with a giant grin resonating in her voice.

"Close your eyes," says Dick, and she does.

Dick uses the mug to pour water over her hair, and she moans a little as he runs his hand from the top of her forehead, backwards down her hair. In his mind, Dick tells his body to be quiet because the moaning isn't necessarily a sign he'll be getting any bedroom action out of this.

The moans continue to get a little stronger as the shampooing and conditioning processes take place, and when everything is rinsed off, Jaclyn runs her own hands through her hair.

"I cannot even recall the last time my hair has felt this smooth," she says.

"You're welcome," says Dick, even though it hadn't been a proper thank you.

Then Dick exits the bath first, grabbing a towel and holding it open for Jaclyn to step into before drying himself off.

Jaclyn smiles at Dick, which reminds him of her very yellow teeth. She really should see a dentist, but that is far too complex to organise at this particular juncture.

"Remember how I said we have different hygiene practices now?" Dick asks, rummaging through his toiletries bag again. "There's something else I forgot to mention."

He pulls out a fresh toothbrush, thanking his overzealous organisation trait that packs such items just in case of emergencies. A number of years earlier, Dick had accidentally dropped the only one he had in the toilet bowl and he didn't want to be stuck in that sort of situation without a toothbrush again. That was the first time he wondered if perhaps women were right to put the toilet seat down after using it. His focus is drawn back to the fresh toothbrush, and he squeezes toothpaste onto the bristles.

"Hold this," Dick says, handing Jaclyn the toothbrush. "I'm going to teach you how to clean your teeth."

Then Dick pulls out his own toothbrush, and demonstrates with toothpaste just how it's supposed to be done.

Jaclyn watches at first, then says, "That certainly explains why your teeth look better than my own."

It's not long before Jaclyn masters the craft of teeth-brushing. She becomes so skilled, in fact, that Dick thinks if she could go back to her time, she could make a living from teaching people how it's done. And selling her people toothbrushes and toothpaste. He suspects this is not, however, what she would want to do.

Jaclyn's gums bleed a lot whilst brushing, what with them never having been brushed before, which Dick notices is a little revolting when he watches. At least her teeth look a lot better after she spits the blood and toothpaste out.

With Jaclyn now clean, shaved, and smelling fresh, Dick is comfortable enough to return to the beach with her for their photography session.

A lot of Jaclyn's poses, kneeling on a towel on the sand and such, start out stilted. Dick tries to get her to lighten up a bit, but his lack of professional experience as a photographer means this actual skill eludes him.

Eventually Dick decides to go the way of advice for people who have trouble speaking in public.

"Imagine me naked," he says. "But not in a sexual way.

Imagine I'm the lone person on this beach who is naked, amongst hundreds of others, all gawking. These people aren't paying attention to you because all they see is me. It makes it easier to be yourself. Maybe you spot someone in the crowd who appeals to you and you want to attract their attention, make eye contact."

Jaclyn starts cracking up with laughter, which is not quite the response he wanted, but he snaps as many pictures as he can of her laughing.

As her laughter dies down, he says, "Okay, why don't you start walking into the sea?"

She does as he instructs, and he snaps more photos as she walks, admiring the sun beginning to set in the distance behind her.

When Jaclyn turns around, Dick says, "Okay, let's ignore the nudity now. Just imagine I'm someone you find attractive and you want to get my attention, but you can't use words because we don't speak the same language."

This time Jaclyn is much looser, perhaps because he had made her laugh. Whatever it is, she relaxes into Dick's advice, and he manages to capture plenty of photos with various camera settings.

When he's satisfied with the number, he calls Jaclyn back out of the sea, and they sit together on the towel. Putting the camera in playback mode, Dick previews the photos on the LCD screen, working backwards, showing them to Jaclyn.

"You have remarkable talent," Jaclyn says, admiring the pictures. "If I did not know otherwise, I would think this were your profession."

He may have been able to accept Jaclyn's earlier compliment, but this is a subject he does not agree with, so he finds it harder this time. He places his camera in his lap and says, "That's probably because you haven't seen professional photos. I honestly don't have the experience to do this professionally."

"I disagree," Jaclyn says. "You do not need experience when you have talent and interest. You are capable of doing whatever you believe you can."

"Sounds like something my mother would say," Dick says, and then the thought of his mother begins to choke him up, so he expels that thought from his mind.

It's easier for Dick to do when Jaclyn looks Dick directly in the eye, holds his gaze, and says, "I am serious." Then she looks away, at the sunset and adds, "I live it. You should know, there are very few female pirates."

"I can do anything?" Dick asks.

Jaclyn looks Dick in the eye again. "Anything," she says.

The eye contact is what Dick senses as encouragement to take things with Jaclyn further, so he leans in to kiss her. Unfortunately she places her hand on his lips before he gets the chance.

"That," she says, "would be the exception. My apologies, Dick. You may take me to New York, but the odds of you achieving that favour are incredibly low."

"Why?" Dick's response is automatic. He kicks himself every time he asks a question where he knows the answer will hurt him, but he still does it.

Jaclyn looks around the beach for a moment until she sets her eyes on an attractive, redheaded woman in a purple bikini.

"Because I am more attracted to her than I am you," she

says.

Dick follows Jaclyn's gaze and sighs. He agrees that the redhead is indeed attractive, but curses a little in his head that this woman he thought might be into him is actually a lesbian. Just another sign that he really has no idea how to read women.

Two

"Oh, Jack, will you let me tell you about this most incredible story Prue shared with me?" Katherine gushed, laying in the arms of her lover.

Jack was silent, but looked down at her hair, then traced an index finger along her hairline, combing it back behind Katherine's ear.

"Oh, dear, I fear it was too soon for me to mention her again," Katherine added, feeling the awkwardness of the silence. She swallowed, but after some silence continued on her course. "I apologise, Jack, though I confess this time the story she shared with me was not her own. As you know, she cannot pen her own words, and this was a piece I read from parchment." She paused, and hesitated somewhat, speaking softer when she added, "It was written by a faerie with whom she has become acquainted. A most beautifully crafted work. Oh, Jack, I would love to read it to you."

"A faerie?" Jack asked, ignoring Katherine's other words. "Kitty, you know there are no such things. Prudence is taking advantage of your credulity, inventing stories to capture your interest."

Katherine sighed. Jack knew she did not like when Jack invalidated her beliefs or her 'desire to see more than the educated men and women of South Britain would see', as Katherine often phrased it. Yet, Katherine had no evidence of the imaginary meeting reality herself, just stories from her former chambermaid. To Jack's mind, it made sense for the help to believe in such things, but it was not proper for someone of Katherine's status.

"I might also suggest you reconsider using her informal name in my company. It makes me feel as though you would rather like to invite her back to your bed," Jack added.

Katherine's eyes worked their way up Jack's curves until they met her gaze. "My lady, I love you so, yet I fear you will never break free of this jealous mould."

"She desires you, still," Jacqueline retorted, pulling away from Kitty's embrace. She left the bed, removing some of the bedclothes to wrap around her nakedness.

"That may be so, but I am with you, here, now. I choose not her."

Jacqueline wandered slowly to the window and looked out at the street from the second story, gazing at the horse-drawn carts. She quietly wondered to herself where the passengers and supplies were going, and whence they came.

"Darling Kitty, I hoped this to be true."

"Past tense, Jacqueline?" Kitty's tone was fearful now. She sat upright in the bed. "You are ending things with me?"

Jacqueline simply shook her head. She did not turn around, as she did not wish for Kitty to see her eyes glisten from the tears that were forming.

That evening, after Katherine departed, Jacqueline reflected on some of their history. They met at a party held by Jacqueline's parents, two years earlier when they were but fifteen. The purpose of the party had been to find Jacqueline a husband, and thus she entertained everyone that night by singing, accompanied by an organist.

After the first song break, a man took her hand and said, "You have a beautiful voice, and for that reason I have asked your father for your hand in marriage." He kissed her hand and added, "I am Francis Marshall, and it is a pleasure to make your acquaintance this evening."

Jacqueline sized him up and estimated that he was likely in his late twenties, or perhaps early thirties.

"Mr Marshall," Jacqueline said, giving him a shallow nod. "Did my father accept your proposal?"

He nodded and told her, "We are to marry in the new year, on your sixteenth birthday."

She smiled graciously at him, but excused herself to return to her music.

During the second song break, a girl of about her age walked up to her. She curtsied and said, "Good evening; I am Katherine Grayson, daughter of Lord Thomas Grayson, the writer."

Jacqueline smiled at the girl and asked, "I suppose Lord Grayson brought you to this event in the hope he would find you a husband, too?"

"Well, yes," said Katherine. "In truth, I cannot say I like the idea all that much. Men are such vile creatures, do you not think?"

Jacqueline shrugged. "I have not met too many in my lifetime. Mr Marshall seems pleasant enough."

"Who is Mr Marshall?"

With a quick look around the room to find him, Jacqueline pointed him out for Katherine to assess.

"Hmm," she said. "I may have to see for myself."

Jacqueline watched the girl walk over to Marshall and talk to him, but was interrupted by her organist playing again.

During the length of her engagement to Marshall, Katherine would write love letters and read them to her, trying to court Jacqueline herself. Jacqueline did not give in, as she had been promised to another, though she confessed that it had been very difficult. The romance of it all appealed to her more than the behaviour of her betrothed.

The wedding went ahead on her birthday in January. She could not help noticing the disappointment on Katherine's face once she had stated her vows, and looked into the crowd.

If her husband had not died of yellow fever only months later, she had feared that she may have had to be unfaithful to him. Katherine's attention did not disappear simply because she married.

When Jacqueline became a widow, she knew it unlikely that another man would want her, having already been used. Thus she did not feel like there was anything wrong with giving in to her desire, with Katherine's attention still strong. The night they first laid together, Jacqueline asked what it had been that kept her interest so long.

"You never told me to stop," Katherine said. "Yes, you said you could not be with me, but I could see in your eyes that you wanted it more than the life made for you. I see you dream but not know how to take action. I want to be the person who helps you become the woman you want to be."

Again, it felt romantic, having someone who truly wanted to know who she was.

Weeks after that first night, Katherine invited Jack to her own chamber. It was then that Jacqueline met Katherine's chambermaid, Prudence. The look in Prudence's eyes told her that she, too, loved Katherine.

"Why does she look at you so?" Jacqueline had asked Katherine when they were alone.

"We have been together," Katherine confessed. "It started when I was fourteen… but then I met you, and I put a stop to it all. I do not desire her as I desire you."

"You need a new chambermaid," Jacqueline insisted. "I do not like the thought of her being in your chamber."

Katherine accepted the terms, but refused to remove Prudence from her life completely, since they had been such good friends. It was only with some reluctance that Jacqueline agreed, knowing that it was not a good idea to control her lover too much, lest she leave her. That was the last thing she wanted.

Yet, here she was, reflecting on that decision and wondering if it really had been the best choice.

One morning, several days later, Kitty had made plans that did not include Jacqueline. Jacqueline often worried about Kitty during these absences, but on this occasion, decided to remove Kitty's pistol from its hiding place beneath her bed. She recalled the day when Kitty had taught her to use the thing, though at that moment, had no expectation of ever having to cock it, let alone fire the weapon. Indeed, she hoped she would not need to, even this day.

"My father did not want to see me suffer the fate of my mother," Jacqueline remembered Kitty had told her. "And now I want you to learn that which he taught me, so that you may also avoid that fate."

Jacqueline threw on some stockings, breeches, and other clothes she had removed from her brother, James's wardrobe, disguising herself so as to avoid recognition. Everything she needed for her outing was packed into a satchel. She set out upon her journey to the garden where she knew Katherine liked to venture for thoughts that inspired her writing. Prior to this moment, Jacqueline had refused to join Katherine in the garden, as Jacqueline's only introduction to it had been too much to bear a second time.

The garden was on privately owned property belonging to the Bromley estate, fenced off with stone walls, and the only easy passage into the garden was protected by two guards to prevent trespassers. Thus, Kitty had packed some rope in her satchel, and when they had arrived at one of the side walls, Kitty had tied one end into a noose, and thrown it over one of the merlons that decorated the top of the wall. Jacqueline recalled wondering what in God's name Kitty had intended to do next, but she need not have thought long, as Kitty was soon scaling the wall with the rope's assistance.

When Jacqueline approached the very merlon she had previously encountered, she struggled to believe she had once followed Kitty over the wall. It also looked to her that the wall had increased in height.

Jack took a deep breath. "You can do this," she said to herself.

At least this time she was wearing trousers. Then she pondered why Kitty had not thought to warn her what to wear that first visit.

Jacqueline consciously took another breath and drew open her satchel. She gathered the rope in her hands, and pulled one end into a noose, remembering how Katherine had done it.

Once over the wall, Jacqueline snuck along the perimeter, behind the oak trees, with a quickened pace. She slowed down when she began to hear voices, though this was not entirely unexpected. After all, the purpose of her venturing out here, outside her level of comfort, was entirely due to the desire to confirm her suspicions.

Upon arriving close enough to hear the voices audibly, Jacqueline sat herself down behind the trunk of one of the larger oaks, and listened.

"These clouds insist upon my penning my dreams."

Though Jacqueline had not yet seen to whom the voices belonged, she immediately recognised the first as Kitty's.

"Dreams are, of course, best when shared."

The second voice, Jacqueline was less sure about. In any case, it was not solely important who was speaking, but what might be said.

"I am wont to share them with you."

"Be mindful of your utterances, Kitty, lest Jacqueline discover your unfaithfulness."

"Oh, Prue. Jack could nay hurt a fly. I would chance the risk; she will do no harm."

If it had not been clear by that point, Jacqueline thanked those upon whom she was eavesdropping for their frankness. They so easily provided her with the evidence she had come for. She surveyed her options for the next move, and opened the satchel once more, removing Kitty's pistol from within. Jacqueline eyed the pistol and brandished it about in front of herself. Her body trembled.

"I will not falter," Jacqueline said to herself, standing.

Jacqueline calmed her nerves and dipped her head out from behind the oak, looking immediately at the two young women before her. They did not notice her, so she took in their positions. Kitty lay flat on her back, viewing the sky. Prudence sat with her arms hugged around her knees, watching Kitty. She was faced away from Jacqueline, which turned out to be of some luck, for they were only a few feet ahead of her.

Returning to her place behind the tree, she loaded the pistol with ball and gunpowder. The flint was already in place, so she cocked the weapon and stepped out. In three quick strides, Jacqueline held the weapon to Prudence's back and fired the trigger without a second thought. Blood spattered over Jack's hand and sleeve. Prudence fell limp to the grass before Katherine had time to notice what happened.

Jacqueline turned and fled the scene just as Katherine's shock wore off. Instinct overcame her and she was up and over the wall before Katherine even managed to stand. Only when she reached her home did Jacqueline find herself able to rest and process what had just transpired.

She sprawled herself out on the floor of James's room, wishing it had all been a terrible nightmare.

"I suppose now I shall ne'er see another opera," Jacqueline whispered to herself, imagining the worst. She shook her head and laughed. "Nay, that is the least of my worries."

Jacqueline held the pistol above her head, admiring the weapon. Soon there was a noise just outside the room and Jacqueline knew her brother was about to enter. She returned the pistol to her satchel just in time to meet James's gaze.

"Dreaming, dear sister?" James asked. "For whatever reason would you be dressed in my clothes?"

Jacqueline sat up and crossed her legs. Then she removed the cap from her head, allowing her long hair to flow down her back, and return her feminine appearance.

"Men do seem to have more opportunity to be merry," Jacqueline replied.

James strode over to Jacqueline's place on the rug, squatting to be closer to her eye level. He grabbed her right forearm and spoke, "Do not let me find you in these again."

As James loosened his grip, his fingers felt the material more carefully. He looked down, noticing where Prudence's blood had dried on the dark material.

"What is this?" he asked. Then his eyes trailed down to the white cuffs around her wrist, and he ran a finger along Jack's stained hand. "Is this blood?"

Jacqueline's lower lip trembled.

"Jack, what happened? Are you hurt?"

She slowly shook her head, but she did not know what to say. How could she lie to her brother after he found her like this?

"If it is not your blood, then whose is it?"

"James, I…" Jack's hand shook, despite James continuing to hold her forearm.

Brushing hair out of her face, her older brother prompted, "Who did you hurt?"

"It was Kitty, she…"

"You hurt Katherine?" James interrupted, eyes wide.

"Nay, I meant…" Jack started sobbing. "Kitty was… she was unfaithful to me."

James dropped his jaw. "What did you do?"

"I shot her lover."

"Is she dead?"

"I do not know. I believe so."

James grabbed her other arm. "Jack, you could be hanged for this." He pulled her up, and started pulling her toward the door. "We have to get you out of here."

Stopping him, Jack said, "Where am I to go, James?"

"France. You can go live with Mother and Father."

"And leave my Kitty?" More tears escaped her eyes. "They would not allow her to come."

Scratching his head, James asked, "Do you believe Katherine will remain with you after this?"

Jack paused for thought, trying to replay the scene of the murder in her head. "Why would she not? I do not think she recognised me."

"I know you love her and you do not wish to leave her, but," James said, showing concern on his face, "I still think France would be best. You cannot survive elsewhere on your own. What would you and Kitty do for money? We cannot have you whoring yourselves to men."

"James, please, I beg of you." She embraced him, and laid her head on his shoulder. "I cannot face them after what I did. There must be another way."

"Let me think." James cracked his knuckles, then pulled her in front of him so he could get a better look. "For now, I believe it would be wise for us to discard what you are wearing where no one will find them. I will leave you to undress, then take the clothes to the Thames for you, and sink them."

They stood together, and embraced again.

"Thank you, my dear brother. I do not know what I would do without you."

He smiled at her. "Then perhaps we can sail to New England together? I have already considered travelling to the New World, but had not yet enough desire to go."

"Let me see Kitty first. I will see what she desires."

Three days passed before Kitty returned to Jacqueline's bedchamber. Jacqueline paused from her hair combing, stood and turned to face Kitty as soon as she entered. Kitty was not dressed in her usual fashion. Rather, she was in trousers and a doublet. Even more oddly, she wore a cutlass strapped to a belt.

"Where have you been?" Jacqueline asked.

Katherine closed the distance between herself and Jacqueline and replied in a whisper, "Prudence is dead. I fear for our safety here; we may be targeted for our love."

Jacqueline was unsure how to respond, so she remained silent.

"Do you not understand? We have to leave London," Katherine insisted.

Wondering how she could be so fortunate to not even have to argue with Katherine about leaving, Jack thought she should probably give her a believable fight. "Kitty, have you lost your mind? We cannot just… leave. Perhaps you are just scared of what may come to pass once your father finds you a husband."

Katherine turned and collapsed onto the bed. She placed her hands over her face in an effort to prevent her tears from coming. Sensing that there was even more to the story, Jacqueline sat down on the bed beside Katherine and placed a hand on Katherine's knee. Her breathing deepened when she asked, "How much more must I know?"

"Father has promised me to Sir Adam Scott."

"When?"

"Three days past. At the same moment Prudence was murdered."

"Please pause to explain," Jacqueline said, breathing heavier than she ever had in her life. She was nervous because she did not know if this conversation would be possible without her betraying herself, but she hoped that Katherine would see it as her finally worrying about their safety. "Prudence was murdered?" she asked.

Katherine nodded. "Pistol to her back."

"How did you discover this?" Jacqueline asked, curious if Katherine would continue to lie to her about Prudence.

Tears began to form in Kitty's eyes and Jacqueline wondered whether it was because she was stalling for time because she had not come up with an explanation that didn't involve her meeting with Prudence.

"Prue's sister, Cynthia, came to see me." Though Jack knew Kitty had seen the death herself, she could see in Kitty's eyes that this was also true. "Two days past," she added. "She was so upset and she did not know who else to turn to."

"So she sought comfort in someone of a higher class than herself?" Jacqueline asked, almost fuming. "Is she not a girl of only ten? Could she not find comfort in her mother instead?"

"She knew we were friends."

"Friends?" she queried, bitterly. "Or former lovers?"

Katherine reached up to Jacqueline's shoulder and rested her hand there while remaining lain on the bed, "Do not be like that."

This line of questioning was bothering Jacqueline anyway, so she decided to change tack. "Kitty... this is important. You said she was murdered the moment your father promised you to Scott. Do you think that your father played a role in her death?"

Katherine shook her head. "Nay."

"How do you know?"

"Father did not know of my time with her, nor does he know of my relationship with you..." Katherine paused for a moment, assessing the question better. Then she sat up and looked Jacqueline straight in the eye. "However, your brother, he knows..." she trailed off, lost in thought.

"James does not disapprove of our relationship. And what would that have to do with Prudence?"

"He has become a Puritan, Jack. They surely would have taught him our love is wrong. He could be after us next. If not him, then his friends."

Jacqueline considered Katherine's words, realising that Kitty must have at the very least recognised the sombre colouring of James's fashion at the murder scene, if not also that the clothes belonged to him.

Though Katherine did not answer why James would murder Prudence, Jack thought that perhaps it was easier to just help Kitty believe the lie. But how? How could Jacqueline both fight for her brother as she would want to do in any other situation, and sully his name at the same time? Doing so meant she may never see him again, and after all he did for her, she wasn't sure how she could live with herself if she had to risk her relationship with him.

"I hope you are not inventing stories, as Prudence has done with you," Jacqueline decided to say, "just to convince me to leave my family and go with you. I am hesitant to suggest that you are doing this primarily to escape Scott." She pondered for a moment longer and then suggested, "Could we not move to Scotland with your cousin? Brice?"

"You think my father would not find me there?"

"Then what would you propose?"

"Departing from Europe entirely," Kitty said. "I will not see us in New England, though, as I hear even more Puritans are there."

Jacqueline's stomach sank. There went any chance she had to be near James, even if in secret, though it did explain why he had suggested they go there. Then Jack's eyes grew wide in terror at the only alternative she could think of. "I am not going to Africa."

"That is not my intention. We will see the New World, just not New England." Then Katherine admitted, "I have met with Sir Bromley—if you recall, it is his garden I like to go to sometimes—and after much consideration, as well as payment, he has agreed to give us passage to Barbados on one of his merchant vessels."

"Does he know you use his garden?" Jacqueline asked, confused as to how Katherine could have even approached him.

"Oh, my, yes. He caught me there some months ago and welcomed me back any time I wished, leaving my name with his guards. I believe it was because he knew my mother, and missed her so. Had I not shared this with you?"

Jacqueline shook her head.

"My apologies," said Katherine. "There is just one other thing," she added, standing up. "Bromley informs me that his sailors believe it is bad luck to carry a woman aboard their ship. Thus, he has suggested I dress as such," she indicated her fashion, "and pretend you are my wife, and I your husband."

Jacqueline opened her mouth wide in disbelief.

"I know this is not the proper life you expected of yourself, Jack, but..." Katherine started, and held out her hand to Jacqueline, "will you join me?"

In that moment, Jacqueline realised that this was probably the best way for her to get away with murder, and, indeed, remain with her love. She may be separated from her brother, but at least she could also prevent Kitty from enacting revenge on him this way.

After another moment's pause, Jacqueline accepted.

"Mr MacGregor," a voice said.

Katherine was sitting on the foredeck, watching the ship's bowsprit, while Jacqueline was huddled, asleep between her legs.

"Mr MacGregor," the voice said again, and then it coughed before repeating the name a third time.

The cough pulled Katherine out of her daze, and then she remembered she had taken her mother's maiden name, which was the final element of her disguise, after her gentleman's wig.

"Yes?" Katherine asked.

"We shall be pulling into port soon. You may wish to return to your cabin with your wife and make sure all your effects are in order."

"Very well," Katherine said with a nod. The man puttered about on the spot for a little while, until Katherine asked, "Is there anything else?"

"Well, I have been rather curious, whilst watching you these past weeks... if you do not mind me asking, what brought upon your decision to relocate to Barbados?"

Katherine contemplated the question for a moment as she decided how much truth she was willing to share. "I am a Royalist," she said finally, having heard enough discussion amongst the crew to know she would not be abhorred for this answer.

"This does not surprise. Barbados will welcome you graciously," he said, then he bowed his head and continued about his job.

Katherine roused Jacqueline from her sleep by kissing her on the cheek.

"Mmm?" Jacqueline asked, still half-asleep.

"We shall be in Barbados soon. Would you care to join me in our cabin one last time?"

These words were enough to wake Jacqueline completely. She smiled at her lover, took her hand, and led the way.

Once inside the small room, Jacqueline could no longer contain her excitement. "After four weeks on this wreck, I cannot believe I will finally be able to have you back, Kitty."

"Hush!" said Kitty, "Someone may hear you. Please continue to call me Thomas until we arrive."

"Even after all this time, I find it hard to call you by your father's name. I do so look forward to settling down with you."

Jacqueline kissed Kitty, but Kitty took her shoulders and pushed her away. "Listen," she said, "there is something I may have forgotten to mention about that."

A stunned expression crossed Jacqueline's face, and she took a step backwards. "What is with your failing to mention important things to me? Are you leaving me as soon as we arrive? After you brought me all this way?"

Katherine felt a little niggling guilt in her stomach, but maintained her composure. "No," she said, "it is nothing like that. You just need to be aware that, well, I have had to take a position with Bromley's company in order to maintain our standard of living. We can no longer rely on our families to survive."

"What exactly does that mean for us?"

"I will have to maintain this disguise in public, as per Bromley's request. However, in private, you have me as you desire me."

Jacqueline turned and looked out of the window, and Katherine joined her, noticing the island for the first time.

"You sincerely prefer to work, for us, than marry Scott and live a life of luxury, without hardship," Jacqueline noted.

"I do," Katherine confessed. "Besides, and this is not to say that my love for you did not factor into my decision, but have you seen Sir Adam Scott? He is always covered in disgusting pustules. Let us not mention that he is also at least twenty years my senior."

Jacqueline laughed at this, and wrapped her arms around Kitty. "Men are not terribly pleasant to look at even in the best of times."

They smiled together, and Jacqueline snuggled her head into Kitty's shoulder. Kitty reached a hand up to massage her lover's head, then they lowered themselves onto the floor, snuggling quietly until their arrival was announced.

THREE

Dick uses his key card to open the door, and steps in to an empty room. He walks over to the bed and falls onto it, dropping his briefcase onto the desk on his way.

With a heavy sigh, he wishes to himself, "Maybe yesterday was all just a really bizarre dream, and I wasted my day distracted."

Then he hears a noise at the door, causing him to sit up and stare at it as Jaclyn walks in wearing a long skirt and souvenir t-shirt.

"Ah," Dick says to himself, remembering he had collected a spare key for Jaclyn as he left for work that morning. Something clicks in his head and he asks, "How did you get those clothes?"

"Do not worry, I paid for them," she says.

Dick is confused, but quickly comes to a possible explanation. He checks his wallet and finds it devoid of bank notes. Sighing, he says, "I know I showed you where to shop last night, but I didn't mean for you to steal from me in order to purchase things yourself. I just wanted you to look so you could show me what you wanted, making the whole experience quicker for me when we went together."

He sighs again, thinking about his empty wallet. "I just wanted to be able to decide if something was reasonably priced."

She moves in closer and sits down next to him. Placing a hand on his leg, she says, "Do not worry, I will find some way to repay my debt to you."

"How?"

Jaclyn shakes her head, "I confess, I do not yet know."

"Hmm," Dick thinks aloud, but rather than contemplate what the distant future holds for Jaclyn, he considers the immediate future. "Well, it's kinda dinner time, and I'm feeling hungry. Shall we go grab a bite to eat?"

"Only if you promise that we do not return to KFC."

"Deal," Dick agrees, feeling like he could do with something more substantial than fast food himself.

As they walk out onto the footpath, Dick says, "I've been thinking about you a lot today. There's just so much I don't know."

"And to what conclusions did you come?"

"Well, I noticed your scars yesterday, when we were in the bath together," Dick confesses. "They didn't look surgical."

"Piracy is a dangerous profession."

"That was my conclusion, and the evidence I needed to believe you, I guess." Dick shrugs and adds, "But I don't want to make further assumptions. Can I ask you questions about yourself?"

"Perhaps. What do you have on your mind?"

"Well, for example, I would love to know how you wound up here," he says. "It's just so… fascinating, isn't it? I mean, getting to meet a real life pirate, that's one thing, but one from another time? It's crazy to wrap your head around."

They pass a book store and Jaclyn glances through the window as they do.

"It is the thing of stories, perhaps," Jaclyn says. "Though not stories of my time. None printed that I am aware of. Kitty used to talk of it. She wanted to go back into the past to meet Julius Caesar, though I am not sure why. He destroyed the pirates who took him captive."

"Who's Kitty?"

It is a moment before Jaclyn is able to answer.

"She was the woman whom I loved more than anything. I forgot who I was for her."

Sensing a possible tragic end, Dick asks with trepidation, "What happened to her?"

"Dick, I know I have shared much with you, but that is one subject I am not yet ready to discuss. Perhaps in time."

"I suppose that's fair," Dick admits, so he changes the subject back to what he wants to know. "Will you tell me about the day you were having before you got here?"

"You want to know how I came to take that jewellery? Have you not learned of pirates in your history books?"

"Well, I didn't study history, so no. I've seen movies but I'm guessing they're not a hundred percent historically accurate," Dick says. "Given that you don't talk like they do."

"What is a 'movie'?" Jaclyn asks.

"Oh!" he says, realising she wouldn't be familiar with them. "It's like photos, sort of, except that they're captured, moving pictures of people, and there's sound... it's like a story that you watch instead of read."

"And there are moving picture stories of pirates?"

Dick nods.

"How do they talk?"

"Oh, they're all like, 'Ahoy, me hearties,' and 'shiver me timbers' and 'Ye be a right fool,' and stuff like that," Dick says, making a mockery of the few pirate films he has actually seen.

"I was not always a pirate," Jaclyn says. "Perhaps I talk as I do because I did not think you would understand me otherwise."

"Intriguing," Dick says with some interest, "You're like a seventeenth century master of disguise."

"It was not entirely a choice I wanted for myself, but you build upon what you are given."

"I'm sorry," he says. "I would still like to know about what you were doing," Dick adds, trying to get the conversation back on track again.

"Ah," she says, and clears her throat before beginning her story. "After some weeks of plotting and discovering the secrets of one Sir Nathaniel Bromley's home, an hour before dawn, I sneaked in and lifted his wife's jewellery from their safe." She pauses for a moment as she lets the memory flow in her mind. "Unfortunately I became too cocky and thought I could deviate from the plan to find other items in their bedroom. Bromley awoke from his slumber and called upon his guards the moment he saw me. I had to make haste my escape. I believe the guards were on my tail until moments before I passed into your time."

"You must be quick on your feet," Dick says.

"It is of utmost importance when one lives and serves with pirates," Jaclyn says with a smile. "Not only in the body, but also the mind."

Dick simply stares at Jaclyn in awe. "There is so much I want to learn about you."

"If you take me with you to New York, then you can."

"We've talked about this," Dick says, turning his attention back to the path in front of him. "I can't help you get a passport."

"Which is where my skills come in. I found some men who can. They said it would be ready on Friday. How many days away is that?"

"Two," he says, then moves in front of Jaclyn and stops her in her tracks. "How did you *do* that? And how are you paying for it?"

"I offered them my jewellery."

Dick shrugs. "I suppose that makes sense," he says, "but that doesn't explain how you managed to find them in the first place."

"There are some things that are better if you do not have all the details."

He shakes his head, "Yeah, well, I'll believe it when I see it."

She pushes past him and changes the subject. "I found a place I would rather like to dine this evening, if you do not mind. It is this way."

Once seated in an Italian restaurant, a waiter brings the pair some menus to peruse. Dick hands one to Jaclyn and says, "Choose a drink from this menu, first. That tends to be the etiquette in places like this."

Jaclyn looks at the menu, but it's all words, no pictures.

"I do not understand this menu," she says.

"Why not? You speak English... that's just the wine list," Dick responds. "Oh... maybe you didn't have so much variety in your time?"

"That is not the problem," she says, and she folds in on herself a little. "I cannot read," she confesses in a whisper. "There are few words I can recognise by sight, but that is all."

"Never mind... I'll read it to you and you can just stop me once you hear something you like the sound of."

Jaclyn graciously accepts, and after being read the beverage list, chooses a hot chocolate.

The waiter returns to take their drink order, then gives them more time for their meal selections. Jaclyn finds herself grateful that the food menu at least includes photographs. She points to one of the pictures that looks particularly appetising, showing it to Dick so that he may order for them both the next time the waiter makes his rounds.

"I have never been to New England," Jaclyn says, making conversation. "Is it still populated by Puritans?"

Dick chuckles a little and then says, "No, I'd say the states that make up New England are a lot more liberal in their thoughts than the Puritans were."

"States?"

"Sorry, I guess I'm going to have to explain my country better to you..." Dick starts, but is interrupted by the waiter.

"May I take your order?"

"Yes, thank you," Dick says. "I'll have the Alfredo linguine, and my companion here will have the chicken lasagne."

Dick returns the menus to the waiter, who then departs

from their table.

"Where was I?"

"Your country?"

"Oh, yes," says Dick. "Right, well… New England and New York make up just a small portion of the country we now call the United States of America. New England is just the northern most point of the country and… do you know Florida?"

Jaclyn nods.

"Right… Florida is the southern most point on the east coast, and the country spans west out as far as the Pacific Ocean."

There's a moment of silence as Jaclyn considers this news. "They are no longer colonies owned by the King?" she asks. "Though I confess I am not surprised the Spaniards were overthrown in Florida, considering how my people took Jamaica from them."

"Florida used to belong to Spain?" Dick asks, not bothering to conceal his ignorance. "I'm not sure how that came about. Maybe we'll have to introduce you to someone who can tell you these things. Or I could Google it. Wikipedia should have the answers."

Dick takes out his phone and starts tapping away at it, all while Jaclyn watches him incredulously.

"Aha!" he says finally. "Looks like we made a deal with Spain that gave us Florida after we became a country."

"Your magic box can inform you of such events?"

"This is where technology has taken us," Dick says with a shrug.

Their drinks arrive, and Jaclyn takes a sip of hers.

"Hmm," she says with some confusion.

"What's wrong?"

"This is much sweeter than I am familiar with."

"Do you still like it?"

"It may take some time to enjoy." Jaclyn looks at the little bubbles popping about in Dick's dark drink and asks, "What are you drinking?"

"Coke," he says. "Would you like to try some?"

Jaclyn nods and Dick hands her his glass. She takes the straw out, not realising what it's for, and takes a big gulp. Dick watches her face become confused.

"It is... interesting. I am not sure what I think about the taste, but maybe with time I could come to enjoy it. For now, my chocolate is fine." She turns her attention back to the phone, since Dick is fiddling with it again. "What else does that box do?"

"You might've asked an easier question with, 'what *doesn't* it do?' Well, I guess its main function is communication over long distances in a variety of methods. So where in your time the only way to do that would have been to mail someone a letter, these days you can send someone a letter instantly. Or talk to them through a phone like this, no matter where they are in the world." He pauses momentarily and starts tapping at it some more, then says, "Look," and shows the screen to her, "it even plays movies."

A video of a cat's crazy antics begins to play.

"I love YouTube," Dick says.

"Is this considered entertainment?" Jaclyn asks.

Dick sits back in his seat, taking the phone with him and putting it away.

"For many," he says dryly, "though I suppose you wouldn't get it, would you? What did you do for entertainment? Did you even have time for any?”

“There were many dull days on the sea; we had music, played cards, drank…”

“But didn’t keep cats around to laugh at,” Dick finishes for her.

“No. Do you?”

Dick shakes his head. “I travel too much to keep pets. I grew up with a pair of them, though.”

The food arrives, and, now presented with the option to eat her food, Jaclyn notices the cutlery at her place.

“What odd cutlery. Is this a fork?” she asks, picking it up.

“Yes,” Dick says, looking at her strangely.

“How odd. I am familiar with them only having two tines; at least that was the case the last time I used one.”

Then Jaclyn stares rather blankly at the silverware until Dick pulls his chair around to her side of the table and decides to demonstrate how to use her knife and fork.

“Thank you,” she says, and picks up the method for her own use rather quickly, slicing the lasagne with her knife, putting it down, and then using the fork with the same hand.

Dick returns to his side of the table, and Jaclyn watches him using his fork in a completely different way to her, twirling the pasta around the tines before shoving quite a lot into his mouth.

“Did you grab anything to eat earlier?” Dick asks.

“Yes,” she says, swallowing her food. “I found apples at the shop you showed to me.”

“I can’t get past how observant you are; how you figure out how to do things just by watching others do them.”

Jaclyn shrugs. "It is how I learned to wield a sword. Kitty taught me. She was incredible with her skills, and still to this day I do not know how she had the strength to overpower any man she encountered."

"Sounds like quite a woman."

"She was."

When Dick returns to his room Friday evening, he finds Jaclyn laying on the bed, flicking through a small red book in her hand.

"What's that?" he asks.

She shows him the lion and unicorn emblem on the front cover.

"European Union, United Kingdom of Great Britain and Northern Ireland passport," Dick reads. "Wow, I guess you did know what you were doing."

"So you will take me with you?"

"Listen… airfares are kind of expensive, and I barely know you. Do I even trust that you'll pay me back?" Dick lightly shakes his head, and shows her a serious expression. "I don't think you need me—look at what you've accomplished on your own already!"

"Where will I go, Dick? When you leave, I lose my place to sleep. Have you not appreciated my company?"

There's a sadness in her eyes so different from the puppy dog look she gave him the day they met. Dick considers that maybe she actually sees him as a friend, the only friend she has in this world, and would miss him if he leaves her here.

He finds himself wishing he had a friend he could call for advice, but how close is he to any of them, really? Jason makes jokes about his perpetual bachelorhood with zero prospects. Aiden only ever talks about himself. Sue is at least friendly enough, but they still aren't terribly close. He can't even remember the last time he saw anyone else.

As for his parents? Forget it, they have too much else to worry about right now.

Struck by the realisation of how lonely he is living in a city of eight million people, he can't help thinking that spending three days in Jaclyn's company has actually meant she has seen him more than the majority of his friends have seen him in the last six months. Jason is the only exception because they work together.

He may not know her that well yet, but if he invites her to live with him, maybe it would be an opportunity for him to actually make a new friend. Dick then acknowledges how much easier it has been to talk to her since she revealed her sexuality to him, and that it is a good foundation for forming a friendship if he's not worrying about whether or not he will have the chance to sleep with her.

"If I take you with me," he says, "we're going to have to set up some ground rules. For example, you can't go stealing my money to buy things yourself."

"The consequence of which would be marooning me?"

"What?" Dick asks. "No. Why would you think that?"

"It was the consequence of such actions according to the pirate code I agreed upon."

"Oh."

"I promised I would repay my debt to you. How am I to do this if you leave me here?" Jaclyn may look sincere as she says this, but Dick isn't so sure.

"How will you even if I do take you with me? You're going to have a bigger debt to me if I pay for this flight, you know. And I'm not going to allow you to just rob people to pay for your expenses."

"You want me to be an honest woman?"

"I want you to be morally responsible. America is in an economic crisis right now. Lots of people losing jobs. I don't even know if you'd be able to find work," Dick says. "But that's all the more reason why I don't want you stealing from anyone. You don't know their situation, but chances are, they need everything they've got. Robbing people could be the difference between them having somewhere to live and being homeless."

"If you leave me here, I, too, will be homeless."

Dick cannot argue with that logic. How can he lecture this woman on being morally responsible if he is not also willing to be the same?

"Okay, fine. Consider yourself lucky I'm going home tomorrow. Let me get my computer out and see if I can't book you on the same flight," he says, fiddling with his laptop bag. "Can I have a look at your passport? I'll need the details inside when I'm making the booking."

Jaclyn gets up off the bed and hands her passport to him. As Dick is waiting for his laptop to start up, he opens her passport to the photo page and reads through the information.

"Born January twenty-seventh, nineteen eighty-four, huh?"

"That is my real birthday," she says.

"I didn't know you could make your own customisations with these things, but what do I know about passport forgeries?" Dick muses. "Were you also born in Bristol?"

"Well, no."

"I can't believe you used your own name on this. Oh, well, I suppose they're not going to track you back to the seventeenth century."

Once the computer is on, Dick puts the passport down on the desk next to it, and connects to the Internet.

"Bring me your things," Dick says to Jaclyn as he's packing his suitcase the next morning.

She dumps her pirate clothes down on the bed, along with her flintlock, some new clothes she had bought with Dick's money, and some jewellery—including the elephant necklace she showed him the day they met.

"I thought you paid for your passport with this?" Dick asks.

"Dick, I did not show you all the jewellery I took, nor did they need it all as payment," Jaclyn says, though he's not entirely sure if he believes her.

Despite his doubts, Dick puts the jewellery and new clothes in with his things, then says, "I can't pack your gun. They won't allow it through airport security."

"Why?" Jaclyn asks.

"You just aren't allowed to take guns to an airport. They want to avoid crazy people shooting up the place."

"But I cannot even fire my weapon," she says with some disappointment.

"Doesn't matter."

"Then what will we do with it?"

Dick shrugs. "Maybe we can bury it like you would've done with your treasure."

"Is this another of your ideas from one of your pirate

movies?"

"You didn't bury your treasure?"

"No. Do you not think that if I had, I would be out there digging it up and paying off my debt?"

"Jesus, these writers really make a lot of shit up for their stories."

"That does not mean it is a bad idea to bury my pistol," Jaclyn says, snapping it up. She heads for the door. "Do not leave without me."

It's too early in the morning for there to be very many tourists on the beach when Jaclyn finds herself there. The flintlock is tucked into the back of her jeans, with the handle hidden underneath her t-shirt. She walks barefoot along the sand, the tide occasionally hitting her feet.

A few hundred metres away from the hotel, she takes out her pistol and holds it in front of her, taking in every detail for her memory.

Jaclyn closes her eyes and is transported back in time, seeing Kitty's face as she hands her a pair of matching pistols—one of which she is holding now.

"These are for you," Kitty says to her, "for luck. They have served me well."

A tear rolls down Jaclyn's cheek as she remembers that moment.

"I apologise, my love," Jaclyn says. "This is the last thing I have of yours, and yet I cannot save it."

She opens her eyes and throws her pistol as far as she can, into the sea.

"May no one else retrieve it," she adds, and sits down in the sand. It doesn't matter that it gets her jeans a little wet, she just needs to be able to look at the Caribbean water one last time before leaving.

Ten years, she thinks. That's how long she's been in the West Indies. Even when she had an opportunity to leave it all behind before, she chose to remain. Despite the fact she knew she was probably headed for the gallows, she never wanted to leave. As long as she had her crew, she was content.

"Where are they now?" she wonders. "I should not have left them in Port Royal. Maybe then I would not have found myself here."

For all that Dick has told her about New York, and all the insistence she has shown him, she cannot help feeling a little nervous at the thought of leaving behind the last thing that is even remotely familiar to her world.

Then she remembers Dick still has her clothes, so perhaps not all is lost. She picks herself back up, out of the sand, and returns to the hotel.

Dick proceeds to the check-in counter with Jaclyn at his side.

"I know these tickets weren't booked at the same time, but is it possible for you to seat us together anyway?" Dick asks the clerk.

"Let me see what I can do," the woman says. "Passports?"

Dick hands over his passport, then more tentatively provides Jaclyn's.

"Any bags today, sir?"

"Ah, yes, just the one," Dick says, and drops his suitcase onto the conveyor belt.

He notices Jaclyn looking around rather than paying attention to the check-in process.

After only a couple of minutes, the clerk returns their passports with their boarding passes. Dick checks their boarding passes to make sure they're seated next to each other before thanking the clerk and pulling Jaclyn away from the counter.

"That was easier than I expected," he says.

As the pair head towards the security screening process, Jaclyn notices a man with a weapon holstered to his belt.

"I thought you informed me that pistols were not allowed to be brought into the airport?" Jaclyn says to Dick, just before walking toward the uniformed man with her hand stretched out.

"What?" Dick asks from behind her, and in the next moment, Jaclyn finds herself being tackled to the floor.

"What's all this about?" a security guard asks after a pair of them rush into action.

"Sorry, nothing, I thought she was about to fall," Dick lies. "I was going to try and catch her but I guess I tripped instead."

"Very well," says the security guard, and he and his partner return to their posts.

"What on earth are you doing?" Dick asks Jaclyn through gritted teeth as they move into sitting positions on the floor.

"He had a pistol; you said they were not allowed here, so I thought it was my duty to relieve him of it."

Dick places a hand on his head and starts massaging the side of his face with his thumb. "Do you want to get arrested?"

She shakes her head. "Would it help you to know that I have never been arrested?"

"Not really, no. This is a different time, Jaclyn. The police have a lot more resources at their disposal now. Just keep close to me and you'll be fine," Dick says, picking himself up. He reaches out his hand to help Jaclyn up, then adds, sternly whispering into her ear, "*Don't* take someone else's gun. You won't be celebrated as a hero. Those men work here and it's their job to stop the public who do carry guns."

"That hardly seems fair, allowing some men to carry weapons and not others," Jaclyn comments.

"Yeah, well, I don't make the rules, and I feel safer knowing this one exists," Dick says. Then he looks at the metal detector and adds, "Now it's time for you to use your observation skills again. We have to go through this one at a time."

"JetBlue flight eight seven two bound for JFK Intentional Airport is now ready for boarding."

"That's us," Dick says, standing up.

Jaclyn looks around at all the other people in the departure lounge standing up around her, and so follows suit. Dick shuffles her toward the queue, where they remain until their boarding passes are collected.

Once they reach the aircraft, Dick walks in first, heading down the aisle, but Jaclyn just stops in the middle of the entrance, holding up everyone behind her.

"Can I help you?" a flight attendant asks, but Jaclyn doesn't hear him because she is too busy looking around the cabin in awe.

Dick rushes back up the aisle to grab Jaclyn, and only then does she follow him to their seats.

"I suppose it is too much to ask for our own cabin?" Jaclyn asks Dick.

With a laugh, Dick informs her, "I think there are very few commercial planes in the world that let you have your own cabin, and the ones that do cost a fortune to use."

"I am not sure if this chair is more or less comfortable than a hammock. Are we expected to remain seated the whole time?"

"Pretty much, but that's okay because they bring meals to you. It's only really necessary to get up if you want to use the bathroom."

Without knowing how long the flight is supposed to take, Jaclyn cannot help feeling a little nervous about this lack of movement.

"I suppose there is one advantage to this circumstance. It will be nice to travel without having to help handle the vessel."

FOUR

Alone in a small room, Jacqueline swished a sword back and forth in the air, practicing her skill, trying to get a better control of its weight. This inn was not up to her preferred standards but they were in Tortuga now, where pirates were abundant. Barbados was but a distant memory, and even her accommodation there had not been as grand as her home in London in which she was raised.

When Jacqueline accidentally stuck her cutlass in the wall, she was startled as the door swung open.

"Kitty!" Jacqueline said with her voice raised. "Whatever are you wearing those breeches for? I thought you were done with that."

"We must disguise ourselves, Jack. I will not allow for another pirate to take you and have his way. This is our only choice." With that, Katherine threw more men's clothing onto Jacqueline's bed.

Jack looked at the clothes, realising Kitty expected her to wear men's fashion, too. The last time she had worn such items, she murdered someone. Kitty had not recognised her then, but she wondered if donning them now would make the difference. Not wanting to take the chance, she knew she had to try and find another way.

"Is this to be our life now?" Jacqueline asked, pulling the sword out of the wall and placing the tip on the ground so she could lean on it a little like a cane. "Whatever happened to your dreams? To continue Lady Mary Wroth's legacy and become a writer?"

"To write, one must experience life, Jack! I did not know it before, but being here in Tortuga has made me desire to write about these rogues. We must join with them willingly and live a life on the high seas."

"But why can we not simply stay in Tortuga to observe them? Surely that is enough."

Katherine shook her head. "Nay. I cannot take down Cromwell's Navy from here."

Jack dropped her sword on the wooden floorboards. "You want to risk our *lives* for that?"

Crossing her arms across her chest, Katherine firmly said, "He is responsible for my mother's death. He needs to pay."

Though shorter than Kitty, Jack stood tall with her hands on her hips. "What if I refuse?"

Katherine was immediately in front of her, and took her hands in her own. "Then I would miss you so."

Embracing Jack in her arms, Katherine closed her eyes and kissed Jack softly on her lips.

When they parted, Jack asked, "Can you promise me that we shall come to no more harm?"

"I have doubts I can protect you from pistol or cutlass." Kitty ran a hand through Jack's hair. "Yet you should know I will do all I can to prevent any man from taking you."

Jacqueline sat down on the bed, closed her eyes and

nodded solemnly.

"Come now," Kitty said, "let us prepare ourselves." The sound of Kitty removing her cutlass from its scabbard roused Jack in time to see her grabbing a chunk of her red hair, and start sawing at it. She was reducing it to the length of her shoulder.

Jack stood as Kitty returned her cutlass to its scabbard, and then found herself at Kitty's side.

"Oh, Kitty," said Jacqueline, running her fingers through Kitty's hair. A tear escaped her.

Heading down the pier beside Kitty, Jacqueline admired the sight of the large, square-rigged two-masted vessel that they were approaching. Though she had never been on a boat quite like it before, having seen similar designs in harbour and at sea, Jacqueline recognised it to be a brig. It was painted black, with a red stripe around the middle, and featured a figurehead underneath the bowsprit that looked like a skeleton wearing a skirt.

A man guarded the gangplank which led to the vessel, but he was still too far away for Jack to notice anything particular about him, beyond his clothes. The tan breeches he wore were so dirty and fit him so snugly that it looked as though he hadn't worn anything else in years, and the once-white shirt covered his body but not his bulging arms.

Jack looked down at her own clothes and hoped they were enough to disguise her body shape so that no one could tell she was a woman. The red scarf she had wrapped around her head was all she had to hide the length of her hair, and she didn't want to think about what would happen if it should accidentally come undone. It didn't matter that Kitty had given her several lessons about how to walk and carry herself as a man would, Jack was still afraid of being caught.

She stopped Kitty in her tracks and whispered, "I am not sure I can continue."

In her mind, Jack wanted to ask Kitty to hold her and tell her everything would be okay, but that sort of behaviour even in front of one meagre sailor could easily give them away.

"Allow me to be the one to converse with them," Kitty said, "and all will be well. The quartermaster has already warmed to me."

Trying to take this reassurance as it was intended, Jack continued toward the boat, followed closely by Kitty.

When they arrived, Jacqueline stared directly into the eyes of the bearded man who waited there, and couldn't help feeling a little revolted. He was filthy, and his biceps looked close to bursting they were so big, but she needed to not react. As long as she stared directly at him, the man did not flinch.

Though this was not their first voyage at sea, it was the first time they were to intentionally join the crew of a new vessel. Jacqueline was not quite sure what to make of this man, so she turned her attention to Katherine.

Kitty pushed Jacqueline aside and threw out her gruffest voice possible, "Eh, this here be *Mary's Revenge*?"

The name of the boat was likely painted on the stern, but that was out of their view.

"Aye," the bearded man replied.

"We be the new crewmates," Kitty said. She elbowed

Jacqueline and added, "This here is Jack, and I be Kit."

The bearded man nodded the pair on board. As they hurried up the gangplank, Jack spotted two men waiting to greet them. The first was wearing a black tricorn hat over his shoulder-length copper hair, the curls of which did well to obscure his ears. His red and black coat fell open over a grimy white shirt, and black breeches. He was about two inches shorter than the second man, who stood beside him on the right, further from the gangplank.

As they got closer, Jack could see that the taller man was bald and had a beard that only barely covered his chin. His facial hair was light brown, and with the way the sun had tarnished his skin, it made it difficult to distinguish where his face met his hair from a distance.

When they met the men on deck, Kitty greeted the first man with a nod and, "Captain." Then she turned to the bald man, nodded her head, and greeted him by name, "Mr Higgins."

On closer inspection, the captain's hair was sprinkled with a few grey strands, and his moustache and goatee made him look more distinguished than the other man, especially when comparing the captain's blue eyes to Higgins's near-black irises.

"The quartermaster here tells me ye both barely escaped from the Royal Navy with yer necks. Said everyone ye sailed with sank with the ship."

"Aye, Captain." Kitty nodded.

The captain moved in to stand nose to nose with Kitty. "And just how did ye escape, then?"

"'Tis better answered by example, sir," Kitty replied. "Just give me the chance to fight the first scum ye finds."

"Very well. Welcome aboard, men." The captain turned to Higgins and issued him an order, "Mr Higgins, take these men to lock up their pistols before showing them the fore-castle."

The quartermaster nodded at the captain, but Jack didn't like the sound of that. No privacy amongst men sounded atrocious to her. The pirates she had previously met may have been close to taking advantage of her at any time, but at least when they had known she was a wo-man, they hadn't forced her to sleep in the same quarters as them. They smelled bad enough when she stood next to them; Jack didn't want to imagine how much worse it would be below deck.

When Jacqueline shook herself out of her thoughts, she noticed Higgins had his hands out in front of them. She didn't know why he was doing this until she watched Kitty disappointedly pull her two flintlocks from the sash around her waist and place them in Higgins's possession. When Higgins turned to Jack, she realised she had to re-trieve her own pistol for him.

With his full hands falling at his sides, the quartermas-ter nodded across the deck as an indication to the women to follow him.

The forecastle was strung with hammocks—many hanging above others—and it smelled of bad body odour, sweat, and a hint of vomit just near the entrance. Jack presumed that had come from one of drunken sailors, and though there was no longer evidence of the contents of someone's stomach on the ground, the sea air clearly could not pen-etrate the room enough to entirely remove the stench. The lighting was such that they made do with whatever sun was able to stream in from the windows.

Higgins left Kitty and Jack there to meet some of the other crew who were already on board. They dropped their canvas knapsacks on a pile of others in the corner before joining the three men who were standing there talking. As Jack worried about giving their identities away just by opening her mouth, she relied on Kitty to converse on her behalf.

"Ye must be the new crew," the blond one said with a French accent. "François," he added, introducing himself.

"Kit," said Kitty, then pointed to Jacqueline. "And this is me mate Jack."

"He don' talk?" François asked.

Jack shrugged, then nodded toward the other two men who hadn't said a word.

"Henry," the shortest one said. Even though his long black hair was tied back in a ponytail, his curls were visible on the top of his head. "Or ye can call me Baker."

The man with the scarred face introduced himself as Turner. Jack tried to take in their names and faces, wanting to remember them, because she was sure she wouldn't be able to do that with the entire crew, even if it appeared like it could be a relatively small one.

It would be so much more preferable to Jack if she could associate with as few of them as possible. She looked around the room and saw a tall black man sleeping in one of the hammocks, and her immediate thought was, *Especially that one.*

A few days into the voyage, Jack was amongst the rest of

the crew, busy with the menial task of swabbing the deck when she heard the lookout's call from the crosstrees. "Sail ho! Starboard side!"

Jack paused from her duty, mop in hand, and looked toward the captain who was standing on the quarterdeck, looking through a spyglass of his own. Through experience on her previous vessel, she knew the captain was likely to issue new orders, and she wanted to be able to hear what the plan was before dropping sand over the deck to soak up the water.

"It be a merchant vessel," the captain yelled.

Jack looked starboard, but the craft was too far out for her to deem anything in particular about it.

To the men not busy manoeuvring *Mary's Revenge*, McDonald ordered, "Clear for action." He then turned to the man nearest him and said, "Turner, get below and tell the rest of the crew."

Turner ran off, passing Katherine—who had been busy swabbing on the port side—on his way. Captain McDonald looked at her.

"Gray," McDonald yelled, "this be yer chance to show us yer talent."

"Aye, Captain!" she yelled back, ignoring the other men who were scrambling about the deck, making sure they were prepared to launch an attack.

Both Katherine and Jacqueline cleared what they could so that no one would trip or slip on what they had left to do before Kitty met with Jack.

"To the arms lockers," Kitty said, obviously aware of this being the first time Jack was expected to engage in an attack.

Jacqueline nodded and followed Kitty below.

Fetching their weaponry, the women stocked themselves up with the pistols they had arrived with, along with a powderhorn and shot bag each. The blades of their choosing were a cutlass for Kitty, whilst Jack took a small dagger, worried about her ability to use something heavier in this sort of situation. They then headed to their sleeping quarters to fetch their stockings and boots, wanting to make sure they were appropriately dressed for the attack.

They were much closer to the merchant vessel once the women returned to the main deck, and Jack could finally see it was flying English colours. She smiled, knowing how pleased Kitty would be to take down the men on board.

Wondering if their brig had raised their own colours yet, Jack looked aloft, and for the first time was able to see how McDonald's flag looked, since it had not been raised the entire time they had been sailing on the *Mary's Revenge*. From what she could tell of its design as it waved in the wind, it was black and pictured a white cutlass dripping with blood. There was another image on it, but with the limited time Jack was able to look at it, she couldn't make out what it was.

It was about another hour before the brig had sailed close enough to the merchant vessel, which surrendered at that point. Not that Captain McDonald cared.

The scene reminded Jacqueline of the numb feeling she had when she was in the position of being a passenger on the merchant that was taken by pirates as it was en route to Virginia. The scarred bodies of the pirates looked so evil, so she knew exactly how the sailors on this merchant must be feeling. Hoping for survival.

On their merchant, the captain had been merciful, allowing the sailors and passengers a choice between death and joining the crew, which is how she and Kitty ended up surviving the take over. Captain McDonald had something else in mind when he ordered his crew over.

Higgins, being the quartermaster, was the first across, but was closely followed by Katherine. Jack held back until most of the crew had gone across, and she tried not to cringe as she watched the pirates slaughter the defenceless sailors.

A bout of bravery fell over the merchant's captain and led him to pull a cutlass on Higgins, since he had been the one to lead the charge. Higgins was caught off guard, and only narrowly managed to avoid the sword in his side thanks to Katherine's perfect aim. She shot the captain in his chest, and left the rest of him to Higgins.

Aside from shooting the captain, Kitty slit a dozen throats on her way to relieve the ship of its tobacco and sugar.

Jacqueline managed to avoid harming any of the men she encountered, but then she was relegated the duty of burning the ship as soon as the pirates had taken all they could plunder.

A lot of laugher was shared amongst the pirates as they watched it burn until it sank.

After their fourth attack on an English merchant—one in which the sailors had been much braver than the first they encountered—Jack and Kitty were given the duty of storing all the plunder in the hold while the rest of the crew tended to the wounded—both men and vessel alike.

Once everything was secured, they couldn't help themselves from taking advantage of the privacy. They embraced, and Jacqueline's heart pounded. Katherine pulled away Jacqueline's scarf to reveal hair that fell halfway down her back. She ran her fingers through the strands and pulled Jacqueline in for a warm kiss.

Jacqueline cautiously looked over at the door, yet passion stirred within her body. Kitty allayed her doubts with another kiss, bringing her attention back to the moment. It consumed her and she fell backwards onto a crate of tobacco, pulling Kitty with her.

Jack's back rested against another crate while Kitty tore at the masculine clothes Jacqueline wore, exposing her breast. The lantern's candle light flickered over Jack's body, which caused her to smile as she watched Kitty thumb around her large areole, perking up her nipples.

"What be this?" Kitty asked. "Ye are warm for me, begging for mercy."

Planting a kiss on Kitty's lips, Jack mused, "I do so love when you speak as they do."

"Aye," Kitty replied as a smile crossed her face.

Katherine's hands moved Jack so that she was laying on the crate, then slowly made their way down Jack's body, across her curves and beneath her breeches. The kisses Jack received as Kitty's fingers moved back and forth between her legs only intensified the experience.

When Jacqueline climaxed, she rolled off the crate and collapsed painfully onto the slimy ballast rocks below, still breathing quite hard. The rocks were cold against her skin, and Jack had to start massaging her breast where one had scraped it as she carefully turned herself back around. She expected her thigh would probably be bruised horribly by the next day.

Suddenly, they heard the quartermaster's screechy voice call, "What be taking ye?"

There was no time for Jack to act in her panicked state. All she could think about was the idea that they were sure to be disciplined. Katherine threw her leg over Jacqueline's breast, resting her foot against the ceiling. The best Jack could hope for was that Higgins had not uncovered their secret. She then thanked Kitty's sense that she had kept everything of her own on, no matter how uncomfortably hot the doublet probably made her feel.

Jacqueline's heart thumped more intensely than it ever had before.

Higgins snarled when he was closer. "What is this? Jack is a woman?"

There was barely enough room for Katherine to move on him so swiftly, but somehow she managed to immediately raise her pistol to the quartermaster's forehead. "Speak of this to no one," she said, "or I will not hesitate to shoot ye."

With her breathing getting heavier by the second, Jack found herself thankful that they hadn't been asked to lock up their arms before relocating the plunder. She didn't know what the consequences would be if Kitty followed through with shooting such a high ranking officer, but she didn't think it could be worse than having her secret exposed.

Higgins swallowed, which was followed by a hesitant nod, probably wondering why he had thought to trust Katherine in the first place. She returned the pistol to the sash around her waist.

"Could at least share," Higgins added, baring his teeth.

Barely a second passed before Katherine grabbed hold of the quartermaster's neck and struck him up against the ceiling. His hands gripped her arms in retaliation and he tried to thrust her backward. Katherine stood her ground, though her arms began to weaken.

"Ye will not defile her," Katherine said in her harshest tone imaginable.

When Higgins's arms fell to his side and he began to choke, Kitty loosened her grip enough for him to answer, "Ye have my word."

Katherine removed her hold completely. "Let me finish things up here,"—she looked over her shoulder at Jacqueline, and then back to Higgins—"and then we will meet ye on deck."

The quartermaster backed slowly out of the hold and shut the door behind him.

Jacqueline finally let out the breath she had been holding from the intensity of the situation.

"Whatever would I do without you, Kitty?" Jacqueline asked.

"Hush," Kitty replied. "Let us not speak of such things."

"I admire you," Jacqueline replied. "I fear I have been silenced in front of these men for far too long. It is time I come into my own."

"Yes, perhaps. But you are increasing in weapon-wielding skill. I would not have escaped those other pirates solely on my own. Your mastery of the flintlock alone fills me with admiration."

Jacqueline sat up, shifting uncomfortably at Kitty's

words. "It would not have been necessary to fight them had you not lured the Navy."

"Was there another way to rid ourselves of the constant torment?" Kitty shot back, upset.

"We could have perhaps escaped at any time we made land." Jack was quiet, not wanting to start an argument.

"There was less assurance in that sort of situation; we would have likely been caught again. It was only a matter of time before one of the crew, or—Heaven help them—the captain completely had his way with you," Kitty said resolutely, running her fingers through Jacqueline's hair once more. "And having the Navy on our side, our names on the passenger list, simply made it easier to have them take us to the nearest port."

"Perhaps you are right," Jacqueline agreed. "That aside, we *are* amongst pirates again. I believe I would benefit much from talking for myself. Will you help me speak as they do?"

"Aye," Kitty replied. "I will help ye talk like them," she said.

With that, Jacqueline arose and thanked Kitty with a kiss.

"By the by, I also love the way you alone are able to sate my lust," Jacqueline said with a smile. "Now, let me dress."

As she did so, Kitty took the lantern, positioning it in a place to make it easier for Jack to see what she was doing.

Tentatively, Kitty said, "I should warn ye that there is a chance Mr Higgins will have us—or at least me—in chains when we return to the main deck, for what I did when he was here."

Jack's stomach was immediately in a pit of nerves again,

but the tried to ignore it as she tied her scarf back around her head.

Attempting to reassure Kitty, Jack took her hands in her own, and gave her a short kiss on the lips. Jack took the lantern from Kitty and carried it, walking ahead of her in the hope Higgins's desire would prevent any kind of action when they returned. She blew the candle out when there was enough light to see without it, knowing it was hazardous to have the flames around particularly when it wasn't necessary.

When the women reached the main deck, nothing happened. Higgins was nowhere to be seen, but the wounded were still being tended to. Jack considered that if it had not been for the fact they'd just been in a battle and more hands were available, this reappearance may have gone quite differently.

The following week, Jacqueline and Kitty were working different watches. Jacqueline was eating some pineapple when Higgins brushed up against her back. As he sat down beside her, he slid the palm of his right hand along her backside in a fashion that would not alert to the other men in the mess to his actions. Once seated, Higgins slipped Jacqueline a note beneath the table and started eating his own food.

Later that day, Jacqueline found herself knocking on the quartermaster's cabin door. When Higgins answered, he quickly grabbed her wrist and pulled her inside, slamming the door shut.

"I presume you rose to quartermaster due to being one of the few men aboard this vessel who can read and write."

Jacqueline's words were said far too calmly for someone who had been treated just as she had, but she was well-adapted to hiding when she feared for her safety now.

There was even a slight smirk in her tone, which left Higgins speechless.

She added, "I, however, am like those men. I did nay ask Kit what yer note says, and simply thought it meant you were wont to see me."

Jacqueline looked around the small cabin, wishing she had the kind of privacy the quartermaster enjoyed. Then she spotted something familiar in the corner. After walking over to it, she picked up a golden goblet.

Turning to look at Higgins, she asked, "Where did ye get this?"

A smirk found its way across Higgins's face. "Me beauty, did Kit not tell ye that I only agreed to take ye on board with payment?"

Jacqueline was shocked to silence for a few moments, and then she asked, "Does the captain know?"

He shook his head and gave her a cocky smile. "Though I may say, you and Kit do stun Captain McDonald. It is a mystery that ye escaped from a sinking vessel and survived alone."

Jacqueline pondered Higgins's words, worried that he and the captain could uncover the lies, then removed the scarf from her head. She attempted to highlight her femininity as best as possible whilst dressed as she was, and then walked up to Higgins. They stood face to face, though Jacqueline was nearly a foot shorter than Higgins. Jacqueline reached her hands around the quartermaster's neck and pulled him down enough to plant a kiss on his lips.

"Aye, and likely to remain as such," Jacqueline replied with a coy smile.

The quartermaster seemed not to hear, looking entranced from the kiss. He wrapped his arms around Jacqueline but before he could attempt to lift her, she placed her hands on his arms and moved them away.

"Not now," Jacqueline said, hoping to be able to milk him for what she could without ever having to give him what he wanted. "I first desire a favour."

Before she explained what she meant, she again hid her hair in the red scarf and left the cabin.

About a week or so later, after attacking and looting another English vessel, as well as a Dutch merchant, Jacqueline and Katherine met in the galley at a time Jack informed her that no one, not even Noah the cook, would be there. Jack had pinched some rum from the lockup for their enjoyment, though Kitty had no idea how Jack had managed that.

It was not too long before the women were feeling tipsy. Katherine stood by a window, bottle in hand, and looked out at the sunset tinted sea. All she expected to see was water, but, on first glance, she thought she saw a woman's face, framed by blonde curls. Katherine looked back at Jacqueline, who was still drinking merrily away. She turned back to the sea, and the face was gone, only to reappear moments later from beneath the ocean.

Katherine blinked a couple of times to be sure her eyes were not deceiving her.

"Jack," she said, "ye must see this."

"Aye?" Jacqueline replied. "What be it?"

"There be a mermaid out there," Kitty replied.

"Ye know I believe in no such creatures," Jacqueline insisted, but drunkenly walked to join Kitty at the window anyway.

The head bobbed beneath the sea again moments before Jacqueline arrived.

"I see nothing," Jacqueline said, matter-of-factly. "Perhaps the setting sun is playing tricks with your eyes."

"Wait. She will return," Katherine contended.

Katherine was wrong, or at least the head did not reappear before the women were interrupted by a loud, forced cough.

The women turned away from the window and were met with a glare from Higgins. Katherine firmly held her bottle of rum behind her back.

"What are ye doing in the galley?" Higgins asked accusingly.

"Admiring the view," Katherine quipped.

Higgins was not impressed. He pulled out a pistol and paced back and forth in front of the disguised women, brandishing the weapon and occasionally glancing over at them.

"Hmm..." he pondered.

The quartermaster paused his pacing and eyed Katherine more suspiciously. He wiped his brow with the back of his pistol equipped hand. The man breathed in deeply and moved his eyes down Katherine's body. She made a move toward the side where she kept a pistol during battle before remembering it was in the arms locker. Katherine's breath became heavier as Higgins's eyes moved in on Jacqueline's face, and thus she tightly gripped Jacqueline's hand beside her.

"Ye be a beauty," Higgins said, speaking to Jacqueline alone. "Be not with this… *boy*," he added, attempting to insult as he pointed to Kitty. "Do ye fancy a trip to me quarters yet?"

Higgins was almost salivating as his empty hand fingered the barrel of his flintlock. His words sounded more like a threat than an invitation.

"Take this further now and I will come for ye," Katherine said, feeling her heart tighten in her chest. She was less sure of herself without a weapon to protect them from this foe.

Though Katherine could not see Jack's face, the way Higgins was looking at her made Kitty wonder what sort of expression she held. When he turned his attention back to Katherine, she could not tell if he was responding to the way Jack looked at him, or to the strength in her own eyes.

"Very well," he said, raising his pistol and continuing to idly play with it in his hands, admiring it. "I shall let ye off this time," he added, "but no more sneaking around this here vessel. Now get ye back to yer quarters."

"Aye, sir." Kitty saluted with the hand that had been holding Jacqueline's, her heart still not quite free from fear.

Higgins stood his ground, so Jacqueline and Katherine walked slowly in his direction. Once past the man, Kitty brought the bottle around to her front, and the pair quickly ran out of the galley before Higgins was able to notice the stolen rum.

Hoping the next day that Higgins wanted to call a truce, Katherine knocked on the quartermaster's cabin door.

"Kit Gray, sir. The bosun says you desired to see me," Katherine said.

"Aye, come in," came Higgins's voice from within the cabin.

When she opened the door, she was met with an entirely unexpected sight. The quartermaster had a man bent forward over his bed; the man's face was obscured. Katherine turned away from the thrusting. She felt like she was going to be sick if she watched any longer.

"Sir, if yer busy, I can return later," Katherine said.

"Not at all," the quartermaster said with a sly grin. "Care to drop yer breeches and join me?"

Kitty wondered if this was what Higgins considered an appropriate way to resolve their differences. However, when she turned her attention back to him, feeling even more disgust, she found Higgins grasping Jacqueline's hair and making sure Kitty could see her flushed face. There was a stream of tears running from Jacqueline's eyes but Kitty could not determine whether they were from pain or guilt.

As Kitty stood, finding herself speechless and, for once, unable to take any action, Higgins finished up and withdrew from Jack. After fixing himself up, he practically threw Jacqueline at Katherine.

"Ye can have her back now," Higgins said smugly.

Katherine wiped away Jacqueline's tears as she pulled her breeches up before the pair left the cabin together. She then immediately dragged Jack back to the forecastle.

Closing the door behind them while Jack sat on a hammock, Kitty asked, "What happened? How did he overcome you?"

Only silence and tears replied, and Kitty concluded that Jack must have been too traumatised by the event to talk about it. This was by far worse than the taunts Jack got from their former crewmates, and so Kitty knew there was no way she could live with herself if she did not somehow avenge Jack being defiled. She just needed to figure out how she could do that without being blamed for it.

The following evening, the *Mary's Revenge* was at anchor, and Katherine was charged with the duty of keeping watch while the rest of the crew slept. She was thankful for the opportunity because she thought it would give her enough downtime to think about what she could do with Higgins.

Pacing the main deck didn't help. She found it hard to conceive a way to get rid of the man who was taunting her by making her lover suffer without being caught. If anyone saw her murder him, she knew there would be consequences. Facing the pirate court and likely receiving severe punishment was no way to save Jack.

She climbed up to the quarterdeck and looked out at the sea, hoping the water would somehow give her some extra insight. In the moonlight, Katherine could see something round bobbing in and out of the water. Then she could've sworn she heard "Katherine Grayson" being carried through the air with a sing-song voice. Moments later a large fish tail breached the surface. Forgetting all other thoughts, Katherine stared in awe, hoping for another glimpse.

Minutes passed with no sighting, so she climbed higher to the poop deck and glanced from port to starboard. Then there was a whistle coming from immediately beneath her.

Katherine looked down and saw a blonde-haired woman's face.

"Evening, Kitty!" the woman of the sea shouted up at her.

Confused enough to forget her pirate tongue, Kitty shouted back, "Hush! How do you know my name?" Realising she didn't want the answer shouted back at her in case they woke the captain in the cabin below her, she added, "Wait!"

Kitty looked at the lines hanging down past the back of the taffrail, which led to a few skiffs below. The small boats were not far from the woman in the sea, so her eyes wandered back to the blonde.

"Allow me a moment to bring myself closer," Kitty yelled.

The next thing she knew, Kitty was climbing down the line that lead to the skiff nearest the woman. Once settled in the boat, the mermaid immediately found her arms on the closest side. Kitty stared deeply into her eyes. There was something familiar about her face but she could not place it.

"How do you know my true name?" Kitty asked again.

The only response she got from the mermaid was a smile.

Kitty decided to try a different approach. "Do you have a name?"

"Prudence," the mermaid replied, flipping her fins above the surface of the sea.

Kitty sighed deeply at the sound of her name. "I knew someone who shared your name."

Prudence's face lit up with glee. "Was she special?"

"Aye."

"I sense sadness," Prudence said. "Whatever happened to her?"

Katherine wept into her hands.

"Ah," Prudence nodded, knowingly. "She is no longer with us." The mermaid bobbed beneath the sea again. When she resurfaced, she added, "Or so you assume."

Finding herself confused again, Kitty said, "She died in my presence. There is no doubt in my mind."

"I wonder if you may help me?" the mermaid said. "Because if she is dead, I do not know who I am."

Prudence lifted herself up onto the side of the skiff and joined Kitty inside. Moments after her body no longer touched the sea, Prudence's fins transformed into legs.

Gasping at the sight of the mermaid's nakedness, Kitty couldn't help but notice the complete lack of hair on her body as her eyes were first drawn between the mermaid's legs. As Kitty's eyes rose upwards along Prudence's shimmering body, she caught sight of an unmistakable birthmark on her stomach, just to the left of her bellybutton. Kitty's mouth began to spread broadly, as she then admired the firm and perky breasts in her view.

"Prue!" Kitty said, wide-eyed. "This... what... how...?" she spluttered.

"I do not quite know nor understand myself," Prudence replied.

Kitty examined Prudence's face more closely, trying to figure out why she had not previously recognised her. "Whatever happened to your smallpox scars?" she asked.

"Part of the magic of the transformation—a mermaid's goal is one that required all that was ugly about me to be removed. I am supposed to be pure beauty, now. However…" Prue paused, clearly not happy with something that should make the average woman thrilled to tears. Soon tears did start to form in the corners of Prudence's eyes, but Kitty could tell they were not borne of happiness.

"Whatever is the matter, Prue? I wish to help you in whatever manner I can," she paused, wondering whether she should say exactly what was on her mind. She shouldn't be thinking it. Not when she had been with Jacqueline and without Prue for as long as she had. Yet she found she couldn't help herself. Her words came out in a whisper. "I still love you."

"This… beauty. This life…" Prue said, not really knowing where to start or how much time she had to talk.

Kitty encouraged her, "Tell me everything. From the beginning."

Prudence nodded. "I shall try," she said. Closing her eyes, she began to recall from her memory. "When I found myself surrounded by water, at first I could not breathe. I do not know how much time had passed between when I was shot and when I was there, but to me, it felt instantaneous." She paused then to look at Kitty's reaction—a mixture of awe and shock. Prue continued, "A woman came—she was like me, with fins. Though I did not yet know I had my own, I noticed hers as she was swimming toward me. As she neared, she placed a hand on my cheek to calm me. This allowed me to breathe. 'Welcome,' she said, and took my hands in hers. 'You are mermaid now,' she told me, and I looked down, noticing my fins for the first time.

"Then we swam together, with her keeping hold of my

hands while I got used to my new body, and she took me to Miranda. She is like our Mother Superior.

"Miranda explained that mermaids are formed out of revenge, though even she does not know all the details of how that works. It is a punishment for me—a punishment for certain women who choose to lay with those they should not. My behaviour in my life made me what I am now."

Prudence sighed, and Kitty sensed regret. "This is my fault," Kitty said, understanding.

"Nay," Prudence disagreed. "Perhaps in part, but I also had a choice, and I needed you in my life. I would not change a thing."

"You said this is a punishment. I do not understand. Eternity as a mermaid? Is that what you mean?" Kitty asked.

"That is not all. For I am not a mermaid alone; I am a siren. I do not know how long I will have to live like this, though I do hope it is not eternity." Prudence paused, trying to decide how to convey the rest of the story. "As a siren I... I must deliver men to my community. Kitty, I do not know what I am doing. I have not yet had any success."

"How much time has passed in this quest?" Kitty asked, worried Prudence had been at it since she had died.

"A month, maybe two."

Kitty was stunned to silence.

"What is it, Kitty?"

"Prue... you have been gone nearly two years."

With that comment, Prudence burst into tears. "What... happened... to... me...?" she asked between sobs.

"I do not know," said Katherine. "What I do know is that I love you, and I wish to help." Katherine processed the information she had. "You need a man from this vessel," Katherine said with understanding. "Aye, yes. I know just the pirate." She then proceeded to give Prudence a description of the quartermaster.

It wasn't the way she had expected to resolve her objective, but it did seem to be the only solution that would not put her personally at risk.

Prudence threw her arms around Kitty and planted a kiss on her lips. When she pulled away, she said, "I wish I could stay up here with you forever, but I do not know if these legs expire, and I do not wish to take that risk."

Kitty shook her head. "It means more to me to know you are alive. May we meet again."

With that, Prudence dove back into the sea, her fins reforming the instant her hands touched the water.

Days later, after a bloody battle aboard a Spanish galleon, the surviving pirates had anchored the brig close to a small island so the injured could have some time to recover from their wounds. Some of the less-injured crew had gone ashore in search of meat, whilst the others who remained aboard enjoyed the fruits of their success, sharing rum between them. Jack and Kitty leaned against the gunwale, humouring each other whilst Kitty focused on the thought of killing more Englishmen rather than the recent Spaniards. Watching the sun set the sky on fire while musicians played on the quarterdeck on the opposite end of the brig had a calming effect on them.

Out of the corner of her eye, Katherine could see Higgins pacing the starboard side.

"What do ye suppose he be doing?" Katherine asked Jacqueline when the pacing stopped and Higgins stared over the side, into the sea.

"Perhaps he caught a glimpse of yer mermaid," Jacqueline mused in jest.

"Dare not tease me, Jack."

They stared longer at the man, but he did not stray. It was as if his eyes were transfixed on something at sea. Soon he lowered his head, closer to whatever he was observing, and then...

Jacqueline jumped to her feet to make toward Higgins, but Kitty held out her arm to keep her from moving. They watched as the quartermaster fell.

At the sound of the splash, other crew members turned their heads in that direction. Four men ran to the side of the brig and looked overboard.

"What was that?" one of them shouted.

Katherine stood and shouted back, "I think that t'were Higgins."

It was then that Kitty realised she might seem suspicious if she did not try and do something to save him. In the midst of screams of "Man Overboard!" from the men around the place the quartermaster fell, and the musicians putting their instruments down, Kitty scrambled up to the poop deck, and followed the musicians down the line to the only skiff that remained with the brig.

François Bertrand—the first of the crew who formally introduced himself to her, and turned out to be the brig's flautist—rowed the boat to the area below where the other pirates were looking. Along with Henry—the man who played the hurdy gurdy—Kitty jumped into the water, and pretended to search for the missing quartermaster.

"Find 'im?" Thomas Grant—the bearded fiddler—called from next to François when Kitty popped her head above water again.

"Nay," she replied, and looked around for Henry to see if he had any luck. When she couldn't find him, her heart began racing and she asked, "Where did Baker go?"

"Bastard!" Grant yelled, obviously realising he hadn't come back up, before quickly pointing to the place he'd last seen Henry.

Kitty dived back under the water, hoping Prudence hadn't taken Henry as well. That hadn't been part of the deal, and she happened to like Henry. Though it was hard to see as the saltwater was burning her eyes, she caught a glimpse of an air bubble and swam in that direction.

Finally she noticed Henry's recognisable long black curls, and was soon able to dig her arms under his and swim back to the surface. She was glad Baker was a short—albeit stocky—man, or she may not have had the strength to carry him back to the skiff.

Once she got back to the boat, Grant and Bertrand pulled him in. Grant started slapping him to try and get him to wake up as Kitty pulled herself back in to join them.

"Let me try," Kitty said, and took over from Grant by thumping Henry's chest.

When Henry spat out a mouthful of seawater, the other three on the skiff collectively breathed a sigh of relief.

"Did ye see the quartermaster?" Grant asked as Henry sat himself back up.

"Aye, barely," he replied, and Kitty found a knot forming in her stomach. "I tried to reach 'im, but t'were like he wanted to drown 'imself. He just kept going deeper and I could nay keep up."

The only thing Kitty could think about was how lucky she was that Henry hadn't also seen Prudence. There was no reason she would want the crew to perceive mermaids as a real threat, because at this point the stories she had heard around the brig had been minimal and based on myth.

"Better report back to the captain now," François said, beginning to row back toward the stern.

"What happened out there?" the captain shouted at Katherine in his cabin.

"I cannot fathom what Higgins was thinking, Captain," Kitty offered. "I only saw it t'were him just before he fell."

"But why did ye not stop the quartermaster going overboard?" McDonald gritted his teeth in frustration.

"There was no time!" Katherine protested.

"Please, Cap'n," Grant said, "least Gray helped us try to save 'im. 'S more than the rest o' the crew."

"And he saved me in the meantime..." Baker added.

McDonald kicked his boot against the cabin door, and Katherine worried if he was somehow contemplating disciplinary measures for her, despite the words spoken in her favour.

The captain turned to face the four who had attempted rescue, and tried to calm his frustration. "But now I have to rally every man we have to vote in a new quartermaster," McDonald said angrily, "and twenty of them are ashore."

"Jack and me can go ashore for them," Kitty volunteered.

McDonald shook his head. "We shall just wait. They should be back by the morrow." He turned around and looked out the window. "Now get out," he added, not even looking at them.

As the musicians and Kitty left the captain's cabin, François hit her gently on her upper back and squeezed her shoulder.

"Don' worry 'bout the capitaine," he said. "Ye did good out there. He jus' needs time to grieve. Higgins was a well respected man; even saved the capitaine himself more than once."

About an hour after the shore crew returned the following day, Captain McDonald stood on the quarterdeck as his crew gathered on the deck below.

"As ye all well know by now," the captain started, "roughly this time yesterday, Quartermaster Higgins fell overboard."

Silence fell over the crowd.

McDonald continued, "As per the articles ye all agreed to upon this voyage, we must elect a new quartermaster. Do I have any names?"

"Joseph Turner!" one man shouted.

"Bones!" yelled another.

"Kit Gray!" was the third suggestion. Kitty recognised the voice as Henry's, and her heart warmed.

When no more names were called, the captain said, "Ye are all entitled to one vote each. Raise your hand when the name of your choice is called."

Then the captain called each name and counted up the

votes. When the voting was over, anticipation covered the faces of every single man who stood before the captain.

"Please welcome the new quartermaster, Kit Gray."

The crowd was overcome with cheers and applause as Katherine stood in place, stunned. This hadn't been her plan when she wanted Higgins gone. If anything, she might have preferred to keep a lower profile. Jack pushed Kitty forwards, ushering her to join the captain on the quarterdeck.

By the time she reached the captain's side, she managed to compose herself well enough to think this could be a good thing.

"Much thanks for the vote of confidence of ye all," Katherine said with a nod.

As the crowd dispersed, Kitty turned to the captain and asked, "If it is not too much trouble, Captain, I wish to hang a hammock in the quartermaster's cabin for Jack."

The captain looked at Katherine like this was the oddest request he had heard in his life. "Why?"

"I have come accustomed to his company. It would not feel right to separate from him."

"Very well," McDonald agreed.

Kitty thanked the stars for the captain's acceptance, as she felt like Jack was safer by her side, regardless of no one else knowing their secret. Besides which, she liked imagining what they could do with all that extra privacy.

FIVE

The pressure in Jaclyn's ears gets stronger as the plane descends. From her pocket, she pulls out the hard piece of candy that Dick had given her when he explained the ear issue to her before they got on the flight. She hadn't experienced it as the plane took off and thus presumed it to be a fallacy, but now... this experience is all the evidence Jaclyn needs to know Dick hadn't been lying. She unwraps the plastic and pops the yellow candy in her mouth. It doesn't seem to matter how hard she sucks, it does not seem to help her ears, so she holds her hands over them instead and tries to yawn.

Eventually her left ear pops, but she can barely hear anything out of her right. Everything just sounds like a combination of a hum and a whoosh all at the same time. She sticks her index finger in her ear, hoping it will somehow pop that way, but that doesn't work either. She sucks the candy some more, and then yawns again until her ear pops and the pain causes her to use both hands to clutch that ear. Trying to not think about the pain only causes her to notice it more, and she winces.

As the plane touches down at JFK International Airport,

Jaclyn tightly grips her arm rests. Her heart is racing. She looks at Dick, snoozing away in his aisle seat. The plane taxis into the terminal and Dick only awakens when the fasten seat belt indicator flashes off. Jaclyn looks around the plane as the other passengers begin to unbuckle their seat belts and collect their belongings. Her heart starts to slow down again and she turns back to Dick, who is now retrieving a book from the seat pocket in front of him.

"How far did you say we flew?" Jaclyn asks.

"About two thousand miles," Dick replies, nonchalantly.

"In a few hours?"

"Four and a half," Dick says, checking his watch instinctively, despite having flown the route several times and automatically knowing the length of the flight.

Jaclyn shakes her head in disbelief. "That is a month on a ship. I do not believe you have taken me so far in just four and a half hours."

"What's the longest amount of time you've spent on a ship without docking?" Dick asks curiously as he unfastens his seat belt.

Dick retrieves his laptop bag from under the seat in front of him and stands up. Jaclyn is still seated, so Dick coughs to indicate she can stand now too. She tries to stand but her seat belt is still fastened. She looks down at it, handles it for a short while but can't figure it out, having not been able to see the safety demonstration earlier due to her height. Jaclyn looks up at Dick with a sort of embarrassed smile on her face, hoping he can fix it for her. Dick holds back a chuckle as he has to reach down and unfasten Jaclyn's seat belt for her.

"I would say… perhaps two and a half months," Jaclyn finally replies as she stands. "It was supposed to be two, and we barely had enough supplies even for that. It was the worst journey of my life. We lost a lot of food rations and our navigation equipment during a battle with some privateers, which we should have won, and… I do not even want to guess the number of our crew I watched die before we found land again. You have much fortune in your world that you need not concern yourself with such horrors when you travel."

The other seats and aisle are relatively clear now, so Jaclyn enters the aisle and Dick steps out in front of her so she can follow him.

Immigration is cleared with no hassles, and soon they are at Howard Beach waiting for the A train. The subway pulls into the station and Jaclyn looks perplexed as it arrives.

"How many methods of transport do you have in your time?" Jaclyn asks Dick as she continues to stare.

"It's probably better if I don't try to count," Dick replies. "But, obviously, a lot more than horse and carriage and ships."

"Cars… planes… airtrain… what is this one called?"

"The subway. This is what we take to get to my place."

The train's doors open, and Dick grabs Jaclyn's hand to lead her inside while wheeling his suitcase with his other hand.

"It is like the airtrain, but longer?" Jaclyn asks as they take a couple of seats next to each other.

"And generally travels underground rather than over ground."

"Underground travel!" Jaclyn exclaims. "And I thought I had heard everything when you told me about flying."

"Shh," Dick says, hushing Jaclyn. "Keep your voice down. People will think it's strange if they overhear you not knowing about these things."

Dick looks at Jaclyn's clothes, confirming in his head that at least she looks normal in jeans and a tourist t-shirt with a picture of Chamberlain Bridge and labelled "Bridgetown, Barbados."

For most of the subway ride, Jaclyn watches other people entering and exiting the train at each stop. When they reach Ralph Avenue, Jaclyn realises they have already stopped many times and have yet to leave the train themselves, so she starts counting each time the train stops.

"Utica Ave." One. An elderly couple depart the train.

"High Street." Nine. A group of people approximately in their early twenties board.

"Canal Street." Twelve. Two families board.

"Tourists," Dick tells Jaclyn. "New York probably has a lot more of them than Barbados."

"Forty-second Street and the Port Authority Bus Terminal." Eighteen.

"This is where we get off," Dick says, standing up.

Dick takes Jaclyn's hand again as the train is significantly more packed now and he doesn't want to lose her in the crowd.

As they're exiting the bus terminal, Jaclyn accidentally bumps into a man.

"Oof," the man says, turning around to see who walked into him. He instantly recognises Dick. "Dick!" he says, "Been meaning to call you. I'm just heading down to

Byrne's. Why don't you come along?"

"Oh, hey, Lloyd," Dick says. He looks at the suitcase he still has in his hand, and then back to the man Jaclyn bumped into. "I'll think about it. Just got back from Barbados and have to drop my things home first."

Lloyd nods. "All right, then. Hopefully I'll see you down there later."

Jaclyn watches as the man heads off in the opposite direction to where Dick takes her. They only walk a couple of blocks before arriving at a high rise apartment complex. Dick takes Jaclyn up to the fifteenth floor, then opens the door of his apartment.

"Home sweet home," he says.

Jaclyn follows Dick into the main room, fully taking in all of the furnishings—leather couch, television set, coffee table, bookshelves and so forth.

"I moved here with Georgia about ten years ago," Dick says, walking Jaclyn down the hall and stepping into a small room, "and she wanted to make sure we had a spare bedroom we could use for when we had a baby. Even though I didn't really know how I felt about that, she got her way."

Dick pauses to reflect on the day they first viewed the apartment, when he and Georgia stood in the smaller bedroom.

"This would be perfect for a baby," Georgia had said.

He imagined a crib in the corner, special wall coverings with pictures of Winnie the Pooh and Piglet, and mobiles hanging from the ceiling. The image made him cringe, but all he had said to Georgia was, "I suppose so."

Returning himself to the present, Dick says, "Anyway,

after she moved out I rented this room out for a while, to that guy, Lloyd, who you bumped into earlier. He ended up moving on when his wife moved out here with him, and I decided I wanted to live alone after that. I turned this room into a spare bedroom in case anyone needed a place to crash for the night, but it's barely been used. Honestly, I probably should've moved into something smaller years ago and saved myself on rent. At least I have a decent place for you to stay so we no longer have to share a bed?"

"Do you miss her?"

"Huh?"

"Georgia. You have referred to her several times in the short time you have known me."

"Oh. No, not most of the time. Only when I dig into the depths of my wardrobe and find some of her old clothes that she left behind. Whenever I remind her they're there and she should come pick them up, she ignores me."

"Then why do you bother to keep them?"

Dick blinks a couple of times; donating her clothes had never even crossed his mind until Jaclyn asks this question of him.

"I don't know."

"Perhaps you believe it is your only chance to see her again?"

"Why would I want to see her again? I broke up with *her*, not the other way around. She asked too much of me," Dick says bitterly.

"You complain far too much. I would like to suggest that it may be time for you to move on."

He frowns at her, and decides she might have a point, so he puts a positive spin on the conversation and says, "Well, you know… you could probably fit into her clothes. That's gotta be good, right? Saves me money."

Obviously trying not to laugh, Jaclyn says, "As long as you do not mistake me for Georgia. I would rather prefer it if you did not try to kiss me again."

Dick raises his hand, saying, "Scout's honour." He then turns to head out of the room and adds, "I'll bring them in for you now."

After heading into his own bedroom, he opens the wardrobe doors and slides all of his clothes to the right. Then Dick reaches in and pulls out a few hangers full of clothes.

The first dress in Dick's hand, he remembers as the red dress Georgia wore on their very first date. It was one of the things that first drew him to her; the way her cleavage looked in it. She stopped wearing clothes like that after they moved in together. Dick wonders if that was the reason she left it behind, or if it was because she didn't want to be reminded of their first date like he was just now.

He files through Georgia's clothes, realising they were all worn on significant dates. Georgia wore the blue strapless dress to their engagement party in 2003. The red sweater and black skinny jeans were worn on their three year anniversary when they took a vacation to Park City, Utah in the winter of 2002. Dick picks this outfit out to carry in his other hand, then carries the clothes to Jaclyn's room.

After dumping the big pile of clothes on the single-sized bed in the room, Dick holds up the sweater and jeans for Jaclyn to see.

"We're going to go out tonight," he says. "You can wear

this. Go ahead and put it on; I'm going to go freshen up."

Dick walks into Byrne's first, with Jaclyn close behind him. His height should allow him a more optimal viewing position to find his friend, which is why Jaclyn stands beside him, looking absolutely clueless.

"This is far more crowded than the taverns I am accustomed to," she says to herself.

Before Dick finds what he's looking for, though, a man joins them, shaking Dick's hand.

"Dick," he says.

"Sean," Dick nods back. "Been a while."

"Indeed," says Sean. "I am here to inquire about the nature of your relationship with this woman."

Though Dick normally finds Sean's speech a little jarring, this time he breathes out a strong puff of air as he thinks about how much he sounds like Jaclyn, and can't help wondering if he has also been transplanted from the past.

"Strictly friendship," says Dick.

Jaclyn extends her hand to greet the man. "Pleasure to meet you, sir."

"Her name's Jaclyn," Dick adds, then he leans over and whispers in Sean's ear, "If you're asking because you're interested, don't bother. She's a lesbian."

"How unfortunate," says Sean.

"You do not care for my name?" asks Jaclyn. "Perhaps you would prefer Miss Rousseau."

"French?" Sean inquires.

"Nay," says Jaclyn, "Though my father was." She pauses to observe Sean more closely and adds, "Dick has shown me air travel and its advanced accessibility, but still I did not expect to find a Chinaman here. You are Chinese, no?"

Sean blinks at her a few times before responding, "My lineage is Japanese diaspora."

Silence comes between Sean and Jaclyn as they continue to observe each other, trying to form some greater understanding of the other one. That is, until Dick interrupts and tells Jaclyn, "Japan is a country to the east of China."

Jaclyn can't quite contain herself when the word, "Fascinating," escapes her lips.

Still in a state of some confusion, Sean says, "Please excuse me," and retreats into the crowd.

Dick wipes his hand over his face in embarrassment. "Great," he says to himself, considering how the term 'Chinaman' is usually considered an offensive word. "Now Sean's going to think I'm a douchebag with racist friends."

"Did I say something I should not have?" Jaclyn asks, sensing the embarrassment rather than understanding Dick's words.

Dick turns his attention back to Jaclyn. Their height difference adds to the illusion that he's acting like her father figure again when he says, "Actually, yeah. We're not supposed to notice when people look different from us. Please don't comment on the colour of someone's skin, or the shape of their eyes, or anything like that..."

Before Dick can continue his rebuking, a short Hispanic man who had made a beeline for them interrupts.

"Hi," he says, "I'm Max."

"Dick Grayson," replies Dick. Slightly stunned, he looks over to Sean, who rejoins them and shrugs.

Jaclyn starts to open her mouth to say something, but Max gets in first, "Can I call you Richard for short?" he asks. "My brother-in-law is named Dick."

"Indeed," says Sean, startling Max, who hadn't noticed Sean following him. "His brother-in-law was responsible for rearranging the topography of his face."

"To be fair," Max adds, "we were young."

Jaclyn studies Max's face and settles her eyes on his crooked nose. She makes eye contact with him before asking, "You duelled with him?"

"Truth is," says Max, "he duelled, and I fell to the ground, screaming and holding my face."

Dick laughs, noting Max's intentional humour, but Max doesn't seem to notice. He sees that Max is too caught up in admiring Jaclyn's lips when she replies, "Yet you appear to wear the scar with pride."

It's only then that Dick realises Sean's earlier inquiry was for Max's sake.

"Souvenir," Max says, shrugging.

At this point, Dick decides it's best to just observe the remaining conversation between Max and Jaclyn, as there is something amusing about a man trying to impress a lesbian.

"Like a 't-shirt'?" Jaclyn asks.

"Exactly like a t-shirt," Max says, and adds, "I never caught your name."

"Jaclyn," she says, extending her hand again, this time with her palm facing downwards, allowing Max to take her hand and kiss the top of it.

"My pleasure," he says.

Jaclyn's lips curl up in a small smirk on her left side

when she says, "The pleasure is mine."

Dick starts pondering what Jaclyn might be up to, and what she might want to get out of Max. Then he wonders if she's just being friendly because of his brief lesson on racism.

"So," Max asks, "What is it you do for a living?"

"Piracy," Jaclyn says, and Dick wonders why she is being honest now when she hadn't been with him.

"Software? DVDs?" Max replies before clearly realising a normal person wouldn't dream of admitting that to a stranger.

Jaclyn, of course, doesn't understand such words and responds accordingly, "I find you confusing."

"And I find you confusing," Max repeats back to her.

"That, I suppose, is something we then have in common."

Max smirks. "Lebanese or not, I think I'd like to buy you a drink."

This statement causes Dick to think something got a little lost in translation, and decides it's even more amusing to watch a man hit on a lesbian when he doesn't know she is one. As long as it's not him being the ignorant one.

The four of them head back toward the bar to where Sean and Max had been seated, unfortunately discovering that their seats are no longer free.

While they wait for an opening, Jaclyn asks Max, "May I inquire about your profession?"

Max digs into his shirt pocket and takes out a business card, presenting it to Jaclyn. "Max Fuentes, reporter," he says.

To Dick, Max's posture looks smarmy, and he rolls his

eyes at how much he seems to be trying to impress her.

"What do you drink?" Max asks Jaclyn.

"Rum," she says.

"Rum and coke? On the rocks?"

Jaclyn just stares at Max, wide-eyed.

"Just rum, I think," Dick says, assisting them and wondering if Max will catch on that she is actually a pirate.

"Right." Max turns to the bar and places his order.

The moment he returns with Jaclyn's clear spirit, Dick's mobile phone rings.

"Excuse me," says Dick, and he steps away, moving out of the building so he can hear better.

"Perhaps you can enlighten me with the details of your introduction to Dick," Sean says to Jaclyn, reminding Max that he isn't there alone. "I have not known him to be a man who regularly finds the company of a female companion."

"I found him in Barbados," Jaclyn says. "He was taking up residence in an inn."

"An inn?" asks Max. "Barbados?"

"Dick's profession sees him regularly convening there," Sean clarifies.

"Richard," Max corrects Sean, but quickly he turns his attention back to Jaclyn, not caring to learn more about the man she is with, and asks, "What were you doing in Barbados?"

Before she can answer, though, Dick is back and gently takes hold of Jaclyn's arm.

"I'm sorry, gents. We have to go."

"It's fine; we can take care of Jaclyn for you," says Max.

Dick doesn't even need a moment to ponder this. "No,"

he says. Maybe he would be okay with it if she had been in New York more than a few hours.

Sensing trouble on Dick's part, Jaclyn says, "My apologies, Mr Fuentes." Then she downs all of the rum before returning the glass to Max's free hand. "*Adieu.*"

With that, she wraps her arm around Dick's and follows him out.

Once the pair are outside, Jaclyn inquires, "Whatever is the matter?"

"My mother is in the hospital. I have to go see her and I couldn't leave you here without me," he says, walking quickly in the direction of his apartment. "You can't come with me, either, though, so I'm going to drop you home first."

Jaclyn nods in understanding as she walks with him, and then queries, "May I ask you something?"

"Sure."

"Your name is Mr Grayson?"

"Yeah... why?"

"This is but an interesting coincidence. My beloved Kitty... her name was also Grayson. Katherine Grayson."

"That's just weird, but I don't have time to think about that right now. Let's just go back to my place, and we can marvel at it in the morning."

Dick enters the cancer ward and easily spots his father by his neatly-parted auburn hair, though from his rumpled state it doesn't look like he's changed his clothes in days. He approaches his father, who is sitting on a chair in the waiting room with his head in his hands, and sits down next to him.

"How's Mum?" he asks.

His father looks up at him blankly. "Oh, hello, son," he says, sounding tired. "I'll take you in so you can see for yourself. I know she'd like to see you."

Nodding as his father stands, Dick quickly joins him, meeting his eyes. They share a moment of sadness before turning, and Dick follows him down the corridor to his mother's room.

Knocking on the door, Dick's father calls into the room, "Pen, I'm back. I've got Richie with me."

Dick tries not to cringe when he hears the old nickname, but unfortunately his parents never noticed when he outgrew it. He thinks it's not becoming of a forty-two-year-old man, but knows now is not the time to raise that issue... again.

"Come in, Vic," Penelope says.

Her husband opens the door and steps inside the private patient room, then closes the door again once Dick is inside, already moving a chair up to the side of his mother's bed. Dick takes her hand and holds it in his own as he sits down beside her, while his father sits in the corner of the room. It's almost too hard for Dick to bear looking at her face, with how pale she is, and the way her skin sags so noticeably—a sign of how much weight she has lost in the past two months. A sad smile crosses his face when he tries to think of the positive aspect of her not losing her short hair to chemotherapy, but at the same time he knows she wishes she had the opportunity to dye it again to remove the grey.

"Oh, Mum," Dick says, but finds it hard to say anything else.

"Your Dad says you just got back from Barbados again," she says, offering to take the lead in the conversation.

Dick smiles. His mother always did have a way of taking the attention off of herself to shine it on someone else.

"Yeah," he says, nodding.

"Same as usual?"

Dick thinks back to the woman he left in his apartment, and the last few days they shared together. "Yes," he says, deciding he really doesn't want to get into that conversation.

"When are you going to bring me back some photos? Or maybe a nice Barbadian woman so that I can see you settle down soon?"

He chokes a bit at the question, knowing that he did technically bring back both a woman and photos. The question makes him think back to the conversation he had with his mother when she was first diagnosed with pancreatic cancer.

They were sitting in his parents' den, in the home where he grew up in Brooklyn. It was the Independence Day holiday, so he was off work. His father should have been there, too, but had been unexpectedly called in to deliver a baby, so it was just Dick and his mother.

"These odds aren't good," his mother had said to him. "They're going to put me on chemo, but they think the best that'll do is prolong my life maybe a few months."

"You've led a pretty full life, though, Mum. I mean, how many volunteer trips did you take to Asia and South America?"

"I know, and I guess that makes this easier. There's not that much I've missed out on. But... I guess I still hoped

I'd live long enough to meet my grandchildren."

It was a confession that had caught Dick off guard. Before then, he had no idea either of his parents even cared about him producing offspring. Indeed, though it may not have changed his mind about splitting up with Georgia, now that he was being faced with the impending death of his mother, it certainly crossed his mind more frequently.

"I don't know how to answer that," Dick says, snapping himself back into the present.

"Don't worry, you can forget about the lady. However, I would still like to see photos sometime soon. I bet the water looks beautiful."

Dick throws his mother a sad smile, wondering if he even has enough time to make another trip back to Barbados before she passes.

"I'll see what I can do," he says, stroking his mother's hand.

A nurse comes into the room carrying a small container and some water. "It's time for your medication, Mrs Grayson."

Penelope nods and tries to crack a smile. She takes her hand away from Dick so she can hold the water while she's swallowing her pills.

The experience makes Dick feel a little uneasy, so he avoids watching most of it. He'd rather be in high school again, experiencing the awkwardness that came with that, just to get to see his mother when she was still completely healthy.

After the nurse leaves, Penelope says, "Richie, I know I don't talk about my parents much, but I'm glad you could be here in a way I couldn't be for mine."

"Weren't you only a teenager when they died though?"

"Yes, but a very selfish one. I was lucky you weren't as bad as I was at seventeen. I ran away from home when my father got sick. Your Nan seemed healthy then and was able to look after your Pop, but I couldn't cope. Your Aunty Caroline spent days looking for me, even though they sent the police after me, too. I'd made it to Brisbane before they found me."

"From Melbourne?"

She nods. Though Dick has only been to Australia twice to visit his mother's family, he's familiar enough with the geography to know that is like travelling from New York to Florida.

"Wow, Mum. Nan and Pop must've been worried sick."

Penelope nods, and takes Dick's hand again. "It's probably what killed your Nan in the end. She had a stroke, but I think it's because she was worrying about me so much."

"You can't blame yourself for that."

"I don't any more. I've seen her, smiling at me, waiting for me to return to her..." She trails off and her eyes begin to droop.

Dick can barely take this talk any more. His eyes begin to water, and he doesn't want his mother to see him like that.

"I'll be back in a few days, Mum," he says, stroking her hand again.

Sleep overcomes her before he gets up. He nudges his father on the shoulder—who had fallen asleep in his chair—to let him know he is leaving.

As Dick leaves the hospital, he sees a kid selling early editions of the Sunday paper, and decides to pick up a copy as reading material for his subway trip home.

Most articles seem to be about the same old dreary news, a few tributes representing the Twin Tower anniversary, but he skips over those. One article in the World News section, however, catches his eye. The headline reads, *Barbados Bust*. The article goes on to explain that cops were raiding a place meant to have been occupied by passport forgers, but the men had been found dead. Murdered, in fact; their throats had been slashed with a kitchen knife.

"Shit," Dick says to himself aloud. Then in his head, he starts to consider how safe it is for him to be harbouring a murderer in his home. Why had it not occurred to him that Jaclyn was this dangerous before? At least the article also says that police have no leads, or even the murder weapon as evidence, but for how long? What if they trace it to Jaclyn, and then her back to him? *Fuck*, he thinks. Is this really the woman he brought home with him? Maybe it's just a coincidence.

He shuts the paper, which happens to also be good timing since he's about to reach his subway stop anyway. While he walks back to his apartment, he finds himself in two minds. On the one hand, there's no way any authorities would have Jaclyn's fingerprints on file. They don't do fingerprint scanning at airports yet. On the other hand, and perhaps more importantly, *what if this woman gets fed up with him and murders him, too*?

When Dick gets home, he pops his head into Jaclyn's room to find her sleeping, much to his relief. This is definitely something he's going to have to figure out how to deal with in the morning, but right now, he's too tired. He retires to his bedroom, and makes sure that he locks the door behind him. She may have avoided murdering him in his sleep when they were in Barbados together, but back then, Dick still had something she wanted. Passage to another destination and permanent residence. Now? Dick isn't sure she thinks he still has anything to offer her.

The apartment is quiet when Jaclyn wakes up, leaving her to wonder if Dick made it home last night. She wanders around every room just to be sure Dick isn't already awake, but leaves the room where the door is closed. There's only so much puttering about she can do before she finds herself bored and restless.

After sitting on the floor and staring at a wall for a good fifteen minutes or so, Jaclyn stands up and walks into the kitchen, digging through the cupboards to see what she can find that might be edible.

She pulls out a box of crackers, and as she shuts the door, Dick says, "Morning," frightening her enough that it causes her to jump.

Once her heart stops racing, Jaclyn says, "Good morning. Do you normally sleep this late? Not that I know what the time is, but it seems late."

"It's ten," Dick says. "I like sleeping in on weekends. You know, it's impolite to go through someone else's cupboards without asking."

He sounds as though he's accusing her of theft again, so she says, "I was simply looking for something to eat since I had no guidance from you."

"I'm sorry," he says, wiping his head backwards from

his brow, but he still seems rattled by something.

"Do I cause you discomfort?"

"I don't know. I've been thinking, I guess, about how little I really know about you. It didn't occur to me until last night, for example, that you've probably murdered people..."

"Aye," says Jaclyn, accidentally slipping into her pirate vernacular. "That is, I meant to say, does that worry you?"

"Depends; how many people have you murdered?"

"That, I cannot answer, as I did not keep a tally."

"Meaning, too many to count. Yeah, okay, I think I should be scared," Dick says, thinking aloud.

"I will not murder you; you have my word."

"How can I trust you?" Dick asks, frustrated. "I mean, really? What have I got to go on other than your word? And how do I know you're not going to go murdering anyone else?"

"Your magic box can provide you with answers for other matters of historical note, can it not?"

"I don't know how that's going to help you here."

"Kitty was the daughter of Lord Thomas Grayson; he was a rather prestigious writer of my time," Jaclyn informs him. "I suspect your magic box would be able to find him."

"Can you please stop calling it a magic box? It's called a *phone*," he says, and Jaclyn senses that every little thing is frustrating him further.

"If that is not enough," Jaclyn says, "Then my parents..." she sighs and takes a deep breath, knowing that revealing this will be the ultimate disclosure. She isn't really prepared to have to identify herself so much, so soon, but she doesn't feel like she has any other choice. "My parents were also nobles. I would hasten to guess you could find them, also."

"What are their names?"

"Count Leopold and Countess Caroline Rousseau," Jaclyn reveals, then as Dick is pressing away on his phone, she adds, "My father was born in Paris in fifteen eighty-nine, and my mother was London born in sixteen ten. I also have an elder brother, James, who was named in honour of King James, whom I was informed died three years prior to my brother's birth."

"Fuck me," Dick says, looking at his phone in a state of disbelief.

"I thought we had already established that I would do no such thing?"

At this, Dick laughs, and says, "No, that's not what I meant. I mean… ahh, I wish I could just show this to you so you could read it for yourself. No, I meant you're right, or at least I was able to find a record of your family." Dick pauses while he fiddles with the phone some more, then adds, "It says you disappeared in sixteen fifty-one, though. When you were seventeen? I thought you said it was sixteen sixty-one when you left?"

"For this, I think, perhaps we should sit down."

Jaclyn takes the box of crackers and leads Dick to his small dining table, where she takes a seat and starts munching on a cracker while she composes her thoughts.

"That is the last time anyone who knew me by that name would have seen me. Kitty and I ventured to Barbados under false names that year." After this reveal, Jaclyn proceeds to explain the circumstances of her journey with Kitty, and how she then later became a pirate. She did, however, leave out the small detail of how she came to murder Prudence.

"Right, well…" Dick says, taking in all the information. "I guess you have me seeing things differently now. It never occurred to me that someone may not actually choose to be a pirate, but become one out of necessity."

"You have my gratitude," Jaclyn says.

Dick nods, then stands up from the table and says, "I'm going to go pop in the shower now, and then we can work out what we're going to do today."

Whilst in the shower, Dick finds himself reviewing everything Jaclyn had just shared with him. She may be honest about her history, but she's still a murderer. The combination of that knowledge, wanting to avoid thinking about the date, and worrying about his mother causes Dick to decide that he needs to get Jaclyn out of his apartment and somewhere in public. Maybe find her some more clothes that won't remind him of Georgia.

Then it hits him. He can take her somewhere that will accomplish two things: fun, and physical exposure to his line of work. After that, maybe see where the wind takes them, and in the evening, a Broadway show. Dick thinks that maybe if Jaclyn is exposed to the fun side of Manhattan, it could give her something to live for. Something that doesn't involve crime. Perhaps she also needs something to take her mind off Kitty. Then he finds himself wishing she had told him what happened to her lover. Was she killed during a pirate attack? He supposes Jaclyn isn't ready to talk about it in any case, or she would have already.

Dick finishes rinsing his hair, and gets out of the

shower, firmly determined to enjoy the day, despite his mixed feelings.

Both fresh as the late morning, Dick and Jaclyn head out on foot toward Times Square wearing inconspicuous clothes. Georgia had, thankfully, left behind a couple of pieces of casual wear. In the daylight, Jaclyn is able to take a lot more in. The walk is slow to allow for the pirate to look up at all the tall buildings, and wonder why she did not bother to notice them when they headed in the opposite direction the night before.

When they hit Broadway, Jaclyn stops Dick by pulling on his shirt. She slowly turns around in a circle, taking in all the lights and billboards, the roads that intersect here, and the general large crowd of tourists and locals covering the pavement.

"This place is incredible," Jaclyn says, with her mouth agape when words are not coming out of it.

"This is where we'll spend our day, but our first stop is over there," Dick says, pointing across the street to a building with a colourful sign with words Jaclyn can't read. "Toys 'R' Us," he adds.

They cross the street and enter the store, and Jaclyn's eyes are even wider than before.

"First, I thought, since you shared so much about your life with me this morning, I'd show you some of the products the company I work for manufactures," Dick says.

"I would like that," Jaclyn says, and follows Dick upstairs, though she can't help glancing over at the giant wheel that occupies the entire centre of the store. "What is that?" she asks, pointing to it.

"It's called a ferris wheel. We'll go on that next; I'll tell you more about it then."

When Dick finds the action figures, he picks up a box with a toy man inside, and says, "This is the sort of thing we make down in Barbados. It's merchandise from a movie called *Jumping Jack*, which was released at the start of the month."

Jaclyn's eyes light up the way a two-year-old's would the first time he's offered chocolate. She takes the figurine in her hands to study it more carefully. "Can you show me the movie?" she asks. "You have made me very curious to experience these stories."

"Sure," Dick says. "After lunch."

Dick takes Jaclyn through a number of other shelves, explaining which toys he was a part of the process of, and talks about some competing companies.

"I want to know about the ferris wheel now," Jaclyn says, mid-explanation of a board game.

With a sigh, Dick says, "Okay, I'm boring you."

They head down to the lowest floor and line up for the ride. As it comes around to their turn to get on, Jaclyn looks at the carriage before them.

"What are those colourful spheres with faces meant to be?" she asks. "They are... a little haunting."

"You're a pirate, and you're afraid of M&Ms?" Dick muses. He looks at her face and notices her confusion, so adds, "Uh, they're the mascots for some chocolate balls that look like that, but, you know, without the faces, hands and feet."

"Chocolate… balls?" Jaclyn asks. "Now I think you must be speaking in jest. Chocolate is not solid; it is only for drinking."

"I swear to God I'm not. I'll take you to the M&M store next to show you exactly what I mean. Now come on, get in, there's nothing to be afraid of," Dick says, lightly pushing her toward the carriage.

With some hesitation, Jaclyn steps into the M&M carriage and sits down. Dick follows in right behind her, and sits on the opposite side.

Once all of the passengers are on the ride, and the wheel is spinning slowly and continuously, Dick notices the colour begin to leave Jaclyn's face.

"Are you okay?" he asks her.

Jaclyn's cheeks puff up a bit, and she keeps her mouth closed. She simply gives him a nod, but puts a hand on her stomach at the same time.

"Are you sure? You don't look well."

A split second later, vomit escapes Jaclyn's mouth and ends up on Dick's shoes, answering his question for him. Dick's reflexes send him into a standing position, grabbing hold of the blue M&M behind him, and trying to shake his shoes dry. Unfortunately, this causes the carriage to rock even more than it should be, and sends Jaclyn vomiting over the side, onto a kid below.

Immediately, the ride operator pulls their carriage back to the bottom, and Dick and Jaclyn are escorted out of Toys 'R' Us by security guards.

"Great," Dick says sarcastically, standing on the corner of Broadway and 44th Street, still shaking his shoes to try and get the gunk off.

"My apologies," Jaclyn replies with a look of utter despondence.

"How the hell do you survive sailing if you puke from something with as little movement as a ferris wheel?"

Jaclyn shrugs, "Different type of motion?"

"Dick?" a woman's voice calls out from the middle of the street, and Dick looks up to see who it belongs to.

"Hi, Sue," he replies, "What are you doing out here?"

He glances quickly at his shoes again, then looks at Sue. Dick's self-consciousness builds Jaclyn's curiosity for the woman.

"It's my daughter's birthday on Thursday, and I'm a little behind on present shopping," she says, running her fingers through her long dark hair. "You?"

Dick turns to Jaclyn in time to see her wiping her mouth on her sleeve, which sends a shudder into his shoulders. He turns back to Sue and replies, "Showing a new friend the sights. Sue, this is Jaclyn." He indicates the pirate, and adds, "We met in Barbados."

"Oh, I see," Sue replies, sounding a little disappointed. She feigns a smile before directing her attention to Jaclyn and says, "Nice to meet you."

"We are just friends," Jaclyn says, and Dick is clearly confused about why Jaclyn would even bother clarifying that point. "Would you care to join us for our luncheon meal later?" she adds.

Jaclyn enjoys making Dick look lost. He must be wondering why she is being friendly to this Chinese woman after the previous night.

"Thank you for the offer, but I don't think I can. My daughter is only with my ex until four, and I still have a lot

I need to get done today."

"Please. I insist," Jaclyn says, ignoring Sue's discomfort.

Sue turns her attention back to Dick, looking to him for the answer she should give. At that moment, Dick cringes, shifting his weight from one foot to the other. Jaclyn realises his socks must be feeling a little wet at the soles

"It's fine," Dick says, looking at Sue. "I need to go back home and, uh, fix some things first, but how about we meet at Carnegie's in an hour and a half? Will that be enough time for you to find something for Angelina?"

With a smile, Sue checks her watch and nods. "See you at one-thirty."

Jaclyn turns and watches Sue enter the toy store before turning back to Dick.

"She wishes for you to court her," Jaclyn says matter-of-factly.

"What?" Dick asks, stepping off the curb to cross the street. "I don't think so," he adds, with Jaclyn following close behind. "We're not much more than colleagues. She's the person who wrote the screenplay for *Jumping Jack*."

Jaclyn shrugs. "Believe what you wish."

SIX

"Land ho!" Jacqueline yelled from her position aloft in the crosstrees. She peeled her spyglass away from her face and looked down at Captain McDonald on the quarterdeck.

The captain gave the orders to head toward an inlet of the uninhabited island, where they planned to careen *Mary's Revenge* and remove its barnacles, as well as repair damages made to the hull and sails during their last attack.

Jacqueline climbed down the ratlines from the top of the mainmast and met with the captain.

"Fine work, Jack," said the captain, slapping Jacqueline on the back. "Ye will replace Dog as lookout."

"May he rest in peace," muttered Jacqueline under her breath. To the captain, she said, "Aye, sir!"

While most of the pirates worked on the brig's hull, Katherine supervised a group of them on the beach. Some, like Jacqueline, were charged with the task of mending the sails, whilst others wandered into the jungle to see what they could find in order to help them make camp.

When Katherine got tired of standing, she decided to sit down next to Jacqueline, moving in close so that their legs touched.

"Are ye not afraid another may see us in this way?" Jacqueline whispered, taking a break from her stitching.

Kitty shook her head. "Nay. I have endured watching several other men fucking each other over hammocks in the forecastle in their spare time. These men know you share my cabin. They must assume we lie together as those men do."

Jacqueline returned to her stitching as she continued the conversation. "They, however, be acting on lust. They may not take as kindly to our love."

The words resonated in Kitty's mind and made her want to kiss Jacqueline, hearing how she expressed her worry about their safety. She held back her desire, however, and simply said, "They may not like it, but they will not do anything for the same reason they voted me quartermaster. They be frightened of me, and they need me."

A sly smile crossed Jacqueline's face, and she paused her mending for a moment again so that she could grip Kitty's hand to express her appreciation. Returning to her duty, Jacqueline said, "I still prefer to keep much of our affections private."

Kitty nodded, and added, "We will find some privacy in the jungle after sundown tonight."

With that, Kitty stood back up to continue her supervision of the rest of the crew on the shore.

At sundown, the entire crew was on the beach, sitting in small groups, waiting for Noah to finish roasting two wild pigs over an open fire. Jacqueline took in the scent of the meat, and decided to join the cook. She considered the possibility of befriending him, now that she felt a lot more comfortable talking to the rest of the crew without Kitty's assistance.

"How did ye lose yer arm?" Jacqueline asked, watching the pigs as she spoke. Noah had been without his left arm the entire time she had been part of McDonald's crew, and had heard losing it had been the reason he was first given to the role of cook, but never heard the story of how he lost it.

"Sea monster," Noah said with a straight face.

Jack raised an eyebrow at him, "Scurvy dog, lying through yer teeth just because I have so little sea experience."

He shrugged, but Jack wouldn't leave it alone.

"What really happened?"

A smirk formed on the side of Noah's mouth, but then he became serious again before starting his tale. "T'were about fifteen years ago. I were a Royal Navy sailor back then. Not by choice, mind, but were little I could do about that, or so first I be thinking." He chuckled momentarily before catching himself, unsure where that came from. "Ye have to understand that barely four hours sleep each night for months can do things to yer head. I were dreaming up all kinds o' ways of escaping. Then the cook's idea of food seemed to be like eating the ship itself. Were about ready to drown meself when something inside me suggested a better solution might be to *accidentally* get me arm blown off during gunnery practice. Thought for sure they be relieving me of me duties."

Noah shook his head, looking glum.

"Were you relieved?" Jack asked.

"Fortune did not look upon me kindly that day. After I were on the mend, the first mate announced the ship's cook died of scurvy and I be taking his place. The rat bastards." Noah poked one of the pigs with a stick.

"Then how did ye join this crew?"

A broad smile crossed Noah's face. "Aye, well. I had been in the galley cooking and I lug the pot up for serving, but as me eyes adjust to the light I see the crew laying about the deck, blood and guts all hanging out. The captain's head, with holes for eyes, was on the end of a cutlass, being held aloft by one of the many pirates aboard. As I get closer, they all turn and look at me. So I says to them, 'What you lot doing standing around? Vitties not gonna eat itself.'" Noah yawned, leading Jack to believe that the end of his story, until his voice started again. "See, vitties was poisoned."

To that, Jack raised a questioning eyebrow at him. "Ye poisoned them?"

Smirking, Noah said, "Ye be so easy to hoodwink, Jack." He placed his right hand on Jack's shoulder. "Ye gotta fix that if you gonna survive with us."

Jack frowned, trying to avoid a pout, and Noah turned his attention back to the meat.

Before she could ask anything else, the pirate known as Joseph Turner joined them, looking at the spit. "Done yet?" he asked Noah.

"Couple more minutes, I reckon."

Turner turned his attention to Jacqueline and said, "So yer no longer mute, I see."

She tilted her head to the side and looked at him.

"Guess not," she said. "Just shy before."

"Fight well enough for a shy man."

"Never need to talk to kill a man."

Turner chuckled, "That be true."

"Besides, I have yet to earn a scar like yours," she said, looking at the scar that started at his forehead, skipped his eye, but then ran from just below it to his right ear. "Must be better than you."

Noah laughed at this, revealing the few teeth that remained in his mouth as rotten.

"I was a much younger man when I got that," Turner said.

"I be but twenty."

Turner rolled his eyes. "Typical cocky boy. Just ye wait."

At this point in the conversation, Katherine joined them and said, "I hope that not be a threat."

Despite their ten-year age difference, with Katherine the younger, Turner shook his head, slightly fearful but attempting not to show it. "No, sir," he said, respecting his superior officer.

They were then interrupted by a couple of men quarrelling loudly a few yards away. Since the captain was busy elsewhere, Katherine marched over to them and tore a flintlock out of the hand of one of them just before he had the chance to fire. She was too far away for Jacqueline to be able to hear what was being said, so she just observed in silence, until Noah handed her some meat.

Jacqueline took her food and found a place in the sand where she could sit to eat. Shortly after, the lone African pirate known only as Turtle sat down next to her. He was wearing breeches that were torn and frayed at his knees, and a vest that exposed his muscular body. She shifted uncomfortably but tried not to be rude. It was just that she had yet to properly meet an African man, and the things she had heard about them when growing up were not pleasant. These men should be *slaves*, she thought. It was bad enough she found herself caught up with pirates, leaving her wealthy family behind. Not that she had seen her parents for over a year before departing for the Caribbean, since they had left their grown children to care for themselves when they relocated to Paris.

"Evening." Turtle greeted her in such a friendly manner that she did not know what to make of it.

"Evening," she replied, not knowing what else to say.

"Do I scare you?" he asked. "It is just that whenever I see you, you appear to be trying to avoid me."

Since this was the first time Jacqueline had heard Turtle speak, given what he said was true, she was impressed with his use of the English language, especially as it was better than many of the other pirates she had spoken to. It left her rather speechless.

"Shall I take that as a yes?" he asked.

"My apologies," she said. "I be a little shy," she added, figuring that was at least a believable excuse, given her limited speech over the last few months. Then, since Turtle was being friendly to her, she decided to ask, "How long ye been sailing with these gents?"

"More than a decade." He paused to take a breath before elaborating, "I was picked up just before McDonald was made captain. He convinced the crew to let me join them."

From this, and looking the man over more closely,

Jaclyn concluded that Turtle was probably in his late thirties—perhaps even twenty years her senior.

Deciding that she quite enjoyed hearing tales of how and why everyone had turned pirate, she asked, "Why did ye decide to join? Also, how did ye end up encountering McDonald in the first instance?"

"I used to be a house slave in Barbados," he said. "If that were you, would you not also prefer a life where you have a chance at actually getting paid for your work?"

Jacqueline thought back to the time when she didn't even have to work and could afford anything she desired, and how little compensation her servants got. There was a little niggling feeling in her stomach at the thought, but she couldn't identify the cause.

"I suppose being rich and not having to work at all would be best," she said, hiding the reminiscent feeling in the way she spoke.

"I do not know; I may have to disagree with that. It could be rather boring. I find that I need to have more in life than gold and silver. Amongst this crew, everyone sees me as an equal. Is that not better than finding yourself superior to everyone around you without having to lift a finger?"

Jacqueline looked confused, not really understanding what Turtle was trying to say.

"I might ask, how can someone who does nothing be superior to any person who does something?"

Turtle's words were a little much for her to understand immediately, so she stored the quote in her mind and in turn asked him, "So how did ye get away?"

"When I was young, my father taught me that I had to

fight for what I believe in, so I fought and escaped," he said.

Turtle paused a moment and Jacqueline noticed a little water forming in the corner of his eye. He collected himself before continuing.

"I stowed away on a merchant vessel, and McDonald found me when pirates ransacked the stores." Turtle smiled at this memory and then added, "He is a good man."

Katherine interrupted the conversation by sitting down next to Jacqueline and handing the pair of them more meat from the spit.

"What be that quarrel for earlier?" Jacqueline asked.

"Bones accused Tucker of insulting his manhood. I prevented him from shooting Tucker, but only temporarily. They will settle their dispute as per the code, duelling at dawn tomorrow."

Jacqueline rolled her eyes.

"Some men take this freedom a little too far," Turtle noted, punctuating his statement with a frown, and drawing the women's attention back to him.

"That is true," Katherine agreed.

"Turtle has been telling me how he became a free man," Jacqueline informed her lover.

"I imagine it was far more elaborate than our tale," Kitty said.

Turtle looked at her with interest. "I have not heard yours," he said. "At least, nothing is known of you prior to your escaping the Navy when they sank your last vessel."

"He prefers to keep it that way," Jacqueline accidentally let slip, knowing Katherine had not wanted to invent more backstory that could have holes poked into it.

"Only due to the dullness compared to the stories of others."

That was the understatement of the year, thought Jacqueline, though she knew it was not possible for them to share the true account of their move to piracy. Doing so would be tantamount to revealing their sex—or at least hers—and that, according to Kitty, would lead to her being raped every day. As much as she appreciated Kitty keeping her safe, there were times like this that she wished she could just be honest with those who were honest with her. In fact, considering her time on the previous vessel, there were also times she wondered if Kitty's fears were entirely warranted.

Jack thought back on the time when she brought that issue to Kitty a month before, asking if they might be able to test the men on board to see how they'd act around women. Up until that point, they hadn't encountered women on the sea; just in Tortuga. Shortly thereafter, they found a ship with women on board. After violently slaughtering the men, Captain McDonald put it to the vote what should be done with the women.

Remembering the looks on the faces of the women as they were used for the pleasure of the crew brought a sick feeling to her stomach, and she had to put the rest of her meat in the sand, since she could eat it no longer.

"It is a dull story," Jack agreed.

"I am still interested," Turtle said.

Kitty eyed Turtle with a look of some suspicion. "So it would seem."

This could be interesting, Jacqueline thought. They'd never been questioned on their story before, and so hadn't even discussed how they would falsify it. Since Kitty was the storyteller, though, she knew she could leave it up to her to spin something believable.

"We were shipbuilders' apprentices back in Barbados, and became tired of working on the ships without getting to sail," Kitty said, sounding like she was revealing a genuine confession. Jack watched in awe as the lies continued without a hint of their fiction. "So we appropriated one of the sloops we worked on with a dozen other men and set off to find some pirates that would let us join them. What with us not really knowing the waters, and figuring that would be the best way to find our fortunes, it seemed the best choice."

"That is less dull than I expected," Turtle said.

Kitty shrugged.

"Were you also raised in Barbados?"

"Aye."

Jack kept her laughter inside so as not to raise suspicion, but she couldn't help feeling amused at how the lies fell. At least they lived in Barbados long enough to know relevant details if asked.

"I was captured and taken there when I was fifteen," Turtle shared.

"I am sorry for what my people do to yours," Kitty offered.

It was the first time Jack had ever heard anything remotely like an opinion to do with the African slave trade coming from Kitty's mouth, and given all the other lies she had fed Turtle that evening, Jack was unsure of its legitimacy. She decided it was something she would have to discuss with her later.

"And I, too," Turtle said, before excusing himself from their company.

When he was gone, and just Kitty and Jack remained, Jack commented, "I never knew Africans could be so… polite. Father often described them as even too barbaric to be put to use in his business."

"Is it not fascinating the things we have learned through experience these past three years?" Kitty said, standing up.

Jack pulled herself up so that she could retain her whisper and avoid odd looks from the other men. "I am not sure fascinating is the word I would use, but I am not the writer amongst us."

With a smile, Kitty nodded her head to the left, expecting Jack to follow her as she left the fireside. They walked away from the camp toward the jungle, where they could find what could count as privacy away from the crew.

The couple pulled some large leaves off a nearby tree to use for a makeshift bed, and kicked away as many rocks and sticks as they could to avoid as much discomfort as possible.

Kitty removed her doublet to reveal the padded vest that hid her curves, which she wore over a long-sleeved shirt, then lay down on the leaves.

As Jacqueline lowered herself to Kitty's side, she said, "Tell me a story."

She nuzzled her face into Kitty's neck and took her hand, while Kitty noticed how rough Jack's skin had become.

"It has been too long since your last tale. Please tell me

you are still imagining them," Jack whispered softly.

That was the moment that Kitty realised she hadn't been. In fact, the last time she had written anything, they were still living in Barbados. Kitty wondered what was holding her back. Could it be her quartermaster duties? If it were that, she decided, then she would have still written when they first turned to piracy. Could it be that this life on the high seas had completely taken away her identity? Lest Jack begin to suspect the same, Kitty decided to invent a new story as they lay there together. It started out as a romantic tale of courting, rather reminiscent of their first few months.

As she spun her tale, Kitty's fingers wandered across Jack's body. She imagined the story completely in her mind, before she described it, and sent shivers down her own spine until they pooled between her legs. The story became more explicit then, and Kitty eagerly acted out all that she described.

She slowly removed Jack's clothing, piece by piece, her heart pounding from the adrenaline pumping throughout her body as she hoped they would not be found. Kitty wanted to fully experience her lover.

Jack closed her eyes, and Kitty could tell she was savouring the moment, especially when she shuddered every time Kitty whispered suggestively into her ear, or traced a finger around one of her taut nipples.

Though Kitty kept her shirt and vest on, she soon removed her breeches and sat atop her lover, aligning their genitals, and began to thrust. This continued at varying speeds, depending on whether or not Kitty was leaning down to kiss Jack. Short but deep gasps indicated when she had satisfied Jack, and the thrusting continued only a little longer until Kitty had to bite her lip to prevent herself from screaming as she came.

Jacqueline reached her thumb up to Kitty's bottom lip, and wiped away a smear of blood, just before Kitty hastily pulled her breeches back on and collapsed from exertion beside her.

Before the sun even gave a hint of its appearance the next morning, Kitty got up, leaving Jack behind in the leaves. She hadn't been able to sleep well, both because she knew how early she'd have to be up to wake the duellers, and the realisation of how long it had been since she had written anything kept troubling her. After giving up trying to sleep, she scuttled slowly down to the shore and went for a walk along the beach so that she could be alone in her thoughts.

With the tide gently lapping at her bare feet, she mused that it was an experience she never would have thought to describe when she was back in London, or even Barbados. Back in those days, she would not have dreamed to be outside without shoes on. As far as she was aware, no writers had published books about pirates, either. She half-wondered if that was because most pirates were illiterate fools, and thus were not likely to write about themselves. Anyone else would not be able to portray them accurately, she thought, so perhaps that is why none have tried.

Kitty sat down in the sand and allowed the tide to wash over her further as she considered these things. Why couldn't she be the writer to embrace this? She scoffed at herself. Because when would she have the time now, with all her officer duties? Lights out at eight in the evening meant she wouldn't be able to see the paper she was writing on, let alone the words, if she wanted to work on anything at the end of the day whilst aboard *Mary's Revenge*. She supposed she would have to figure out how to fit it in whenever they were on land.

When Kitty began to see a hint of the sun rising along the horizon, she stood up, and brushed the sand off her breeches as best she could. She headed back to the camp, passed the dying embers from the fire that cooked their meal the night before, and found the place where Tucker laid himself to rest. His filth bothered her, despite the fact that was not uncommon amongst the crew, so rather than wake him with her hands, she kicked him in his ribs. Tucker stirred, and swatted his hand in front of his face out of reflex.

Frustrated, Kitty kicked him again, rolling him over to his front so that when he finally roused, he got a mouth full of sand. Tucker continuously spat it out as he stood up, then looked at Kitty with resentment.

"Jesus, Tucker," Kitty swore. "Not my fault yer in this mess. Bones is already up, and dawn approaches." She nodded toward the horizon, indicating both the sun rising and Bones's silhouette. "Least ye could do is make it harder for him. This rate, yer gonna be too slow to even have yer pistol out and yer shot in the back."

These words sobered Tucker right up, and he marched over to the duelling site, with Kitty close behind.

Jack woke up to the sound of a pistol being fired and started hyperventilating when she sat up in a rush. Her breathing calmed as she felt around her body and determined that she wasn't wounded. Only then did she notice that Kitty was no longer beside her, so she stood up and walked out of the jungle.

It wasn't long before Jack spotted the crowd of pirates gathered along the beach, facing the sea. She jogged toward them and slipped herself in between Turner and Noah, wondering what had captivated their interest so much. Then she saw the unmoving body lying just in front of her. Jack's eyes followed the blood on his chest to the hole it seeped from, then turned away.

"Tucker never stood a chance," Turner said, and Jack looked up at him. He looked back at Jack and added, "Ye do not want to start a conflict with Bones. Mark my words."

Jack just nodded at him.

Shortly after, while they continued to stand in silence, even though the rest of the crew started to move off and get back to their duties, Jacqueline could sense a new, somewhat overbearing presence behind her. She turned around, hoping to see Kitty, but instead found herself face-to-ribs with Turtle. Though she knew he was tall, having seen him standing at a distance next to other pirates, this was the first time she had been able to compare him to herself side-by-side. She slowly raised her head to get a glimpse of the expression on his face, but she couldn't read it.

Turtle was looking past Jacqueline, and then she noticed some movement out of the corner of her eye. When she turned, she realised Turner was patting Turtle's back. Her eyes narrowed in on the action, confusion setting in.

The feeling dispersed somewhat when Turner said,

"Sorry for your loss."

He was *comforting* Turtle? Jacqueline had no idea pirates even grieved for the loss of their crewmates. She hadn't seen it amongst all the other deaths in all the fights they've had procuring food, wares, and gold from other vessels. Add to that the complication that Turtle was *African.*

"Were you friends?" Jack asked Turtle.

Turtle nodded. "Tucker was the first man to agree with McDonald and welcome me amongst this crew. Bones is a senseless bastard."

"Do not dare go after him for this," Turner warned. "We need you more than we need him, and I do not trust his scruples."

Turtle shook his head. "As much as my blood boils for it, revenge is not the answer."

A quick glance at Turtle's right hand tightly gripping his cutlass, and Jack wasn't sure she believed that he really meant to stay away from Bones. With mixed emotions, she resigned herself to the idea that she may have to acknowledge him as human after all.

SEVEN

"Ahoy thar, landlubber," a voice says, coming from behind Dick as he walks down the street. "What ye be doing here?"

Dick is only about a block away from his office, but he stops walking and turns around, hoping he hasn't been ambushed by yet another pirate.

Fortunately, he sees a man in a business suit. "What are you doing, Jason?"

"Arr! Don't ye know it be International Talk Like a Pirate Day?" Jason asks.

Dick rolls his eyes. "You're an idiot," he says, then turns around and continues walking.

Jason follows, mumbling things like, "Ye be no fun, landlubber."

It's not that Dick is disinterested in having fun, but he gets enough actual pirate at home. He's just afraid listening to trite and overused pirate phrases at work might send him over the edge.

Jaclyn is watching some video hits show on the television when she hears a knock on the door. The only thing she knows for certain is that the person on the other side is not Dick, since it's his apartment, and he doesn't need to knock. She is thankful for the interruption, though. Not yet being familiar enough to understand the remote control, she is rather tired of listening to the same songs over and over again, especially when, for the most part, they all sound like noise to her. That is, except for, "Sure Thing" by Miss Spring, which reminds her of a seventeenth century ballad, and actually has the sounds of instruments she recognises—an organ, and a violin. She's listened to and enjoyed it enough to have the lyrics memorised now.

When Jaclyn opens the door, she leans on the door frame and greets her visitor, "Mr Fuentes."

He doesn't respond immediately, too busy looking over her clothes, until he reaches her bare feet, and his eyes work their way back up her body again.

"May I ask how you found your way here?" Jaclyn asks, snapping Max out of his trance.

"Please, call me Max," he says, responding to her greeting rather than her question. "That is a stunning corset," he adds. "Is this what you usually wear at home?"

"I find more comfort in my own attire," she says. "It is much preferred to that which clothed me when we met the other night."

"Who *are* you?" Max asks, intrigued.

"Did we not already exchange introductions?"

"We did, but..." Max pauses to look around the hallway a moment, then changes the direction of the conversation to ask, "Do you mind if I come in and sit down?"

Jaclyn looks him over, and finds his stature and appearance to be completely non-threatening, so she swings the door open to allow him to pass her. Once Max is seated on the black leather couch, Jaclyn shuts the door behind her.

"Do you mind if I switch this off?" Max asks, indicating the television. "I'm not especially fond of Nym-B$$. I had to interview him once. He's a bit of a dick."

"Please," Jaclyn says. "I wished to have done that an hour ago."

Max looks at her, confused. "You don't know how to turn off the TV?"

She shakes her head.

"Come here," he says, and she joins him on the couch, scooting right up next to him so their legs touch. Max shivers a little before drawing Jaclyn's attention to the remote control he collected from the coffee table. "It's pretty easy," he says. "Just press the red button."

As Max does so, silencing the hip-hop music and causing the television to go black, Jaclyn says, "There is so much magic in your world."

Max considers this, then looks over her outfit again. Connecting the dots, he says, "So, when you said you were involved in piracy... did you mean to say that you are an actual pirate?"

Jaclyn shrugs. "How honest do I appear to you?"

He shuffles further over on the couch so that he can get a better look at Jaclyn when he responds. "I wouldn't expect a real pirate to admit to being one."

"Perhaps, then, it was said in jest."

There's only slight movement when Max shakes his head, disagreeing with Jaclyn. "I don't know. You don't even know how to work a TV..." He pauses, remembering the date, and adds, "Then again, it is International Talk Like a Pirate Day..."

But before Max can continue his train of thought, his phone rings, and he pulls it out of his inside coat pocket to answer it. He uses the index finger on his spare hand to indicate "one moment" to Jaclyn.

"Chief," he says. Then he nods a few times before saying, "I have to what?" A pause, then, "Take the bus? Why can't I fly?"

Jaclyn watches Max roll his eyes a few times until he notices her watching him intently. Then he smiles, an idea crossing his mind.

"Fine, Chief. I'll take the bus." Max hangs up his phone and returns it to his coat. "Well, Buccaneer," he says, finding a nickname for Jaclyn. "How'd you like to go on a little adventure?"

Jaclyn looks around the trappings of the apartment, wishing Dick would trust her enough to let her out on her own. After all, she's already been there a week.

"When will we be departing?" she asks.

"Uh," he says, momentarily thrown. "Immediately."

Jaclyn smiles and quickly runs into another room, spitting out, "Wait here," as she goes.

The next minute, Jaclyn is back, having thrown on her stockings and boots, wrapped her scarf around her head, and adorned her waist with a black sash that is decorated at the ends with gold baubles.

Max raises an eyebrow at her, but doesn't comment on the additions to her wardrobe.

"Ready?" he asks.

Pulling a small bag off the coffee table, Jaclyn says, "Dick left this for me 'in case of emergency,' though did not actually specify what he meant by that. I am presuming leaving his home may count as such." She hangs the strap around her neck and adds, "Now we may depart."

Jaclyn leaves the apartment first, and Max, realising she had not bothered to lock the door—because she didn't know how—locks it for her.

Once they're in the lift, Jaclyn asks, "What will this adventure entail?"

"Well, apart from the press conference in Washington I have to get to in just over five and a half hours, I don't know yet. That'll be part of the excitement."

At the Port Authority Bus Terminal, Max leads Jaclyn through one of the many gates to their bus. When the ticket collector takes their tickets, he pauses to admire Jaclyn's bust.

"Do you not know it is rude to stare?" Jaclyn asks, snapping the ticket collector out of his trance.

"Sorry, I was just, uh, admiring your corset," he replies, handing the tickets back to Max.

They head toward the bus and Max passes his hand out for Jaclyn to take as she steps onto the bus. Once they are comfortably seated somewhere near the middle, Max leans his chair backwards.

"Why do men do that?" Jaclyn asks.

"Do what?" Max replies.

"Stare at me."

"Have you seen yourself?" Max asks, bewildered. "Especially today? You do realise it's *Talk* Like a Pirate Day, not *Dress* Like a Pirate Day, right?"

Jaclyn shrugs. "You are being confusing again. Can we discuss another subject?"

"Sure," Max says, preparing himself for small talk. "So, first time to America?"

"What do you mean when you say 'America'?" Jaclyn asks. Being more familiar with the term 'the Americas,' but having learned the country she's in can also be referred to as 'America,' she just wants to clarify.

Max looks somewhat confused himself, but answers, "Ah, the United States of."

Jaclyn considers the question, thinking back on her only previous chance to travel to this land, and how that came to be. Business in Barbados had treated her and Kitty well, despite the brief war with England. After a year there, Katherine—under the name of Thomas MacGregor—was living in good stead on the island.

One evening in late May, 1652, Katherine and Jacqueline had headed into the Spitting Dog Tavern, as had been a customary excursion for them every other week since the Charter of Barbados was ratified in January.

"Mr and Mrs MacGregor," greeted the tavern keeper.

"Mr Jennings," said Jacqueline.

"It is good to have you with us again this evening."

Jacqueline nodded.

They took a seat at a table in the corner of the main tavern room, and Mr Jennings brought them complementary drinks. As they drank, Jacqueline noticed her friend Jan Roosa enter the tavern with his hurdy gurdy, head straight for his stool in the corner, and begin to play for the crowd.

Slowly the crowd came to notice the music, which sounded like a blend of bagpipes and a violin. After a couple of songs, Jacqueline stood up and opened her mouth to accompany the music with her melodious voice.

Jacqueline noticed the eyes of a few of the tavern's regulars turn to watch her, and their smiles spread from ear to ear. She then observed a few unfamiliar faces staring at her in awe as she sang, causing her to smile all the wider.

It was not all that uncommon for a new Barbadian resident to introduce themselves to Jacqueline after a performance, not realising that she lived as a married woman. Therefore, on this particular night, when she noticed a new gentleman walk into the tavern as she was performing, and stare at her intently the entire time, without even ordering a drink, that is precisely what she expected him to do. When this gentleman did not behave in such a manner, it completely blindsided her. She returned to her seat next to Kitty without a single greeting from anyone in the audience, though he did continue to stare.

"Have you seen that man before?" Jacqueline asked Kitty, indicating the newcomer.

Kitty looked at the black-haired man and shook her head.

"He is causing me some discomfort," Jacqueline added.

"Would you like me to duel him?"

"Oh, no, I do not think that is necessary."

"Very well; perhaps we should bid our farewell to Mr Jennings and be on our way," Kitty suggested.

"Yes, please."

The couple found the tavern keeper, and just for good measure, Kitty pointed out the man and asked, "Would you please inquire about his interest in my wife?"

Mr Jennings said, "But of course, Mr MacGregor."

"Farewell," said Kitty.

"Thank you again for giving me the opportunity to sing," added Jacqueline. "Until next time."

The women exited the tavern and started walking in the direction of their home, but after a short time, Jacqueline noticed that she started feeling a little queasy. She took hold of Kitty's arm to steady herself.

Unable to shake the feeling, she told Kitty, "I am unsettled."

Kitty stopped them and turned Jacqueline to face her.

"Why?" Kitty asked, but Jacqueline was unable to answer. Seeing the gentleman from the tavern only a few yards away left her speechless, though explained her feelings.

Kitty tried shaking Jack to snap her out of her trance with no success. Next she turned to see what Jack was looking at.

"Lady Grayson?" the man asked, and Jack fainted.

Jaclyn was later told by Kitty what happened whilst she was unconscious.

"No," Kitty said, looking at her fallen lover on the street. "No, this is Jacqueline MacGregor. My wife."

She had been nervous hearing her true name from a stranger, but she refused to show him that she had any inkling what he was talking about.

"I know that," the man said, "she is not to whom I refer." He held out his hand to greet Kitty and introduced himself, "Charles Bromley. My father sent me out here to find you."

"Oh," said Kitty, and paused to think a moment. "In that case, would you mind helping me carry my wife home?"

"You do not need to refer to her as your wife around me."

"Force of habit," Kitty said. "Will you help?" she asked again.

Charles nodded, and lifted the woman up from her armpits, while Kitty took her legs.

Jacqueline recovered sitting in the main room of her home to a view of the tavern gentleman fanning her face. Still in shock, she found herself retreating into her chair as far as she could.

"Jack, this is Mr Bromley, my employer's son," Kitty informed her.

When Jacqueline turned her attention toward Kitty, she noticed she had changed into her women's fashion, which eased her worries some. If Katherine was comfortable exposing her identity in front of this man, then she knew they must be safe.

"What brings you to Barbados, Mr Bromley?" Jack asked.

"My father is expanding his business. He wishes for me to take over from you here, and move you on to Virginia."

"No!" Jack yelled, standing to emphasise her point.

"Please, Jack, settle," Kitty said calmly, taking Jack's hands.

"I do not wish to leave again," Jack said softly, directing her attention solely to Kitty. "We are happy here, are we not?"

"I am afraid that matters not to Sir Bromley," Kitty replied. "We must go."

Jacqueline frowned at Kitty, glanced at Charles just long enough for him to notice her frustration, and then stormed out of the room, retreating to her bed chamber.

After recalling the memory, Jaclyn tells Max, "I was supposed to travel to Virginia in sixteen fifty-two, but the brigantine I was on ended up being taken by pirates."

Max doesn't reply.

"That is how I became a pirate," she says, then tells him the story of how she and Kitty ended up in Barbados in the first place.

"Did you just explain all this to me to make sure I know you're a lesbian?" Max asks.

"A what?" she asks in return.

"Lesbian. Dyke. Homosexual..." Max trails off when none of these words ring a bell. He ends up rephrasing, "Interested in women, only."

A smile crosses Jaclyn's face. She told him about how she became a *pirate*, and the thing he chose to focus on was her relationship with Kitty?

"That was not my specific intention, though if it will prevent you from trying to court me, I see no harm in saying yes."

"It won't," Max replies.

Jaclyn isn't really sure how to respond to that—mentioning her interest in women seemed to prevent Dick from trying to take things further with her, so why is Max different? On the other hand, she thinks, perhaps it will be amusing to watch Max try.

Curiosity getting the better of her, she settles on asking, "Why?"

"You referred to Kitty as if you're no longer together. Plus, she's not here," Max admits. "And I've seen the way you've been looking at me."

Jaclyn puts a hand to her chest and lets out a gasp, despite the fact she's not entirely sure how she's been looking at him. Could curiosity be mistaken for attraction by a man? She laughs mildly to herself, because in her experience, men will find any reason to think she's attracted to them. Rather than gratifying him with a response, she turns to face the window beside her, and notices that the skyscrapers are no longer around.

When Jaclyn turns around again to change the topic, she finds Max with a notepad and pen in his hands, writing something down. Instead of commenting on the scenery, Jaclyn asks, "Is it common for people to read and write here?"

Max puts his pen down and looks confused again. "You know, just because America isn't England doesn't mean we have poor literacy."

It occurs to Jaclyn that Max hasn't been taking her piracy story seriously, and thus the concept of her not being as well educated as him may not even cross his mind. She confesses, "I do not know how."

"Really?"

She shrugs. "I recognise some words, but nothing more."

"Well then," says Max, "I think we found our travelling activity."

For the rest of the bus ride to Washington, Max uses his notepad to tutor Jaclyn. They don't get much further than the alphabet, but that's because they only have three-and-a-half hours by that point, and Jaclyn struggles a lot.

Immediately after jumping off the bus, Max leads Jaclyn to an old building. They step inside to a large banquet hall.

At one end of the room, there is a long table and five empty seats behind it, and microphones at each place. In front of the table are rows of chairs. Crowds of people are gathering in clumps and finding seats in the audience. Various people have video and still cameras; others have sound recorders; then there are the people like Max, who just have a notepad and pen.

"This really is the least efficient way of getting an interesting story," Max whispers in Jaclyn's ear.

"Then why did you come?"

As Max leads Jaclyn to some chairs toward the back of the audience, he informs her, "I don't normally do these sorts of events, but the person who was meant to be covering it called in sick, so I didn't really have a choice."

Not long after taking their places, the moderator comes out onto the stage in front of the long table and asks everyone to sit down.

"We'll be talking about *Washington Spring* very shortly," the moderator announces.

"What is *Washington Spring*?" Jaclyn asks Max.

"A soon-to-be-released movie."

"Oh."

"I'm sure this press conference will tell you more."

With everyone now seated, the moderator introduces each of the speakers as they join the stage. "Mark Wong, the director; his sister, Sue Wong, the screenwriter; producer Adrienne Walcott; and leading actors, Emily Brand and William McCormack."

"I have met her," Jaclyn states, pointing out Sue Wong.

Max shrugs, "Big deal, she's just the screenwriter..." then after a pause, he adds, "Wait, you've only been in the country a week... how do you know her?"

"She is a friend of Dick's. Although, between you and me, I think she wishes for him to court her."

"This would be much juicier information if either of them were people the public actually wanted to read about," Max says, mostly to himself. When Jaclyn turns to study him, she suspects he's deep in thought.

Throughout the press conference, Max doesn't bother to ask any questions himself. He just jots down notes every once in a while. Jaclyn quietly listens to the information that floods her ears about the film. She learns that it was set in the nineteenth century, and is somewhat of a new American fairy tale. The building they're in was refurbished and used in the production.

Once the moderator announces its end, Max suggests to Jaclyn, "Why don't you go say hello to Sue?"

"I had been considering it," Jaclyn says. "Do you think it would be acceptable?"

Max nods, and adds, "I'll even help you find her."

He takes Jaclyn's hand and dashes off to locate the screenwriter. It doesn't take too long before he spots her, and so he slows his pace, and indicates her position to Jaclyn.

After giving Max her thanks, she walks up to Sue, and Max remains close by her side.

"It is a pleasure to see you again, Ms Wong," Jaclyn says, holding out her hand to shake it.

Sue does so, albeit with a confused expression on her face.

"What are you doing here?" Sue asks.

Taking that as his cue, Max says, "Hi, I'm Max. She's

my guest, though really I brought her down here because I thought she ought to see more of the country than New York."

Sue flashes a smile at Max. "Dick must appreciate you taking her out of his hands for a while, then."

Max doesn't reply, so Jaclyn does instead.

"In actuality, Dick was not home for me to inform him of this journey."

"Oh, gosh, Jaclyn, you can't do that to Dick!" Sue says. "He'll be worried sick, you know, and he already has enough to worry about."

She takes out her smartphone and presses it a few times before holding it to her ear.

Jaclyn looks at Max, and he shrugs.

"Hi, Dick," Sue says, sounding flushed. "Are you home yet?" A short pause. "Oh thank God. Listen, Jaclyn's ended up down here in Washington, and she says she didn't tell you she was coming."

After a couple of short pauses and *uh-huh*s, Sue hands her phone to Jaclyn. It's her first time holding one of these things, but having observed Sue just now, she figures she's supposed to hold it up to her ear, too.

"Jaclyn?" Dick's voice says.

"Yes, Dick?"

A little irritated, Dick asks, "How on Earth did you get to Washington?"

"Mr Fuentes brought me."

"Who?"

"Remember the man who was with your strange friend?"

Max chuckles.

After a moment of silence, Dick asks, "How did he even find you again?"

"I am not sure."

"Oh, never mind. Did you take the emergency bag I left you?"

"Yes."

"Okay, good. I put an old phone in there for you. Can you call me when you get back? I didn't have a spare set of keys for you so that's really the only way you'll be getting back in."

Jaclyn takes the phone out of her bag and looks at it.

"But I do not know how to use it," she says.

"If Sean's friend can drag you to another part of the country, he can show you how to use a phone." Dick's frustration is still present, though toned down. "Can you hand me back to Sue now?"

"Uh, yes. Thank you, Dick."

Jaclyn hands the phone back to Sue.

"Did you get in trouble with Daddy?" Max asks.

Baffled, Jaclyn says, "Dick is not my father."

Max smirks. "He acts like it, though."

After a moment's consideration, Jaclyn realises he's probably right.

No longer on the phone, Sue chastises Max. "Leave Dick alone; it just means he cares."

"Jaclyn's right—you do have a thing for Dick."

Sue's jaw drops and she takes a step back from the unexpected statement. After composing herself, she says, "You're not going to tell him, are you?"

Jaclyn watches the sly grin cross Max's face.

"Not if you get me an exclusive interview with your

brother," he says. "I have a source that says Emily Brand got her role because she slept with him, and I thought he might like the opportunity to defend his name."

Sue frowns and turns to Jaclyn, pulling her to the side so Max can't hear what she has to say. "For future reference, you need to not bring this man anywhere near me or my family."

"My apologies," Jaclyn says. "I did not know he would cause you any discomfort."

They return to Max, and Sue says, "I'll introduce you, but nothing more. I don't think he'll appreciate the blackmail."

As Sue wanders off to find her brother, Max says to Jaclyn, "It always amuses me what you can find out by lying about sources."

"I hope we may depart soon," Jaclyn says, changing the subject.

"As soon as we've met Mr Wong."

On that note, Mark wanders up to the reporter and the pirate, and shakes Max's hand. He then turns to Jaclyn to do the same, but pauses to compliment her, "That really is an incredible outfit."

She smiles at him, taking in his features. Something about his skin and eyes reminds her of someone from her past.

"Thank you," Jaclyn says.

"You're not from around here, are you?" Mark says, and Jaclyn shakes her head. "I thought not. It's your accent. Very pretty."

"She's a lesbian," Max pipes in.

Jaclyn smirks at the obvious jealousy, but otherwise ignores him. Hoping it will help Mark ignore the comment also, she asks, "What about yourself? Are you from, uh, *America*?" She emphasises the last word mostly for herself, as a reminder of what the country is commonly referred to.

"No, I'm from Malaysia originally. I came out here to study film and never left."

"This is all very interesting," Max interrupts, "but not as interesting as the way Ms Brand was cast in your film. . ."

Ignoring Max, Mark looks over Jaclyn's outfit again and says, "You know, I think you could have the eye I need for a new costume designer. Can I have your number to discuss a potential job offer?"

"That is such an obvious line if ever I heard one," Max interrupts again.

"My number?" Jaclyn asks, confused. Does he mean her age? "Uh... twenty-seven?"

Mark smiles. "I meant your phone number."

"Oh..." Jaclyn says, thinking about the phone Dick loaned her. "I am not sure what the number is. However, your sister knows my friend Dick. She will be able to help you find me."

"All right, then," Mark says, then reaches into his pocket and pulls out his wallet. "In the meantime, if you would like to maybe meet up for a drink later tonight, here's my card." He hands Jaclyn a card, and adds, pointing to the bottom corner, "And that's my number."

"Thank you," Jaclyn says, taking the card and putting it in her bag.

Mark nods, and says his goodbye before wandering off again.

A little bewildered, Max can't help saying, "What. The.

Fuck."

"What?" Jaclyn asks, not understanding the expression.

"That's never happened to me before."

"I do not understand."

Max shrugs. "Never mind, let's just go."

As they exit the building, Jaclyn pulls out Dick's phone. She looks at it curiously.

"Mr Fuentes, could I ask a favour?" she queries.

"I told you, call me Max. What sort of favour?"

Jaclyn passes the phone to him. "Will you show me how to use this?"

They stop walking, and Jaclyn senses some disappointment in Max.

"Was that not a favour you were hoping I would ask? If it causes less concern, Dick asked me to have you teach me, so that I could tell him when I return to New York." After attempting to read Max's face, she adds, "I do not plan on talking to Mr Wong with it."

This seems to be enough for Max to accept, though Jaclyn wonders if she can read him well enough to guess what kind of favour he would ask of her in return. She quickly wipes the grin off her face so that she can give Max her full attention when he shows her exactly what to do.

After dinner, Max finds them a motel to stay in for the night. Jaclyn decides to amuse herself by finding out how much Max will do for her, by going as far as pretending not to know how to get into the room. After all, she didn't lock the door at Dick's apartment either.

Max takes the cards for both his and Jaclyn's room from the check-in clerk, and bounds up the stairs. Jaclyn can't be bothered following him too closely, so by the time she reaches the top of the stairs, she finds Max holding a room door open for her.

"You have my gratitude," Jaclyn says, entering the room. She notes that Max must have placed her room key in the magic slot that turns the lights on for her.

"I've organised to have tomorrow off so that I can show you around some of the sights while we're here," Max says. "I'll collect you at eight for breakfast. Then we'll find our adventure."

Jaclyn smiles at him and agrees, then closes the door on him, amusing herself with the final glimpse of his stunned expression.

Since Jaclyn is without a change of clothes, what with her immediate departure that morning, and not knowing how long they would be away, she removes every item she is wearing. She is also thankful for the privacy, as she can't even remember the last time she was afforded the opportunity to walk around naked without worrying about peering eyes or someone accidentally walking in on her. Even when she was at Dick's apartment, while he was at work, she found she couldn't get that comfortable. What if he happened to come home earlier than expected for some reason?

When she catches a glimpse of herself in the mirror on the wall opposite the double bed, she does a double take, and walks closer. Her eyes trail over the scars on her arms and stomach, and she finds herself frowning at the imperfections.

She shakes herself out of the feeling, and walks into the bathroom to fill the bath.

Whilst enjoying the comforting heat of the water, Jaclyn looks down at her stomach scar. This time, though, rather than seeing it as an imperfection, she remembers the moment she got it.

Jacqueline was amongst the crew to storm a Spanish galleon, looking for gold. At first, the ship had appeared to be abandoned, so Captain McDonald hadn't sent too many men aboard to check it out. Then a group of Spaniards ambushed them—or at least they tried, pretending they were more than four.

The one who caught Jacqueline by surprise would have killed her if he had pushed his blade any further into her, but thankfully Kitty rushed at him and stuck her own cutlass in his side. The speed at which she was running meant she was unable to stop when she hit him, and ended up throwing him overboard.

Turner and Bones slaughtered the other three Spaniards, and they later discovered the rest of the crew all dead—most likely from scurvy and other diseases—below deck. The *Mary's Revenge* certainly got a good haul from that robbery, but Jaclyn remembers enjoying what came after that even more. The combination of being saved by her beloved, and Kitty getting two shares of that lot of treasure, meant that the intimacy that came after Jack was patched up warmed her soul.

Jaclyn smiles at the memory, and touches her fingers over the scar. It's not an imperfection. It's a sign of how much Kitty loved her.

After stuffing themselves for over ninety minutes at the motel's buffet breakfast, Max takes Jaclyn's hand and leads her out into the brisk Washington air. He leads them to the nearest Metro, explaining to Jaclyn that the place he wants to take her is too far away to travel by foot.

The train isn't very full, so Jaclyn bounds in excitedly and slips herself into one of the seats. Max is a little slower to board, and pauses by a pole in the middle of the train's doors. He shoots Jaclyn a smile, and retrieves his phone from his pocket.

"You're cute," Max says, looking at the pirate leaning over the seat in front of her, holding her own pole. "I just want to capture this moment."

Max holds the phone up in front of him and presses it.

"What did you do just now?" Jaclyn asks, holding the pole with one hand and leaning back now, as Max walks toward her.

He scoots Jaclyn over, sits down beside her, and shows her the photograph on his phone.

Impressed, Jaclyn then asks, "You can take photographs on that thing?"

Max chuckles to himself, and nods.

"Can you take more?" Even though Max tries to hide his smirk, Jaclyn catches it, and playfully pushes his shoulder. "What? I have only been here for two weeks. I still find photographs fascinating, and I want more to document my time here."

"I thought you got here a week ago?" Max asks.

"To America, yes. Two weeks ago is when I arrived in two-thousand and eleven."

Silence overcomes them, and Jaclyn notices a woman on the other side of the train staring at her, until the woman turns away after being seen.

Eventually, "Huh" escapes Max's lips.

"I really am a seventeenth-century pirate," Jaclyn whispers, figuring Max probably hadn't really taken her completely seriously before.

Max then surprises Jaclyn by jumping back out of the chair. "Well then," he says. "Let's take some more photos."

Rather than try to convince him any further, just in case he's only pretending to believe her, Jaclyn simply smiles and makes the most of it. She poses in various positions for Max, until they reach L'Enfant Plaza.

It's only a short walk to their destination, and once they arrive, Max announces the name of the large grey building. "The National Air and Space museum."

Upon entering the building, they are greeted by security and a metal detector. Recognising the device from the airport, Jaclyn doesn't even bother questioning it. She simply hands Dick's bag to the nearest security guard and walks through.

One guard looks at Jaclyn's outfit and smiles. He asks Max, "Acting exercise?"

"Yeah," Max replies rather automatically, but Jaclyn's not really paying attention.

As soon as she collects her bag, she looks up and around the large room, looking in awe at all the spaceships. The expression on her face is much like that of a blind person having their sight restored.

When she manages to stop slowly spinning around the room, taking everything in, she walks toward the large grey disc centrepiece. Jaclyn holds her face really close to it, taking in every detail. Then she spots something else, enclosed in a metal frame.

Wandering over to it, she stands by the notice, but she cannot read the words. Max pauses from his phone photography and walks up behind her.

"That's been to Mars," Max informs her.

Jaclyn turns around and stares at Max with disbelief.

"It's true," Max confirms.

"That is incredible."

"So what would you like to see first?" Max asks. "The history of air travel, or space travel?"

"Oh, air, please," Jaclyn says, curious how humans came to design and construct the large passenger planes like the one she had flown to America on.

Jaclyn follows Max to the correct room, and the first thing she finds is a model of a golden ship with a giant white sphere on top. Her hands touch the glass case as she admires it.

"Do these exist?" Jaclyn asks.

"No."

"Oh," Jaclyn says with some disappointment. "That is a shame. I would love to have sailed on one."

She spends a few more minutes admiring the model, before moving along and looking at all of the early model planes that hang from the ceiling in the room.

Once they exit the room, Max asks, "Would you like to see an aircraft carrier ship now? It's much bigger than the ships you would be used to."

Jaclyn nods, so Max leads her up the stairs. As they enter the room to their right, it's like they're entering the deck of an actual aircraft carrier. Jaclyn admires the small plane she immediately encounters, walking slowly around it, until she spots a moving picture of the sea and a helicopter.

Walking over to the picture, Jaclyn places her hands around the metal railing, and crouches down to watch.

The helicopter is completely ignored in favour of the deep blue ocean.

"I miss the sea," she says with a hint of sadness.

"I'm sorry."

Jaclyn stands up and faces Max again. "Why?" she asks. "It is not your fault I am here."

"Whose fault is it then?" Max asks.

With a frown, the memory of how she got to this century starts to push its way back into her head. Jaclyn shakes it out and says, "Not now. I am not ready to think about that."

Max shrugs, and leads Jaclyn through the rest of the aircraft carrier section of the museum. When they reach a model enclosed in glass casing, Jaclyn spends a lot of time focusing on the details, looking at the size in comparison to the miniature people on board.

"That deck is enormous," she says, wide-eyed.

Max glances down at his trousers, and rubs his thighs with his hands, then looks back up again.

"Oh, you said *deck*," he says sheepishly. "I thought you said..."

Jaclyn immediately interrupts him, smirking, "You men, do you always think with what one might find underneath your clothes?"

"Only when we're around particularly sexy women," Max confesses.

Though she had been looking at Max through the glass,

this seems to be subject matter that would be better to see him face-to-face with. Jaclyn wanders around to the other side of the model and says, "Define 'sexy.'"

After all, the word is yet another she is not exactly familiar with. She could take a wild guess that it has something to do with *sex*, but what? Are sexy women those who open their legs for every man who comes along?

Max takes a finger and brushes some of Jaclyn's fringe away from her blue eyes so he can look into them much deeper. "A woman," he says, stroking her cheek, "whose features," he adds, moving his finger down her neck, "causes men," then her chest, where it runs along the top of her corset, "to want to undress her." He picks his finger back off her chest, then places both of his hands at the top of her shirtless sleeves, pulls her close to him and whispers in her ear, "Even in public."

There's a tight gasp, and it takes a moment for Jaclyn to realise it came from her mouth. She wonders what exactly this man is doing to her, especially after noticing the tingling sensation within her breeches.

After catching her breath, Jaclyn pulls Max's arms down and says, "Let us move on. I want you to show me about space travel now."

"Right," says Max, turning around.

He leads Jaclyn back down the stairs and across to the opposite side of the building. As Jaclyn approaches the space shuttles, her pace slows, and she begins to wobble. The sight of these ships cause her to lose her balance a little, just because to Jaclyn, they're so unfathomable. She turns around slowly, much in the same way she did in the entrance, just taking it all in.

Max watches her from a distance, but catches up when she reaches some objects inside glass casing. Jaclyn places her hands on the glass, looking intently at the object shaped like a person within.

She asks Max, "Is this like a suit of armour?"

"Yes, I suppose so," he replies. "It's what people have to wear in space to protect themselves."

Jaclyn spends a little more time looking through the other glass cases. Occasionally she'll glance at the signs and wish she was able to read the words on them, but she refuses to ask Max to trouble himself by doing it for her. It feels odd for her to accept that reading is *normal* for *everyone* these days, to the extent that there are so many signs around.

Leaving the largest space room, she walks toward the moon lander. Her eyes scan the material it is made from, and she sheepishly asks, "Is it made out of *paper*?" Because that is certainly what it looks like.

"Something like that," Max replies. He moves in closer to her again, right behind her, and whispers, "So, this may have been to the moon, but would you like to see a rock that is from the moon?"

Jaclyn wonders whether she should be bothered by Max invading her personal space like that, but the innocence of the question helps her avoid the feeling. Instead, she takes a deep breath, and nods, since his presence has somehow rendered her speechless.

As they ride the escalator back up to the second floor, Max says, "You know, I can't help but wonder if the reason you like women is because you haven't experienced sex with a twenty-first century man. I imagine the men you're used to would be more than a little selfish."

"If you mean they are only interested in their own pleasure, then you would be correct," Jaclyn replies.

"I, on the other hand, take a great deal of pride in being able to pleasure a woman."

Max steps off the escalator.

"Are you suggesting you would like to lay with me?" Jaclyn asks, following Max onto the second floor.

"I wouldn't say no."

"Oh," Jaclyn says, following Max, "so, it would be your expectation that I seduce you, would it?"

Max turns and raises his eyebrows at her. "Always the woman's decision."

With a smirk, Jaclyn walks past Max, despite the fact she has no idea which way to go to find the moon rocks, and just waits for Max to catch back up with her so he can continue to act as her guide.

When they arrive at the moon rocks, Jaclyn spends a good ten minutes looking at them all, trying to find something she can classify as evidence that they did, indeed, come from the moon. She gives up when she realises she hasn't really studied Earth rocks all that carefully.

Jaclyn turns away from the rocks and asks Max, "How often do people travel to the moon? How long does it take to get there? Until I flew on a plane, I had no idea people could travel in five hours what would have taken a month on the sea."

After a short pause, Max answers her second question. "Well," he says, "if I recall correctly, it takes a few days to get to the moon…"

"Have you been there?" Jaclyn asks, interrupting.

"No," he admits. "No, the last shuttle to the moon was before I was born, in nineteen seventy-two."

Jaclyn frowns. "Why did they stop going there?"

With a shrug, Max replies, "Dunno. NASA also just had to decommission their shuttle program completely this year. Government cutbacks."

Confusion spreads over Jaclyn's face. "In language I can understand?"

"Right..." Max says, obviously unsure of what words Jaclyn doesn't understand. Of course not, Jaclyn thinks, since they're all probably normal words to him. Still, he indulges her, "That just means the National Aeronautics and Space Administration—that is, the people America funds to put things in space—had their budget reduced. They may not have been sending people to the moon, but they were still sending shuttles outside Earth's atmosphere. Now they've stopped that, too, because the costs were too high. Understand now?"

Jaclyn nods, and says with some disappointment, "I suppose it would not be in your king's interest."

Max laughs, though Jaclyn has no idea why.

"What is so amusing? Do you not have a king?" she asks, scoffing at the thought.

"No."

"Oh." Now Jaclyn feels a little embarrassed. Under her breath, she affirms for herself, "I do not think Kitty would like it here."

Fortunately for Jaclyn, Max ignores the comment. She supposes he may also be entirely ignoring the fact that she's apparently meant to be what people refer to as *lesbians*, what with him being fairly direct with his interest in her. This keeps her somewhat amused, and plants a smile on her face.

"May we dine now?" Jaclyn asks.

Max says with a shrug, "Sure."

They head further away from their previous Metro station, since they had not passed any restaurants on their way to the museum. On the first street corner, Jaclyn notices a large post that kind of reminds her of a mast. She finds herself unable to stop from jumping up onto the base of the lamppost and looking out across the street while the walk light remains red. It reminds her of her time as the lookout on *Mary's Revenge*, and she smiles.

When she turns to find Max, she sheepishly notices that he is pointing his phone directly at her, presumably taking more photographs.

The walk light turns green, and Jaclyn jumps back down onto the pavement. She walks with confidence as she and Max cross the street. When they arrive at the other side, Max holds his arm out to stop her in her tracks.

"Okay," he says, "we're about to pass by both the Washington Monument and the US Capitol. We can't come all this way without you getting photos with them."

Though Jaclyn has no idea what these sights are, she has never turned down the opportunity to have her photo taken yet, and so obliges Max. She poses for him where he tells her to stand.

They continue on their way when Max is satisfied, and over the next couple of blocks of their journey, Max points out various men who are staring at her. Jaclyn just smiles.

When they reach one street corner, Jaclyn notices a

word she recognises on the other side. She turns to Max and points to the building, saying, "Let us dine at the tavern."

Max smirks a little, but agrees.

Arriving at the tavern, Jaclyn climbs the stairs to the second storey, with Max following behind her. She chooses a table for them, and they seat themselves while waiting for the waitress to bring them the menu.

"You might be interested to know," Max says, accepting a menu, "that earlier this year, New York made it legal for lesbians to marry."

Jaclyn's eyes suddenly light up, but then just as quickly she feels deflated.

"This would be more welcome news if Kitty were still with me," she says.

"Maybe you'll meet someone else you want to marry instead," Max replies. "In the meantime, you're welcome to enjoy my company."

Jaclyn ignores him. She instead opens her menu and notes that there are again no pictures to explain the items. When she looks up, she asks Max, "Will you order something for me that you think I would like?"

He nods, and calls back the waitress to take their order.

"... and fish and chips for the lady," Max says, after voicing his own order. The waitress takes their menus away, and Max adds, "I thought it might make you feel more at home. It's the most *English* thing on the menu."

Jaclyn decides that it is probably best not to tell Max that, whilst she has obviously eaten fish before, she has no idea what chips are. If she has learned anything from being surrounded by men over the last nine years—well, nine years of her life—it's that it is not in her best interest to embarrass a man by suggesting that he has done something he thinks is right, but is, in fact, utterly wrong. Especially if she actually likes the man, and this one has not only started giving her literacy lessons, but somehow also provided her with tingly sensations in her breeches.

While they wait for their food to arrive, Jaclyn turns to the television screen over the bar, and watches for a few seconds as several men run around on some grass.

"What are those men doing?" Jaclyn asks.

"Playing football," Max replies. "It's a sport."

"People find this entertaining?"

Max nods.

"How strange," Jaclyn says, then turns away from the screen to look around the rest of the room. Her eyes settle on a red box on the wall next to her. "And what is this?"

"Fire alarm. In case of fire, smash that."

Jaclyn muses, "I have started fires to avoid paying bills before. Would you like me to do that this time?"

He looks at her with some confusion. "I wouldn't. It'd be much harder to get away with something like that here. They have cameras everywhere, filming you. They'd know it was you."

Feeling somewhat defeated, Jaclyn learns the first downside to this new invention she otherwise adores. Then, as she considers the repercussions of this news further, her eyes dart back and forth, wondering if there were any cameras watching her when she met with her Barbadian forgers.

Their food arrives, pushing the thought from her mind. Jaclyn examines her dish—well, basket—picking at the crumbed yellow coating of what she presumes must be the fish, because the other items in the basket certainly don't look like fish. She wants to say, "*This* is fish?" but reminds herself not to embarrass Max, and settles for silence instead.

Upon tasting the food, she discovers that it is as described and, in fact, she even likes it.

"Thank you for this delicious selection," she tells Max after swallowing her first bite. She brushes a hand over one of his to emphasise her point.

"No problem."

During the course of their meal, Max throws in a few more flirtatious comments, to which Jaclyn feels fluttering in her stomach.

After Max pays the bill, he leads Jaclyn to the Naval Heritage Center.

"Last stop for photos," Max claims when they arrive. "How are you with maps?"

Max nods his head over at the ground, and Jaclyn's eyes scan the gigantic world map. When she realises her mouth is agape, she shuts it, and walks over various parts of the map.

"Can you find anything you're familiar with?"

Jaclyn's eyes settle on the Caribbean islands, and she nods. She crouches down and points to the largest of the islands, saying, "This is Hispaniola."

"Beautiful," Max says, stepping backwards. "Stay there."

He walks back farther, and pulls his phone out again, snapping a photograph of her right by the island. After capturing her image a few more times in the area, Max suggests they head back to the Metro, and their motel.

"I should probably tell you that not all plastic cards work like money," Max informs Jaclyn, following her up the stairs of the motel. "So you should return the one you swiped from me."

"This, you mean?" she asks, pulling the room key from her pouch and holding it between her middle and index fingers, without turning around to face him.

"Yes."

"You think I do not know how to use this." It's not a question. She just seems amused when she turns around, bites her lip and raises an eyebrow.

"Fine. Show me."

A big grin crosses her face before she turns away again, and confidently walks towards room 246. Jaclyn unlocks the door and lets herself in.

Max wants to ask, "How did you know what my room number was?" but instead chooses to let it slide. He can't ignore the fact that this sexy woman just entered his hotel room, so he simply follows her in instead.

The door closes behind Max, and he finds Jaclyn standing by the bed. He walks towards her and, as soon as he's close enough, she pushes him backwards onto the bed and immediately climbs on top of him, legs either side of his waist, her hands pressing down on his shoulders.

"I suppose this is what you have been wanting all day," Jaclyn says with confidence.

Max looks from side to side and then back at Jaclyn. "Yes," he squeaks.

Then Max tries to struggle out of Jaclyn's hold, wanting to regain control of the situation, and finds that he can't. Jaclyn grins slyly to herself. His exertion bought her enough time to remove the scarf from her head, and she uses it to tie Max's arms above his head. She moves her lips closer to his, while continuing to hold one of his wrists with her hand.

"Is this what you wanted?" Jaclyn asks.

Max tries to reach his head upwards to kiss Jaclyn, but she pulls away.

"This isn't quite how I anticipated this going," he replies.

Jaclyn starts grinding herself into Max's growing erection. He whimpers, which is all the incentive she needs to stop grinding and pull at his necktie. Not being familiar with the removal of such an accessory, it frustrates her momentarily, but she manages to loosen it enough to pull it over his head. Then she gets to work on his buttons. With every one she unbuttons, she notes that he is not struggling against his bindings. She suspects her behaviour at the museum has given Max enough reason not to fear her, and wonders whether she needs to fix that.

Once Max's shirt is open, though not off, since it can't be removed while he's bound, she gets to work on his belt, and pulls it apart and out of his trousers with ease.

"You know, if you'd let me have control, I could show you how twenty-first century men treat women," Max suggests. "As I've said, I suspect it's a whole lot better than what you're used to, Buccaneer."

Jaclyn raises an eyebrow. "Are you certain you do not wish for me to unbind you such that would allow for your escape?"

"I don't need you for that," Max replies, tossing her scarf away and revealing that he's managed to free his hands on his own.

Unfortunately for Max, as he begins to make a move to assert his control, Jaclyn grabs his wrists again, placing them back above his head. She holds them in place with just one hand, using her other hand to remove the decorated scarf from her waist, which she then uses to re-bind his wrists. This time, to make sure it's harder for him to escape, she spreads the scarf so that there is about a foot and a half gap between his wrists, which she places behind his neck. Max proves this greater difficulty when he tries to reach his arms forward again.

"You really enjoy being in control, don't you?" Max asks.

"One must learn to enjoy what one must do to survive," Jaclyn confesses, satisfied that she has bound Max more successfully this time.

Jaclyn then gets started on Max's trousers. She unbuttons the top, then looks at the fly, recalling the time Dick taught her how to zip and unzip when he got her a pair of jeans. She closes her eyes and grinds herself against Max's groin again, eliciting a moan from him.

"You don't know what you're doing, do you?" Max asks, seemingly frustrated at Jaclyn's pause in removing his pants. "Untie me and I can get the zipper for you."

Jaclyn doesn't respond. Instead, she leans forward and runs her top teeth down Max's chest and stomach, until she reaches his pants. She grabs the pull-tab with her teeth and pulls down, eliciting another moan from Max.

"Or you could do that," Max says.

After Jaclyn sits back on top of him, she removes her boots, one at a time, dropping them to the floor.

Max adds, "I was serious when I said I could pleasure you in ways you weren't used to."

"I imagine you are enjoying yourself too much for that now," Jaclyn says, grinding again. Max shrugs, and Jaclyn offers, "You do know that I could kill you, do you not? Why do you not fear me?"

Max shrugs again. "Maybe this is worth it."

"Let us speculate for a moment. Perhaps I want to test your theory." Jaclyn leans forward again, her mouth inches from Max's. She rubs the bonds of his wrists. "What would that entail?"

"Hands. Fingers. Tongue."

"Tongue?" Jaclyn asks, intrigued.

"Not even Kitty used her tongue on you?" The blank expression on Jaclyn's face is all the answer Max needs to add, "Well then, if you want to learn more, you'll have to untie me."

Jaclyn starts removing the bonds, giving in to her temptation. As soon as one hand is free, Max takes it upon himself to help with the other one, then keeps the scarf, flips Jaclyn onto her back and binds her wrists, several times, as tight as he can.

"That is because I don't trust you," Max says. "In fact, I think I could just leave you like this and run."

Before Max has the chance, though, Jaclyn wraps her legs around Max's waist and pulls him closer.

She hides her fear with a threat, "You run now and I will hunt you down and kill you. You know this will not hold me long."

He rolls his eyes. "You don't even have a gun."

"I am a pirate. I am resourceful."

Whilst Jaclyn is being serious about her resourcefulness, she knows her heart isn't in the actual threat. She just hopes Max doesn't notice.

"You really don't give a man much choice, do you?"

She's not quite sure whether he's just playing along, but responds anyway. "Well, you are a man. I know what men are capable of."

"You know what pirate men are capable of. I am not from your time and that is not me."

"You have already bound me," Jaclyn disputes. "I am trusting that you will make good your promise rather than raping me. Do you consider that an easy decision to make?"

In that moment, Jaclyn releases Max, allowing him to stand upright while he ponders Jaclyn's words. Jaclyn's previous unfastening of his trousers causes them to slip partway down his legs.

Max looks at her vulnerability, combined with the sex appeal of a woman in a corset and immediately gets to work at removing her breeches. He momentarily admires the fact her stockings are held up by garters before removing both of those articles of clothing, too.

Jaclyn watches as Max runs his fingernails up the front of her legs. When he reaches her thighs, he switches to the inside, causing Jaclyn to close her eyes and gasp. This spurs Max on, using a thumb on her clitoris. He watches Jaclyn bite her bottom lip and wonders what kind of effect his tongue will have.

As much as Max might usually be inclined to take his time to find out, he is far too curious. His tongue switches places with his thumb and Jaclyn moans, then starts breathing deeper as Max works his magic on her.

"Kitty… has… never…" Jaclyn says between gasps. "I… do… not… think… I want… to go… home…" But that's all that manages to escape her lips before Max brings her to orgasm.

Max looks up at Jaclyn, wiping his moist lips. "Can you handle more?"

"That was not the end?" Jaclyn asks.

"Not unless you want it to be."

"You did promise to show me how a twenty-first-century man treats a woman."

And that's all the incentive Max needs to keep going. He slides his shirt off his arms, removes his wallet from a pocket in his trousers, and a condom from within that as quickly as he can, before discarding the rest of his clothes.

Jaclyn watches intently as Max positions himself over her, unwrapping the condom.

"What is that?" she asks as he starts rolling it on.

"It's called a condom," Max says. "We use them to prevent pregnancy," he adds, without admitting he's a little afraid of possible seventeenth-century STIs she might have. She's probably unaware of such things, and even if she understands that diseases can be transmitted sexually, that's not the kind of thing you discuss when you're in the process of having sex with someone if you actually want to keep going.

Max is gentle when he pushes himself inside her in a way

that she has never experienced from another man. She closes her eyes and just lets herself go to fulfilment. Just minutes later she climaxes again, shortly followed by Max's own orgasm.

As Max collapses on top of Jaclyn, she shows him how easily she is able to untie even his difficult knots.

"I never completely surrender control," she says.

Yet after discarding her scarf, she fails to admit that her hands and arms are now paralysed. Part of her wonders if this is the behaviour all men expect, or at least *desire*, when they encounter a woman. Then she wonders if that is the reason Kitty so long wanted to protect the secret of her sex.

EIGHT

Jacqueline sat in the Tavern of the Horses with Turtle, Grant, Turner, and Noah—four of the pirates with whom she spoke with most often. Katherine had remained back on the brig with Captain McDonald.

This tavern was most welcoming to pirates and their ilk, and it was their regular haunt in Tortuga. It was not too far from the harbour, which often made it the first stop after leaving a vessel. They were still part of the *Mary's Revenge* crew, and Katherine was still the quartermaster, though it was nearly three years after she had been promoted to the position.

They were having a good laugh around a square table inside the tavern, reminiscing about the time Turner had become tangled up in some ropes on the main deck before the quartermaster found him.

"Weren't me at fault," Turner said. "Bones done me in. Gray would nay believe me, though."

"He be hard on all of us," said Noah.

"Except Jack," Grant mused. He eyes Jacqueline suspiciously. "Why be that?"

Jacqueline's hands quivered beneath the table before

she made an abrupt decision. Sick of the lies, she threw her hands on top of the table, leaned in close to the other four, and said, "I have a secret."

Her companions looked at her with curiosity more than anything else, as Jacqueline removed the scarf from her head, revealing long but unfortunately matted hair. Since it was not uncommon for other male pirates to have long hair, Turner, Grant and Noah were confused. Turtle instead looked into Jacqueline's eyes, and she knew he understood.

"Ye call me Jack, but that is not me name." Then Jacqueline surprised even herself by standing up in the crowded room and shouted, "Call me Jaclyn. And find me some women's clothes."

Jack scanned the crowd but most of them ignored her, likely thinking she was just some man who had gone a bit cuckoo after too long at sea. Then she noticed Katherine standing in the entrance, astounded. Once Jacqueline retook her seat, Katherine rushed over to their table, and grabbed her wrist.

"What are ye doing?" Kitty said through gritted teeth.

"I be sick of this disguise, Kit," said Jacqueline, simply.

"It is not safe to dress another way," Kitty whispered.

"I think I can look after meself and wear a corset," Jacqueline retorted with a smug grin, and noticed the smiles of her crewmates.

Katherine shook her head and stormed back out of the tavern.

"The quartermaster been lying with ye?" Noah said with a chuckle. "Probably wants ye all to himself."

"Aye," Jacqueline said with a smile.

"And now ye want to share yerself around?" Grant asked

with a strong implication that he would like to be part of it.

Jacqueline immediately whipped out her pistol, cocked the weapon and held it directly to Grant's forehead as a warning to what the outcome could be if any other man dared to suggest such a thing.

Grant swallowed hard. "Let it be known that this here woman knows how to handle a weapon."

Turner reached over to the pistol to lower it on Jack's behalf. "We get yer point," he said. "No fucking without yer say so."

"And make sure every wretched soul knows it," Jack said.

Noah pulled out his only hand to shake Jacqueline's. "Well," he said, "I guess it be good to properly meet ye, Jaclyn."

They shook hands, and that was that.

Katherine found herself on the end of the pier in a crouch, looking out at the sea, which was glimmering under the moonshine. She needed some time alone to think about what Jacqueline had done. In the distance, a head bobbed up out of the sea every so often, getting closer. When Katherine noticed it, she squinted, trying to get a better look, wishing she had a spyglass on her. After a few seconds, she spotted the fins, and got to her feet.

Before long, the mermaid's head breeched the surface again, just below the pier. Kitty quickly glanced around to make sure no one was watching her before she sat down and hung her legs over the side.

"Prue?" she asked.

"Kitty? Have I finally found you again?" Prudence asked

in return.

Kitty nodded. "You have been searching for me?"

"Since that day I lured your pirate to the sea. I thought you would have returned to London."

"Hush," said Kitty, and she looked around again. "Let us not talk here. Follow me while I look for a dinghy and then we can talk in the sea."

Prudence followed Katherine from a distance, watching as Katherine moved closer to shore and walked out onto a small jetty. That's where she found her dinghy and paddled her way out of the harbour, meeting Prudence halfway.

When they reached a calm spot distant enough from the pier so as not to be seen by anyone who might be wandering out there, Prudence pulled herself aboard the small boat. Her fins transformed again, baring her naked body before Katherine.

"Kitty, what are you doing here?" Prudence asked. "This is pirate territory."

"I know. That is precisely why I am here."

"I do not understand."

"I have been documenting my time, here in the West Indies. You remember my dreams, do you not? I want my story to be memorable and accurate."

"You are writing of pirates?"

"Aye," Kitty said with a grin.

"Why not then, write of a pirate love story with a mermaid?" asked Prudence, leaning forward, presenting her breasts for show. "I would be only too happy to help with the accuracy."

Prudence reached her hand out to stroke Kitty's face, and Kitty closed her eyes. When she took a deep breath, enjoying Prudence's touch, she was taken back five years, remembering their time together before Prudence died.

"I love you," Kitty said then, opening her eyes and feeling herself get a little moist between her legs.

They both leaned in closer to each other and kissed as passionately as they used to. Kitty quickly discarded her doublet and hat behind her, and continued to disrobe until she was as naked as Prudence. They kissed again as Kitty gently pushed Prudence backwards, and her hand found its place between Prudence's legs.

Prudence gasped as Kitty's middle finger entered her, and her thumb rubbed Prudence's clitoris. They were careful not to move too much, though, lest the boat capsize.

Another gasp emerged from Prudence, who then bit her lip to prevent herself from crying out. Her body stiffened as the orgasm overcame her.

Upon catching her breath, she said, "I love you, Kitty." She took a few more deep breaths before adding, "When next we meet, I shall return the favour."

With that, she dived out of the dinghy, rocking it slightly, and returned to her half-fish form.

"I still do not know how long I can be with legs," said Prudence, resting her head on her arms, crossed over on the side of the boat.

"Please find out, for me?" Kitty asked, and planted a kiss on Prudence's forehead.

Prudence closed her eyes and nodded.

"Find me whenever you are able. I shall remain here, in this New World, until I tell you otherwise. Though I hope not to venture too much farther north, it may depend on my captain's intent," said Kitty, not wanting to say goodbye. "Watch for the brig you found me on before. *Mary's Revenge*, be its name. I shall provide you with men when you need them."

This elicited a smile from Prudence, and she said, "You have my gratitude. Until next we meet."

When Kitty smiled back, Prudence dived under the sea. Kitty remained there a few minutes longer, deep in thought while she clothed herself, until she remembered Jacqueline back on shore. Then a strong sense of regret washed over her.

"What am I doing?" she asked herself. "How can I do this again?"

Katherine rowed back to the jetty to return the dinghy, trying to push the thought of Prudence and what had just occurred between them from her mind.

After repairs were made to the brig, McDonald's crew set sail again, heading toward Hispaniola. When they were becalmed, much of the crew found themselves aboard the main deck, being entertained by the same pirates who were playing when Mr Higgins fell overboard. With Thomas Grant on the fiddle, Henry on the hurdy gurdy, and François on the flute, the music was familiar to all who were listening.

The music stirred Katherine and Jacqueline in their cabin and brought them out to share in the entertainment. When the band started playing a particular song the crew were familiar with, many pirates began to sing along. Then a woman's voice was heard amongst them, which startled the band enough to stop. Grant nodded over at Jacqueline, and the whole crew looked at her. For many, this was the moment they discovered they even had a woman aboard *Mary's Revenge.*

"What is this madness?" one man shouted.

Much noise erupted amongst the crew as they argued amongst themselves, some excited at the prospect of getting laid, but most arguing their superstitions.

When Captain McDonald overheard the noise, he was drawn out of his cabin. "Avast!" he yelled at the crew. "Will someone explain the commotion?"

"Captain, sir!" Bones yelled. "There be a woman aboard."

"Ah, I suppose I should have mentioned that to you lot before we set sail," said the captain.

"Ye knew of this?" asked another man. "Damn your eyes! Ye risk our very survival!"

A few men mumbled in agreement, and the captain had to shout again to silence them. "Men! This woman be sailing with us for three years and I think ye all will find we have had much luck in that time. So quit yer superstitious whining."

"Three years?" Bones yelled again, decidedly being the most vocal of the bunch. "Who is she?"

Jacqueline ran over to the captain's side and announced on her own behalf, "Jack Rousseau."

Then Grant carried his fiddle with him as he joined the captain and Jacqueline. "She do fight as well as the rest of us," he said, "if not better than some." He narrowed his eyes at Bones. "'Sides," he added, "that's some voice she has on her. Could be a good mermaid repellent."

That instigated some murmurs amongst the crew.

"Men!" shouted the captain, hushing the crew again.

"We need to stop these ridiculous mermaid rumours. Has anyone here ever seen one?" He looked around his crew but did not get a single answer. "Then there is no evidence they exist."

"What about Higgins?" Bertrand asked. "He looked like he had been enchanted before he fell overboard."

The few men who remained alive from the crew back then, and had been on deck to see Higgins fall, agreed with Bertrand.

Then Jacqueline chimed in, taking the captain's side, "If ye all spent less time believing in hogwash, maybe ye would have had time to see through me disguise."

A number of pirates admitted she may have had a point, but Jacqueline was not paying attention to them. She was watching Katherine shift a little uncomfortably in her place, which made her realise it was not the best idea to suggest the pirates take more notice of their surroundings, lest they listen to her and discover Kitty's womanhood. It was not as though she needed to say it to convince the captain to keep her around.

As the murmurs started to die down again, the captain returned to his cabin, and Bertrand and Baker returned to their instruments and started playing again.

Grant turned to Jacqueline and asked, "Will ye join us to sing?"

She smiled and accepted, admitting, "This be the way me first pirate crew accepted me amongst them, as a woman."

"Ye were known to them?" Grant asked.

"Aye," she said, "When they took our vessel—the one the quartermaster and me was on before we joined this one—I was not disguised as a man. We were given the usual choice of becoming pirates, or death, so Kit signed us up to save our hides. There was an awful amount of leering at me, so I suspected they only accepted me at first because they thought they could fuck me any time they desired."

Grant snorted, remembering his behaviour the night she revealed her sex to him. "Aye, that be why ye learned how to wield yer weapons."

She smiled at him again, and then they joined Bertrand and Baker as the next song started.

As the song wound down, those on the deck cheered for Jacqueline. However, she did not notice them as much as she noticed the smile that was plastered so clearly across Katherine's face.

The wind had still not found them by that evening, which allowed Jacqueline and Katherine to privately celebrate Jacqueline's new role on the vessel in their cabin. Kitty held the singer's hand and walked her into the cabin, but as soon as she was inside, Kitty kissed her mouth, and pushed her backwards into the door, slamming it shut with the force of her passion.

Kitty took a breather to say, "It has been far too long since you have shared that voice. I have missed it so."

"Then you are no longer unsettled by my disclosure?" asked Jacqueline, taking Kitty's hands in hers, and looking directly into her eyes.

"I must have forgotten how much you have grown since we entered this life. You know how to handle yourself well amongst these men. Watching you this afternoon filled me with much pride." Kitty paused, kissing Jacqueline on the lips again, and added, "I love you."

Jacqueline spun them around. "You taught me well," she said, pulling Kitty to their bed.

Kitty placed her palm on Jacqueline's cheek as she climbed on top of her, and said, "I must apologise," they kissed, "for keeping you," and again, "from yourself," another kiss, "for so long."

The singer attempted to put a finger to Kitty's lips to silence her, but Kitty pulled her hand away.

"I must also apologise for refusing to lay with you for so long," Kitty added.

"You did what you thought was necessary to protect me, and for that alone I know how much you love me," Jacqueline said, shaking her head. "You do not need to apologise."

"Perhaps not, but I still wish to repair that damage," Kitty replied, and started removing Jacqueline's corset with some difficulty.

Jacqueline laughed at this. "It has been some years since you last had to disrobe such fashion," she said, and Kitty laughed along with her, giving up and rolling onto her back.

After the laugher died down, they laid in silence, until Jacqueline decided to speak her thoughts.

"Do you ever wonder… might we ever… marry?"

Katherine rolled onto her side to face her partner. She said, without much thought, "No." When she noticed the frown, she added, "There will never be a law that allows such heresy."

"But no one knows you are a woman," said Jacqueline with some passion that meant her eyes began to water.

"We could make it possible."

Katherine shook her head. "I do not wish to remain a man forever; it is just not possible."

"Then disrobe now."

Kitty grinned coyly at the implication of this comment, and got off the bed to lock their cabin before removing her doublet.

"Announce yourself to the rest of the crew as a woman," Jacqueline added, which stopped Katherine from undressing.

"You know I cannot do that. I will return one day, but not in front of these men. I do not trust them. You may be safe due to your own strength... but what if the reason is, in actuality, due to having the quartermaster's protection?"

Jacqueline conceded the point, and joined Katherine in the middle of the room to help her continue disrobing.

Early the following morning, the women awoke to the sound of cannon fire and splashing, both of which seemed to rock the vessel to an extent they had never before felt. Jacqueline jumped off the bed first and threw all of Kitty's clothes at her before throwing on her own. Of course, with the complexity of the corset, Kitty finished first and headed straight for the door. She turned and looked back at Jack.

Even though Jack's eyes were on her corset, she knew Kitty's pause meant she did not want to leave the cabin without her. "Do not concern yourself with me," Jack said. "Go find the captain and discover the details of this conflict."

When Kitty did not act, nor reply, Jack looked up at her. "I love you," Kitty affirmed, then passionately kissed

Jack on the lips before finally running through the door.

Once dressed, Jack squinted as she looked around the cabin, hoping it would help her find her flintlocks in the dark. The first one turned up under the ratty blankets on the floor, and she decided to give up finding the second one, knowing how even three seconds could be the difference between life and death for one of her friends. Instead she grabbed her cutlass and hoped that would be enough for this battle.

The brig's main deck was almost as dark as the cabin. Jacqueline determined it was still at least a couple of hours before dawn. This in turn caused her to wonder who was attacking them, as she would not have expected the Navy to find them at this hour. She ran across the deck to see if she could find Kitty, or the captain, or *someone* who could fill her in on the details, but this focus led to an inability of noticing her surroundings. Jaclyn tripped over a corpse and landed at Turtle's feet.

Another cannon blast from *Mary's Revenge* rocked the brig.

Turtle reached down to Jack, so she took his arm and let him help her up.

"Where be the captain?" she asked.

"Killed from a blast on the gun deck."

Jack tumbled backwards from shock. If the captain could die… "What about Kit? The quartermaster?"

"He has been issuing the orders. But we are in bad shape…" he trailed off, looking distracted, paying more attention to the starboard side.

Jack jumped up to slap Turtle across the cheek. "What are you doing?"

He snapped himself out of his daze, but didn't look at her. "Do you hear that?"

Numbing her other senses, Jack opened her ears. Not only had the cannon fire ceased from both sides, but it was almost eerily silent.

"I cannot hear anything. What caused everything to stop?"

Turtle shook his head. "You cannot hear the song?"

Closing her eyes, Jack tried again to listen, but all she got was silence. She then opened her eyes and looked around the deck to see if it looked like anyone else could hear what Turtle did. The men who remained standing all looked frozen in place.

Jack couldn't understand it. What on Earth could be causing them to behave in such a way? She turned her attention back to Turtle and shook her head. "I cannot."

By this time, though, Turtle had lost his focus on her. His eyes were closed and he gently swayed back and forth on the spot. As the only clearly sane person on deck, Jacqueline knew she had no choice but to investigate.

Since Turtle's head was tilted more towards the starboard side, that's where Jack rushed to first. She leaned her head right over the gunwale to look directly into the sea. She couldn't see anything in the direction of the head of the brig, but when she turned to look toward the stern... she could have sworn she saw something bob beneath the water. Jack pulled herself back to the deck and ran toward the stern.

Whatever it was that went below, she needed to find out. Was it one of the crew, drowning? If timing did not seem so crucial, Jack might have tried to look for Kitty to see if she was encountering the phenomenon. Instead, it was a conversation she would have to save for later.

When Jack reached the taffrail, rather than throwing herself over the edge like she did with the gunwale, she pulled out her spyglass from the sash around her waist. With that, she was less exposed, just in case there was an army of rival pirates waiting below who might try to shoot her. Not that they would be able to hit her at that range.

Through the spyglass, Jack could see the surface of the ocean at much closer range, though the peripheral angles were rather limited, so it took her longer to scan the area. If it weren't for the moonlight, it would have been hard for her to see anything at all.

When she was about to give up, she saw something that sort of shimmered. A fin of some sort. A sea monster? She never used to believe in such nonsense, but she found it hard to know what to believe now that she had encountered something for which she had no explanation.

Jack kept searching the sea, trying to get a glimpse of whatever it was again, but instead got a bit of a shock when she felt something on her shoulder. When she turned around, she saw that it was a hand. Her eyes slowly followed along the arm it was attached to, until she discovered Kitty.

"What are you doing?"

Despite knowing that Kitty believed in the unbelievable, without a proper understanding of what was happening, Jack decided not to give away the truth. "The other vessel stopped firing at us. I was trying to find out what happened."

Kitty looked out over the taffrail at the sea, then back at

Jack. "That is not where the vessel was." Then Kitty turned Jack's attention to port, and pointed. "It has always been there. Though I do not know why they stopped either."

It occurred to Jacqueline that she should ask why the men on the brig had all frozen in place, but when she turned her attention back to them, that was no longer the case. Though curious if Kitty had seen them that way, she thought better than to ask.

Instead, she focused on the other vessel. "Who are they?"

Kitty shrugged. "It is hard to tell from this distance, in this light, but I have heard some of the men exchanging comments about some privateers calling themselves pirate assassins."

"The murderous pirate assassin army?"

"You have heard of them?" Kitty looked confused.

Jack supposed Kitty was not used to her knowing things she didn't. She nodded. "Guess I hear more from the crew than you do. Some of the newer men are what was left of other crews attacked by them."

"I suppose it would do me good to talk to the men more." Kitty sighed. "What else do you know about them?"

Jack turned slightly so she could rest her arms on the taffrail and look back out at the sea on that side. "Turner says they be Cromwell's puppets and ye can be sure he is paying their wage to destroy as many of us pirates as they can, and letting them keep any treasure they be finding."

"That blasted son of a whore Cromwell! I do not think this be them, but you can be sure that when I am made captain, I will make it my business to find them. No one who supports Cromwell…" Kitty trailed off.

Wondering what distracted Kitty, Jacqueline turned back and looked in the same direction as her. Though it was still dark, there was at least enough light from the moon to see that a lot of objects... *men?...* were falling over the other vessel's port gunwale.

"Let us not speak of this to the crew," Kitty said. "I dare not wish to scare them further." She turned her attention away from the other vessel and back to Jack. "Please help me rally the men to get us out of here, in the event that there are still men on that brig who will return to attacking us soon."

"Would it not be better to attack them while their defences are down?"

Kitty narrowed her eyes. "You are not the captain."

Jack wanted to spit in Kitty's face at that statement, but instead she opted for a little less hostility. "Neither are you."

"Not *yet*. But the captain is dead, and I am quartermaster, so who do you think they will vote for?"

Though unsure exactly where the courage to challenge her lover came from, Jack couldn't help opposing her. "Not you, if you dare not attack that other brig and take their treasure."

Katherine looked at her blankly, and Jack didn't know what she was thinking.

"Let me go over first. I need to prove to these men that I am still capable."

As soon as grappling hooks were used to pull the other brig closer—but before the lines had completely secured both vessels together along their gunwales—Jaclyn breached the enemy ship. She held a cutlass across her chest, guarding it, in her right hand, while her left held a pistol at her side. Though the sun was now clearly visible over them, the main deck was eerily empty as she searched, leading her to believe all the men had fallen overboard.

Returning the cutlass to its scabbard, and her pistol to the sash around her waist, she reported back to Kitty on *Mary's Revenge*, "I think we should take this brig. They be gone, and ours is in bad shape from their guns."

Katherine looked at the crew nearest to her. With her pistol in hand, she waved them over. "Turner, Bertrand, Baker, search below deck with Jack. Make sure no one is left alive."

Thankful that Kitty gave her men she felt more comfortable around, Jaclyn led them below deck.

"Do ye suppose these cowardly prigs just hid in the hold when the realised we was gonna come aboard?" Baker asked.

"Bet they can nay handle a proper fight," Turner added.

They reached the gun deck and Jaclyn turned around. "Let me go in alone. I can manage anyone who be waiting."

Whilst the other three held back, Jaclyn wandered in slowly, accentuating her hips as she walked, and kept her weapons in place along her sash.

She could see the top of a dark-haired man peering out over one of the more distant guns. Tilting her head to the side, Jaclyn asked, "What are you afraid of?"

As the man stood up, she noticed his tan arms, muscles curving out of a sleeveless shirt.

"Were–were you that voice I heard, singing that haunting song?" he asked in a whisper as she neared.

Jaclyn shook her head. "What be your name?"

"Juan."

"Juan," Jaclyn said, and lowered her corset, enhancing her cleavage. "I will not hurt you; I just want to know why you attacked my brig."

"I... Captain's orders, he said you was pirates."

Jaclyn lifted her breasts out of her corset, and closed the rest of the gap between them, pressing herself up against the Spaniard. Looking at him in a way that might encourage sympathy, Jaclyn asked, "Do I *look* like a pirate?"

Her lips were close to his. As he shook his head, looking deep into her eyes, she lifted her right leg backwards and pulled a dagger from within.

"So what am I to do now? You killed my crew."

"We could sail for–" Juan didn't get to finish his thought, because that was the moment Jaclyn stabbed him in the stomach.

Freeing the dagger from his body, Jaclyn said, "Your captain was right. Having letters of marque do not make him better than us. Now that brainless, black-hearted cur will pay with his brig."

She turned around to head back to her crewmates and found herself being applauded by them. When she was finally standing at Turner's side, Baker gave her a grin and squeezed her left breast. She slapped him across his cheek.

"Do that again, and ye end up like Juan over there," she said, nodding her head backwards. "Dolt."

"Ye may wish to put them away, then," Turner suggested.

Jaclyn raised an eyebrow at him. "And risk being unable to use my best weapon against any other fiendish privateer aboard?"

Bertrand grinned. "This is what we been missing by not allowing women around."

"They are distracting," Baker said, still looking at her nipples.

Jaclyn didn't know if she wanted to punch him in the face or thank him, but she didn't have time to decide before she noticed a topless, fair-skinned man come up behind them, swinging a cutlass.

Pushing past her men, she flashed her breasts at the privateer. Though it confused him at first, he still managed to tear her arm with his sword before she stabbed him, too, with the dagger she still held.

Returning her dagger to her boot, she held her bleeding arm with her hand, and turned around. "And that, sea snakes, is how a woman fights."

NINE

Early on the Saturday following Jaclyn's return from Washington, she and Dick take the subway to Battery Park at the southern tip of Manhattan. They stand next to each other by the fence, and Dick points out the Statue of Liberty and Ellis Island, providing Jaclyn with a brief explanation of the cultural significance of both.

It's a lot for Jaclyn to take in, and though Dick may not know a lot about history in general, she is still appreciative of what he can tell her about America's past.

However, more than the historical references, Jaclyn finds herself being thankful that Dick lives a reasonable distance to water. There is just something about the sea air that she can't help but need. It may not be exactly the same as she's used to in the West Indies—the air in the north being cooler than that of the tropics—but breathing in the salty tang still gives her a sense of calm and familiarity, which helps her feel more grounded in a place where little else reminds her of the seventeenth century.

"When you finally allow me to explore this city on my own," she says, with a hint of frustration in her voice, "I think I shall come here often."

Jaclyn had hoped that when she returned to New York, Dick would see her as quite capable of getting by without him. Instead, she recalls his anger with her when she called him to announce her arrival. Apparently he had been in some big important "meeting" and forgotten to turn his phone off.

He doesn't reply, and Jaclyn supposes that he's sick of that conversation. It then occurs to her that perhaps a little extra friendliness wouldn't hurt, so she changes the topic. "I would appreciate the opportunity to have you photograph me again whilst we are here." She looks at the bag that is hung over Dick's shoulder, which she had insisted he bring with him. "Mr Fuentes photographed me in Washington, but I dare say that I much prefer yours."

"I have a better idea," he says.

Half an hour later, Jaclyn finds herself on a ferry heading out to the statue. She stands by the railing, closes her eyes and takes a deep breath. It's not remotely like sailing any of the vessels she has been on, but with her eyes closed, she can almost pretend it is. The speed of the ferry blows her hair around in a way that reminds her of sailing in strong winds.

When she opens her eyes, all she can say is, "This is extraordinary."

"But you've been on boats before. How is this different?"

Jaclyn can't help thinking Dick must be displaying a special kind of ignorance. "Dick... this boat has no sails, nor oars."

"Oh," he says, in a tone that indicates he's been made aware of his own stupidity.

In that moment, Jaclyn catches a flash of something in the corner of her eye. "I need a moment," she says, hoping Dick will take the hint.

She watches him take his seat before turning her attention back to the Hudson, trying to spot what she thought she saw again.

"There is nothing out there," she whispers to herself. "I am seeing things."

Even so, this event causes Jaclyn's mind to wander to the memory of the evening Kitty was voted captain.

The sun was setting, and Jaclyn had her telescope out, searching the water for unwanted visitors. Years earlier she had not believed Kitty when she talked of mermaids. As Kitty's fantasy talk had died down, so did Jaclyn's understanding that Kitty continued to believe. Yet, when Kitty's name was announced, and Jaclyn distractedly raised her hand to vote, she saw a blonde woman in the sea. The woman was calm, and Jaclyn thus decided she was unlikely to have fallen from the rival vessel they had just defeated. If she had, she probably would've been splashing about and screaming for help.

Jack moved to the back of the crowd to get a better look. She did not understand how or why the woman remained at a distance from their brig, watching.

After a few more names were put to the vote, Turner said, "Welcome our new captain. Kit Gray."

Quite unexpectedly, Jaclyn swore to herself that she saw the woman smile. As the crowd cheered for Kitty's appointment, Jaclyn discovered that the woman was nothing of the sort. She jumped up, and dived under the water. The last thing Jaclyn glimpsed was the sun reflecting off the woman's fins.

This time, though, the shimmer Jaclyn had seen was not so clear. It could have been anything. She glances out across the water once more, but gives up. She couldn't possibly have spotted a mermaid here. Jaclyn decides that they are likely extinct by now.

As the ferry draws nearer to the statue, Dick takes out his camera and instructs Jaclyn on where to stand so he can get the best framing for the photos.

Jaclyn hopes this is Dick's way of apologising to her for being mad when she returned on Wednesday, but decides against asking. She doesn't want to ruin the moment.

Arriving back on Manhattan Island, Dick suggests they walk up Broadway so Jaclyn can get more of a feel for the city. "Especially since you've been so cooped up at my place."

"Is that an apology?"

Dick shrugs. "I'm not very good at apologies."

With a smile on her face, Jaclyn throws her arms around Dick in the biggest hug her small frame will allow.

"If we followed this street far enough, we'd reach the toy shop I took you to a couple weekends ago," Dick informs her once they reach Broadway. "Of course, that's probably *hours* away. I'm not sure exactly, as I've never done it myself. Too far."

Jaclyn chuckles at the idea of a few hours walk being too far, considering some of her experiences, but notes that she still has so much to get used to living in this time now. Then she notices the Charging Bull. "What an odd statue to idolise."

As they walk for the next ten minutes, Dick does his best to explain what the bull is supposed to represent. He only stops when Jaclyn makes him by resting a hand on his stomach. They find themselves standing still on a street corner, stunned at the sight of the crowd ahead of them.

"What is this?" Jaclyn asks.

Dick shakes his head. "I don't know; looks like a protest of some sort."

They start walking again to get a closer look.

"What do you read on their signs?" Jaclyn asks.

Looking over them, Dick picks a few to read. "Occupy Wall Street. We are the ninety-nine percent. We want our country back. Banks got bailed out, we got sold out. Regulate the banks. Banks for Democracy, not Plutocracy..." He trails off.

Jaclyn eyes the protesters, and admits, "I do not understand what any of this means."

Turning away from the crowd, Dick shakes his head at Jaclyn. "Apart from the common banking theme, I'm not entirely sure either."

"You may have to explain 'banking' to me."

Dick opens his eyes wide with surprise. "Even banks weren't around in your time?"

"Perhaps we called them something else? I will not know until you explicate."

With a chuckle, Dick suggests, "If you want that much detail, this is likely to take up the rest of the afternoon."

Jaclyn looks back at the protesters. Many of them appear to be beginning to march north. "I could stay and ask these people if you would prefer."

Another shake of Dick's head. "That's probably not the

best idea. Come on, we should probably avoid this in case things get nasty. I'll find us a subway."

Whilst Jaclyn follows Dick away from Zuccotti Park, she finds she can't help looking back over her shoulder at the protestors. Seeing their passion fills her with interest, and she just wants to learn more about why they're there. After all, she and Kitty left London in part because it was the best way to protest against Cromwell without getting hurt. That is, until they became pirates.

After an entire afternoon of explaining banks and the state of the economy to Jaclyn, Dick decides to get online and do a Google search about the protest.

"Wow," he says to himself. "This thing has already been going for eight days. Why isn't the news covering it?"

Overhearing him, Jaclyn sits down on the couch next to him and asks, "Eight days? For how long do they plan to protest?"

"Looks like they're not planning on leaving at all." Dick clicks a few more links, and plays a short video on YouTube. After a few seconds of silence, he says, "They're not even letting the cops intimidate them, despite pepper spraying some women today. God, I'm glad we didn't follow them all the way to Union Square. This looks crazy."

"You *sound* crazy. Cops? Pepper spraying?"

Dick plays the video again, this time with Jaclyn paying attention to it, so he can pause it to point out and explain the details. When it finishes, Jaclyn smirks.

"I hardly think this is a laughing matter," Dick says.

"My apologies." Jaclyn shrugs. "But I have seen far worse at the hands of the Navy, which I believe is roughly the sea's equivalent to your 'cops.' At least these women survived."

Dick rolls his eyes. "You may have noticed we don't carry swords these days." He purses his lips while he thinks how else to explain the significance. "Also, the police force operates under a strict code of conduct. Violence and immobilising people should only be used in the case of resisting arrest, or against those attacking cops first. There was none of that here." He sighs. "Those poor women. I may not know enough about this protest to know if I agree with them or not, but they were already sectioned off. There is no way they deserved that treatment."

A minute passes before Jaclyn responds. "You are right. This is another time, and it would do me well to remember to expect better behaviour from men."

Dick can't help but wonder if she means to include him in her statement.

When Dick hands Jaclyn copies of his keys, she can hardly believe her eyes. She didn't expect him to trust her to that extent already, and so she figures it must be a test to make sure she doesn't do anything stupid. For that reason, for the week that follows, she decides to play it safe. Her activities mainly include wandering around the city, recording a map in her head, and figuring out how to use the subway on her own. Since she still can't read, she pays careful attention to the stop names to keep up her awareness. Though, increasingly, she does find it would be easier to get by if she could read. By Friday, she calls Max to see if he would be willing to help tutor her some more. He agrees to find time for her.

Meanwhile, Jaclyn notices that Dick is becoming increasingly withdrawn from her, like he doesn't even seem to care to find out what she's been up to. That's when he's even home, which isn't particularly often, despite the fact Jaclyn tries to return to his apartment by sundown.

"Is there something on your mind?" Jaclyn asks when Dick finally emerges from his bedroom Saturday morning.

"Huh?" Dick is still a little groggy from sleep.

"You have not been interrogating me these past few days. I am not sure I believe you trust me to that extent."

Dick sighs, but instead of answering, heads into the kitchen and switches the coffee machine on. Jaclyn follows him in.

Without looking at her, or even turning away from the machine, Dick says, "I don't want to talk about it."

Unsure of the appropriate gesture, Jaclyn tries placing a hand on Dick's arm. "You can talk to me. Being a pirate does not mean I lack emotion."

He turns and looks her in the eye. "How did you lose Kitty?"

"That is not up for discussion. We are examining you." Her tone is curt.

"See, you don't want to talk about her either." Dick looks pretty pleased with himself.

Jaclyn shakes her head ever so slightly at Dick. "Perhaps we can try again in a week."

Without a sufficient response, Dick turns back to his coffee, and Jaclyn leaves the room.

Five minutes later, Jaclyn enters the main room with a satchel over her shoulder, and finds Dick sitting blank-faced in front of the television with his coffee. "While you refuse to engage in conversation with me, I shall continue to head out on my own."

The only sound that exits Dick's body in response is a *pfft*, and Jaclyn can't tell from which orifice it originates.

Jaclyn scoffs in response, and ventures out of the apartment alone.

A couple of hours later, Jaclyn manages to find her way back to Zuccotti Park. Curiosity over the past week had gotten the better of her, and she wanted to find out more. She wants to understand. There is a part of her that wonders if this might be a way she could reconnect with her feelings for Kitty. Is the protest at all similar to the one that got Kitty's mother killed? She decides that the best way for her to find out is to get to know some of the protestors. Armed with hope, Jaclyn sets about trying to find some who would be willing to clue her in.

The first person Jaclyn sets her eyes on is a young woman with ginger dreadlocks, sitting on the pavement with cardboard signs in front of her. The thick eyeliner the woman is wearing particularly captures her attention. Though this woman may be a few years younger than Jaclyn, she can't help feeling like this is what Kitty might have resembled had she not chopped off her hair, and deliberately hidden her femininity.

With her best attempt at acting casual, Jaclyn walks up to the woman and says, "Hi."

The ginger stands up and throws Jaclyn a curious look. "Hi?" She looks Jaclyn up and down. "Do I know you from somewhere?"

Embarrassment floods Jaclyn's system, feeling like she

did something wrong, though she has no idea what. Still, she needs to find a way to rectify her mistake, and fast. "No." She holds out her right hand. "Jaclyn Rousseau. I am new to New York. I was simply hoping you may be able to tell me more about what this is all about."

"Cute accent," the woman says. "Nikki Porter." She takes Jaclyn's hand and shakes it casually. "And I would love to."

They let each other's hands go, and Jaclyn delivers her sharpest, toothy smile to Nikki.

Nikki smiles back. "How much do you already know about American politics?"

The question causes an immediate change of expression in Jaclyn. She's almost shy when she admits, "I know you do not have a king?"

Nikki can't help letting a smirk escape, but quickly quietens down. "Where are you from?"

"England, originally." Jaclyn figures it's best not to admit the century, too.

"I'm surprised that's all you know, then."

Jaclyn bites her lip while she tries to come up with a response that makes sense, and isn't entirely dishonest. "I have been exploring the West Indies over the last ten years. I have not had much opportunity to hear of news in your country."

This answer seems to satisfy Nikki enough for her to continue. "Well, our country isn't really run by the president any more, either." She huffs. "Fucking banks and fucking corporations buy their way in and get the laws they want. They don't give a shit about ninety-nine percent of the population. We're losing the middle class. They'd be fucking thrilled if we all lived in poverty."

As Nikki settles down, Jaclyn chews on the word *poverty* for a while. Growing up in London, it was an issue she never heard acknowledged. What did she care about the poor? They were beneath her. Then she was introduced to piracy, where no one was beneath her. Whilst she may not have been poor much of the time, given the robberies she'd been involved with, it had given her a different understanding of the world.

Nikki adds, "They've turned us all into fucking slaves."

Jaclyn chokes. She's not sure if she heard Nikki properly. *Slaves*? Really?

"I do not understand," Jaclyn says, looking around at everyone. "If you are all enslaved, why are you not out working on plantations?"

Nikki raises an eyebrow at Jaclyn, but answers her question anyway. "They give us the illusion of freedom, pay us money, but only so we buy more crap, grow our debts, and never find a way to climb out of the hole they encouraged us to dig."

"Hmm." Jaclyn doesn't say much, trying to process this information. "Then... how do you think things can change?"

"We want to bring the power back to the people. We're the rightful rulers of America."

The passion that fills Nikki's face as she speaks reminds Jaclyn of the way Kitty used to talk when she told her if they robbed enough English merchant vessels, they'd be taking away Cromwell's power. The similarities in the situations are uncanny, and Jaclyn can't help feeling a little hot under the collar.

"Are you staying here?" Jaclyn asks.

Nikki nods, and then points to a blue tent. "That's my tent over there."

Jaclyn mouths a "Wow."

"Yeah."

"Why protest here?" Jaclyn asks, curiosity getting the better of her.

"Wall Street." Nikki points down Broadway. "That's where the major decisions were made that crashed the economy. Every single person who works down there is a fucking thief as far as I'm concerned. They all need to pay for what they did."

That, too, sounds familiar to Jaclyn. It was how Kitty justified her murders. She always said that anyone who still worked while Cromwell ruled must have supported him, and so they deserved what they got for not supporting the king.

"Can I get your number," Jaclyn says, remembering how she was asked for hers, "in the event I want to learn more?" She takes out her phone.

"Instead of asking me out on a date?" Nikki smirks.

Jaclyn looks at her blankly, not understanding what Nikki means by 'date.' She doesn't ask, though, as she would rather not embarrass herself further. She's not sure she could dig herself out again.

Nikki takes the phone. "Sure I can." She starts pressing buttons. "But I want you to meet me for coffee when you do have more questions."

"Thank you," Jaclyn says, taking her phone back, but still not getting the underlying meaning of Nikki's words.

While Jaclyn heads back toward the subway, she calls

Max, but he doesn't answer, so she decides to leave a voice-mail message. "When next we meet, I will want you to show me how to write 'Nikki,' and 'Wall Street.' Can you do that?"

The apartment is void of any life when Jaclyn returns. She sighs, and sits down on the couch, wondering if Dick just didn't want to be around her after the morning they had. In case that is the reason for his absence, she calls Max again. This time, he answers.

"Who's Nikki?" he asks immediately.

Jaclyn hopes he can't hear her blushing through her voice. "Just a woman I met."

"Did you fuck her?"

"Max!"

"I think that's the first time I've heard you use my first name."

Jaclyn smirks. "I think we misplaced the need for formalities when you fucked me."

"Knew you weren't really offended by that language." His tone is very obviously sure of himself.

Even though she knows he can't see her, Jaclyn shrugs. "I am no stranger to it. I simply hoped to leave it behind when I came here. My thoughts were such that it was not respectable to use such words in polite company, and I did not want people gaining an accurate impression of me so soon."

"I wouldn't worry what other people think of you," Max says. "So tell me about Nikki."

"Do you have the time to meet with me at Dick's apartment to talk? Now?"

"Is he home?"

"No; I do not know where he is."

"Then I do now. Be right there."

'Right there' turns out to be about forty minutes, but that's considered making good time for Manhattan.

When Jaclyn answers the door, the sight of Max causes her to bite her lip.

"What's this for?" Max asks, pointing to her teeth.

Jaclyn shakes herself out of it. "I was remembering what you look like undressed."

He smiles at her, and lets himself in. "I can help you remember better later." He turns around to face her, and opens his jacket a little. "Or now."

"That will not be necessary," Jaclyn says, walking toward the couch.

Max lets go of his jacket and follows her as she sits. "So I was right, you did fuck Nikki?"

"No." Jaclyn bites her thumb.

"You want to, though."

"Yes." She pauses. "I believe so." Then she shakes her head, sure her confusion must be apparent on her face. "I do not know. She reminds me of Kitty. That may be all this feeling is."

Max finally sits down next to Jaclyn. "How did you meet her?"

"At a protest. Near Wall Street."

"Well I suppose that answers why you want to know how to write that as well."

"Mmm," is all Jaclyn can mumble. That's not entirely accurate, but she doesn't really want to go into detail about that with Max.

"How can I help, then? You want to ask her out on a date?"

Jaclyn's eyes sort of light up at hearing the word 'date.'

"What do you mean by that? Nikki said something similar to that, but I did not understand what she meant by 'date.' Could you explain?"

"It's part of the courting process. You go out together, have some drinks, then go back to their place, or yours, and fuck."

Jaclyn stares at Max, unblinking. Max looks confused.

"What?" he asks.

"It would seem she may already want to lay with me and I did not even realise."

"It happens. Not to me, of course, but I hear some people have trouble recognising that sort of thing." Max looks amused. "I'm surprised, though. You seemed to figure out I wanted to fuck you easy enough."

Jaclyn shrugs. "I have only been with one woman. Men make their intentions known in a far more obvious way."

"Sounds like Nikki was pretty obvious, too, you just didn't notice because you're not familiar with current social conventions." Max stands. "That all you want from me?"

The expression Max flashes Jaclyn next is not one she is unfamiliar with. Yet she can't help but feel dragged into its implications.

About thirty minutes later, Dick returns to his apartment and hangs his coat up on a hook next to the front door. It's quiet, so Dick assumes Jaclyn must still be out, which is just what he wanted.

He starts to walk toward his bedroom, figuring he could do with a nap after the day he's had. When he sees Max Fuentes emerging from Jaclyn's bedroom, and beginning to walk toward him, he stops dead in his tracks.

"Richard," Max says, flashing Dick a smug grin on his way past him.

By the time Dick manages to get over the overwhelming feeling of 'What the fuck?' and 'Did he smell like sex?' long enough to turn around, all he catches is the door closing behind Max. He turns back around and heads to Jaclyn's room.

"Jaclyn?"

She pops her head out of the door. "Yes?"

Dick moves closer to her and leans against the wall before asking the first thing on his mind. "Did you just have sex with that guy?"

"Oh." Jaclyn stands up straight. "*Now* you want to interrogate me again?"

Dick matches her pose and shakes his head. "I'm sorry. It's none of my business." He starts to head toward his room, but curiosity gets the better of him and he can't help himself. Facing Jaclyn again, he says, "But he's a *man*."

"I never said I only lay with women."

Barbados was long enough ago for Dick to have forgotten what Jaclyn's exact words were, but in the end he decides it doesn't matter. He has too much else to worry about with his mother right now to have any interest in sex anyway.

With a shrug, Dick says, "I suppose even if you had, there was nothing stopping you from lying to me about it. You are a pirate, after all." Then he turns back to return to his nap goal, though he's not sure how he'll be able to sleep with this on his mind now.

"Hey!" Jaclyn strides forward and jumps up to grab Dick's shoulder, turning him around again. "Engaging in pirating does not make a liar. I discontinued lying when I stopped disguising myself as a man." In a softer voice, she adds, "At the very least, I try to be honest. There is no harm in withholding certain details."

Dick shrugs again.

"Is this why you have been staying away from me?" Jaclyn sounds a little bitter this time. "Because I have not been sharing your bed?"

"You want to know why I've been so distant?" Dick asks in a huff. "I'm losing my mother. Okay? Not that it's any of your business, but my mother is..." he chokes on the last word, "*dying.*"

With that, Dick's hands form fists, and he gently hits the base of one against the wall before crumbling to the floor. He does his best to prevent himself from crying, too.

Jaclyn gets down on her knees. Dick doesn't know what inside her causes her to react in such a way, but she wraps her arms around him and pulls him close to her. He finds himself appreciating the lack of words. This, he thinks, is what real friends do. Yet, he's getting it from a pirate instead.

"Would you like to tell me about her?" Jaclyn asks, hoping he'll react better than the times she tried to get Kitty to talk to her about her mother. "It may be worth losing yourself in a good memory."

Though Jaclyn may, in part, be asking to get Dick's mind

away from being upset with her, she is also genuinely curious. She wasn't very close to her own mother, and finds it hard to understand others who are.

Roughly five minutes pass before Dick calms down enough to talk again.

"Okay," he says. "Here's something. This is from about twenty-four years ago, back when I was still in high school. I thought I was madly in love with my best friend, Julie. When Mum realised how upset I was when she started dating this guy I hated, she listened to everything I had to vent about. Then she asked me if it was really Julie I wanted, or was I just upset at the thought of losing my friend and not having a girl like me."

Jaclyn can't relate to the experience, considering every person she has been attracted to has been interested in her, too, but she supposes she needs to keep the conversation going somehow. "How did you respond?"

"I rolled my eyes at her." He pauses to smirk at his immature behaviour. "But, then, a few days later I confessed that I wasn't sure, and maybe I was just bothered that I didn't have any girls who wanted to date me."

Not knowing what she should say next, she tries, "Did that change?"

"Funnily enough, we had a vacation booked for Christmas that year, so we could see Mum's family in Australia. She suggested I might find a fling there, seeing as how Dad's accent was what attracted her in the beginning. This was back in the eighties so it turned out Mum was right. She even bought me condoms to make sure I was careful." He shakes his head and laughs at the memory. "I don't know how many teenage boys were lucky enough to have a mum like that back then."

"It sounds like she means a lot to you," Jaclyn says, stroking his arm.

She finally stands up and takes his hand, pulling him over to the couch where it's more comfortable, and asks for another story. His are not like the stories Kitty used to share with her, but it's nice to be able to listen.

Dick ends up sharing memories there until they both fall asleep where they sit.

At Nikki's suggestion, Jaclyn meets her back at Zuccotti Park on Tuesday morning. This way Jaclyn can't get lost looking for the name of a coffee shop when she can't read anyway—not that she has admitted that to Nikki yet. Nikki's reasoning was that Jaclyn was new to the area, and that suited Jaclyn just fine.

Jaclyn follows Nikki several blocks, including various turns, which Jaclyn tries to keep track of in her head in case she needs to return sometime.

"I like this place because it's not a chain like Starbucks," Nikki says as they arrive. "Fucking corporations and all that."

All Jaclyn can do is smile, because how else is she supposed to respond when she's not entirely sure what Nikki is talking about?

They enter the establishment, and Nikki gets Jaclyn to save them a table. "What would you like to drink?"

"Hot chocolate?" Jaclyn asks. When Dick had tried to give her some of his instant coffee at home, she spat it out because it tasted like burnt horse shit to her, and she doesn't want a repeat performance of that in front of this woman she likes.

Nikki smiles, and adds a slight laugh from her nose. "Not a coffee drinker, huh?"

"I prefer chocolate."

"Fair enough. Wait here." Nikki heads to the counter to place their order.

When Nikki returns, she's still closing her purse as she sits down.

"So you're thinking of joining our cause, huh?"

"I cannot think of a better reason for me to be here right now," Jaclyn says. There's a hint of sadness in her voice, but there's a part of her that wants to believe that maybe this is what she was sent into the future to do.

"There's room in my tent if you want to see what it's like on the front lines."

A female barista brings the women their drinks, interrupting them momentarily.

After she leaves, and with not a care for the impression it will make, Jaclyn asks, "Are you inviting me to bed?"

Nikki smirks. "In a manner of speaking... I don't have a bed in the tent, obviously."

Biting her lip, Jaclyn can't think how to respond.

"You're cute," Nikki says.

Jaclyn bites harder, then switches to her thumb when it begins to hurt.

"Nervous, too." Nikki smiles. "But interested, or you'd have left by now." She runs a finger in circles over the back of Jaclyn's hand that remains on the table.

"I am not exactly new to *this*, but it has been a little over a year since I was last with a woman."

"We can take it slow."

Though a little shy about it, Jaclyn confesses, "I would like to try tonight."

"Or, not so slow." Nikki laughs.

Dick checks his phone as soon as he leaves a proposal meeting. He had felt it vibrate in his pocket several times whilst talking to his clients, but he couldn't exactly answer it then. There are several missed calls from his father, followed by one voicemail message.

Listening to it, his father says, "The nurse is saying it doesn't look like your mom will live past sunset tonight. Try and get down here if you want to say your final goodbye."

He checks his watch; it's a little after three, and the message was left about ten minutes earlier.

After ducking into his boss' office to let her know he has to get to the hospice, he heads right over.

Dick slowly opens the door to his mother's room. She's lying on the bed, eyes closed, but she's not sleeping. His breathing slows almost to a stop as he senses that he's the only person alive in that room. Whatever made his mother the woman she was is no longer in her body. She's nothing more than an empty shell now.

Feeling a presence behind him, Dick turns around and finds his father. Victor opens his arms for him, and the men embrace in their sadness, but do not weep.

When Nikki and Jaclyn return to the protest camp, Nikki introduces Jaclyn to a few of the people she's met since joining the movement, since they happen to be sleeping in nearby tents.

The first person Nikki presents Jaclyn to is Mike, who is apparently a former lawyer who got sick of drawing up patents, whatever that means. His dark skin reminds her of Turtle's, though his facial features are quite different, which Jaclyn assumes indicates he must be from a different part of Africa, except that Mike's voice sounds like the other Americans she has met. Mike is also noticeably shorter than Turtle by about six inches. Jaclyn notes that Mike is dressed more sensibly than her African friend, and admires the fact that he has more hair on his head.

Sarah is a blonde woman who seems old enough to be Jaclyn's mother—if she doesn't take into consideration the missing centuries—due to her wrinkles and the strands of hair that had faded to grey. She and Jaclyn are about the same height, though Sarah is considerably chubbier. Before Sarah came to Wall Street, she had been an elementary school teacher. Jaclyn admires the fact that in this century, women have that right, when in her time girls couldn't even receive the kind of education that boys got.

A few other people are introduced, but Jaclyn gets too overwhelmed to remember all of their names.

Most of the time, Jaclyn finds it better to listen rather than speak. There is a lot of discussion about individual beliefs, and they don't always line up with others in the movement. A lot of points tend to fly through Jaclyn's head without time for her to analyse or understand what is being said. She thinks she has missed a lot by not being born in this century, and Dick's understanding of capitalism seems to be different from those talking about it here.

Part of her wonders if anyone truly understands what capitalism is anyway. Whilst Nikki seems to want to take it down completely, Mike and Sarah argue that capitalism isn't in itself evil. Their reason for protesting is purely for more regulations, which is yet another thing Jaclyn doesn't understand the meaning of. The government in this time sounds a lot more complicated than anything she's familiar with in the seventeenth century.

As the day draws on, Nikki walks Jaclyn down to Wall Street so she can get a better look at the type of people who work there as they leave for the day.

"So, this is Wall Street," Nikki says. She points to a group of men and women in mostly black and grey business suits, carrying briefcases. "Those guys there, laughing amongst themselves. They're the type who would've made decisions that crashed the economy. And then gave each other pats on the back and giant bonuses when the government bailed them out."

Jaclyn watches them. Empathising with Nikki, she begins to feel the rage circulating in her blood. She finds herself wishing there was something—anything—she could do to help.

"And look at those women with them," Nikki says, shaking her head and pursing her lips. "I hate them even more, going along with the patriarchy, not caring to defend the rest of our rights."

Jaclyn doesn't quite understand every word Nikki shares with her about this 'patriarchy' as she continues to speak, but finds herself agreeing with what she can comprehend. How abhorrent that, in an age where women seem to have more opportunities, more choices, they're going out there and making decisions that ruin the lives of many! She frowns.

"I have seen enough for now," Jaclyn says.

With a nod, Nikki takes her back to camp.

Inside the tent, Jaclyn asks, "What did you do with your time before you came out here?"

"I spent four years studying computer programming, and couldn't get a job in my field because of the economy." Nikki sighs. "Debt slave like everyone else. Had to stay in waitressing. It sucks. People don't tip as well as they used to."

Jaclyn makes a mental note of the words and phrases that don't make sense to her so she can ask Dick later. She's tired of not understanding things that should make sense to any normal person, but she would rather not have the 'from another century' conversation with anyone else.

At least she understands enough to offer sympathy. "My apologies," she says, and places a hand on top of one of Nikki's. "Is there nothing else you could have done? You look like someone who would enjoy adventurous activities."

Nikki smirks. "What, like exploring the Amazon jungle?"

"Perhaps." Jaclyn shrugs. "I have a friend who has been." She is thinking about Turtle, who told her a story once about a journey he and Captain McDonald went on to look for gold to take from the Portuguese up the Amazon River.

"It's okay, you're not the first person to make that kind of assumption about me." Nikki takes Jaclyn's hand and holds it in hers. "I've considered it, I guess. Travelling, I mean. But I don't think about it much because it's an expensive dream."

"Have you considered sailing?" Jaclyn asks, feeling a little coy. "It can be hard work, but it is wonderful to experience."

"You've sailed?"

"It is why I spent so long in the West Indies." Jaclyn smiles. It may not be the whole truth, but she appreciates the opportunity to tell Nikki more about herself.

"That's incredible. No wonder you didn't have access to the news." Nikki laughs. "Not for me though. I got seasick just going on the ferry to the Statue of Liberty."

Jaclyn begins to consider that Nikki may not resemble Kitty as much as she thought. That idea is washed away almost as immediately as it comes when Nikki leans forward and brushes her lips against Jaclyn's.

When Dick wakes the following morning and Jaclyn isn't up and moving about, all kinds of thoughts fill his head. Was she there last night? Dick was too tired to even check on her by the time he got home that he just went straight to bed. Has something happened to her? Has she gotten herself into some kind of trouble? Well that would be just perfect timing, he thinks with much sarcasm. At least he already called in to work for a mental health day for his mother's passing. He just wishes he didn't have to go out looking for this woman when he could be taking the time for himself.

That's when he remembers she has a phone. He looks up her number in his phone and calls it.

Jaclyn is startled awake to the sound of her phone ringing. Nikki laughs at the awkward noise Jaclyn makes, then hands her the phone.

"I think it's for you," she says.

"Mmm?" Jaclyn mumbles into the phone, not really registering what's going on.

"Where are you? Are you okay?" Dick asks. Then he starts rambling. "Oh, I suppose since you answered, you're not in jail at least..."

"You worry about me far too much," Jaclyn interrupts. "I was sleeping."

"Not in your room."

"No, you are right, not in my room." She sighs.

"Parents?" Nikki whispers.

Jaclyn shakes her head and whispers back, "I will tell you later." Then louder, and to her phone, she says, "I came back to the protest."

"What are you doing down there?" Dick sounds even more confused than he was when they met.

With a shrug, Jaclyn says, "Curiosity."

"I hope you're not doing anything weird in public..." Dick starts, but changes tune. "Never mind; can you come home? I could use a..." he hesitates on the next word, "a *friend* right now."

Before replying, Jaclyn focuses on the word *weird*. She wonders why Dick would say that. He hasn't come across as the type of man to believe in fate or destiny. However, since he shrugged it off, Jaclyn supposes she will too. "I shall be home as early as the subway allows."

After Jaclyn ends the call, Nikki muses, "I love the way you talk."

Jaclyn smiles at the compliment. "Thank you for... everything. I will try to return soon. My... *roommate* needs me."

It's the first time Jaclyn uses that word to refer to Dick,

but after the 'Daddy' incident with Max, he insisted she use it if she ever needed to talk about their relationship.

The apartment is quiet when Jaclyn gets home. She tiptoes through in case Dick has gone back to bed, but finds him sitting in his room reading a book instead. He looks up at her and puts the book down as she stands in the doorway.

"What do you need?" Jaclyn asks.

Dick pats the bed beside him.

"I am not having sex with you simply because you found out I fuck men as well as women."

His expression changes to one of frustration, and he throws a pillow at her, but it misses. "That's not what this is about, but if you want to bring it up, I don't think you should be sleeping with a guy like Max."

Jaclyn walks over to Dick's bed and sits down. "Why?"

"I know his type. He's a sleaze. He'll end up hurting you."

"No, he will not. I am not looking for a man to marry, Dick, and I think I know him better than you do." Now Jaclyn's frustrated, too. "I also think I know men who only want to fuck better than you do. Lived with them for years. They never cared enough to teach me to read."

"*Could* they read?" Dick asks with a smile.

"Perhaps not, but that is not the point."

Dick sighs. "Maybe you're right. I'm sorry. I don't want to talk about this right now anyway." He pauses to sigh again. "Mum died yesterday."

"Oh, Dick." Jaclyn wraps her arms around Dick and rests her head on his shoulder. "You could have called me sooner. I would have come."

"I wasn't home anyway. Didn't notice you weren't here until this morning."

Jaclyn leaves the embrace and asks, "Can I sing you something?"

"You sing?" Dick looks skeptical.

"There is a lot about me that you do not know."

Dick smirks. "I have a feeling there's a lot that would be best if it stayed unknown."

"Though you want to know about Kitty."

"Well, there's that..."

"It is fine. I am going to sing you the song I wrote when I lost Kitty." She recalls the sadness she felt when she came up with the lyrics. "I hope it will help you relate. Maybe we can talk about our losses after."

With a smile, Dick can't help acknowledging Jaclyn's kindness. "Thank you. This is more than I could have hoped to expect."

Jaclyn stands, clears her throat, and begins to sing. "You have gone away... left me here, in this place, without you..."

TEN

"I am returning to London," Kitty confessed to Jaclyn.

They were sitting in a chocolate house in Port Royal. Kitty had chosen this establishment over one of the many taverns that littered the town because the pirates she knew did not frequent there. This in turn meant she could shed her men's clothes, which allowed her to feel normal again for a while. Jaclyn may have had the courage to dress more feminine, but Kitty had not allowed herself to. Here, though, they both wore dresses that were unfamiliar to their crew.

When Kitty had announced this news to Jaclyn, there was no, "Will you come with me?" or "Can we discuss our next move?" Jaclyn didn't want to think of them as parting ways, but she didn't know how else to take it.

"With whom will you be sailing?" queried Jaclyn, at least hoping she would be included in the response.

"I have bought passage on one of Sir Bromley's merchant vessels."

"And he accepted? Does he know how much you have helped plunder from him?"

"Jack, not one person beyond you would think Katherine Grayson could possibly be a pirate, nor, for that matter, a captain," said Kitty. Then she paused before adding, "Now do you see why I had to continue to conceal my identity, even after you revealed yours and survived?"

"I am confused as to why you wish to return at all," Jaclyn said, changing the subject slightly. "Is this because of Prudence?"

"Yes and no," Kitty confessed. "With the monarchy restored and the Puritans with less control... I feel safer again."

"No," said Jaclyn. "That is not to what I refer."

"Then I do not understand."

"I know you have been seeing her."

"Jack, she died nine years past. Unless you think I am talking to her ghost?" she spoke as calmly as she could, but Jaclyn could sense her nervousness. She knew Katherine was lying. Of course, she had good reason to.

"I have seen you with her. The mermaid."

"A mermaid? Whatever would make you believe she is a mermaid?" Katherine tried to keep herself steady, but Jaclyn noticed a nervous twitch in her left hand. She added, "I thought you did not believe in such fanciful ideas?"

"It is hard to remain unbelieving of that which you see with your own eyes," said Jaclyn.

Katherine shifted in her place, but realised there was no sense in lying any longer. When she next spoke, she averted her eyes, "How much time has passed since you first saw her?"

At this point, Jaclyn wasn't really sure whether she wanted to continue the discussion. Still, since she figured Kitty was leaving her anyway, there was no better time to alleviate the tension she had felt for Prudence in all these years.

"Three years," she said, remembering the moment she had caught them together.

When Turtle had told her he had seen the captain with a fair-haired woman, Jack didn't believe it until that moment. She had sat up in bed one night, wondering why Kitty wasn't laying with her, and heard voices travelling through an open stern window. When she looked out of it, that's when she saw them.

Kitty sat in a skiff, while Prudence's arms rested on the side of the boat, with the bottom half of her body in the water. It dawned on her that this was the woman in the sea she had seen when Kitty was made captain. Saltwater began to seep from her eyes, and streamed down her face faster the longer she watched.

She didn't recognise Prudence physically without her pock-covered face, but she knew it was her with the way Kitty behaved. Hearing her call the woman "Prue" only confirmed it.

Once Prudence's head dipped beneath the sea, and her tail emerged, Jaclyn knew it was time to return to her bed and hide what she had seen.

"Why did you not say anything?" Kitty asked, looking at Jaclyn's eyes, wanting to understand; wanting to know if they would tell her a different story than Jaclyn's words.

"I needed you," said Jaclyn, and her eyes began to water. "I needed you, and I thought if we discussed her, you would leave me."

Katherine took a sip of her hot chocolate drink while she processed her thoughts.

"Jack," she started, then took another mouthful of chocolate before continuing, "Prue is not the reason I wish to return in London."

Jaclyn's response was immediate: "But you are carrying on an affair with her." Then she stood up, requesting loudly, "Do not deny me!"

"Hush," said Kitty, "You are making a scene. Sit."

Jaclyn did as she was told, but continued to display her displeasure by crossing both her arms and her legs, frowning at her lover.

"I would never leave you for Prudence."

"Yet you refuse to choose between us."

"I love you both," Katherine confessed. "However," she added, "I must leave you, Jack. You have changed. You love the sea far too much to stay in one place, but I still wish to follow my dream of becoming a writer."

"So you are leaving me for her," Jaclyn said quietly.

"Nay," Katherine objected. "I am doing this for myself."

"Then there is something you should perhaps know," Jaclyn said, realising there was no sense in arguing. She closed her eyes and confessed, "A Puritan did not murder Prudence."

"I do not understand. How do you know that?"

Jaclyn stood, and whispered in Katherine's ear, "It was me."

But Jaclyn did not want to see the pain in Katherine's eyes when she learned the truth, so she turned to leave the chocolate house without looking back. She faked the confidence in her walk just long enough until she reached the exit, but as soon as the door shut behind her, she ran as fast as she could to a deserted jetty. She did not want to risk

Kitty following her. She did not want Kitty to see the tears streaming down her face or the regret in her own eyes.

A tearful hour passed before Jaclyn noticed a Dutch fluyt mooring not too far away. Whilst she had encountered such ships, having helped attack and steal from a number of them, this was the first time she had actually seen one anywhere near to a place pirates trade. She wondered if that was why it didn't pull in to dock in the harbour.

Minutes later, Jaclyn watched as two people manned a small boat and slowly rowed in to the jetty she was sitting on. One of the men was very obviously Dutch, but the other man did not look European at all. In fact, his ancestry was clearly unlike that of anyone she had ever met or sailed with.

"Welcome to Port Royal," Jaclyn said as the Dutchman tied the boat to the jetty.

"Miss," the Dutchman said with a nod.

"You speak English?"

"I do."

"What about that man?" Jaclyn asked, indicating the man who was storing the paddles.

"No," he said. "He is Chinese, however he does speak Dutch."

"Chinese?" Jaclyn asked, being unfamiliar with the word.

"Ah. We found him in Malacca, over in the East Indies, about ten years ago," said the Dutchman. Jaclyn still looked clueless, so the Dutchman added, "Of course, I gather, you have not sailed that far east." After climbing onto the jetty, he changed the subject and asked, "How does a woman with your beauty find herself in the West Indies anyway?"

"I am not a punk, if that is what you are thinking," Jaclyn said defensively.

"A what?"

"A whore," Jaclyn said, realising the Dutchman probably wasn't familiar with the slang. "There are a lot of whores here. I just thought..."

"No need, Miss," the Dutchman interrupted. He then held out his hand to greet the woman and introduce himself, "Captain Dries van der Lawick."

Jaclyn took Dries's hand and shook it. "Jaclyn Rousseau," she said, adding, "pirate."

Dries looked affronted. "I am not!"

With a smile and a bit of a chuckle, Jaclyn said, "I was referring to myself, though I can see why you may have made that mistake. I dress differently when sailing." She paused a moment to make sure Dries was not going to attack her for confessing to her profession, and added, "You do not appear outraged."

"That would be due to the fact we took this vessel off the coast of Java," Dries said with a smile. "We are kindred."

Jaclyn looked at the Chinese man in the dinghy again, admiring his features somewhat.

"Come," said Jaclyn, "let me take you and—"

"Li Cheng Wu," Dries offered, as the Chinese man finally pulled himself up onto the jetty.

"Cheng Wu," Cheng Wu clarified.

"Let me show you and Cheng Wu to the Frigate Anchor Tavern."

Jaclyn had decided this would be a great diversion from

thinking about losing Katherine just over an hour before, and now that Katherine had decided to leave piracy behind, there was not a chance Jaclyn was likely to find her in a tavern.

As they arrived at their destination, Jaclyn remembered what she was wearing, and decided she did not want to be seen amongst her brethren in a dress.

"I will return to you in a moment," she said, and quickly walked into the inn she had been staying at, which happened to be the building opposite the tavern.

Once in her room, Jaclyn noted that Kitty had already taken all of her belongings, though left much of her treasure behind. This act left Jaclyn wondering why she would have done something so nice for her after the way she left things. She also wondered how Kitty was going to survive on the little amount she kept. Then she considered that it made sense, if Kitty had chosen not to reveal her career in piracy. She wouldn't want to be asked questions about where she got such items. Suddenly leaving it behind didn't seem like an act of generosity, and Jaclyn felt a little sick to her stomach.

"I need a drink," she said to herself, figuring that was the best way to wash away these thoughts.

Jaclyn threw her dress off and into the corner of the room before dressing herself back into her breeches, shirt, bodice, and boots. She then trudged back over to the Frigate Anchor to find Dries and Cheng Wu.

When she found them, she noticed a smile on Cheng Wu's face as he whispered something into Dries's ear. He nodded just as Jaclyn sat down to join them.

"My friend here is curious how you ended up pirate.

Did you marry one?"

"Is he asking because he wishes to make a proposal if I did not?" Jaclyn asked, picking up on Cheng Wu's facial cues.

Dries and Cheng Wu exchanged some words in Dutch.

"Because," she added, "I am unmarried, and he is a fine looking sailor if ever I saw one." She confessed to herself that it may have had something to do with wanting to find a quick way to forget about Kitty.

Cheng Wu mumbled something in a language she was unfamiliar with, and even Dries didn't seem to understand him. They exchanged more Dutch, and Jaclyn started to feel a bit frustrated at the lack of English spoken.

"Does he speak French, perhaps?" Jaclyn asked, hoping they could find a common language.

Dries laughed, "Actually, we have taught him French. I would bet that he is the most knowledgable Chinaman in the world. He picked up the language with ease."

With a sigh of relief, Jaclyn continued the rest of the conversation in the language of her father, and the others followed suit.

As the evening drew to a close, Jaclyn asked, "Do you plan to keep your fluyt? I have never thought of it as a good pirate vessel."

Dries nodded, "You are right, my dear. Taking the ship was the easiest way of transporting the cargo, but we will be looking for another."

Thoughts about the vessel Jaclyn helped appropriate the first time she attacked one as a woman entered her mind, for that was her home now.

"Your crew is small. Why do you not invite them to join

with us on the brig *Medusa's Wrath*?" Jaclyn asked, feeling comfortable with these foreign men. "We are in need of more men after so many died during a raid on a Spanish galleon near Hispaniola."

"And lose my captain's post?" Dries asked.

Kitty's quartermaster, Turner, entered Jaclyn's mind. Though he might have been a decent quartermaster, she didn't think he was fit to captain their brig.

"We also lost our captain," she said, before wondering if Kitty had informed Turner of that.

"And quartermaster?" Cheng Wu asked. "Captain here will trust no one but me."

"I will talk to ours. See if we can come to an arrangement."

"Hmm," Dries said. "Let me talk to my crew." Standing, he added, "Come, Li."

As Cheng Wu stood, Jaclyn said, "Wait. I wish to speak with you further." A coy smile crossed her face.

"Captain?" Cheng Wu asked.

Dries nodded at him, and left the tavern as Cheng Wu sat back down.

"I did not mean for us to stay here," Jaclyn said. "Let me take you somewhere more private."

It was only as Jaclyn was leaving the tavern that she noticed Noah watching her, but she decided she would deal with that conversation later. She was too focused on taking Cheng Wu back to her room at the inn.

Maybe it was a rash decision for Jaclyn, so once they were in her room, she decided to give Cheng Wu a way out.

"I should perhaps warn you that the last time I fucked a man, he ended up mermaid food," she said, maintaining her French.

"I do not consider myself superstitious," Cheng Wu replied, and Jaclyn was amused that he had even understood her crass language.

Cheng Wu fell asleep immediately after their three minutes of intercourse, which left Jaclyn to reflect on her time with Higgins, and compare the differences between her sexual encounters with men. Recalling the look on Kitty's face when she was caught in the act caused her to weep a little. No matter how much Higgins had tormented her, and no matter that Kitty had been unfaithful to her, she still felt so much guilt. Asking Kitty for help probably would have been better.

The circumstances were entirely different this time, but apparently you don't need to be in a relationship with someone to feel like you betrayed them. Drowning herself in false love didn't seem to do anything to alleviate the pain of losing Kitty, either.

She wanted to go out for a walk to clear her head, but she didn't trust leaving Cheng Wu alone with her treasure. If she hadn't been so exhausted, she might have considered counting her coins to see if she had enough to buy a place and settle down. Maybe open her own tavern. Port Royal wasn't that bad of a place, even if it was filled with pirates.

Left with no other options, Jaclyn laid down next to Cheng Wu, but had a mostly restless night. Any time she felt the man move, she worried he was going to steal from her.

The next morning was when she wondered if Kitty may have had a point to leave a world where she couldn't really trust her friends. However, by the time she managed to get

Cheng Wu up and down to the harbour with her, she found that Bromley's vessel had already departed.

Jaclyn mentally kicked herself for thinking she even had a chance to join Kitty on the journey back to London. There was no reason she would have accepted Jaclyn back after the way she had severed their relationship.

Those thoughts were pushed from her mind when she noticed Dries's fluyt docked in the harbour now. Jaclyn was going to board the vessel with Cheng Wu to find him, when a disheveled Turner came stumbling towards them.

"Ye look like a cow shit all over ye," Jaclyn said to him, glad Turner had become a friend she could talk to like that before he was voted quartermaster.

"Too much drink; too many whores," was Turner's explanation. "Need to sleep 'em off in my cabin."

"Ye should probably stop spending your share of the booty the minute we dock, even if ye do get more than the rest of us," said Jaclyn. "Meanwhile, our captain's deserted us. Can we have a word in private?"

Turner held his head and simply nodded in response.

After turning back to Cheng Wu, Jaclyn said, in French, "Tell Captain van der Lawick to meet me outside the Frigate Anchor in an hour."

Cheng Wu nodded, and returned to his ship as Jaclyn and Turner walked further along the dock to find their current brig.

"So, let me make sure I understand what yer trying to say," Turner said, "Captain Gray decided to leave us in favour of King Charles?"

Jaclyn nodded, and decided that perhaps it was time

for her to talk to someone other than Katherine—someone she trusted—about how she and Katherine ended up as pirates in the New World. "He started out justifying his killings by saying anyone what trades with England was just supporting Cromwell's illegitimate government," she cited. "I think he sort of saw himself as some sort of self appointed hero for the crown. Never believed it until now."

"Sounds more honourable than the rest of us. No wonder he only told you," Turner said, and paused on that thought, focusing clearly on Jaclyn. After processing, he added, "'Course, he must not be that honourable if he decided to leave you behind. How long ye been together?"

"Since we was but sixteen in London," Jaclyn answered, and stopped to calculate. "God blind me, that was nearly ten years gone now."

"If ye do not mind my saying, and maybe this will nay mean much coming from me, what with my reputation and all, but he clearly be a bastard here."

"Aye," said Jaclyn, not sure whether she actually agreed with him. "But we all has our faults. If ye decided to make good of yer life, would ye want a pirate for a wife?"

Turner smirked. "Should make that one of yer songs."

With a shrug, Jaclyn leaned back in her chair and rested her boots on Turner's desk. "Regardless, we be needing a new captain. And that man ye saw me with has a captain in need of a vessel. What say we talk with them?"

It was a strange feeling for Kitty to be back on a merchant vessel—without killing the crew—after all her years in piracy. Yet, some things didn't change. After lights out, she found herself on deck and being whistled at from the sea.

Just as with her first encounter with the mermaid, and many others since, she lowered herself into a skiff on the calm ocean.

Prudence joined her immediately, scales disappearing as she did, and kissed her lover, until Kitty pulled away.

"Wait," she said. "Jack knew about us."

"When?" Prudence looked confused.

Kitty couldn't stop herself from letting her emotion out—it was the first chance she had to be with someone she trusted since leaving Jaclyn. First, her lips and cheeks began to quiver. Then tears formed in the corners of her eyes. "All the time. She knows about us now, and she knew about us when…" she choked back some tears, "…when you were still human. Oh, Prue, that's the reason you died. She killed you."

"We both knew I was murdered." Prudence sounded calm, but Kitty could see the fire start to burn behind her eyes. "Perhaps she did me a favour. Had I died any other way, I would not be a mermaid."

It was Kitty's turn to look confused. "I do not understand."

Prudence sighed. "Becoming a siren, I have learned, is a curse reserved for the murdered adulteress."

"So you can live on to continue to commit the same act? That does not seem fair."

With a shrug, Prudence revealed, "The theory is that we are most likely murdered by resentful spouses, and we will want to take revenge on them by luring their husbands into the sea."

Kitty raised a skeptical eyebrow. "How successful is that?"

Prudence shrugged again. "Moderately. It seems that whichever sorceress cast the curse clearly did not consider the exceptions."

"You mean me." Kitty's voice was quiet. She still hated after all these years that she had been part of the reason Prue was in this situation, even if Prue didn't blame her herself.

With a smirk, Prudence kissed Katherine's cheek. "You would be one of many exceptions, yes. I do not think women are the intended targets. After nine months, I have yet to see my magic work on one."

"Prue… you were murdered nine *years* past, not months."

"When will you learn that time works differently for me?" Prudence smiled, but Kitty could see the sadness hidden beneath it.

"Is there a way to remove the curse?" It was not the first time Kitty had asked Prue that question, but she figured it was worth another try, now that she was being presented with other new information. Perhaps now Prue had discovered a cure of some sort.

Seeing Prue shake her head, however, did not fill Kitty with any comfort.

"Do not let this get you down." Prue brushed a hand across Kitty's cheek, then left it to linger on her jawline. "I may not be able to see daylight, but I will continue to accompany you back to London." She kissed Kitty again; this time their lips met, and Kitty kissed her back. "We will be together as much as possible. I can meet you on the banks of the Thames."

Though she still felt a little melancholy, Kitty couldn't

help letting her eyes wander down Prudence's chest. Distraction took over.

Charles Bromley awaited Kitty's arrival. He was, after all, one of the few people who knew her true identity when she had dressed as a man.

"My father insisted that I meet you here, and that I may assist with your transition back to England," Charles informed her the instant she left the vessel.

Kitty frowned, but knew she had little choice but to follow Charles. "I suppose he is also insisting that you find out how I survived when his vessel to Virginia was attacked by pirates."

"Nonsense!" Charles exclaimed. "He does not wish to further shame you by inquiring about how you…" he lowered his voice to a whisper, "were forced into becoming one of their…" and quieter, still, "*whores.*"

She shuddered at the word. It was one of the things she abhorred most about the company she kept—that they partook in such activities with such women. Their only saving grace was that they at least appeared to show respect toward Jack, but all other women seemed fair game to them, to attack, to fuck, to rape.

"My apologies; I should not have said anything." Charles looked at her with a mixture of sadness and compassion.

"I was not sure he believed my story when I wrote to him."

Charles gave Kitty a sympathetic smile. "How else would you have got your hands on pirate treasure to pay for your safe return?"

Knowing the question was rhetorical, and figuring it was best ignored, anyway, Kitty asked Charles the question that had been burning on her mind the entire journey. "How is my father?"

Charles bit his lower lip. No response did not seem like a good sign.

She tried not to cry, and wiped a tear away. "How is he?"

"His funeral was yesterday."

That was all Kitty needed to hear for her to drop to her knees, throw her head in her hands, and openly weep. She did not care who saw her like that.

Charles, too, got down on his knees, and wrapped an arm around her shoulder. "I am so sorry."

She shrugged off his gesture, and stood. "Take me home. I need to be alone at this time."

It had been many years since her mother passed, and at least five since she spoke of her to anyone, but the comfort Charles attempted to provide reminded Kitty of Jack. She hadn't appreciated it from her, either. Kitty quietly wondered to herself if that was the reason she didn't tell Jack that she had heard her father was sick. It wasn't Jack's job to mother her. Jack was *her* responsibility, not the other way around. She did not need to be pitied.

Before her departure meeting with Jack, she had planned on seeking her out and bringing her back to London, once she knew she need not deal with her father's affairs any longer, but she knew that was no longer possible. How could Jack forgive her for betraying her trust? How could *she* forgive *Jack* for murdering Prue?

Jack's voice entered her mind, accompanied by Baker's hurdy gurdy, singing lyrics Jack had written for her.

"Pirates are we, tearing your flesh, because ye have something we desire. When ye be dead, the plunder be taken, we set your vessel on fire. Evil, ye calls us, but away from your eyes, our captain honours us all. With equal shares, double for he, for without him, none of us would stand tall."

Her words felt like a lie now, piercing Kitty's heart. Yet, she knew she would miss that voice.

ELEVEN

Dick spends longer than normal dressing this morning, making sure the formal black suit fits just perfectly. His mother may not be physically there to see him, but a small part of him thinks her spirit may attend her funeral.

"Is this acceptable?" Jaclyn asks, walking into Dick's room wearing a long, respectable black dress.

With a short smile, Dick nods. "Thanks for coming with me." He turns back to the mirror he's standing in front of.

Since his attention is away from her, Jaclyn moves her reflection into Dick's view. "I do believe you could have invited Ms Wong rather than me."

Dick scrunches up his face at Jaclyn. "Why? We're not especially close."

"She would like to be."

Jaclyn's words cause Dick to stop paying attention to his own reflection again. "I highly doubt that."

"Dick, I could even see it on her face when she talked of you in Washington."

With a scoff, Dick says, "Even if that were true, my mother's funeral is not the place you take someone for a first date."

"Perhaps you are right." Jaclyn brushes a hand down Dick's arm, and adds, "You look perfect."

"Who is that woman you brought?" Victor asks his son. "I didn't think you were seeing anyone."

"I'm not; she's just a friend." Dick takes a sandwich from the table in front of them, then changes the subject because he'd rather not talk about Jaclyn. "You know, Dad, while we were organising this, finding phone numbers for family to inform and invite... it made me realise how out of touch with everyone I am."

"And your mother's wake is a little too sombre to reconnect with them properly." Victor sips his red wine. "Do you want to organise a family reunion?"

Dick shrugs. "No, I don't think it's that. I'm feeling a little curious about my family history though. The Grayson line in particular."

"Your grandmother should have that information. She was interested in genealogy when you were born; said she wanted to trace things back as far as she could so she could pass it on to you one day."

"I wonder why she never mentioned it to me then..."

"Just a minute," Victor interrupts, squinting over Dick's shoulder. "What is your friend doing?"

Dick turns around, finding Jaclyn dipping a glass into the fruit punch bowl, and swallowing down gulps of it, over and over.

"I have no idea; I'm sorry, I'll be right back."

He rushes over to the punch table and pulls Jaclyn away from it before snatching the glass out of her hand.

"What are you doing?" he asks through gritted teeth.

"You're making a scene, and my *dad* noticed."

"My mouth was burning. It felt as though it was on fire."

"What did you eat?" Dick is a little more concerned now.

Jaclyn points to a glass of chilli peppers. Dick bites his lower lip with a large intake of air. He turns around briefly and notices his father watching them, causing Dick to feel like he's a disappointment. It reminds him of the look his father had when he found out Georgia had taken hedge trimmers to his father's garden, apparently in retaliation to something Victor had said, though Dick hadn't thought his father had been offensive. His father's numerous displeased reactions to Georgia's actions had been one of the factors that influenced Dick to end his relationship with her.

Turning his attention back to Jaclyn, he becomes stern with her again. "Okay, if you can't figure out what's on the table purely for decoration, and what you can eat, I think you should leave."

He starts to wonder whether Jaclyn should continue to be his responsibility.

Jaclyn looks up at Dick with worry in her eyes. "Did I embarrass you?"

"What do you think?" he says with sarcasm. "I don't even know what possessed me to bring you."

She lowers her eyes to the ground, and her voice is a whisper, "If you desire me gone, it would be preferable if you allowed me to wait outside. I do not know how to get home."

Dick takes her wrist and gently pulls her outside to avoid causing a scene in front of his family and his mother's friends. He really doesn't think he can cope with seeing Jaclyn for a while.

"Find your way back to Wall Street instead. You clearly don't need me any more if you can camp out there."

"Dick..."

He cuts her off. "Just take this and go," he says, giving her twenty dollars for the subway, assuming she can remember her way back there. They may be in Brooklyn, but she seems to have figured out how to use the subway system on her own.

With that, Dick leaves Jaclyn and returns to the wake.

Unsure of how serious Dick is, but also being in an unfamiliar part of New York, Jaclyn finds herself in a moment of indecision. However, she inevitably decides that she is better off leaving, just in case he's still sour by the time he heads home. After walking a few blocks and not finding the subway—not having realised earlier that she would need to pay attention on her way in—she decides to dig her phone out of the handbag Dick had her carry.

"Max," she says into the phone, "Dick has abandoned me. I do not know where I am. Can you find me, and allow me to stay with you for a while?"

After a moment's pause, Max replies, "I'm working right now. If you can read me the letters on a nearby street sign, I'll be able to find out where you are and give you directions to somewhere you're familiar with."

"Will you find me afterward? I do not know where else to go."

Max hesitates. "I don't think it's a good idea if you stay with me. My roommates think I'm gay. Have you tried

Nikki?"

With a sigh, Jaclyn says, "Perhaps if you can get me back to Wall Street, I will." Then she proceeds to give Max the names of the streets she is on the intersection of.

When Jaclyn manages to make it back to Zuccotti Park, she finds Sarah before she can find Nikki.

"That is an interesting dress to wear to Occupy," Sarah says. "Or are you going on another date with Nikki?"

Jaclyn can't help smiling, because her dating Nikki was not mentioned when she met Nikki's friends. This means she must be liked enough to be talked about, which is certainly a change from feeling like her relationship with Kitty had to be such a secret. Sure, part of that was because Kitty kept her own identity a secret, but there were times Jaclyn wondered if there was more to it. Was Kitty ashamed of her?

She dampens her grin and replies, "No, though I am looking for her. Do you know where I may find her?"

"She'll be back soon."

"Thank you; I shall be back soon, too. If she arrives before me, can you inform her that I am around?"

Sarah smiles at Jaclyn. "Sure."

Leaving Sarah, Jaclyn heads south. Though she doesn't carry a watch, or even know how to read the clock on her phone, the position of the sun in the sky suggests to her that it's near the end of the work day. She finds herself back by Wall Street, watching bankers and secretaries alike leave the buildings. The more time she spends down there, the easier she finds it to tell them apart.

It's like she's channelling Nikki's rage, which brings

comfort to her in the way it did when she slashed the throats of Navy men. "I am doing this for you, Kitty," were the words that ran through her mind every time she killed a man.

After about ten minutes of watching, Jaclyn heads back to the park to find Nikki, and is greeted with a passionate kiss.

"I didn't expect to see you down here today. I thought you were looking after your roommate in his time of grief?"

Jaclyn bites her lip while figuring out how to respond. "He did not appreciate my company, and has decided he needs some space. May I stay with you for now?"

"Of course you can!"

Nikki's enthusiasm causes Jaclyn to smile widely. Then she's dragged into the tent, and promptly finds herself underneath Nikki, being smothered with kisses.

They're interrupted when Jaclyn's phone rings. Thinking it might be Dick wondering where she is, Jaclyn decides to stop Nikki to answer it.

"Hey, I felt bad I couldn't let you stay with me. I'll buy you a drink if you want to meet me at Byrne's tonight."

Jaclyn finds herself feeling a little relief that it's not Dick, because she's not sure she can face him right now.

"Byrne's?" Jaclyn asks.

"The place we met."

She looks at Nikki. "I am not sure. I am with Nikki now."

Nikki whispers, "It's fine if you need to go patch things up with your roommate."

The assumption makes it easier for Jaclyn to accept. She decides it's not technically lying if she hadn't told Nikki who was on the phone, and it's not like she plans on meeting Max to have sex with him again. Not, she thinks, now that she's actually got something with Nikki. She's not like Kitty was. She can't face herself as an adulteress.

It's only the second time Jaclyn walks into Byrne's, and the first time alone, but she feels more at ease despite that, because she's meeting Max. The fact she's been in New York longer than a day probably helps, too.

Max sees Jaclyn enter, and meets her halfway between the door and the bar stools.

"Hey, Buccaneer. Nice dress," he says.

"Thank you." Jaclyn runs her long-sleeved gloved hands down the silk of the long black dress. "I have not had the opportunity to change it since this morning."

"And the gloves are perfect, because if you ever want to break any laws, no one would be able to find you."

Jaclyn isn't really sure how gloves would help with that, but she makes a mental note of this useful information.

After they walk over to the bar, Max orders a straight rum for Jaclyn, and a scotch for himself. He turns to Jaclyn and asks, "Have you heard from Richard yet?"

She shakes her head. "I am not sure I will. However, I can stay with Nikki in her tent."

"Nikki lives in a tent?"

"I believe so. She has not shown me any other place of residence." Noticing the appalled expression in Max's eyes, she adds, "It is fine that you could not allow me to stay with you. I have slept in far worse places than a tent. Have you tried sleeping on leaves in a jungle?"

The bartender places their drinks on the counter.

Handing Jaclyn her rum, Max says, "You can't stay in a

tent if all you have is that dress."

Jaclyn shrugs. "It is only temporary. I can go back to Dick's apartment when he is working tomorrow to get my clothes. I do not know what else I can do. I have no money."

"So you're going to trade that dress for your pirate clothes?"

After taking a sip of her drink, Jaclyn comments, "I may not know New York as well as you do, but taking into consideration the other fashion I have seen down where Nikki is, I do not believe anyone would consider it odd to see me in a corset and breeches."

"Where is this tent?"

"Down near Wall Street."

"Ah. I forgot you mentioned you met her at the protest." Then Max promptly asks her something else. "If you're not at Richard's, do you still want to continue your lessons?"

Jaclyn wonders if the subject change means Max isn't interested in the Occupy movement at all, but figures that's for the best, since she doesn't really want to talk to him about it either. She considers Max's question. As Dick only gave her the boot a few hours earlier, she hasn't really had time to think about where else she might be able to meet Max that would be conducive to learning to read.

"I do, but I know not where," she says.

"Do you know Battery Park? It's not too far from your... tent."

Jaclyn nods. "Dick took me there."

"Then we can meet there. Call me when you're ready for that." Max takes a sip of his scotch. "In the meantime, would you care to join me in the restroom for a quick fuck?"

Smirking, Jaclyn shakes her head. "There will be no more of such behaviour."

Whilst at work the following day, and checking his email, Dick finds himself drawn to the one from Natalia Grayson. His grandmother—ninety years old, and knows how to use a computer. Attached to the email is the genealogy information his father said she had. He sends a quick thank you reply, and resists the urge to open the document then and there. After all, he only has an hour to wait before he can head home.

It's hard for Dick to focus on the latest prototype he's working on. He may not have talked to Jaclyn much about Kitty—Katherine—but he finds himself morbidly curious about the fact they share a surname now. It is surely just a coincidence. Jaclyn was, if anything, just a stroke of bad luck that he found himself having to care for. But if that is truly the case, why is he wanting to research his family tree?

His mother. He thinks about her again, and the way he felt when he walked into that room; the way he just *knew* her essence was gone. Where did it go? Would he have felt this way, questioning what he believes in, if he had encountered death in such a way at a younger age? He hadn't known time travel was possible back then, so perhaps not. No wonder he finds himself questioning everything. He wants answers.

Curiosity getting the better of him, he opens his web browser and types "Catherine Grayson" into the search bar. The first page of results is made up of various profile pages on sites such as LinkedIn and Facebook.

"Well, that was pointless," he says to himself.

He sits back in his chair, takes a deep breath, and decides to get back to his work. Perhaps when he gets home, he can see if his family tree shows him anything else, but that, he thinks, will probably be pointless, too.

Jaclyn returns to the Occupy camp from her mission to Dick's apartment dressed in exactly what she finds most comfortable, minus the scarf and sash. She also carries a satchel with a few other clothes, in the event it is necessary to change. However, given the stench of the park, she finds herself feeling at home with the lack of hygiene, and is aware that she may not need them. As long as she has her gloves.

When Nikki sees her in the purple corset, she almost lets out a squeal.

"This is what I find comfort in wearing," Jaclyn tells her.

"Well it looks very sexy on you."

Jaclyn smiles, though is unsurprised. This particular outfit seems to have worked in that way to attract the attention of many others. The men with whom she sailed often commented on how it was the highlight of their days to get to see her in it—especially when she sang. Remembering that, Jaclyn realises she hasn't sung for Nikki yet. It was the thing Kitty appreciated about her most, and yet, she thinks, perhaps that is something she should keep between her and Kitty. Singing to Dick was different.

Then Nikki adds, "Isn't it uncomfortable to sleep in, though?"

It's only then that Jaclyn realises that she's only ever

seen Nikki in t-shirts and jeans. "Oh," she says, "I have slept in this with such frequency that it is like being wrapped in a blanket to me."

"You are a curious piece of work." Nikki scratches her head, then adds, "I do like that in a woman."

After the lack of results at work, it takes Dick a few days before he downloads software he can use to access his family tree. Jaclyn's absence also means he doesn't have the physical reminder of his curiosity.

Once the work week is out of the way, Dick orders Chinese, and then sits down at his computer at home, loading up the family tree program.

"Jesus," Dick swears, looking at the number of people in the database. "This might take a while."

He gets up from the computer to make himself a coffee, then continues to stay away from the computer.

When the buzzer rings, he answers the door, and pays the delivery man for his dinner. After dumping the rice and sweet and sour pork onto a plate, he takes it back to his computer to eat while making another attempt at checking out the program.

This time, Dick notices the search box, and figures it would be best to start with his father, since the chance of there being other Richard Graysons in the database is higher than discovering another with his father's name. He types in "Victor Grayson," and finds his assumption to be correct.

Clicking on the name reveals Dick's father, associated with himself below, then his grandparents above, and their parents, then lines reaching up indicating there is more information there. He takes a couple of bites of his dinner while quietly wondering to himself how far back the information goes.

When he looks at his grandmother Natalia's name, there's a part of him that is curious to find out how many generations back it would take him to find when that side of the family came out from Italy. He decides he can save that for another day, however.

As Dick continues to eat, he clicks backwards along the males in the Grayson line, such that he loses count how many generations there are. Like synchronicity, when Dick takes his last bite, he finds the final name. Charles Grayson, born in 1665.

"What now?" he wonders aloud, and decides to take a break to return his plate and fork to the kitchen. While he's there, he pours himself a glass of orange juice.

Dick soon decides that Google would be a waste of time again, so instead he calls his grandmother. It's only a little after 7:30pm, so she would still be awake.

"Nonna, can I talk to you about the stuff you sent me?"

"Of course you can, darling," Natalia replies.

"How were you able to trace so far back into the seventeenth century?"

She takes her time before responding. "Are you referring to my husband's side? Mine only goes back to the eighteen hundreds."

"Yeah, Grandpop's side."

"They researched, and kept good records, because when they came out to America in the mid-nineteenth century, they joined the Latter Day Saints."

"I come from a family of Mormons?" Dick can hardly

believe the surprise in his voice.

"Your Grandpop was one, until he converted to Catholicism to marry me."

"Huh." Dick doesn't really know how to take this information.

Clearly he didn't make much effort to get to know his family history before now, but then, his grandfather passed away when he was only ten, so he wasn't talked about all that often after that.

Dick thinks about how far back those records went. "How come they don't go further back than sixteen sixty five?"

"Did you read the notes associated with the last person in that line?"

"What notes?" Dick isn't sure what she means. "I didn't see any notes."

His grandmother's reply is soft, "There should be a way to find them, but if you have any problems, you can come visit me tomorrow."

"Thanks, Nonna," Dick says. "Love you, bye."

He hangs up the phone and heads back to his computer.

There aren't a lot of notes on Charles Grayson's profile, but Dick is still impressed with the content he reads.

Charles Grayson was raised by Brice and Mary MacGregor. His actual parents are unknown, but one is believed to be related to one of his adopted parents.

"MacGregor?" Dick asks himself, wondering why that name rings a bell with him.

"It's my birthday today," Nikki announces. "And I want to

ignore the fact they want to evict us from sleeping here. So I hope some of you can join me for... a night of karaoke!"

This is one of those times that Jaclyn decides to keep her mouth shut. Chances are, she thinks, karaoke is something she should know about, if she had grown up in this time period.

"Happy birthday!" Mike gives Nikki a hug. "Finally old enough to vote now, huh?"

Nikki lightly punches him on his arm. "Don't be silly; I'm twenty-three."

This is the first time Jaclyn has heard Nikki's age, but she's not particularly surprised by it. *Four years*, Jaclyn thinks of their age difference. *That's about what Kitty and Prudence had.* Then she silently wonders to herself if she is turning into Prudence, preying on someone that much younger than her. But Nikki isn't fourteen like Kitty was when Prudence first seduced her. This is far different.

"I'd love to come," Sarah says. "Let me belt out some Celine Dion."

Nikki turns to Jaclyn, "You're coming, too, right? It wouldn't be the same without you!"

"Sure, I will follow," she replies with a smile, but feels a little apprehension with the lack of knowledge of what's in store that evening.

The four of them end up on the subway to reach their destination, a karaoke bar called V.H. Won. When they arrive, a Korean woman who appears to be about Jaclyn's age rushes over and gives Nikki a hug.

"It is good to see that you decided to come here for your birthday," the woman says.

Nikki puts her arm around the woman and faces her

Occupy friends to make the introductions. "Everyone, this is Yun Kim. She owns this place. Yun," she points at each of her friends as she's naming them, "Jaclyn, Sarah, and Mike."

When Nikki doesn't remove her arm from Yun's waist afterwards, Jaclyn starts to feel some butterflies in her stomach.

Yun addresses Nikki, "So what are you going to sing for us tonight?"

"Oh, you'll see!" she replies with a smile.

This is enough for Jaclyn to establish that karaoke is related to singing. Her heart sinks, because she really hadn't wanted to share her voice in front of Nikki. Finally, her hand drops to her side, but only as Yun walks away.

"How long have you known Yun?" Jaclyn asks.

"Oh, ever since I started coming here to work off the stress of college."

Jaclyn takes Nikki aside and asks in a whisper, "Have you been intimate with her?"

"Oh my God, no!" Nikki says, appalled. "She's, like, forty, and like a second mother to me. I'm from Colorado, so I don't have any family out here."

Despite the fact Jaclyn has no idea where Colorado is, she's smart enough to discern it's a reasonable distance away from New York.

With a sigh, Nikki adds, "She could tell when I was sad, that I was missing them, because of the songs I sang. So she wanted to comfort me."

"My apologies," Jaclyn says.

Nikki smirks. "Why do you talk like that? You should just say 'sorry' instead."

After a quick bite of the lip, Jaclyn repeats, "Sorry." Then she adds, "It was how I was raised to speak."

"Fair enough." Nikki turns to address everyone in the group. "Let's get this party started!"

A few minutes later, Yun takes the stage, and holds the microphone, announcing the start of the evening. "And tonight, I'm going to lead you off with 'Sweet Home Alabama.' So start signing up with your own songs!"

The music starts, but the electric guitar sounds like screeching to Jaclyn, which essentially drowns out whatever Yun is singing. She can't even detect the drum beat in the background. To Yun's side, a video is projected onto an otherwise white screen, and words Jaclyn cannot read appear at the bottom.

As other singers take the stage, it becomes clearer to her that the words on the screen are the song lyrics, because she sees people reading from the screen when they need to. Jaclyn can't help wondering how this is some form of entertainment for these people. She thinks that, especially when it's impossible to understand so many of the singers, what with their terrible singing, or choices of songs using whatever passes for a musical instrument these days, they would be better off going to watch a professional sing. It's been a long time since she last went to an opera, but this is the point she finds herself in desperate need of one, to remind herself what counts as good music.

Then Jaclyn realises it might not be the activity that is the problem so much as she's nervous about being asked to get involved.

How could I participate, if indeed I wished to? she wonders. She can't read. She doesn't know popular music. There's probably no option to sing a song she actually *knows.*

"I guess I'm up next," Sarah says, getting to her feet.

Jaclyn isn't sure how she knows that, given no one came up to her to say anything.

Sarah adds, "Wish me luck. I tend to get a little emotional singing this one."

"Luck!" Nikki and Mike collectively say.

The music opens with the sound of a violin, followed by what sounds like panpipes to Jaclyn. Finally some musical instruments she recognises. The softness of the underlying music makes it easier for Jaclyn to understand more of the lyrics as Sarah sings them. Even though she doesn't recognise the song, she can't help being moved as she watches the emotion in Sarah's eyes as she sings.

By the end of the song, Sarah's eyes are glossy. When she takes her seat back at their table, she says, "'My Heart Will Go On' makes me think of a boy I loved during my adolescence. He died in a car accident when he was eighteen."

Nikki reaches out to Sarah and lightly strokes her hand.

"Only one song between Sarah and me, so I'd better get ready," Mike says, standing up. "I hope you're all up for a bit of reggae, because I'm singing..." he pauses for dramatic effect, and shakes his shoulders, as well as his fists in front of him, "'One Love' by Bob Marley."

As Mike sings, Jaclyn finds it hard to discern any of the lyrics, especially over the drum beat. She finds herself wishing she could, though, because from the look on Mike's face, he's singing about something he believes in. *Why does this music have to be so loud?* she wonders.

When Mike returns to their table, Nikki asks Jaclyn, "So, what are you going to sing?"

Her stomach churns. "I do not know this music."

"Seriously?" Nikki raises an eyebrow at her. "You didn't even get music when you were exploring the last decade?"

Jaclyn bites her lip out of nervousness, but shakes her head anyway.

"But aren't you, like, twenty-seven? Surely you listened to stuff in high school."

High school? Jaclyn isn't sure what kind of school that is, but needless to say, girls didn't go to *any* school in the time period she's from. She shakes her head again.

"Well, if you don't pick something by the time I'm finished, I'm going to choose something for you, and you can read the lyrics and figure out the tune as you go along."

Nikki comes across as being friendly in her suggestion, but it makes Jaclyn want to throw up a little. How on Earth is she going to be able to fake reading?

There are a few more songs before Nikki's turn, but each passing song is another Jaclyn does not recognise. Though she wonders how she should be expected to when the music tends to drown out the voices of the amateur singers. She eventually finds herself in the bathroom, coughing up the alcohol and peanuts she'd been consuming at the table.

When Jaclyn gets back, Nikki is about ready to leave to sing. She nervously tells the group, "Okay, this is a bit embarrassing, showing you guys what music I like after seeing you all sing. Just... don't laugh at me, okay?"

"Honey, there is nothing wrong with having different tastes in music," Sarah says, trying to calm her down.

"Even when I like Top 40 stuff despite hating the corporations that release it?"

Mike lightly pushes Nikki out of her chair. "Just go sing. Have fun. It's *your* birthday. Who are we to judge?"

"Okay, okay," Nikki brushes herself off and heads to the stage.

For Jaclyn, she's becoming aware of how important music seems to be for people today.

Just before the song starts, Nikki announces, "I'm dedicating this one to Jaclyn."

The music starts off with some high-note piano—an instrument Jaclyn only recognises from watching a concert on the music channel where it was the only thing that accompanied the singer. Over the piano, she can hear a vocal harmony. Soon, a steady drumbeat is introduced.

Jaclyn focuses on the lyrics, which she can thankfully understand only because the background music is quieter than it has been for the other singers; perhaps because it sounds like Nikki can actually sing. She likes the complimentary nature of the opening verse.

It's only when the song reaches the chorus that Jaclyn realises she's heard this song before, back when she watched a number of music videos in Dick's apartment. She didn't like the song at the time because it was too hard for her to hear all the lyrics over the instruments that played in addition to the piano, which makes her appreciate the fact Nikki is more intelligible than the original artist—Mars something, if her memory serves her.

As she continues to listen, knowing Nikki is making the song about her, it makes her feel something she can't describe. After being told to hide who she was for Kitty when she joined McDonald's crew, and Dick telling her she had to shave her legs and armpits—which she has temporarily ignored at present—it's nice for her to hear that there is someone in the world who thinks she's amazing, and that she doesn't have to change anything for her. The longer she watches, the more she imagines that this must be what it was like for Kitty when she listened to Jaclyn sing.

Nikki doesn't come across as a professional the way Jaclyn feels she herself is—there are some sections of the song that Jaclyn can tell aren't quite at the right pitch—but it's the passion in the way she expresses herself that moves Jaclyn the most.

As Nikki heads back toward their table, Jaclyn meets her halfway with a kiss. Out of the corner of her eye, she can see Yun smiling at them the way a proud mother might.

When they part, Nikki immediately asks, "So, what's your song?"

Jaclyn takes a deep breath and considers the name of the only song she memorised from her days in front of the television. "If you can find 'Sure Thing' by Miss Spring, you can put my name down for that."

She hopes Nikki doesn't notice that she's requesting such a task, because she doesn't want to have to admit she can't read, let alone write, such things.

"Sure thing," Nikki smirks, and wanders over to the song book to look it up.

When she returns to the table, she announces, "You're on the list."

Jaclyn thanks her lucky stars that there was a song she had memorised. To be on the safe side, though, she goes over the lyrics in her mind while the next few people sing their songs.

Then it's her turn. The butterflies return to her stomach. She's never used a microphone before, but hopes observing the other singers is enough for her to get it right.

The organ sounds and video begin to play at the same time, and she starts out by watching the words, pretending that she's reading the lyrics. "I was your yes girl," she sings, "Doing everything that you asked me to. Because I loved you. I never questioned you at all." Then she stops looking at the screen right when the violin starts up, and performs for the audience, belting out the ballad. "But then you changed. And so did I. Suddenly I am not a sure thing any more..."

The passion in Jaclyn's performance as she sings is so strong that by the time she finishes, the audience erupts into a spontaneous applause. Jaclyn is so overcome by the reaction that she faints on the stage.

When she comes to, Jaclyn finds herself in a booth, being fanned with paper by Nikki. "Are you okay?"

"What happened?" Jaclyn asks, still feeling a little groggy.

"Well, before you fainted, you performed the most awesome rendition of 'Sure Thing' I've ever heard here! I'd go as far as proposing you did an even better job on it than Miss Spring." Nikki's excitement is swapped for a more serious tone. "Do you relate to the lyrics?"

Jaclyn shares a sad smile, and gives a tentative nod.

"I'm sorry," Nikki offers. "But, hey, now you have me!"

The enthusiasm is enough to pull Jaclyn out of her state, and she can't help smiling along with Nikki.

Dick bolts upright out of bed at the early hour of

5:34am—on a Saturday. In his sleep addled state, it occurs to him that MacGregor was a name Jaclyn had mentioned to him. However, he doesn't want to have to talk to her to find out for sure. His only way around that is, perhaps, to talk to Sean, who could ask Max to ask Jaclyn. He's presuming she would still be in touch with Max, considering their sexual friendship.

It's too early to call, though, so he writes Sean a text. *'Can you talk to Max about getting some info from Jaclyn for me?'*

He hopes sending it will expel the thought from his mind enough to go back to sleep.

About an hour later, just as he's about to really drift off, his sleep is interrupted by his phone receiving a text. He groans and rolls over, picking up the phone off his bedside table.

'Why would Max be talking to her? Was she not staying with you?'

Since Sean is clearly awake, and so is he, Dick sits up in bed and calls him back. "Long story, but she's not here any more, and I don't really want to talk to her right now. But Max befriended her after we left Byrne's, so I figure, much as I don't like the guy, this is the only way I can get the info I need."

"What exactly is it that you *do* require?"

After Dick shares the details, he hangs up, and finally manages to go back to sleep.

Various missed calls, and messages later, it's not until early Sunday afternoon that Sean, Max, and Jaclyn are able to meet at a small café for lunch. After they find a table, Jaclyn stays with it while Max and Sean line up to place their orders.

"It is fortunate to discover that terrible odour is not being emitted by you," Sean says to Max. "Though that would indicate it belongs to the woman."

"Yeah, about that. She's been living with protestors in a tent. It's probably best you don't say anything to her."

"Noted."

They move up in the queue.

"Is that the reason for which she is no longer residing with Dick?"

"No, he kicked her out."

Reaching the front of the queue, Sean places his own order, and Max recites items for himself and Jaclyn. Then they return to the table and wait for their food and beverages to arrive.

"For what reason did you assemble us here today?" Jaclyn asks, speaking mainly to Max.

Max looks at Sean, waiting for his answer.

"Dick."

"Dick?" Jaclyn looks confused.

Max turns back to Jaclyn. "Richard. Not cock."

"Dick is another word for male fowl?"

"No, another word for penis," Max informs her.

"What is a penis?"

Neither Max, nor Sean, seem to know how to respond. Then Sean suggests to Max, "Perhaps her ignorance of said anatomy is the reason she is only interested in women?"

Their meal arrives by the hand of a waitress.

"Never mind that, I'll show you later, when we have more privacy," Max says to Jaclyn. He turns back to Sean.

"You were referring to Richard."

"Yes." Sean directs his attention toward Jaclyn. "Your acquaintance has requested some information."

"Why are you even helping him?" Max asks. "I feel like we're the kids of divorced parents here. You should know what that's like."

Sean clenches his teeth. "I shall pretend you did not say that."

"It's not really like you, though."

"I was feeling charitable."

Jaclyn interrupts the pair of them. "Dick still does not wish to speak with me himself?"

"Precisely," Sean says.

"Then why should I help him?"

"Perhaps it would place you back in his good graces, and he would provide you with an opportunity to shower."

Max throws Sean a look that gets him to change his phrasing.

"That is, he may amend his dismissal and allow you to return to his lodging."

"What information is he seeking?" she asks, before taking a bite of her panini.

"Does the name 'MacGregor' have any relevance to you?"

"It seems odd for Dick to be asking that." Jaclyn can't even comprehend why he would, but answers anyway. "Yes, that is the name Kitty and I used when we travelled to Barbados. She took MacGregor from her mother, and Thomas from her father."

"He was also curious about the name Brice."

"Brice MacGregor?" she asks, and Sean nods while she

takes a sip of her hot chocolate. "How could he possibly even know that name?"

"Perhaps you should discuss that with him," Sean says.

"Who's Brice?" Max asks.

"A cousin of Kitty's."

Dick places his pen down on the table and looks at his notes. "Thanks, Sean," he says over the phone.

"You should be informed that Jaclyn was inquiring as to how you came by that name."

"I'll deal with that when I'm ready. Anything else?" Dick picks the pen back up and starts tapping it.

"Please allow the woman the opportunity to shower." Sean's tone is rather serious. "Her odour is appalling."

Dick frowns. "I highly doubt it's as bad as it was when I met her."

"Just… consider it, for the sake of those who encounter her."

"We'll see. Thanks again for doing this for me, Sean."

"Mmm."

They hang up, and Dick takes his notes into his room, fetches his laptop, and sits down on his bed to continue his search. In the web browser's search bar, Dick types "Thomas Grayson MacGregor." He thinks that maybe he'll get results for Kitty's parents this way, especially since Jaclyn told him they were wealthy.

One of the first results is a Wikipedia entry on a Lord Thomas Grayson, an influential writer born in 1602. "This must be her father," he says to himself. Reading further confirms it. He was married to Lady Beatrice MacGregor. They had three children, though only Katherine Grayson survived past the age of two.

Katherine with a K, Dick thinks. *I spelled her name wrong before.* He clicks the link over her name for the Wikipedia entry on her.

Katherine Grayson was born in 1634 to parents Lord Thomas and Lady Beatrice Grayson. She went missing between 1651 and 1660, resurfacing only after her father passed away. Possibly inspired by her father's legacy, she was an early female writer, and authored the book, A Pirate's Reverie, *which was first published in 1664.*

"Hmm." Dick rubs his chin. "I wonder how hard it would be to find her book?"

He continues reading.

Assumed to be in retaliation for the book's release, Katherine reported she had been raped, in which the encounter produced a child. As she had been unmarried, this was not questioned. Shortly after the child's birth in 1665, she disappeared again. What happened to both her child and her after that is unknown.

Dick doesn't know how to react to this information. First of all, it was almost too easy to discover this. Maybe Max edited the Wikipedia entry so he'd be spooked by it? This is otherwise far too big a coincidence for Dick to handle, even if he had had his curiosity leading him down this path. He didn't actually expect it to be true.

When his phone rings, Dick puts his computer down on the bed and follows the music to the main room. He finds the phone on the dining table, where he had left it half an hour earlier.

"Hello?" he answers, too quickly to notice the caller's name.

"Dick, I ran into Jaclyn again, earlier today. She was with that asshole reporter." It's Sue's voice.

"Yeah, I know." Dick walks into the kitchen to pour himself a glass of water.

"Is she not staying with you any more?" Sue asks. "Because she doesn't seem to be looking after herself very well. It was like standing next to a durian."

"What's a durian?"

"Oh, you Americans." Sue smirks. "It's a Malaysian fruit. I just meant that it was hard to get past her smell, but the way she talked sort of made me want to taste her anyway."

Dick groans, and realises Jaclyn must've been messing with him when she said Sue was interested in him.

"I didn't know you were a lesbian."

"In a metaphorical sense, Dick! I have a daughter, remember?"

"Yeah, but you're not with the father." He didn't mean to let that slip out, and hopes that he doesn't live to regret it.

"Trust me, I'm straight." She sighs, and adds, "Really, really straight."

Feeling a little awkward at this conversation now, Dick changes the subject. "Hey, I just had a thought. There's something you might be able to help me with. Would you be free to meet me for dinner Tuesday night?"

"Is this your way of asking me out on a date?"

Dick thinks about his answer for a moment, and how Sue might want him to respond. "…No?"

"Oh." She sounds a little dejected.

"Do you want it to be?"

"It might be nice." *Was Jaclyn right?*

"Um… okay then… I guess we can try that," Dick says, feeling a little flustered. "I have to warn you I might be a little more nervous than usual though. How do you feel about Friday's?"

"They do a good mojito."

"Meet you at the Times Square one at eight?"

"Sure."

"Okay. See you then." Dick hangs up the phone, hardly believing he has a date. With Sue Wong. The screenwriter.

It's been ten days since Jaclyn last saw Dick. Ten days since she moved into a tent with Nikki. She might have expected to hear directly from Dick after the way he indirectly extracted information out of her, but the reality is, she has been too busy to think about that. She has been too busy plotting, just as she had in the lead up to robbing Sir Bromley in Barbados. Which is how she ended up here, in an apartment belonging to a woman she does not know by name. Following the executive home from Wall Street over the last few days helped her secure the plan she intends to follow through on now.

She jimmied her way in only moments before, knowing the dark-haired woman would not be home for at least an hour. She looks out the window and finds that the sun is at approximately the height it is when her target would be leaving Wall Street. Since this is the first time she has actually entered the apartment, Jaclyn casually wanders through it, using her gloved hands to pick up any objects that she may be able to use as a weapon, analysing them with care.

Jaclyn pauses in the lounge room when she hears a ringing sound. It takes her a few moments to get out of her mindset to realise it belongs to her phone.

"Hello?" she answers.

"Are you doing anything right now?" It's a male's voice.

"Dick?"

"Yes."

"I am presently occupied. I do not mean in the *intimate* sense."

"Right. The Wall Street protest. You know, you don't have to stay down there all day, every day."

Jaclyn figures it's best to let Dick believe she's still down in Zuccotti Park.

"I am aware of this. However, if you recall, you desired nothing more from my presence." She walks into the kitchen to continue her search.

"I hate to say it, but… I think I kind of miss you." He takes a deep breath. "You were right about Sue."

By the sink, Jaclyn finds a knife block similar to the one Dick has at his place. "You spoke with her?"

As Dick replies, she starts pulling out the knives. "We went on a date a couple of nights ago. The thing is… I've got no clue what I'm doing."

She pulls out the butcher's knife. "Could we discuss this another time?"

"Come home?"

Wandering deeper into the apartment, Jaclyn says, "I will consider your request."

"I'm sorry."

"Thank you," she says with a smile. Then she repeats, "I will consider your request."

"You wanted to know how I knew about Brice Mac-Gregor."

She'd almost forgotten about that. It's been four days since that meeting.

"Then I shall be there, tonight, when I am finished here."

Jaclyn hangs up the phone, and turns it off before Dick can get another word in. She's found the bedroom, which she enters, and starts searching drawers in the tallboy, then boxes on the dressing table. She finds necklaces and ear-rings filled with various precious gems—diamonds, emer-alds, pearls—but as much as she's tempted to take them with her, that's not why she's here.

She surveys the rest of the room, and finds the perfect hiding place—a walk-in closet, with horizontal gratings on the doors. Slipping inside, she sits down, and places the knife on the carpeted floor.

As she waits, she finds herself thinking about Nikki, and the reaction she got the first time she was seen in the clothes she's wearing now. It makes her smile. Nikki has done so much for her, which causes her to want to do everything she can to show Nikki how much she cares back. She doubts she would be in this room for any other reason.

Her thoughts are eventually broken by the sound of laugher coming from another room. There are two people. This is not something Jaclyn had planned for, but she's dealt with more people at once before.

"So when does Brian get back from Paris?" the male asks.

"Not until Thursday week," the woman answers.

The male laughs again. "And Kelly's still visiting her family out west until God knows when. Her father dies, I guess. So I've got you for the next seven days."

A laugh from the woman. "That you do."

There are various shuffling sounds then, and soon Jaclyn hears them entering the bedroom. Peeking through the grates, she can see the couple undressing. Jaclyn clenches her fist around the knife handle. If she had known these people personally, hearing and seeing these things would probably have made her vomit right in the closet. After what Prudence did to her, there is no way she could ever forgive anyone of those actions.

She continues to hide well over the next hour of foreplay and sex acts. Only after the couple has completely worn each other out does Jaclyn stand, holding the knife.

Jaclyn quietly steps out of the closet, knowing that the slightest noise could wake the adulterers. She walks over to the woman's side. When the man lets out a loud snore, indicating to Jaclyn a deep sleep, she places the knife on the bed, and pulls off the scarf from her head, which she then uses to quickly tie around the woman's mouth, muffling her as she begins to wake to prevent her from screaming and waking the man. The initial shock also forestalls the woman's ability to use her arms or legs to wake her partner, giving Jaclyn enough time to grab both of the woman's arms behind her back, pick up the knife, and drag her out of the room.

The naked woman struggles against Jaclyn's embrace, and as she pulls her past a mirror, Jaclyn sees the woman trying to take in every inch of her appearance.

"Do not worry about trying to identify me," Jaclyn whispers in the woman's ear. "You will not survive this."

With that comment, she uses the mirror to her advantage, finding just the right place to slice the woman's throat. Blood starts gushing out over Jaclyn's gloved hand, and she immediately drops the woman face first in the hallway. After untying her scarf and pulling it out from beneath her face, Jaclyn runs, leaving the woman to bleed out.

Not knowing how much time she might have to get away from the crime scene before the man wakes, and hearing her heart pounding in her ears, she heads to the kitchen only long enough to dump the knife in the sink. Looking at the blood on her gloves, she concludes that Max was right to suggest she wear them when committing a crime. It's easier to discard gloves than wash it off her bare hands. She should know.

After discarding her gloves and scarf in a dumpster on the way to the subway, and calling Nikki to let her know she needs to see her roommate on the way to his apartment, she finds herself knocking on his door. She could let herself in, but figures this is the polite way to handle seeing him again. Dick answers the door and scrunches up his face at her.

"I thought you wished for me to come?" she says, thinking he must have changed his mind.

"I did. I'm glad you're here." He opens the door wide enough to let her in. "I should probably let you freshen up with a shower before we talk."

"That is very kind of you," she says with a smile, oblivious to his reasons.

Though she's familiar with worse conditions living

aboard pirate vessels, after the last few hours, she wants nothing more than to rid herself of the clothes she's been wearing for the past several days. She feels filthy, not from her living circumstances, or the fact she just murdered someone in cold blood, but because she watched her so clearly cheating on her spouse.

As she showers, she closes her eyes and lifts her head up, immersing her face in the raining water. A memory flashes into her mind, and she stumbles backwards. "Prudence," she says to herself.

Just in case of any more flashes, she lowers herself to sit on the cold tiled floor. She supposes it makes sense for Prudence to enter her mind in this moment, now that she has had more time to process what she witnessed this evening. In the midst of thinking about it, she feels sick to her stomach, and evacuates the contents of it onto the tiles.

"Curse you, Prudence," she says. "I do not need this."

Her tears mix with the shower water so that it's impossible to tell the difference between them.

By the time Jaclyn emerges from the bathroom, wearing fresh clothes, her eyes are so sore that she knows there must be red rings around them. Dick is waiting for her on the couch in the main room, but he thankfully doesn't comment on the state of her face.

"Feeling better?" Dick asks.

Jaclyn shrugs, and walks over to join him on the couch.

Though he looks a little awkward doing so, Dick moves closer to her and embraces her in a hug.

Confused, Jaclyn asks, "What is this for?"

He pulls away. "I found out Kitty didn't die, but left

you."

"How could you possibly know *that*? Have you learned to read my thoughts?" Though Dick is clearly just trying to comfort her, all she feels is frustration.

Dick rolls his eyes. "Don't be ridiculous, people can't read minds."

"Maybe *people* cannot," Jaclyn accidentally thinks aloud. When she realises, and remembering Dick doesn't believe in fantasy, she says, "Then where did you get this information?"

"Remember when you told me she and I shared the same name? I got curious when you left, and couldn't help myself. I had to research her."

"Is that how you found Brice?"

"Not exactly. There's not much in the way of a family tree for her on the Internet, beyond her and her parents..." he trails off in thought, then says, "Wait a minute, what did you mean before?"

"When?"

"About the mind-reading." Dick starts nervously tapping his foot.

"Ignore me. You do not need to trouble yourself with understanding the world I come from."

"I'm curious now."

"You would not believe me." Jaclyn stands, not wanting to be part of this conversation any more.

Dick stands, too. "I eventually believed you travelled through time."

"You had evidence," she says, looking up at him.

"Does it relate to how you got here?" he asks cautiously.

"I thought I suggested I did not know how I arrived in

your time?"

Dick takes her hands and sits her back down. "I don't believe you. You seemed to realise pretty quickly that you were no longer in the past. That's not how someone would react if they had no idea what was going on."

With a sigh, she says, "Are you sure you want me to tell you what happened?"

He nods slowly.

"I still do not think you will believe me."

Somewhere in the depths of the Atlantic, a dark-haired woman is gasping for air, but swallowing water instead. A blonde swims toward her, and covers her mouth when she reaches her side. Though she can't see the blonde's lips move, the dark-haired woman can hear her in her mind.

Welcome. I am Prudence. This may be too much for you to understand immediately, but you are mermaid now.

The new mermaid opens her eyes wide with shock. Somehow, she finds herself answering back telepathically. *What happened? How did I get here?*

Come with me and I will explain all.

TWELVE

Captain van der Lawick's crew had only been back in Port Royal about a week since their last voyage. Though it had been Jaclyn's suggestion that Kitty's crew join with his, life with van der Lawick as captain of *Medusa's Wrath* hadn't been what she expected. He had not proven to be better than Turner might have been if he had assumed command of their vessel instead. The only consolation was the fact van der Lawick wasn't a drunkard.

Rather than stay in an inn this time, Jaclyn headed up the Jamaican coast with Turtle, where they made camp on a beach. Jaclyn convinced him to do this with her because he was about the only person left that she still trusted, and she thought it might be better to have some protection.

"Can you help me get to Barbados?" she asked him that evening, as they sat by a campfire on the sand.

"If I go back there, they will enslave me again."

"I know it is asking much…" Jaclyn sighed. "It is just that… I want to get the man who lured Captain Gray away from us. I want to make him pay."

Lure might have been too strong a word for Jaclyn to use to describe what actually happened, but only she and

Turner knew the real reason Kitty left. Regardless, Sir Bromley was involved, and Jaclyn hated him for it.

When Turtle didn't respond, she realised she was going about her plan the wrong way. She leaned into him, and apologised for her insistence. Turtle put an arm around her in forgiveness.

"We could get away from all this, Ejiogu," Jaclyn said, using his real name. She placed a hand on his thigh. "Make a better life for us both." She turned her head around and looked him directly in the eye. "They will want you dead once they discover what you did to Noah. You will be safe from them in Barbados."

"Perhaps you are right."

"Have I thanked you for that yet?" she asked, taking his hand in hers.

"Not in words." Though his tone was serious, Jaclyn could see the twinkle in his eye, the thought of him remembering how she thanked him obvious in the way he looked at her.

She leaned upwards and kissed Turtle on the cheek. "You have my everlasting gratitude."

"Have you a plan?" he asked.

Jaclyn simply smiled at him.

Dressed as a man once more, Jaclyn pulled a wrist-bound Turtle along with her to the merchant vessel she had bought passage for.

"Transporting a slave," she announced. "Thomas Mac-Gregor," she added, to get her name marked off the passenger list as she and Turtle boarded. She had been unable to think of an alternate pseudonym, so she used one of Kitty's.

Once they were safely on board, and away from anyone who may eavesdrop on their conversation, Turtle said, "I cannot believe I let you talk me into this."

"It will work," she said. "People already believe you are my slave."

"It is still Barbados. If my former. . ." he choked on the next word, "*owner* should see me, then it is over."

She sighed. "Then you can spend all your days locked inside for all I care. However, you have been gone nigh on twenty years; you are probably no longer recognisable."

"You still have not explained how we will afford to live."

"Then I am fortunate that you have trusted me this far." She squeezed his thigh for good measure.

"I confess that I have desired to live as a husband to you, even if only in mind and action."

Jaclyn knew what he was referring to. She was aware that there was no way anyone would perform a marriage ceremony between them. Just as she would not have been able to marry Kitty. She didn't really know what it was about her that made her find herself only attracted to those she could not legally be with. Perhaps it was God's punishment for looking elsewhere after her husband died. She hadn't even thought about Mr Marshall in roughly a decade.

Turtle added, "I would still like to know how you propose to support us."

With a smile, Jaclyn answered. "I formerly sang at the Spitting Dog Tavern. I am sure Mr Jennings would have me back, and pay me to work for him."

A few days into their voyage to Bridgetown, Jaclyn noticed Turtle starting to ignore her mid-conversation. His head was pulled to the side. She'd seen this before.

"Stay here," Jaclyn said, trying to keep his attention. "You can hear the singing again, can you not?"

He nodded, but he could not speak.

"Zounds!" She began pacing the room, muttering to herself about Prudence. "I would guess this is her again. What does she want now? She already has Kitty to herself."

Knowing she was probably the only woman aboard the vessel, she left Turtle and found herself in the fresh air on deck. It was already after lights out; a crescent moon shone in the sky. Jaclyn looked around. There were only two men out there with her, both frozen in place. She followed the direction of their gaze to the port gunwale, and leaned out over the edge.

"Where in the world are you, Prudence?" she yelled.

The blonde mermaid popped her head out of the water with a sly grin spread across her face.

"I know you are here for me. What do you want?"

Your life.

What? Jaclyn had no idea how Prudence had been able to dump her words into Jaclyn's mind like that. Her mouth hadn't even moved.

"Have you not already taken enough from me?" Jaclyn yelled. Then, to herself, she thought with some sadness, *You have already influenced Kitty away from me.*

Kitty made her own choices.

Jaclyn wasn't sure if Prudence's response was to what she said aloud, or what she said in her head. She decided to test her with her thoughts. *You should be dead.*

You would know; it was by your hand. Somehow Prudence's sly smile got even wider.

Is that why you are here? Jaclyn was thinking mostly to herself, but she was also aware that Prudence could hear her thoughts now.

Only so you know I know. And to warn you. Continue down this path you are following, and there will be consequences.

That was the last thought Prudence put into Jaclyn's head before she disappeared beneath the sea again, and life aboard the merchantman resumed as normal. She had no idea what Prudence even meant. Had she been following her, reading her thoughts? If so, for how long? She couldn't even think what she might be doing that Prudence wouldn't like. It's not like she was planning to go to London to find Kitty again. She knew Kitty would not have her back.

The rest of the journey was uneventful. Jaclyn supposed it could be because Prudence knew she had to at least stay on the merchantman until she and Turtle arrived in Barbados. Another part of her thought it was just an empty threat, because what could Prudence even do to her, as long as she remained on land? Prudence was a woman of the sea. If it was using Kitty's pseudonym that bothered her, then she had planned to give that up as soon as she arrived in Barbados, and found herself in women's clothes again.

It did not take long for Jaclyn and Turtle to find themselves a small house they could rent. Once they were settled there, Jaclyn requested that Turtle stay behind while she go to check out the Spitting Dog Tavern.

Jaclyn stood in the doorway for a few minutes, assessing the room. It had changed a lot since she was last there, become a little fancier. She started to feel a little under-dressed, but soon forgot about that when Mr Jennings came over to her.

"Mrs MacGregor, it is wonderful to see you again." He took her hand in his and planted a kiss on the back of it. "Where is your husband?"

"He is no longer with us," she replied. She didn't want to say that Kitty had *died*, since that would be outright lying. It was much better for her to imply it instead.

"Is that what brings you back here?" Mr Jennings asked, leading her to a table for them to sit at.

"Quite. I was hoping to be employed by you again."

Mr Jennings frowned at her, and started tapping his fingers on the table. This made Jaclyn feel a little nervous.

Leaning forward, Jennings said, "It would be lovely to have you back, but I am afraid that I already have a full entertainment schedule."

"Oh." Jaclyn was disappointed, but didn't want to be discouraged. "Is there anything else I could do?"

He leaned back in his chair and contemplated the question a long while before answering. "Your husband is no longer with us, you said?"

Jaclyn nodded. Jennings rubbed his chin.

"There may be something you could do…"

"Please tell me," she said, leaning forward. "I do not have a lot of money."

Jennings leaned forward again, too. "You could make a small fortune on this. If you recall, you are pleasing to the eyes of the men who have frequented this tavern in the past."

"What is your point, Mr Jennings?"

He replied in a whisper, "I offer the men here high class prostitutes. You would be welcome to become one."

She scoffed, disgusted, and stood up immediately, slamming her hands down on the table. "You make me ill," she whispered to him, so as not to disturb the patrons. "Inform me only if there is an opening for a singer," she added. "Good day to you."

With that, she stormed out of the tavern and headed back to Turtle.

As much as she wanted to cry, as soon as she walked into their house, the only thing she saw fit to do was tear Turtle's clothes off, as well as her own, and sexually ravage him.

After their excitement died down, Turtle asked, "What was that about?"

"I am no punk," was all she could say. That's when she finally broke down in tears.

Turtle pulled Jaclyn close to him.

"Where are my pistols?" Jaclyn asked the next day, after searching all the places she could think of.

Turtle was laying on the floor, meditating with his eyes closed. He opened them and turned toward Jaclyn.

"What do you need them for?" he asked, and she felt like he could see right through her.

She sighed, and walked closer to him. "Kit gave them to me."

Sitting up, Turtle replied matter-of-factly, "He abandoned us."

Her lip wobbled a bit. "I still miss him," she said, hoping not to make him jealous. "I need the memento."

When Turtle stood up, he towered over her. "Is that all you want them for?"

Asking this while looking down at Jaclyn intimidated her into answering completely honestly. "No."

"I thought we agreed to stop using violence," he said taking her hands in his.

"Sometimes it is necessary."

"*Why* is it necessary?" he asked, dropping her hands.

"I am a *singer*, not a damned whore."

"Thus you have to murder someone so you can take their place?"

Jaclyn shrugged.

"This is not the answer."

"Where are my pistols?"

"I will have no part in this."

"Where are my pistols?"

Turtle sighed. There was no reasoning with her, and Jaclyn knew her point would be made.

"They are in a box, under the bed. But I will not help you this time." He sighed again, and made himself clear. "Noah deserved what he got for what he did to you. A defenceless singer does not."

Jaclyn shrugged again and headed to the bedroom to find her weapons.

About a week later, Jaclyn returned to the Spitting Dog. She didn't want to be obviously involved in the death of one of the tavern's singers, so she didn't approach Mr Jennings at all. Instead, she simply sat at a table and waited for him to find her.

"May I sit here?" a voice asked when she hadn't been paying attention.

Jaclyn looked up to see who the voice belonged to. "Mr Roosa?"

He smiled at her. "So you do recognise me," he said, and took a seat, setting his hurdy gurdy on his lap. "It is good to see you again, Jacqueline. Jennings said you had been in. I told him to bring you back immediately, but he said he did not know how to find you."

Jaclyn's stomach sank about a hundred feet. She could've had her job back without murdering anyone.

"I think I may be ill," she whispered.

Jan looked worried. "Please do not be sick! We need another singer *tonight*." He got up and went around to her side to rub her back. "Is that better?"

She nodded at him, so he stood up and took her hands, walking her over to his stage so they could return to their old routine.

About mid-way through their performance, Jaclyn noticed a very important looking man walk into the tavern, with a woman on his arm. They sat down toward the back of the room. Jaclyn couldn't help watching them through the next couple of songs.

During a break in songs, Jaclyn asked Jan, "Do you know who they are?"

He nodded. "Sir Nathaniel Bromley, and his wife, Anne."

Jaclyn caught a gasp in her throat before Jan could realise her surprise. She smiled her thanks to Jan, and they moved on to the next song.

When the evening was over, Jaclyn stealthily followed the Bromleys home, just so she could find out where they lived.

Before she headed back to her own place, she found herself walking down to the beach, thinking it was the best way for her to clear her head. Why did she still care about chasing the Bromleys? She had Turtle now, and he didn't believe in revenge unless rape was involved. Perhaps she should be listening to him. It wasn't as though taking revenge on Bromley would bring Kitty back.

As she watched the waves, which reflected the moonlight, she decided to find somewhere comfortable to sit down. The sound of them crashing and the repetitive movement had a calming effect on her, and she realised Kitty had been right about her needing the sea. Was that why she returned to Barbados instead of London?

When a wave washed up a naked blonde woman, it distracted her from her thoughts. She quickly got up and rushed over to the woman. Only then did she notice the tail in the water. Prudence pulled herself up on her hands, and that same sly grin spread across her face. As she dragged herself forwards, Jaclyn stepped backwards.

"You cannot get me here, Prudence," she said, attempting confidence, but sounding more nervous.

Prudence raised an eyebrow at her. "Is that so?" she asked, continuing to move forward. As her fins left the water, the scales dissolved, leaving her with legs.

Jaclyn gasped, and tripped backwards. Then Prudence stood up, and started slowly walking toward her. This unexpected turn of events, coupled with Jaclyn's lack of weaponry, caused her to stand up as quickly as possible, and run in the opposite direction.

As soon as Jaclyn got home, she slammed the door shut, and slid down against it. The noise woke up Turtle in the next room, and he came out to see what was going on.

After catching her breath, Jaclyn said, "It is not safe here."

"What do you mean?" Turtle asked, joining her on the floor.

"We need to leave Barbados. I apologise, Ejiogu. We made a mistake to come here."

"We cannot afford to leave now," he said with a frown.

Jaclyn's eyes darted around the room, trying to think of a solution. Her eyes narrowed on her pistols on the table, and then the idea hit her.

"I know a place we can plunder. That will buy us passage off this island."

Turtle took her hand. "What is causing you to be so fearful?"

She opted for complete honesty. "The source of that singing you first heard on *Mary's Revenge*."

Her answer caused Turtle's breathing to deepen.

"You are also fearful?"

"I cannot protect you from that."

Jaclyn smiled sadly at him, thankful that he still wanted to be her protector. "I know."

Over the course of the next few days, Jaclyn staked out the Bromley residence, looking for ways in. There were guards everywhere, so eventually she took in their faces, and tried to see if she might recognise them somewhere in the town when they were not working. Most of her evenings were spent at the tavern, singing.

About a week later, she did recognise one of Bromley's guards at the Spitting Dog, watching her sing, and getting drunk. He was in uniform, and was recognisable for his fair hair and scruff of hair on his chin.

When Jaclyn was done for the night, and bid farewell to Jan, she wandered over to the guard's table. She bent over him, making sure he had a clear view of the cleavage popping out of the top of her corset.

As the man swallowed, Jaclyn sat down on a stool next to him, looked into his green eyes, and said, "I could not help but notice the way you looked upon me as I sang."

She smiled at him, and he smiled back.

"Your voice is almost as mesmerising as your beauty," he said.

"May I have your name?" Jaclyn asked, running her hand down his arm.

The man quickly took a swig of his ale before answering. "Simon. Simon Ainsley."

"Well, Mr Ainsley, how would you like to buy me a drink, and you can tell me about what it is you do here in Bridgetown?"

Simon immediately ordered over another ale to the table.

Squeezing Simon's biceps, Jaclyn commented, "You seem so strong and rugged." She smiled. "I like that in a man."

After smiling at the compliment, Simon said, "It helps me keep the riffraff away from Sir Bromley's residence."

"Oh? You are one of his guards?" She took a sip of the

ale.

He nodded.

"You must be very good, then, for him to keep you around. I heard he does terrible things to his staff if they disobey him."

Simon puffed out his chest. "Not me, Miss. I am one of his finest guards. He even welcomes me inside to guard the house from trespassers when he and Lady Anne are away in London."

Jaclyn switched from the stool to Simon's lap, and wrapped an arm around his neck. "Mm," she mumbled, "I did find me a nice specimen tonight."

He grinned at her, and she kissed him on the cheek.

"I do so love the jewellery Lady Anne wears around town. Have you ever seen it up close?"

"Have I? Ha! I have to know where she keeps it," he boasts. "The first room on the left, once you get upstairs. It is right next to their bedchamber."

"Oh, Mr Ainsley," Jaclyn said, pressing her chest up against his. "You are such a big, important man." She kissed him on the cheek again. "I would love to talk with you more, but it is already so late. Perhaps you could come see me sing again soon?"

"I would like that," he said.

"Until next we meet," Jaclyn replied, getting up off of him. She waved with just the tips of her fingers, and left the tavern.

When she returned home, the place felt eerily quiet. She couldn't understand why. Normally, she should be able to hear Turtle snoring in their bedroom. She walked slowly to the room, but when she arrived, he wasn't there. Her breathing sped up, and then she found it difficult to keep going.

"No," she said. "No, Prudence." She took a deep breath. *You cannot do this to me again.*

Though she still found it difficult to breathe, she left the house, and immediately ran down to the sea.

"Prudence!" she screamed. "Prudence!"

The mermaid's head rose from the sea, that same sly grin on her face.

"Why are you doing this?" she said, exasperated.

You deserve it.

"Stop putting your words in my head." Jaclyn could no longer stop herself from screaming at Prudence.

Prudence only obliged after she pulled herself from the sea again, standing naked before her. "Or what? What will be my consequences?"

That's when Jaclyn realised she'd been too angry to even think of grabbing her pistols to bring with her. She couldn't reply.

"I know what yours are."

That damn smile again.

"Oh?" Jaclyn asked, trying to find some courage within. "Then answer me this. What do I deserve?"

"To be alone."

"Is that why you took Ejiogu, also?"

"He was easy. He wanted to join me."

Jaclyn did her best to hold back her tears. Though she knew in her heart Prudence had taken him, hearing the truth from her still stung.

"So I am alone now. You can leave here."

Prudence shook her head. "I know what you are planning."

All Jaclyn could feel was confusion and numbness.

"Steal from Bromley, and you will find your consequence in the future."

Jaclyn dropped into the sand. "I do not understand you."

The mermaid dropped to the sand and crawled to Jaclyn, then lifted her chin with her finger. "You will find yourself having missed the next few centuries."

With a scoff, Jaclyn spat in Prudence's face, and said, "Test me, witch. I do not believe you have that kind of power." Then she shrugged, and added, "Besides which, you have taken everything that means anything to me. What else do I have to lose?"

Your mind.

Jaclyn grabbed her own head after she heard Prudence's words in there. Maybe she was right. Jaclyn could lose her mind, if she let Prudence have that kind of control. If she hadn't been so busy massaging her headache, she would've attacked her then and there. Unfortunately, Prudence disappeared back into the sea before the throbbing went away.

With Turtle gone, and Prudence's threats, Jaclyn knew she couldn't be too careful. She spent a few more days planning everything out, but she didn't want to be discouraged. Jaclyn was determined not to let Prudence completely destroy her. For all she knew, the threats could still be empty. So Prudence could stand on the beach. That did not necessarily mean she could walk further ashore.

About an hour before dawn, less than a week after her

last encounter with the mermaid, Jaclyn put her plan into action. She donned some breeches, knowing they would be easier to escape in than a dress. Then she pulled on the only corset that remained from her pirate days, and added the rest of her former pirate clothes—sleeves, sash, stockings, scarf, boots. Both of the pistols Kitty had given her ended up in the sash. Her cutlass was left behind primarily because she wanted to keep her load relatively light.

She snuck past a sleeping guard to get beyond the perimeter, making it into the Bromley estate. The front door was unlocked, and the house was silent. She crept upstairs and found the room the guard at the tavern told her about with ease. After rifling through various belongings, Jaclyn pulled out an elegant necklace—fashioned with an elephant carved out of black onyx, and decorated with diamonds and gold. Other necklaces soon followed, and they ended up in the pockets of her breeches.

That was all she had intended to do, but being this close to a sleeping Bromley—with a couple of ready flintlocks on her—increased her courage. She wandered down the hall to the bed chamber, and opened the door. After pulling out a pistol and raising the weapon, she walked a few steps, and fired. The shot missed, and woke the Bromleys. Jaclyn didn't know what to do, so she dropped the no-longer-usable pistol on the floor and ran.

"Guards!" Sir Bromley yelled.

Jaclyn managed to get out the front door before she actually saw any of Bromley's guards, but soon two of them found her, and started chasing. By the time she got out of the front gates, there were six tailing her. She ran through the streets of Bridgetown, relying on her superior speed and stamina. Eventually she found herself needing to catch her breath, so she ducked into someone's cottage, hoping not to be seen. After all, it was still dark, and most of the town was sleeping.

Whilst inside, she readied her second flintlock, just in case she might need it. Then she heard a noise inside the cottage, and figured it was time to escape again. She slowly crept down the street, hoping that by now, the guards had passed her by. When she turned a corner, however, she found herself face-to-face with Prudence. The flintlock accidentally went off because of Jaclyn's shock at finding her like this. On top of that, Prudence was still naked. How could she get away with that?

I warned you.

Jaclyn held her empty hand to her head, and returned her pistol to her sash.

Return what you stole.

"You are insane." Though her head was aching, Jaclyn attempted to spit at Prudence again, but narrowly missed her.

"If you do not believe, then turn around now. Run away. Find yourself in the future." There was that same sly grin again.

Jaclyn still didn't believe Prudence had that kind of power, and getting out of her head long enough to speak gave her the chance to run.

She didn't have time to think about her surroundings, or how scared she was. All Jaclyn could do was run, and keep on running through the streets of Bridgetown. She didn't notice when the streets changed, or the buildings around her looked different from what she was familiar with. Nor did she notice when the sun suddenly appeared in the sky, without the breaking of dawn.

When she found the staircase, a part of her thought she could climb it, and if Prudence was following her, perhaps she could push her off the height and kill her that way.

It was only when she got to the top of the staircase that she realised something was different about her surroundings. She still didn't have time to think about that. She needed a place to hide.

THIRTEEN

"So… a mermaid sent you here?" Dick looks at Jaclyn like she told him he had a carrot growing out of his shoulder.

"I knew you would not believe me." She sighs, and stands up, knowing there's no point in continuing the discussion. "I need to sleep now." She turns around and starts heading for the hall.

Jaclyn stops walking when Dick says, "I might just need a few days to process this, is all."

Without turning around, Jaclyn shrugs in response, then continues on to her room.

In the morning, neither Dick nor Jaclyn acknowledge the story she shared the night before. The conversation at the breakfast table focuses instead on Dick.

Jaclyn asks, "Do you wish to tell me about your date with Sue now?"

A deep sigh escapes Dick's mouth before he replies. "It was a disaster." He sips his coffee.

She eyes him with disbelief. "Do you have another date planned?" she asks, and takes a bite of her buttered toast.

"Tonight."

"Then it could not have been as bad as you think." She leans in closer. "What happened?"

Dick takes his time contemplating how to explain the details while eating a few bites of his own piece of toast.

"I talked business too much, and tuned out when she started talking about her daughter. She must've been able to tell I wasn't paying attention."

"Is that the extent of your error?"

"I didn't stop her from paying for her own meal." Dick sighs. "I should've been a gentleman and paid for the whole thing. After all, I've been paying for your meals since you've been here, and we're not even dating."

Jaclyn considers Dick's words. If Sue presented her own money, then would that mean it's expected for women to share the cost of a meal these days? "If she presumed you would pay, would she not have kept her money to herself?"

"I don't know what these social conventions are these days. With feminism and all that, sometimes, I guess women want to be able to pay their own way." He stands up and starts collecting the breakfast dishes. "But then you hear about the ones who still want romance and chivalry. How am I supposed to tell the difference?"

Jaclyn follows Dick to the kitchen, where he starts the washing up. "Do you wish to pursue this relationship further? If you are not interested in having children of your own, then perhaps she is not the woman for you, as she already has a child."

"I don't know." He shrugs, but doesn't look up from the sink. "It's not like anyone else is interested in me."

She looks at him sternly. "That is not a good reason to be with someone."

"I don't really know her well enough yet to know if I'd want a relationship with her."

Jaclyn picks up a tea-towel and starts drying the dishes. "Then you need to be able to listen to her, and find out what she cares about most. If that is her daughter, then you need to care about her daughter. I do not know anything about children, so I cannot help you with advice on that subject."

As he finishes with the last plate, Dick turns to her and asks, "Do you want children?"

It's a question she's never seriously considered before. Being with Kitty, she knew that biology dictated that they would not be able to conceive with each other. Even when she had been with men, she didn't consider children as a possible consequence of her actions, until Max brought up the reason condoms were invented. Because of this, Jaclyn shrugs.

"I thought I would be with Kitty forever, and as such, the possibility has never entered my mind."

Thinking more on the topic, Jaclyn realises that's not entirely true. When she had married Mr Marshall, there was a certain expectation that she would bear his son. However, given the fact their marriage had been cut so short, she hasn't needed to think about it since.

"You know, there are other ways lesbians can have children these days," Dick says, leaning on the bench. Then he corrects himself, "Sorry, I forgot, you're not a lesbian. Well, anyway, there are other ways to have children if you're in a relationship with another woman. Surrogacy. Adoption. IVF…" he trails off. "I suppose you'd only understand adoption, huh?"

"I think it is not necessary for me to know about these methods right now. I have only known Nikki for a few weeks, and do not know whether she will want me to stay, nor if she wishes to have children."

After Jaclyn puts the last plate away, they head back into the main room, where the subject moves on to advice for Dick's date that evening.

Dick stands at the entrance to Applebee's, waiting for Sue. He checks his watch; 6:08pm. They'd arranged to meet at six, so Sue's tardiness makes him nervous that she might not show up, or be too late to surprise her after dinner. He nervously taps his foot to distract himself from checking his watch again. He checks his phone instead, thinking that maybe she tried to call or send him a text to let him know she would be late, but there's nothing there either.

Suddenly, a woman's hand covers his phone, and he looks up to see who it belongs to.

"Sorry I'm a little late," Sue says.

Dick hides the fact he'd been worried about being stood up just seconds before. "It's okay." He turns his attention to the host and asks for them to be seated.

She shows them to a table for two people, and hands them their menus before disappearing.

"You have a thing for restaurant chains, don't you?" Sue asks while perusing her menu.

Dick looks up from his. "Do you have a problem with that?" he worries.

She puts the menu down and nervously taps a finger on the table. "It's just that when I call my mum back home and tell her how things are going, I'm not sure how she'd react to me eating at restaurant chains. So many of them are there too, and we're in *New York*. There's so much more to choose from here."

"Really? You have the same chains as us in Malaysia?" She nods.

"When was the last time you went back there?" Dick asks, genuinely curious.

Sue bites her lip. "About five years ago."

"Do you miss it?"

Their waiter interrupts, "Are you ready to order?"

"We need a few more minutes," Dick tells him, and he wanders off.

"Sometimes," Sue says, getting the conversation back, "but this is home now. It's hard to explain. I feel like I can be myself here in ways I can't when I'm back there, parents looking over my shoulder." She picks up her menu again and scans through it. "I guess the thing I miss most is the food. I've yet to find a *nyonya* restaurant in Manhattan."

Dick makes a mental note of this. Perhaps if he survives this date and manages to arrange a third, he can try to find a Malaysian place to take her to instead.

Not really knowing how to follow up Sue's statement, though, Dick takes the opportunity to decide what he wants from the menu. Not that he needed to look, as he predictably chooses his usual order of nachos.

After the waiter takes their order, Sue says, "I found the book you asked me to look for."

"Really?" Dick asks, bewildered. "That was quick."

"There are web sites that host all sorts of old books; even really obscure things like *A Pirate's Reverie*."

Dick raises an eyebrow at her. "And you knew about

them before I asked?"

"Sometimes it's good to read old stories to get inspired. After all, that's pretty much how Walt Disney started." She smiles. "He's kind of my hero."

A short laugh escapes Dick's lips before he can stifle it.

"What?" Sue asks.

"My parents took me to see *Pete's Dragon* for my ninth birthday. I know Disney himself was dead by then, but that movie made me dream big, you know? For a while I believed in dragons, and I wanted one just like Elliot for a friend." Dick delves further into his memory. "Wow... you know, I haven't thought about this for such a long time, but... we went to Disney World on vacation a few months later, and I got a toy Elliot there. Come to think of it, that might be when I started to think about wanting to make toys for other kids." He laughs. "I've been at this so long that I kind of forgot I used to actually love the idea of it more than I do now."

"Have you ever gotten to work with Disney?"

Dick shakes his head. "No, unfortunately."

Their meal arrives, temporarily interrupting the conversation. Dick looks at the kid who is serving them, and assumes he's probably working there only to put himself through college. He looks bored, and doesn't even bother to say anything as he puts their plates in front of them.

After he walks away, Sue says, "You know, we can still be Disney-like, without the branding. I think we might even be able to one-up them."

"How?" Dick asks, then gets started on his nachos.

"*A Pirate's Reverie* is a pretty unique story, and no one's done it before." Scooping up a spoonful of her orange chicken, Sue says, "I could adapt it for the screen."

"You read it?"

Sue nods, unable to respond with her mouth full.

"What's it about?" Dick asks. "Other than the obvious pirate aspect."

"A pirate captain who is torn between two lovers: a woman who lives on the surface, and a mermaid."

Dick doesn't know how to respond immediately, as he needs time to process this. Didn't Jaclyn say Kitty was taken from her by a mermaid, before the mermaid sent her here? Could it be based on Kitty's life? If he hadn't already been curious, this would be enough to make him read it himself.

Realising he's taking a while to respond, and not wanting to raise a question from Sue about the expression on his face, he asks, "What did you like most about it?"

Sue considers his question as she eats. After swallowing, she says, "Probably the mermaid. Did you know Langkawi in Malaysia even has its own mermaid story?" She smiles at the opportunity to tell Dick a little more about the country she's from. "There's a beach there called *pantai hitam*. Legend suggests people built up wood to burn there, to scare the mermaids away from their oncoming war. Then the sand was burnt black, and was scarred forever. I find it fascinating that these creatures have been part of the mythology of so many different cultures."

Curious for more thoughts on the movie version, Dick wonders, "Would you want it to be an animated or live action film?"

"Probably live action. It's not really suitable for younger children, but I think we could target the teen to mid-forties market."

"I guess I can work with that. I've done action figures for that age group. Do you think there's still time to cash in on Disney's pirate popularity, though?" Dick asks. "Pardon the cliché and pun, but I thought that ship had sailed. Everyone seems more interested in vampires, werewolves, and zombies."

"My brother, Mark, will know how to make it work. He can build an audience from the ground up." She smiles at Dick, and reaches her hand across the table toward him. "I don't know if you've seen *Washington Spring* yet, but when I wrote that, people told me there was no market for an historical American fairy tale. Do you know how much it's grossed in the month it's been out?"

Dick shakes his head while finishing off a handful of nachos.

"A hundred and forty million in the US alone."

Not expecting such a large sum, Dick chokes on his food.

"Are you okay?" Sue asks, getting up from her seat and going around the table to pat Dick on the back.

All Dick can do is wince and nod.

"I'm sorry, I didn't mean to brag. That's not like me at all."

Dick finally swallows his food and catches his breath. "It's okay, I was worse the other night."

"You were?"

"I was surprised you wanted to see me again, that's how bad I was talking about sales."

Sue smirks at him.

He raises an eyebrow at her. "What?"

Still with a grin, Sue says, "I didn't notice."

"Really?"

She shrugs. "Maybe I was too busy worrying about Angelina. If you recall, she was at her dad's with an icepack on her face after soccer training."

Dick doesn't recall, but he nods to pretend he does anyway. That must have been one of those things he had tuned out for. However, with Jaclyn's advice, he realises he should probably try and remember this information for the future.

"I'm impressed you let her play. If I had a daughter, I'm not sure I could handle the bumps and bruises of sports." Dick has no idea where that thought even came from. Something he'd considered back when Georgia wanted children with him?

"It wasn't easy to let her go, but she was pretty insistent on it."

They continue talking about Angelina for most of the remainder of their meal, and Dick finds himself being more interactive this time. Perhaps it was because Jaclyn talked to him about his mother earlier in the day, and that reminded him that she had wanted grandchildren. He then decided he should probably at least consider whether or not he could change his stance on wanting them.

When it's time to pay the bill, Dick slips his credit card to the waiter.

"Oh, Dick," Sue says, laughing at something he's said just as the waiter returns.

"Dick?" the waiter asks, then he checks the credit card, and looks back up at Dick. "Dick Grayson?" He laughs. "You know, Robin?" He chuckles some more, then stops when he notices Dick's frown. "From Batman?"

Dick gives him a sarcastic look, then takes his card and the receipts, adds in an appropriate tip, signs that receipt, and hands it back to the waiter.

"I'm sorry, sir, and thank you," the waiter says, leaving them be.

"You get that all the time, don't you?" Sue asks, standing up at the same time as Dick.

"My dad was a fan of the sixties' series, and guess when I was born? I don't know. It makes me feel bitter now, but it was cool for a while when I was a kid. It's why 'Dick' stuck as my name rather than 'Richard' or 'Rick.' Other people liked it." As they make their way back to the entrance, Dick adds, "So, I have a surprise for you next."

"Oh?"

"We're off to see *Avenue Q.*"

Sue smiles at him. "Would you believe I still haven't seen that?"

When Dick checks his email before breakfast the following morning, he finds *A Pirate's Reverie* waiting for him in his inbox. He immediately opens the attachment, but is interrupted by Jaclyn knocking on his door. He swings around in his chair to face her.

"I will be travelling down to the protest again today to spend some time with Nikki. She has not seen me for three days and misses me."

Though Dick noticed Jaclyn had last been down there in her pirate costume, he finds himself relieved that she will be returning wearing jeans and a t-shirt.

"Okay," Dick says with a nod, thinking it will free up his time so he can read. "When do I get to meet her?"

"You wish to meet her?"

He shrugs. "I should probably thank her for looking after you when I didn't let you stay here."

"That is not necessary," Jaclyn says, leaning against the doorframe.

"Why not?"

"I took care of myself. I am not a child, Dick."

Rolling his eyes, Dick concedes, "Alright, alright. But I'd still like to meet her sometime."

"I will consider your request," Jaclyn says, then stands properly. "I am going now, and will be back in the afternoon."

She turns around and walks out, leaving Dick to return to his computer.

It's several hours later before Jaclyn returns. She slowly opens the front door, peeking inside for any sign of Dick. She decides he's either out, or locked away in his room. In either case, she has enough time. Opening the door wider, she allows Nikki inside before her, then pushes it closed.

"Follow me," Jaclyn says, then takes Nikki's hand.

Nikki bites her lip, which Jaclyn can't take her eyes away from as she leads her to her room. The door closes when Jaclyn pushes Nikki backwards into it with a kiss to her lips, which then move down Nikki's neck.

Gasping a little at each peck, Nikki grabs at the base of her own shirt and pulls it over her head, revealing a black satin bra, before stumbling forwards and pushing Jaclyn towards the bed with her own kisses. Nikki then reaches for Jaclyn's shirt, slowly pushing it upwards. Her thumbs rub up against Jaclyn's red, modern-day corset, which she has been wearing beneath the t-shirt she went out in to look normal.

"You're so sexy," Nikki says once she gets the shirt off and has the opportunity to admire the corset in full.

"Is it still sexy if the reason I am wearing this is because my stomach appears to be increasing in size?" Jaclyn asks shyly.

Nikki lightly flicks an index finger over Jaclyn's nose. "Silly. You're sexy regardless, but I'm sure you're just imagining it." She smiles cheekily. "Let me take it off to prove it to you."

As she climbs up onto the bed behind her, Jaclyn can't help feeling a little queasy. Nikki pulls at the ribbons on the back to loosen the corset, whilst Jaclyn becomes acutely aware that this is the first time that Nikki will see her completely naked. Fondling in a tent without really removing everything is not the same thing.

After removing the corset, Nikki gasps, then immediately runs two fingers over the longest scar on Jaclyn's back.

"How did you get this?" she asks.

Jaclyn turns around to face her, and covers her stomach with her arms to avoid showing off her other scars, knowing how difficult it would be for her to tell Nikki the truth. She can't. It's just too much for her to consider trying to convince someone else where she's from.

When Jaclyn doesn't reply, Nikki says, "I've seen the ones on your arms before, but I was afraid to ask about those." She lowers her voice to a whisper. "I didn't want to know if you had a history of attempting suicide."

"Suicide?" Jaclyn accidentally lets a laugh escape. "No, I have not tried to kill myself."

Not wanting to even continue talking about her scars, Jaclyn leans forward and pushes her girlfriend onto the bed with more light kisses to her lips. She distracts Nikki even more when she works her way down her body, licking around her areolae and sucking her nipples into her mouth. Nikki pulls three of her dreadlocks with her right hand, and gasps for air in between biting her lower lip and closing her eyes.

Nikki's hips buckle beneath Jaclyn's stomach, causing her to raise Nikki's skirt and start kissing her way up her left thigh. Then Jaclyn's nerves kick in. She wants to use what Max taught her, but what if she doesn't do it right? Swallowing to steady herself, she reaches for Nikki's underwear. Her hips buckle again just at the moment Jaclyn pulls them down.

The little gasps escaping Nikki's mouth entice Jaclyn to continue, so she licks her lips to moisten them, then buries her face in the small patch of red pubic hair in front of her. She starts off just licking up, like someone would a lollypop, noting a bitter tang. The piquant flavour causes Jaclyn's eyes to scrunch up, mainly because she's unsure if she likes it, yet she wants to please Nikki.

Feeling a little silly and out of place, she decides to change tactics so that the taste isn't so strong. Her tongue starts to dart around, but it has no idea how to find the spot her fingers know so well. Then Jaclyn does something that leads Nikki to squeeze her head with her legs, and thus have to take a break for air.

"Have you done this before?" Nikki asks, clearly trying to conceal her disappointment.

Jaclyn bites her lip and slowly shakes her head.

Sitting up on the edge of the bed, Nikki then asks, "Am I your first? I just assumed that since you're older than me…"

"You are not the first woman I have been involved with," Jaclyn interrupts, allowing Kitty to penetrate her thoughts. Feeling guilty, she shakes her head to force Kitty from her mind, thinking of it as unfair to Nikki. "Only the first I am trying this with."

A smirk forms across Nikki's face, and she can't help blushing a little. "That mean you really like me?"

Jaclyn doesn't know how to reply with words, so instead leans forward to kiss her again.

When she pulls away, she forgets about hiding her stomach, and Nikki immediately notices the scar. She reaches forward and traces a finger along it.

A look of concern on Nikki's face, she asks, "Really, what happened? Do you have health issues that required surgery? I know so many women who've had surgery for PCOS, but I've never seen their scars."

This is not a conversation Jaclyn wants to have. She doesn't even know what PCOS is, so how is she supposed to answer that? "No," she says, because what else could she add? She moves to sit beside Nikki. "Please, you do not need to be concerned." With a sigh, she adds, "That part of my life is over."

Then Jaclyn notices an aftertaste on her tongue. She massages it against the roof of her mouth to try to get rid of the flavour, but is not subtle enough in hiding her behaviour.

Another smirk from Nikki. "Don't worry, you get used to it."

"I hope so; I do not wish to disappoint."

"You don't." Nikki smiles her most reassuring smile. "But I can teach you my techniques."

She reaches for Jaclyn's jeans, unbuttoning them and pulling them off with such ease.

"You'll know what to do in no time."

Once the women are clothed again, Nikki says, "I want to hear more about what it was like sailing in the Caribbean. Did you ever, like, pretend to be pirates or anything? Is that what kind of ship you were on?" After a short pause she adds, "I'm sorry, that's probably a really stupid question, right? I'm just curious because while you were away, Mike invited me to his place and we watched *Pirates of the Caribbean*, so it kind of made me think of you."

Assuming Nikki's talking about one of those movies Dick mentioned to her, Jaclyn admits, "I would have been interested in watching that." There's a part of her that is intrigued to discover how pirates are portrayed today.

"I'm sorry, I should've realised you hadn't seen it and invited you."

She's not really sure why, but something in her brain seems to make the decision to talk for her, like it's a way of admitting the truth without really admitting it. "I did."

"Did what? See the movie?"

"No, pretend to be a pirate." Jaclyn bites her lower lip. That actually is true, she thinks—she was pretending at the same time she was turning into one.

Nikki raises her eyebrows at her. "Really? You're not just messing with me because I asked something stupid?"

"I could sing you one of our ditties if that would help

convince you."

A big grin spreads across Nikki's face. "Go on, then."

Jaclyn stands, and takes a few deep breaths, then starts belting out the lyrics, "It's freedom on the high seas, where we rock—to and fro! Kick the Navy to their knees. Ne'er reap what we sow."

Upon hearing Jaclyn's voice, Dick spins around in his chair. *Is she singing?* He gets up from his chair, and soon finds himself standing outside her bedroom door.

"Watch your back, for we are coming aboard. No matter if ye be peasant or Lord."

That is not only Jaclyn singing, but singing lyrics Dick had read in Katherine's book only minutes before. Dick finds himself with his mouth open wide, dumbstruck, wondering why she's even singing. He knocks on the door, and the singing stops.

"Dick?" Jaclyn calls from the other side of the door.

"Yeah."

"Am I causing a disturbance?"

"Can I talk to you with the door open?" Dick anxiously rubs his thumb against his middle finger.

She opens the door. "My apologies. I did not know you were home."

"Remember, you can just say 'sorry' instead," another voice from inside the room says.

"Is that Nikki?" Dick asks.

A young woman frames herself in the doorway next to Jaclyn. Dick notices how dirty her red dreadlocks look and doesn't need her to answer to figure he's probably right.

"That would be me. Nice to know Jaclyn's been talking

about me. All good things, I hope."

Dick can't contain a smirk at her voice. It sounds a little too cute to come out of a woman who looks like her. It certainly doesn't remind him of Jaclyn.

"Yes, good things," Dick says, because what else is he supposed to say? That he thinks the Occupy movement is pointless? Or that he doesn't understand the ideas she's filling Jaclyn's head with?

Nikki gestures widely. "Nice place you've got here."

"Thanks." Dick pauses, looks at Jaclyn, who shrugs. He turns his attention back to Nikki. "Do you mind if I borrow your girlfriend for a few minutes?"

After having bit her lip at the word 'girlfriend,' and smiling, Nikki says, "No, go ahead."

They leave Nikki in the bedroom while Jaclyn follows Dick into his, and closes the door behind him.

"Why are you singing pirate songs to her? Does she... *know*?"

Jaclyn walks across the room and finds a place to sit on the bed. "Of course not, Dick. I have learned not to speak of such things to anyone else. It is too time consuming to bother."

"Then why?" Dick sits on his computer chair.

"I told her I sailed, and sometimes we sang these songs then." She smiles. "She is young and does not know any better, but she does enjoy my voice. I like to sing to her, but I do not know many other songs."

Dick fiddles with his hands some more as he decides to jump straight to the point. "Who wrote the one you were singing when I interrupted?"

"I did. Kitty encouraged me to come up with new verses

to sing amongst the crew. It was one of my responsibilities once I revealed my sex. I sang for them."

It feels like a few minutes pass while Dick tries to process this information, but it's probably more like thirty seconds.

"Did you know Kitty wrote a book?" he asks finally.

Jaclyn looks confused. "I did not, though did I not mention that one of the reasons she said she was leaving me was because of her writing?" She lays backwards on the bed. "I dare say I should be happy to know she accomplished that goal."

"She used your songs."

Dick's blunt words cause Jaclyn to bolt upright on the bed. "Honest?"

"Yes."

"She never forgot me." She says it mostly to herself.

"Do you need a minute?"

Jaclyn doesn't respond; too busy looking inward. Whilst she's busy reflecting, Dick turns back to his computer and brings up another one of the songs Kitty wrote about. He starts reading it aloud.

This pulls Jaclyn out of her trance, and she walks over to Dick. Her eyes scan the LCD monitor.

"Is this Kitty's book?"

Dick turns to her. "Yes."

After a few moments staring at the screen, she says, "I wish I could read this, but as I cannot, I am going to ask Nikki to leave. I want to know more."

Jaclyn says goodbye to Nikki at the door, briefly kissing her on the lips. After her departure, she immediately heads back to Dick's room at her quickest walking pace. She sits down on his bed and sorts through all the questions in her head, trying to decide what to ask first.

"Do you like the story?" She asks the question thinking his opinion of it will reflect his opinion of Kitty, and thus what he thinks of her.

"I haven't finished it yet, but… it's certainly enlightening."

"To what are you alluding?"

"It has a mermaid in it, who is in love with a pirate captain." Dick waits for Jaclyn to respond.

Jaclyn stares ahead blankly. *She used my songs but wrote about Prudence?*

"Punk." The insult slips out of Jaclyn's mouth before she even realises it was directed at her former lover.

"Pardon?"

"I cannot believe the gall of that woman—to think she could write about Prudence in such a way! However, I suppose she would have thought it unlikely for me to become aware of the story. After all, she had no intention of seeing me again."

After letting Jaclyn spew out her frustration, Dick says, "She wrote about you, too." He coughs. "At least, I assume the character Jane is based on you. She's not a pirate."

"I do not understand."

"The pirate captain is in love with two people." He pauses, then clarifies, "Well, one woman and one mermaid. When he's at sea, he's with the mermaid, but when he's in Port Royal, he's with Jane."

Jaclyn stands and huffs. "Even in her story she could not choose between us. How could she be so cruel?"

With a shrug, Dick adds, "There's something else you should probably know."

She looks at him with a sense of dread, but leans her head upwards to urge him to continue.

"Kitty wrote that mermaids are immortal." He taps a finger on the desk next to him. "If that's true, Prudence could still be out there, looking for you again."

Her eyes are wide, staring more through Dick than at him. "Does it say anything else about the mermaid that I should know?"

"I don't know, like what?"

Jaclyn focuses her eyes on Dick's. "How are they made?"

"I... why would you want to know that?" Dick stands up and places his hands on her shoulders, then looks into her eyes, searching for an answer.

With a whimper, Jaclyn turns her head away. "I murdered her," she whispers. "Prudence. Before she was a mermaid." She turns her attention back to Dick after his hands fall to his sides. Then she raises her voice again. "I know you do not like the idea of me committing such terrible acts, but she deserved it. She was tearing Kitty away from me."

Dick turns away from Jaclyn, and heads toward his bedroom door.

Eyes following, Jaclyn says, "Dick?"

He leaves the room, so Jaclyn does too, trying to understand why he won't respond.

"Dick? Wait," she whimpers again.

After taking a jacket off his coat stand, he exits the apartment.

Jaclyn falls to her knees in the middle of the hallway.

There's something about Jaclyn murdering someone out of revenge that doesn't sit right with him. He finds himself walking to the nearest Starbucks to get his thoughts in order.

"Caffè latte, please," he orders, placing the exact change on the counter.

The barista nods at him and motions for him to take a seat. He turns around and tries to find a free table, but struggles. Then someone in the far corner of the room raises their head up from a newspaper and waves him over.

Dick walks over and sits down. "Hi, Lloyd. Seems like these days we only ever manage to see each other when we randomly bump into each other."

Lloyd shrugs. "Oh, well, you know how things are. The wife and work keeping me busy. You should come down to my comedy club sometime though. Get you out of your place; maybe you'll meet a girl."

"I think I have my plate full with women right now."

"Oh?" Lloyd chuckles. "Dick, you sly fox. How'd you manage that?"

"It's not like that. One's my roommate—*just* roommate—she's the woman you would've seen me with when you ran into me last month." Dick nervously taps a finger on the table. "Then the other is a friend, I guess, who I've just started dating. I have no idea where that's going."

"Caffè latte," the barista says, placing Dick's drink down in front of him.

"Thanks." Dick turns his attention back to Lloyd. "Not looking for pointers, though."

"You could always bring her to the club," Lloyd urges. "Plenty of couples come for dates."

"I dunno. We'll see." Dick takes his first sip. "Anything new with you?"

Dick doesn't particularly care about the answer, but he welcomes the distraction from having to think about Jaclyn's secret.

"Not really. Still trying to get Rini pregnant, but it's hard to tell if she even wants a kid any more…"

Lloyd continues talking, but Dick's no longer paying attention. He doesn't remember Lloyd telling him about them wanting kids before, but now that Dick's dating Sue, and knowing she has a daughter, he finds himself focusing in on every mention of children. It was easier to ignore them when it seemed like no one he knew either had or wanted kids.

"… What do you think?" Lloyd's voice comes back into focus.

"I don't know." It's the only thing Dick can say that doesn't reveal he hasn't been listening.

"You don't know if you'd rather a boy or girl?"

Dick subconsciously thanks Lloyd for repeating his question. "I haven't really wanted children."

"Oh, right. I forgot that was the reason you broke things off with Georgia. I hope you've stopped moaning about her now." Lloyd finishes off the last of the drink he had in his glass. "It got annoying to live with after a while." He stands.

"I hope that didn't influence you moving out."

Without answering Dick, Lloyd says, "Gotta go meet one of my acts for tonight now. I'll see you around."

He departs before Dick has the chance to say goodbye, leaving Dick alone with his thoughts again. The first thing he thinks is that the non-answer from Lloyd is the equivalent of a yes.

Soon his mind wanders back to Jaclyn's confession. She no longer seems so innocent in the mess that led to her being sent here. The reminders of her murderous past are not helpful either. Does this mean he needs to kick her out again? It's not like she's killed anyone since coming to New York, as far as he knows. He berated her once he learned of the murders in Barbados and that seemed to sink in for her.

Yet, Kitty did write about how mermaids were made. Dick figures he should probably give Jaclyn the answer to that question.

On the Thursday that follows, Dick comes home from work with some takeaway Chinese. He sits himself down in front of the television and flips on CNN.

It's in the middle of a story about some gunman in Florida doing something. Dick doesn't pay too much attention until it gets to the next headline.

The newscaster reads, "Wall Street executive Amelia O'Neil was found murdered in her apartment when her husband, Brian, returned home today."

Dick gets a bad feeling in the pit of his stomach. He knows he shouldn't jump to conclusions, but when he knows Jaclyn has been spending so much time with the Wall Street protesters, he can't help himself.

Jaclyn is in Zuccotti Park with Nikki when the news of the murder reaches them.

"Are you sure?" Nikki asks Mike.

"That's what I heard. The police won't release the details of how it happened."

"I hope the mainstream media doesn't try to pin this on us." Nikki starts getting flustered. "Fuck."

Jaclyn tilts her head and looks directly at Nikki. "Did you not say you wanted them to pay for their crimes?"

She looks up at Jaclyn. "Yeah, but I didn't mean like this. They should go to prison."

Nikki no longer seems as similar to Kitty as Jaclyn thought. Kitty would have revelled in the thought of taking someone like Amelia down. Kitty would have said she *deserved it.*

"Oh." Jaclyn doesn't really know what else to say, though she finds herself feeling a little sick again.

It's hard for her to tell what the cause is, though. The memory of Amelia's actions? The now unjustified murder?

"I doubt they'll say it was us," Mike offers. "They haven't got any reason to."

"But you know the mainstream media would love to have a reason to slander us." Nikki scratches a patch of her head between a couple of dreadlocks. "Do the police have any leads?"

Mike shakes his head. "I don't think so. They've already ruled out her husband because he was out of town when it happened a week ago."

"Then I don't see how you can be so sure they won't blame Occupy."

"I must go," Jaclyn interrupts. She can't stand listening to the way Mike and Nikki are talking. She needs some air. "Dick is likely waiting for me." It's not an outright lie, but she also knows Dick doesn't expect her back at any particular time.

"Okay," Nikki says. "See you tomorrow?"

Jaclyn shrugs. "I do not yet know. We shall see."

She smiles solemnly, then turns and heads toward the subway. As she walks, she comes to the conclusion that she should probably keep her distance from Zuccotti Park for a while. The chance of anyone figuring out it was her may be slim, but she would still rather not risk being associated with them while it's being discussed.

When Jaclyn walks in to Dick's apartment, she finds him sitting on the couch, staring at her. There are no lights on, nor sound. She watches him look at her as she closes the door.

"Dick?" Her eyes dart around the room, trying to see if something is amiss, but it's too hard for her to tell. She looks at him again. "May I switch on a light?"

"Did you murder her?"

Jaclyn is taken aback with how forward Dick is. "Pardon?"

"The Wall Street executive. Did you murder her?"

"I am going to turn on a light." Jaclyn walks across the room and switches on the one above the dining table.

Then she goes into the kitchen and pours herself a glass of water from the fridge. When she closes the door, she jumps in fright when she sees Dick standing there, and spills water over herself.

"I said, did you murder her?"

Clearly Dick is not going to back down until he has an answer.

"Why would you think such a thing of me? Is this just because I murdered Prudence? Or because I was a pirate? Did you not ask me to avoid such crimes?" She still doesn't want to lie to him, but how can she tell him the truth?

Jaclyn opens the fridge again and tops up her water.

"You can't even give me a straight answer. Obviously you know what I'm talking about or you would've been a lot more confused." Dick takes the glass from Jaclyn's hand just as she closes the fridge. "That tells me everything."

"Dick…"

He walks away and Jaclyn hears him locking himself in his room. At least he didn't kick her out again, but she's not sure how long that will last. Unfortunately, this time, she hasn't got anywhere else she can go.

Jaclyn pulls her phone out of its carry bag and calls the first person who comes to mind.

"Max?" she asks, when the ringing stops. "I might be homeless again soon, and I do not wish to return to Wall Street."

"I already told you that you can't stay here."

She sighs and rubs her forehead. "I understand. Perhaps we can instead meet in Battery Park again soon?" She thinks about Kitty's book, and how she wishes she could read it for herself rather than relying on Dick for the information. "I would like another lesson."

"I can do late Monday afternoon."

"All right," she says, hoping her disappointment isn't heard. "I shall see you then."

Jaclyn hangs up the phone and finds herself wondering why Max didn't jump at another opportunity to see her. Was it because she stopped having sex with him when her relationship with Nikki became serious?

That doesn't help her with her situation with Dick. If he were someone else, she might have considered killing him to keep her secret safe, but she couldn't do that with Dick. Not after everything he's done for her. Could she?

Dick sits cross-legged on his bed with his palms on his temples. The only words running through his head are, *harbouring a fugitive, harbouring a fugitive, harbouring a fugitive.*

He snaps himself upright and asks aloud, "Am I stupid? Why did I even ask her about it?" *Now she has every reason to kill me, too.*

Getting off his bed, he heads for the computer and sits down. He opens a browser and places the mouse cursor in the search bar.

Dick's fingers are poised a couple of inches above the keyboard. *Now what?* Anything he could think of wanting to look for made him worry that his search would have the FBI knocking at his door. *There's no such thing as privacy on the Internet.* He stands again, and spins his chair around in frustration. *I guess I'll just have to make amends. With a murderer.*

His bottom lip quivers at the thought. He has to slap himself across his face a couple of times to snap himself out of it.

By the time Dick has the courage to face Jaclyn again, he discovers she is no longer in his apartment. Unsure what to think about that, he supposes he could call her. He returns to his room to fetch his phone, and looks up her number.

When Jaclyn answers, she doesn't give Dick a chance to say anything. "I thought it best to gift you with my absence for a few days."

She hangs up without any further information.

The Statue of Liberty is visible in the distance from the bench Jaclyn is waiting on. It's not the same one on which she has slept the past few nights, as the air closer to the river is the coldest in the vicinity. Jaclyn at least had the foresight to find a thick coat she could wear whilst sleeping before she left Dick's. That's what she's currently sitting on, though she expects not for much longer. The chill is already starting to set in, as the sun begins to fall.

Max sits down beside her with a pen and notebook in tow.

"So what's the deal, anyway?" Max asks, avoiding eye contact. "You're even more homeless now?"

With a sigh, Jaclyn shrugs. "It would appear so, but the conditions in which I am living are no worse than I have experienced before."

"What'd you do this time?"

"I do not wish to discuss this matter."

"Are you and Nikki still…" Max trails off once he looks into Jaclyn's eyes.

She hopes her expression is all the answer he needs. Of course they're still together, and he should not be thinking this is an opportunity to get her into bed again. "Can we start the lesson?"

"Of course." Max writes a few words in his notebook. "I want to see how far you've come. Try reading these."

Jaclyn looks at the page, and very slowly sounds out the words. "My… naymee… eyes… makes."

"Good try. I can see why you thought they might sound like that. It says," he points to each word as he says it, "My… name… is… Max."

There's a frustrated sigh, then Jaclyn realises she's the

one who made the noise. "This is impossible."

She stands up and frowns at Max.

"No, it's not." He throws her a smile. "You've made a lot of progress in such a short amount of time."

"I should have been able to guess what it said." She grabs her coat and puts it on, wanting to avoid the chill.

"That wouldn't have been reading, though."

Max starts writing something else. While he's not paying attention, Jaclyn walks down to the river and leans on the fence. The sky is a mix of pinks and purple, and the sun is low enough that she knows it won't be too much longer before it sets. She's inclined to think it was pointless to start this late in the day.

When Jaclyn looks over her shoulder at Max, she sees him hunched over the pad, but his eyes looking out at the river to the right of her. They're unblinking, and his hand is unmoving, though still in a position poised to write.

Watching his frozen body causes Jaclyn to stop breathing. Then it feels like her heart stops, too. She expects there to be a look of horror crossing her face, because there is only one thing she can think of that could cause this kind of phenomenon.

Her heart starts functioning again, at a rapid pace. She turns around to look in the direction Max's head is pointing, and tries to prevent herself from hyperventilating as thoughts of Prudence flood her mind. The glare of the sun is strong, and she can barely see a thing. She takes a deep breath, and lets it out slowly, before lowering herself to the ground, still holding the top of the railing.

A splash registers in Jaclyn's head, and she realises she'd closed her eyes. When she opens them, she sees Prudence looking directly at her from her place in the river. Jaclyn's eyes dart back and forth, whilst the rest of her remains frozen in fear. She can't even speak, or think, for what feels like an hour.

Finally something crosses her mind. *How did you find me?*

Prudence places a sea-battered pistol on the concrete in front of her. The metal parts have a couple of barnacles attached, but aside from that, the handle is still distinct enough that Jaclyn recognises it. This is not the pistol she left in Sir Bromley's bedroom. This is the one she discarded off the coast of Barbados nearly two months ago.

Why are you still doing this to me?

It's the last thing she would want Prudence to see, but she can't help herself. All of the emotion she feels about being found again pours out in the form of tears.

"I am not here to torture you."

"No? Then why did you freeze my friend?" She throws out the words with so much anger.

Prudence doesn't let it distract her. "It was a necessary precaution. I needed only to talk to you."

"Oh, yes, I see that now," Jaclyn says sarcastically. "This is a change from you invading my head."

"I understand this must be very confusing for you. How long have you been here?"

Prudence's friendliness throws Jaclyn off balance.

"Excuse me?"

"I sent you here. How long has it been since you arrived?" When Jaclyn doesn't answer, Prudence adds, "I did not know exactly when you would arrive, but I have been looking for you for over fifty years. Not out of more revenge, but for Kitty."

Jaclyn's stomach drops. "What does Kitty have to do with this?"

"She missed you so." Prudence's upper lip begins to tremble. "She wanted to know what became of you."

"It is a little late for you to make amends." Jaclyn puts on her most scathing voice. "She is dead now."

Prudence shakes her head. "Kitty is in London. She has been there for four years; I sent her here to find you. Now I ask again—how long have you been here?"

The tears from earlier are now dry on Jaclyn's face, and focusing in on how that feels is a way to distract her from the shock of this news. Kitty's in this century. She can't even begin to think about how to process that.

Kitty. Jaclyn hasn't even considered the possibility of seeing her again since she's been here.

"I could tell her how to find you," Prudence offers, "though I am not sure how she will react to knowing you are with child."

Jaclyn snaps out of her trance and focuses on Prudence. "With child?"

"Did you not know?"

The pirate has to steady herself by leaning against the railing, moving her back to face Prudence. "Nay."

"I can hear his heartbeat."

"His?" Jaclyn can barely believe her ears. How can there be a little person growing inside her?

"Yes. I believe you are having a boy."

Jaclyn searches her mind for something to say. This news has made her temporarily forget everything Prudence has put her through. "Do not tell Kitty about the child. I would like to tell her myself." She turns around to face the mermaid again. "Bring her to me?"

With a light blink of her eyes, Prudence smiles at her. "I will."

Milliseconds later, Prudence disappears beneath the sea. It's only then that Jaclyn notices the last shining sparks of the sun. She takes the pistol and hides it inside her coat, then stands up, turns around, and sees Max shaking himself out of a daze. The last several minutes had caused her to forget she was there with him.

Jaclyn runs back to Max. "How are you?"

"When did it get dark? Jesus, is this the effect of years of drug use?"

She doesn't know how to answer that, not without explaining Prudence. That's not a conversation she's interested in having with him.

"Perhaps it was later than you thought when you arrived?"

Max scratches the back of his neck. "Maybe we should try again another time. I have a Halloween party to get to anyway."

"What is a 'Halloween party,' Max?"

He stands up, putting his notepad and pen away. "I'd show you, but you're not in your pirate costume. Sorry, Buccaneer."

With that, Max places a comforting hand on Jaclyn's shoulder, and leaves. She decides it's probably just as well. He's the last person she wants to discuss her apparent pregnancy with right now. Who knows how someone she's had sex with would react to that kind of news?

FOURTEEN

Candles dimly lit the room. Katherine was wiping her teeth with a cloth when Charles Bromley entered her bed chamber. She put the cloth to her side and asked, "Any word of Jack?"

He closed his eyes and shook his head. "Still no one has heard anything of her."

Katherine stroked her dress before standing. "How can no one have seen her for four years? If she had passed on, someone must have seen her."

"Perhaps she fell overboard and drowned?" Charles walked closer to her, and wrapped an arm around her waist.

"Someone would have known she was aboard the vessel and gone missing."

Charles kissed her forehead, then she embraced him in a hug. They parted only when a baby's cries could be heard coming from another room.

"Would you be able to watch him for me tonight?" Katherine asked, looking into his eyes. "I have something I need to do."

He smiled at her, but she could see past the façade and

read the sadness on his face. "I will, but know this, Katherine. This masquerade is wearing on me. I do not wish to keep caring for him when you continue to refuse my proposal. I care not that he is mine. It matters not when no one else knows."

Katherine scoffed at him, ignoring the cries. "A child out of wedlock! We have discussed this before. What would people think of us? No, it is better this way."

"Better than marriage? I think not. People are already gossiping."

Frustration growing, Katherine said, "Go tend to your son."

She couldn't take any more. Katherine stormed out, barely hearing Charles warning her about the plague as she left the room. She left her father's house, determined to get to her destination. It did not matter to her if this argument meant she would arrive early. She needed the air.

The Thames was lit only by the moon. Katherine sat on the banks and waited. The extra time gave her pause for thought about Jack, and how much she missed hearing her voice. The memory of her touch on Katherine's skin as they were intimate together caused her to start weeping.

That's when Katherine remembered coming to the Thames when they were only sixteen. They were probably only a few yards up the river, on the other side, the first time they came. She pictured the two of them, sitting there and holding hands, watching the water flow. Passers-by would have assumed they were just friends, but they both knew the truth. The look Jack had given her spoke a thousand words all at once. It was when Kitty knew she had

Jack. The girl belonged to her then, and barely missed her husband.

Jack's lack of grief for Mr Marshall was the main reason Kitty rejected the notion of marriage. It was not about love, it was an arrangement. An expectation put upon her by society.

Even if Bromley did have some love for her, it would still have been an arrangement. Bearing his son did not change Kitty's feelings for Jack. She liked Charles, and he helped keep her company in the lonely nights when she could not have Prudence at her side, but she did not love him. He did not provide her with the explosive energy she had come to expect from the women she loved.

The sound of a splash pulled Kitty from her thoughts, and focused her attention on the river. Prudence slowly emerged from the water, pulling herself up onto the bank until her tail began to morph into legs.

When Prudence sat down beside her, Kitty said, "It is becoming unsafe for me to meet you here. I am afraid of catching the plague." She sighed and continued, "Before long, the only safe place for me to be is locked up in my house."

"Do you not live only a few streets away?" Prudence used a hand to move Katherine's face towards her, but didn't wait for her to reply. "Have you been crying?"

It took a couple of seconds before Kitty could reply. "I miss Jack."

Prudence flinched upon hearing the name.

"I know you hate her for what she did to you," Kitty murmured, not wanting to acknowledge the history, "but that was, in a way, my own doing." She sighed again, and rubbed her own shoulder. "I have sent someone to look for her. He says no one has seen her for years. I wish to know what happened to her."

As if Prudence hadn't heard anything Kitty said, she pulled her close, pressing her breasts against Kitty's bodice, and kissed her deeply. Kitty pushed her away, increased the distance between them, and studied Prue's face.

"You know." Her voice was just a whisper at first. She watched Prudence's reaction, a mixture of shame and jealousy spreading across her body, from her eyes down to her arms. "You know what happened to Jack... because you took her from this world, just like you do men..."

Kitty started hyperventilating at the realisation. She tried to calm herself down by fanning herself, but in the end what worked was Prudence tearing at her bodice, loosening it for her, and opening her lungs. She slapped Prudence across the cheek.

"That is for Jack, not for saving me." Kitty took a deep breath and closed her eyes. "What did you do?"

She looked at Prudence again, who was already lowering herself back into the Thames. Her tail glistened in the moonlight, and Kitty wondered if she was trying to escape answering.

"I did not kill her," Prue said, sounding bitter. "I could send you to her, but I would not be able to bring you back."

Prudence ducked beneath the water, and stayed there long enough for Katherine to question if she would be back.

When she did resurface, she said, "It would save you from the plague, but you could not take Charles with you."

Katherine didn't know what to say, nor did she know if

she could even believe Prue. Leaving Charles Bromley was not a problem for her, but that's not who Prue was referring to, because as far as she knew, Prudence didn't know about him. Turning her back on her son? How could she do that?

"I need time to think." Katherine grabbed the back of her bodice to keep it from falling down when she stood up.

With a nod, Prudence agreed. "I will return in one month for your decision."

There wasn't any time for Katherine to protest before Prudence disappeared. Was a month long enough for her to decide?

When Katherine returned home, she sat down on her bed, feeling a little defeated. This was not a choice she wished to make. She didn't have long with her thoughts before baby Charles interrupted them. Katherine left her room for the baby's, where she found Bromley sleeping in a chair with a squirming infant held tightly in his arms. She removed Charles from his father's strong grasp, and gently wrapped her own arms around him.

"Poor child," she whispered to him. "Daddy does his best."

Kitty walked him around, patting him gently on his back. When he was settled, she placed him in his cradle. She spent the next few minutes watching him sleep in the dark. It was hard to see well, but she could make out a slight smile on his face.

London was not a safe place to raise a child, not with the plague. His chance of survival was looking grim in Katherine's eyes, and she did not want to do that to one so innocent. She walked over to Bromley and tapped him on the shoulder to rouse him.

Charles sat up, startled at first, until he was able to focus on Katherine. She pulled him out of his chair and into another room because she didn't want their voices to wake their baby.

"I would like you to accompany me to Edinburgh," she said, sitting down on an oak chair in the main room.

He blinked his eyes a couple of times, still half-asleep. "Pardon?"

"My cousin Brice lives there, and I wish to see him. I have not seen my family in so long." She stood up again, and walked over to him. Placing a hand on his arm, she added, "Please. Perhaps we can escape the plague there."

Charles scratched the back of his head whilst looking into her pleading eyes. "Lie with me," he said.

She held back a sigh. They were not even married and he was asking her to perform such duties. Katherine knew she had gotten herself into that mess, and with the baby it bore, she could not regret that decision. Continuing to lie with him was not the problem as much as the guilt that she felt. Would this time just be because she wanted him to protect her from highwaymen?

Taking his hands, Katherine led Charles to her room, and began to undress.

The next day, when Katherine was nursing the baby in the mid afternoon, Charles let himself in. She looked up at the door and greeted him with a smile, because he looked happy himself.

"I have some fortunate news for you, my darling," he said.

She tried not to cringe because she hated when he called her that.

Charles continued, "There is a stagecoach to Edinburgh tomorrow, which is expected to take eleven days. I was able to afford us the best seats, so I went ahead and purchased them. The next coach is not for three weeks, and you appeared to want to depart with haste."

Another smile crossed Katherine's face, and she tried to hide the way her eyes were welling out of happiness. It was times like these that she saw his generosity, and part of her did think he loved her in his own way.

"Thank you." It was all she could say without becoming too emotional.

When little Charles came away from her breast, having fallen asleep, Bromley walked over to Katherine to take him. She thought about their days ahead. This would be her first time travelling by stagecoach, but she had heard it was not the most pleasant of experiences.

Bromley took the baby to his room as Katherine dressed.

Six days into their journey, having expended most conversation topics, Charles placed a hand on Katherine's knee and said, "There is something that has been weighing on me."

Katherine assumed he was going to bring up the marriage discussion again, considering she dragged him along on this trip, knowing it was unnecessary for him to come. She feigned ignorance. "Whatever do you mean?"

"It is about Jacqueline."

This wasn't what she expected to hear. "Do you know

what became of her?"

"Not explicitly, but I believe she stole from my parents."

There was a sudden jolt in the coach, and Charles and Katherine bumped heads with each other. Katherine was thankful that baby Charles remained snug and asleep in Katherine's arms, and that they had not bumped into any of the other rich passengers.

Charles continued, "When I returned to Barbados in September of sixty-one, my father spoke of a woman who trespassed into his bedroom and tried to kill him. He never met Jacqueline, but I could not think what other woman would want to do that. Then he described her to me and I knew it was her." Charles opened up the satchel he was carrying on his lap and removed a pistol from it. "He gave me this," he said, allowing Katherine's eyes to linger on the weapon. "It is what she used to fire upon him, and it could only have come from a pirate. She must have taken it from them."

A knot tied itself inside Katherine's stomach. It would be just like Jack to murder out of revenge, and the pistol was proof. That pistol was Katherine's before she had given it—and its partner—to Jack as a gift.

"You said she stole something?"

He nodded. "My mother's jewellery. There was one item in particular that she treasured above all others. A black onyx elephant necklace from India. It was encrusted with gold and diamonds." Charles looked at her with such guilt that Katherine had to nudge him to continue. "I have been looking for her in the hope of recovering these items."

"Have you recovered them?"

Another large bump along the terrain interrupted the conversation, and woke the baby. Katherine cuddled him to try and calm him, but when that didn't work, she stuck a thumb in his mouth to soothe him.

"No."

Katherine supposed that if Prudence had sent Jack away somewhere, the jewellery must still be with her. Then she started wondering what she could possibly want with it. Had she already wasted all of the treasure Katherine had left behind for her? Or was the looting also out of revenge?

When they arrived in Edinburgh, Bromley immediately hired a carriage to take them to Katherine's cousin's cottage. Bromley knocked on the door, not wanting to let Katherine hurt her delicate hands.

A woman with bright orange hair answered.

"You must be Mary," Katherine greeted. "I am Katherine Grayson, Brice's cousin."

Though Brice and Katherine had exchanged letters over the past few years, she had never actually met his wife.

Mary enveloped Katherine and the baby in a quick hug, then stepped aside. "Do come in."

As they made their way through to the sitting room, Katherine asked where Brice was.

"He went to church this morning, but should be along shortly." Mary's accent was quite thick, but it made Katherine smile, as it was like a reminder of her mother. "Is this your husband?"

Katherine looked at Bromley. "My apologies; where are my manners? I should have introduced you immediately. No, Mr Bromley and I are not married." She looked back at Mary, who appeared dismayed. Realising she probably thought they were living in sin, since she and Brice were clearly religious, Katherine knew she would have to lie to make things right. "He has been caring for me since I was," she lowered her voice for the next word, "*raped*, but we are not together. Charles is not his."

"Your boy deserves a father; why do you not marry?"

Katherine didn't know how to answer that, but Bromley spoke up for her. "It is not for wont of asking on my part." She wished he hadn't.

They were interrupted when Brice entered the room and spoke. "I did not know we were expecting company, Mary."

Mary stood and greeted her husband with a kiss on each cheek. "Nor did I," she said.

Then Katherine passed Charles to Bromley, rose from her chair and embraced Brice in a light hug. "My apologies, cousin. I did not wish to arrive unannounced, but I felt we had to come with great urgency."

Her cousin showed concern on his face. "Kitty?"

"I suppose I must be difficult to recognise after all these years." Katherine acknowledged that she hadn't lived in Scotland since 1638. Brice would only have been eight when her parents relocated to London, and she only knew who he was because of the way Mary greeted him. Her bottom lip began to tremble, and her voice quavered. "May we speak in private?"

Brice grunted an "Mmm," and took her hand to lead her outside. She felt tense at the thought of leaving Mary alone with Bromley and her son, not knowing what Charles might say to her, but this was a matter she needed to discuss with her cousin alone.

They walked for some distance along the cobblestones before either of them said anything. Brice spoke first. "Whatever brings you to Edinburgh must be frightening. What disturbs you, Kitty?"

"The plague," she said. "London is no place to raise a child." She sighed. "Though there is more, I cannot discuss it all."

Katherine had spent the previous twelve days contemplating all of her options, and she hated every one of them. This seemed to be the least horrible, and most likely to guarantee her son's safety.

"I must ask a favour of you." Her voice began to quaver again. "I need to return to London on the next stagecoach, in three days. As Mary has thus far been unable to bear your children, I hoped you might take Charles for me."

"When will you come back for him?"

Katherine stopped walking, and grasped her cousin's upper arms. She did everything she could to hold back the tears she could feel fighting to get through. Even so, the look she got back from Brice was one that told her he felt her sadness. "I do not know," she said, her arms trembling. "Perhaps not at all. If you do not hear from me again after I depart, I want you to raise him as if he were your own." She took a deep breath and added, "The only other request I have is that you keep his name as Charles Grayson, out of respect for both my father and the king."

The concern on Brice's face didn't leave, but he embraced Kitty in the tightest hug she had ever received. It made her wonder why she hadn't made the journey to visit him sooner, since he was the only family she had left after her father's passing. Her tears began falling then, and she was finally able to admit she wasn't as strong as she pretended to be.

"Do you have somewhere to sleep for the next three days?" Brice asked, relaxing his arms and pulling back.

Kitty wiped her eyes. "Not thus far, though we passed an inn on our way here. Mr Bromley—the man who accompanied me on this journey—said we would return there tonight."

With a smirk, Brice asked, "So that is the man who is incapable of winning my cousin's heart?"

She replied by rolling her eyes. "All men are incapable of that." Kitty thought it best to leave that discussion there, and changed the subject. "Has my book made its way here yet?"

"Oh, yes." Brice took Katherine's arm to nudge her back in the direction they had come. "I have been reading it to Mary. She rather likes the mermaid. I had no idea you had that kind of imagination. And pirates! Kitty, how did you come up with such a story?"

"It was not easy." That was the most honesty she was able to provide. "Having Mr Bromley's company helped, as his father is rather involved with trade. They have been attacked by pirates, so I have heard the stories."

Brice nodded. It was times like these that Katherine knew a lie was more believable than the truth.

When the cousins returned to the MacGregor home, Brice took his wife aside to another room to discuss Katherine's proposal. She took Charles from Bromley's arms and held him close, studying his bright blue eyes. It was hard for her to believe that this could be the last time she saw them. If Mary agreed to keep him, Katherine promised they would not return before departing for London.

"Charles," she said, looking down at Bromley, "You may need to say farewell to your son soon."

He quickly stood up, confusion forming on his face. "Katherine..."

"If we are to marry, we should have a fresh start." Lying had become so easy for her. "We will return to London to gather some things, and then perhaps we can travel to the West Indies, searching for your mother's jewellery together."

"But what of the baby?"

Mary returned to the room in time to answer the question herself. "He will stay here."

There was a nod from Brice behind her.

"But..." Bromley tried to object, until Kitty interrupted.

"It is safer for him to remain in Edinburgh. I do not wish for him to catch a death of the plague. Perhaps, in time, I will return."

Her explanation appeared to sate Bromley, at least temporarily. He seemed to be aware that he could not claim his parentage in her family's presence, after the story she told about his conception.

Katherine walked Charles over to the couple and handed him to Mary.

"Farewell, my son." She lightly patted his arm. "I love you."

Then Katherine gave both Mary and Brice a brief hug before turning back to Bromley. He made a move toward the baby, but Katherine threw him a look to suggest it would not be a good idea now to say goodbye. She did not want to raise their suspicions that he was actually the father.

"Farewell all," Bromley said, bowing his head. He turned around, placed a hand on the small of Katherine's back, and led her out of the cottage.

That was the last time Katherine ever saw her son.

"What in Hell was that about, Katherine?" Charles yelled as soon as he shut the door to their room at the inn. Katherine was already sitting on the bed. "How could you pull that on me without talking to me about it? I have to find out about it in a way that means I cannot even say goodbye to my own son?"

"Hush," Katherine said, "You will disturb our neighbours."

"Is all you care about your reputation?" Bromley shook his head slightly, glaring.

Katherine stood and marched over to him, and looked him right in the eye. "You do not think that was difficult for me?"

"You just gave up the one thing that represented my love for you. Considering I know you do not feel as I do, no, I do not think it made a difference to you."

Anger swelled in her body. As much as she didn't want to revert to her pirate past, it came gushing out when she pushed Bromley hard against the door behind him, and held him there. "How *dare* you suggest that? I love Charles perhaps even more than I loved Jack." Finding it hard to see through the tears in her eyes, Katherine lowered her arms and turned around. "Edinburgh is far safer for him than London, or the West Indies."

When Charles didn't reply after a few seconds, Katherine plodded toward the bed. She would have preferred to leave the room entirely, but he was still backed up against the door.

"Never have I seen such emotion from you," Charles finally said.

He walked up behind her and wrapped his arms around Katherine when she was mere inches from the bed, and pulled her close to him. "You are a brave woman, Katherine," he said, and kissed her hair. "But I think, sometimes, too much so. Hiding your fears comes out looking like heartlessness." He pulled his arms tighter. "I wish you would share more of what goes on in that mind of yours."

Katherine turned around, and brushed her lips against his. "I will help you find your mother's jewellery," she reminded him. "It is the least I can do after all you have done for me."

Katherine returned to the Thames right when Prudence had agreed to meet her again. She had told Charles to stay at his home and begin packing for the West Indies so that it would be at least a day before he discovered she was missing.

Holding the pistol she had given to Jack, Katherine sat on the riverbank, and waited. Prudence was late, which caused Kitty's stomach to churn. Could she have been wrong about their being immortal? What if something bad had happened to her? She thought about her son, over three hundred miles away, and hoped she hadn't made a mistake. Those beautiful blue eyes burned into her memory, and she could think of nothing else until she heard a splash in the river.

She shook herself out of her thoughts and focused on the blonde in the Thames. Prudence's wet skin did a good job of masking her, but as she drew herself onto the bank, Katherine was drawn to those eyes. She didn't notice the legs forming, because all she could see was the same shade of blue she remembered her son had.

"Can mermaids have children?" The question slipped out of Katherine's mouth before she'd had the chance to screen her thoughts.

"I am not aware of any such cases," Prudence said.

No, Katherine thought. *What a ridiculous notion to think Charles could be a product of my love for you.*

Prudence took her chin in her hand and lightly kissed her lips. "If nothing else, we are both women. Charles Bromley was a worthy father."

Shuffling backwards, not taking her eyes off Prudence, Katherine could not speak. Instead she automatically pointed the pistol at the mermaid's face.

"Whatever is the matter?" Prudence looked frightened, and Katherine felt it was like looking in a mirror.

"You knew my thoughts." Katherine started breathing heavily. "You know about Mr Bromley..." Her hand began to waver.

"Darling, you needed someone to care for you when I could not be there." The mermaid reached an arm out to her, and lowered the pistol. "I did my best in the only way I knew how." She looked sad now. "You would not talk to me about him, so I had to adapt."

"How long have you been listening to my thoughts?" Katherine's jaw was clenched, and the rest of her body felt stiff.

Prudence didn't react to Kitty's frustrations. "Why did you never marry him? I tried so hard to provide for you."

Confusion overcame Katherine then. *What do you mean by that?*

"If you had married him, you would have stood to inherit his family's wealth. I sent Jack on her way because she was trying to destroy that."

Katherine looked down at the flintlock in her hand, remembering that it had been recovered in Sir Nathaniel Bromley's house.

"Oh, Prue," Kitty's eyes started watering. "I never wanted that."

There was a moment of silence before Prudence replied. "I see now what your decision is." She crawled toward Katherine and kissed her on the lips one last time. "Jack is living in the future."

No more words were exchanged between them as Prudence crawled back into the river. By the time Kitty looked into the Thames, the mermaid was gone. When she raised her head, she saw a lot more bridges crossing the river. Further away from her were buildings taller than she'd ever imagined seeing.

She was no longer in 1665.

FIFTEEN

Jaclyn wakes up as the sun rises, streaming into her face. Her night had not been particularly restful, as thoughts of her pregnancy kept penetrating her dreams. She shivers a little in the early cool air, then sits up on the bench. *What am I going to do with a baby?*

She watches the warm air escape her lips as she breathes out. Her eyes begin to water. It crosses her mind that Prudence could have been lying to her, just to get in her head again. Torment her. She's never felt more alone. Even when Kitty left her, she had friends aboard the brig she left behind. When she herself deserted *Medusa's Wrath*, she at least still had Ejiogu, until Prudence took him. Jaclyn supposes that she might have been more alone then, had she not been filled with so much rage and ended up here. Then she met Dick, and she didn't give him the chance to kick her out until she had other people to fall back on.

Now? She wonders how she can face Dick again. Maybe he'd even turn her in to the authorities. Yet, he's the only person she's met here who knows about Prudence. It's not the right time to talk to Max, and the last thing she wants to do is explain her reality to Nikki. Perhaps calling Dick first would allow Jaclyn to gauge how safe it is to see him again.

After reaching into her coat pocket and pulling out her phone, she presses the 'on' button, but nothing happens. It's been days since she last looked at it, and she largely forgot that it needs to be charged regularly. That could explain why no one has called her in that time. Would Nikki be worried about her? Would Dick?

Without a phone to use, Jaclyn realises she's just going to have to face her fears one way or another.

Since it's a Tuesday, by the time Jaclyn arrives at Dick's, he's already out, likely at work. She lets herself in and looks for any signs she may no longer be welcome there, until it occurs to her that she doesn't know what those signs might look like. It's not as though he could write her a note she would be able to read.

Instead, she goes into her room and plugs her phone in to charge. Maybe once it's ready, she can try calling Dick before he gets home.

This would have been a good plan, except that when Jaclyn leaves her room to go to the kitchen in order to make herself something to eat, Dick walks in the front door. She stops dead in her tracks and just stares at him.

Dick closes the door and puts his keys in his pocket, while looking back at her. There is a good minute's silence between them before anything else happens.

"Where have you been?" Dick sounds concerned rather than demanding, though Jaclyn can tell he's trying to seem neutral.

Jaclyn's fingers start twitching nervously. She's wary

that Dick may be trying to lure her into a false sense of security.

Dick takes a tentative step forward. "Nikki called around, looking for you. We haven't been able to get you on the phone."

"I told you I would give you space," she replies, noncommittal. "What are you doing home?"

He walks a little closer to her, making her feel more nervous. "I've been coming home for lunch since you left, in case you came back but didn't want me to see you."

"Why? To trap me?"

"It is a little hard to trust you out there on your own. I don't know what you're going to do."

Dick's close enough now that he manages to wrap a hand each around her lower arms. She takes a deep swallow. This is *Dick*. Despite everything, she still considers him a friend. She doesn't want to have to hurt him if he gets rough with her.

Looking directly into her eyes, Dick says, "I feel safer knowing where you are, where I can look out for you, and make sure you're not getting into any trouble."

She wants to be sarcastic and say, 'By which you mean not murdering people,' but the sincerity in his face causes Jaclyn to tear up a bit. She looks down, and even though she hadn't intended on saying anything yet, the words just slip out. "Prudence found me."

Dick withdraws a hand from her arm and uses it to raise her chin. He doesn't speak, but his eyes are questioning, prompting her for more. The corner of her mouth begins to twitch, but she doesn't know what to say. Jaclyn pulls her other arm away, and briskly walks past him to get to the couch so she can sit down somewhere comfortable.

After following her to the couch, Dick wraps an arm around her as he sits. Then he leans them backwards and encourages her to rest her head on his chest. Jaclyn supposes this means they're back to being friends again. She likes that he's not saying anything; asking for the details. There's a certain comfort in feeling like he'll just listen when she's ready to talk.

With his free hand, Dick brushes a chunk of her hair away from her face, then starts lightly massaging her temple.

"She was different," Jaclyn finally says. "I do not quite understand why, but she was not so... vengeful."

"You talked to her?"

Jaclyn nods against his chest. With some hesitation, she adds, "She told me Kitty is in London."

"London... back in the seventeenth century, right?"

"No. London, now."

"Now?"

"Yes." She nods again.

"Why would she tell you that? I thought she hated the two of you together?"

Jaclyn swallows, thinking about how much she believed that to be true. "That is why I cannot be certain of her honesty."

"Are you going to go look for her?" The hand Dick had wrapped around her reaches down to hold hers.

"How could I?" She lets out a sigh. "Even if it were true, London was large enough when I was last there. I imagine it would be impossible to locate her now."

When she turns her head to look at Dick, she sees him

looking at the opposite wall. "Crap. I'm going to have to get back to work soon and I still haven't eaten." He glances down at her. "Are you going to be okay? Can we talk about this some more when I get home again?"

"There is only one other thing I wish to discuss." She swallows again, and it feels like there's a giant knot in her throat.

He looks at her curiously, waiting for her to say more. Jaclyn uses her free hand to massage her throat because she wants to get the words out.

They come out in a whisper. "She also said I am with child."

There's a long pause before Dick says, "Well, that is at least something we can test her honesty on. But you have to be here when I get home again."

That evening, when Dick returns, he dumps a couple of full plastic shopping bags on the dining table. Jaclyn isn't in the room, so he walks down the hallway and knocks on her door.

"Are you in there?" he calls.

Though there's no reply, he can hear some sort of rustling sound.

"Dinner's on the table when you're ready," he adds, then heads back into the other room.

Normally when Dick is home alone and gets Chinese, he has a tendency to just eat everything out of the cardboard and styrofoam packaging. He figures it might be a bit inappropriate to do that this time, though, so he grabs a few dishes from the kitchen and sets the table.

When he gets to the disposable chopsticks as he's unpacking the bag, he smirks to himself at the memory of the time he tried to teach Jaclyn how to use them. Dick realises he needs to return to the kitchen to retrieve some silverware for her. A spoon, in particular, since that seemed to be her preferred way of eating rice in the past.

Jaclyn finally emerges from her room about five minutes after everything is ready for her. She's wearing baggy track pants and a t-shirt that looks at least three sizes too big for her. Dick has never seen her wearing anything like that, and wonders what brought on the change, but knows better than to ask a woman about her outfit.

"Help yourself first," he says, indicating the food in front of her.

She smiles but doesn't say anything, then follows his suggestion.

They eat dinner in silence, with Dick not really knowing what to say or how to bring up the conversation they had earlier in the day. Once he finishes off his plate, he decides it's time to open the other bag.

He pulls out a couple of the boxes and shows them to Jaclyn. "These are pregnancy tests. I bought a few, and different types, in case we—er, you—have any problems using them." Dick looks at one of the boxes in his hand. "I can read the instructions to you, but you probably don't want me, ah, watching over you."

"Why? How does it work?"

"Generally... you have to urinate on it. Or in a cup. I think you'll want your privacy, yeah?"

She nods, and he starts opening a box and looking at the instructions.

"Okay, so it says the best results are if you do the test

first thing in the morning." He looks up from the paper. "Do you want to wait that long? We can always try again tomorrow if you get a negative result tonight, just to check. I'm sure I bought enough."

"No, let us not wait. I would like to know now."

He nods at her. "Okay."

About ten minutes later, after accidentally dropping the first two sticks in the toilet, Jaclyn spreads her legs wide and waits. She's a little nervous, knowing Dick is just on the other side and can probably hear every little detail of her in there. Eventually her urine cannot be contained, and she follows the instruction Dick had provided, aiming for only the foam tip.

She emerges from the toilet feeling a combination of tension and relief, then hands the stick to Dick so he can check the result for her.

It's the longest two minutes of her life. She hadn't planned on having children. How could this have happened? Max promised her they were protected. What is she going to do with a *baby*? Then she tells herself a multitude of times that Prudence couldn't possibly have been telling her the truth.

Dick hands the stick to her and points at the two solid pink lines in the window.

"Prudence wasn't lying," he says. "You are pregnant."

Four in the morning is about the only time of day that Katherine can find herself down at the Thames without worrying about being seen with a mermaid. It doesn't bother her too much, as she finds it easier to write at night, when there are fewer sounds to distract her. She tells her-

self the sleep deprivation she experiences on those nights
helps her imagination.

It had taken her a while to adapt to using ball-point
pens, but now she uses them like she's been a professional
all her life. Her favourite place to sit and write while waiting for Prudence is underneath a tree and a spherical lamp,
overlooking the river, opposite the New Globe Theatre.

She looks at the building and knows it is not the same
as the one she used to visit and admire with her mother
when she was a little girl, because the Puritans tore that
one down. It doesn't even look the same, and it's closer to
the river now. The reason she likes being there is not out of
familiarity, but because she finds herself in a place of comfort, knowing that her people wanted to bring it back again.
For Katherine, it's a reminder that her mother's bravery was
not for nothing.

On this particular morning, Katherine is scribbling
words furiously in her notebook.

> *The mermaid had promised to find Sally's prin-
> cess for her, but it had been weeks since Sally had
> seen her. She was beginning to think the mer-
> maid had only come to her in her dreams, and
> that she was going to have to start her own quest
> to find the princess herself.*

Katherine crosses everything out, then tears the page
out of the book and crumples it up. *Why is this so difficult?* She's been supporting herself by writing children's
books for years, but now that her publisher wants her to
write something closer to her heart, she just can't seem to
do it.

A long, drawn out voice calling "Kitty" interrupts her frustration. She looks down at the naked woman on the bank below.

"Any news yet?" Katherine asks, not feeling hopeful.

Every time she sees Prudence, she's acutely aware of how much time has passed since she arrived in this century, under the expectation that she would find Jack. After four years, she's not sure whether she can stand the charade much longer.

"She is in Manhattan."

Katherine stares at Prudence, unblinking. There are several seconds of silence while she processes Prue's unexpected answer. "America?"

About a week after confirmation of her pregnancy, Jaclyn heads down to the coffee shop where she and Nikki had their first date. She's still too wary of showing her face amongst the other protesters, but is glad that Nikki had agreed to see her after Jaclyn had been avoiding her for so long.

Jaclyn nervously waits outside the front, wearing the warmest clothes she could find—two layers of stockings underneath a pair of jeans, and a couple of layers of shirts underneath a woollen coat. She thinks about how London in November never seemed as cold as it is in New York right now, but given the last time she was there was over a decade of her personal timeline before, she supposes she could be wrong about that. Perhaps it's just that she grew too familiar with the warmth of the Caribbean.

A smile greets Jaclyn as Nikki walks around the corner, then jogs toward her. When Nikki reaches her personal space, she cups Jaclyn's head in her hands and plants a kiss on her lips. When she pulls away, she says, "It's really good to see you again. I was worried about you."

She doesn't wait for a response, and takes Jaclyn's hand, walking her inside the coffee shop to get out of the cold.

They find a table with a couple of comfortable chairs, as opposed to the wooden ones, and Jaclyn takes a seat while Nikki goes to the counter to place their order. Jaclyn watches Nikki's animated expressions as she's talking to the barista, making her realise how much she's missed being in her company. She hopes the news of the murder has since died down and been forgotten, because she doesn't want to feel like she disappointed Nikki again. Besides that, there are more pressing things for her to discuss—if she can figure out how.

When Nikki returns to the table, her cheery disposition turns to that of concern. "What's wrong?" she asks as she's taking her seat.

Jaclyn shakes her head, snapping herself out of her thoughts, and plasters on a smile. "Nothing, I was just thinking."

"Oh yeah? The way you looked made me think you dragged me out here to break things off between us." Nikki removes her scarf from around her neck and places it on the chair beside her.

"That thought is very far from my mind." She smiles harder, hoping Nikki can't see through it. "Actually, I was thinking about how much better you are for me than my last girlfriend." Jaclyn is not entirely sure she believes that, but it's what she has to tell herself, considering Kitty has yet to show herself since Prudence announced her presence in this century.

Nikki reaches out to hold Jaclyn's hand. "I'm glad. I've missed having your company, you know. After you left camp, Mike and I argued a long time about why I thought the media would try and pin that murder on us…" Jaclyn's stomach sinks at the topic, but she pulls her hand away and tries to keep calm. "He thought I was kind of insane for thinking they would, but it would've been nice to have had you on my side for that."

"I am sorry." Jaclyn doesn't know what else to say.

"It's okay. It turned out Mike was right. The cops ended up arresting some other Wall Street exec for it. Apparently they were having an affair?"

A barista brings their drinks to the table, momentarily interrupting them. Jaclyn smirks a little into her cup of hot chocolate as she thinks about the result of her crime. It's nice to know she's off the hook for it.

"That is good news," Jaclyn says, then she furrows her brow. "Can I ask you something?"

"Sure, go ahead." Nikki sounds a little too excited for the question that's on Jaclyn's mind.

"I do not know if it is too soon to ask this…"

Nikki raises an eyebrow. "It's not a marriage proposal, is it?"

"No…" It feels as though Jaclyn has a herd of elephants stampeding in her stomach as she thinks about how to get the question out. "I am just curious, what do you think about children?"

She doesn't answer right away, instead opting to take a sip of her chai latte. "Ow!" Nikki puts the mug back down on the table and fans her mouth. "Too hot."

It doesn't take long for Jaclyn to think Nikki might be trying to avoid the question. She doesn't want to press the issue, but she feels like she wants to have an idea how Nikki will react before she shares her news. Waiting for a reply seems to be her best way forward.

Jaclyn catches her gaze once she's done cooling down her mouth.

"Right, your question." Nikki bites her lower lip while she thinks. "I'm not sure I understand what you're asking. Do you mean in general, or do you mean, do I want them?"

Jaclyn's fingers start twitching beneath the table. "Both?"

"Well… I have a niece back in Fort Collins. She's my brother's kid. I get along okay with her, but I think that's because she's family, you know? I don't usually like other people's kids." Nikki hesitates before saying anything else. "As for myself… I've kind of been thinking about that a bit lately. I'm twenty-three and happily childfree. I don't want to raise kids in this fucked up world."

The stampeding elephants in Jaclyn's stomach work their way up to her heart, trampling all over it.

"But the good thing about being a lesbian is I don't have to worry about an accidental pregnancy." She winks at Jaclyn, then notices the horror present in Jaclyn's face. "Don't get me wrong," she tries to backtrack, "I'm not saying never. Maybe if Obama does the right thing and fixes Wall Street… maybe if I eventually see hope in the world's future, and therefore the future of the children on this planet, I could think about it… crap, I've put my foot in it, haven't I?"

Nikki rushes to her chai again, but enough time has

passed this time that she doesn't react to the temperature the same way as before.

After gulping down about half the mug without taking a breath, Nikki awkwardly asks, "So, you want children?"

Jaclyn shrugs and takes a sip of her own drink before responding. "I do not have much choice."

Confused, Nikki asks, "You can't have children?"

Tapping the side of her glass with her thumb, Jaclyn says, "Quite the opposite." She sighs heavily, hoping the elephants don't sit on her lungs next. "I am with child."

The women stare at each other for about a minute, both holding their own drinks, but unable to do anything else.

"With child? Who says that?" Nikki smirks. "You're messing with me, aren't you? That's what this is. You can't be pregnant."

Jaclyn's lungs feel like they're failing. She carefully places her drink on the table in front of her and grabs her chest as she tries to catch her breath.

"Oh, shit, you're not kidding." Nikki looks at her in horror, then puts her own cup down and rushes around to Jaclyn's side and starts patting her on the back.

Coughing out her breath, Jaclyn whispers her thanks.

When Nikki takes her seat again, she calmly says, "We can't see each other any more."

"Pardon?"

"You're pregnant. I did not get you that way, so someone else did. Regardless of whether or not you cheated on me, I can't be with a woman who fucks men."

Nikki finishes off the last of her chai, puts the cup down on the table, and walks away. Behind her she leaves Jaclyn staring dumbfounded at the chair opposite her.

Katherine sits cross-legged on her bed, turning Jaclyn's pistol over in her hands. She lives in a spacious one-bedroom apartment near Paddington Station, so the sounds of trains passing by or pulling in can be heard every now and then.

Looking at the pistol helps the memories flood over her, like the time Jaclyn boarded a Spanish galleon, singing ferociously, before clocking a Spaniard over the back of his head with the handle, then spinning around and shooting another one in the back. Then there was the time they faced the Navy and Jaclyn roared at them about being Cromwell's well paid slaves before discharging the weapons and injuring the sailors she hit. She finished the job with her cutlass.

Those days are far behind her now, and she doesn't miss them. Not the violence anyway. She misses that Jaclyn championed her cause, and stuck by her despite everything. Despite her infidelity. She doesn't know what she'll find when she gets to New York. Prudence hadn't been very clear on the details of what she had been up to since Katherine left her in Port Royal.

Even though there are still a couple of days left before her flight, Katherine locks the pistol back up in her safe, and starts packing for her journey across the Atlantic.

Trudging back into Dick's apartment, feeling defeated, Jaclyn runs a hand through her hair, and heads to her bedroom. She's not expecting Dick to be home for at least three hours, so she digs around in a satchel and pulls out the pistol that Prudence returned to her. For some reason she's feeling drawn to it, like just holding the flintlock will help her figure out what to do next.

She sits down on the bed and holds the weapon in her hands then closes her eyes. Thoughts wash over her. How would Kitty have reacted if she had given her the same news she had just given Nikki? Kitty didn't like men that way either. In fact, any time the subject of sex with men came up, Kitty seemed absolutely horrified at the prospect. Part of it came down to her experiences with Mr Marshall, and Higgins, though at least Kitty didn't hold them against her.

Jaclyn opens her eyes and stares at the beige wall opposite her. It bothers her that she didn't get to explain what happened to Nikki. She was never unfaithful to her, but even if she had been, infidelity can be forgiven. Considering how many years she forgave Kitty for that sort of behaviour, doesn't she deserve a second chance? That's when Jaclyn realises that Kitty never would have left her over something like this. They would have worked something out.

Then she notes the irony of it all. She was attracted to Nikki in the beginning because of how like Kitty she seemed. Some replacement she turned out to be.

Turning her head toward the window, Jaclyn puts her request out to the universe. "Find me?"

SIXTEEN

A knock on the door interrupts Dick and Sue from their brunch. Jaclyn had left the apartment before Dick woke, so it's up to him to answer the door.

"Excuse me," he says, wiping his mouth with a serviette.

He places the serviette down next to his plate and gets up from the table. When Dick answers the door, he's confronted by a redheaded woman he doesn't recognise. From her face, he assumes she's somewhere in her thirties. Looking her up and down, he admires the long, flowing skirt on the red dress she's wearing. It's the sort of smart casual attire that he doesn't expect to be worn by someone trying to sell him something. Besides, he doesn't get people like that knocking on the door of his apartment. They can only reach him by phone.

"Can I help you?" Dick asks. "I'm sorry, I'm not used to strangers knocking on my door. Did you mean to knock on someone else's?"

"I don't think so," the woman replies. "I'm looking for Jaclyn Rousseau. Does she live here?"

Dick looks back at Sue, still sitting at the table, then returns his attention to the redhead. "Who are you?" He asks the question despite thinking he probably already knows the answer. Who else would be looking for Jaclyn?

"Katherine MacGregor, though Jaclyn would know me better as Kitty Grayson."

Dick stares at Kitty blankly as he tries to figure out how to respond. Of course she's using another pseudonym.

"Using your mother's name again, huh?" He slouches against the doorframe, but is still a couple of inches taller than her.

Kitty crosses her arms. "I see she told you about me then. Is she here?"

He looks over his shoulder at Sue again to make sure she's okay, and hopefully not paying attention. Having the author of the story she's basing a screenplay on is not something Dick wants to introduce her to yet, if at all. As far as Sue would believe, Katherine should be dead. Dick pulls the door shut behind him so he can talk to Kitty in the hallway.

"She told me the mermaid said you were here, in our time, but I didn't really believe it. Considering her history, I figured she was just trying to torture Jaclyn some more."

Still with her arms mostly crossed, Kitty bites her thumb. Dick can't tell if he's just made a fool of himself or what. Perhaps this Kitty isn't the real Kitty and doesn't know about mermaids. Or maybe Jaclyn had been lying about that part.

When Kitty doesn't respond, he asks, "How did you get my address anyway?"

"Well, since she's clearly already told you about 'the mermaid,' it shouldn't be as much shock to you if I say Prudence got it from Jaclyn, and passed it on."

"I find that hard to believe." Dick leans backwards against the door and crosses his own arms to match Kitty. "Jaclyn doesn't even know how to read or write properly. She doesn't know the address, she just knows how to get here."

"Yet you believe her word about mermaids."

"I didn't until I read your book."

"My book?" She looks confused. Didn't she write it? Maybe she doesn't think anyone would've been able to find it.

"*A Pirate's Reverie.*"

"Oh." She pauses. "Was there anything in there about mermaids being able to read thoughts? I can't remember if I knew about that before or after it was written."

There's a knock on the door behind him.

"Dick?" Sue's voice asks.

He's not sure what to do. It probably wouldn't be the wisest of choices to let Sue hear him talking about real mermaids.

"Just a minute," he says to Kitty, then opens the door and peeks inside at Sue.

"Everything okay?"

"Uh…" Dick struggles to find decent words. "Just talking to Jaclyn's ex-girlfriend. I'll be back in a moment."

"Okay… just didn't want to let your coffee get cold."

"Thanks." He smiles at Sue, and after she turns around, he closes the door on her again.

"I'm guessing she doesn't know about mermaids," Kitty says in a not-so-quiet voice as he's turning back around.

Dick really hopes Sue's far enough away by then to not have heard her. "No. At least, not that they actually exist, and I'd like to keep it that way."

"You didn't answer my question, about mermaids reading thoughts." She's tapping her fingers on her arm now, clearly growing impatient with him.

"Jaclyn mentioned Prudence could, but it's not in your book. What does that..."

Kitty interrupts him, "That is how Prudence could tell me where you live."

"Oh."

"Now can I see Jaclyn?"

"She's not here." Dick tries to hide a smirk as he watches Kitty's frustration build.

"Where is she?"

"I don't know, I presume she's out with her actual girlfriend. One who *didn't* leave her." At least, not as far as Dick knows. Jaclyn may have failed to mention that to him.

Kitty's arms fall to her sides. "Ouch."

"You really have some nerve showing up here after everything you've put that poor girl through, you know?" He thinks about how this is the woman responsible for Jaclyn's lifestyle. "What were you thinking, turning her into a pirate?" Dick lowers his voice to a whisper. "It's your fault she's murdered people here."

That may not be true, but it's what Dick wants to believe right now. Even the first person Jaclyn killed, before she became a pirate, was because of Katherine.

"She's still killing people?" Kitty asks in a hushed tone.

"Three that I know about. Who knows if there's more? She doesn't discuss it with me."

"I am so very sorry. Please let me stay so I can speak with her. I don't care if she has someone else now, I need to see her. Maybe I can get her to stop."

The desperation in Kitty's eyes, pleading with him, causes Dick to sigh. "I can't right now, I have someone here."

Composing herself again, Kitty stands upright and asserts her confidence. "Then I shall be back in one hour. I do hope that is enough time for you to say goodbye to her."

Katherine then turns and walks toward the lift, not really giving Dick an opportunity to respond.

When Dick goes back inside, he catches Sue racing back to her chair. It screeches as she lands on it, scooting it across the floor.

Shit, Dick thinks. "How much did you hear?"

"Not... a lot..."

"Do you know how rude it is to eavesdrop?" He looks at Sue incredulously.

"What are you hiding?"

Dick is reminded of Georgia asking the same question of him, back when she accused him of cheating on her for no reason. He scratches his cheek, trying to decide the best way to handle this. In all likelihood, Sue isn't asking for the same reasons. They haven't been dating that long, and there's been no discussion of exclusivity.

"Nothing," he finally says. "I just think Jaclyn deserves her privacy." More than that, he doesn't want to be locked up for knowingly harbouring a murderer.

"I should go." Sue finishes the dregs of her coffee and stands. On her way to the door, Sue collects her coat, and once she's beside Dick, she adds, "It would be nice if you wanted to talk to me about her more."

She doesn't give him any time to reply, choosing instead

to leave his apartment without a goodbye. Dick is left feeling confused, speculating on the reason for her abrupt departure.

"It wooled be good to fuck again," Jaclyn reads from Max's notebook as she's sitting beside him on a bench at Battery Park. "Oh, it *would* be good to fuck again." She slaps Max playfully on the arm. "Are you trying to make the most of Nikki leaving me?"

Max shrugs, but smirks at her at the same time.

"I did not tell you why she left. Perhaps you, too, will leave." She looks out at the Hudson.

"Can't leave if we're not together. What happened?"

"I told her I am with child." She turns to face Max in order to see his reaction.

His eyes are wide, stunned into submission.

"Are you going to say something?" she asks, her heart picking up speed.

Max shakes his head until his eyes settle back to their normal size. "Well it can't be mine. We used condoms!"

That isn't really the response Jaclyn was hoping for. She hadn't planned on talking to him that specifically about her pregnancy, but who else could the father be? "Perhaps they did not work?"

"Chances of that happening when they didn't break are slim to none. Trust me, it's not mine." He pauses and looks out at the river himself. "Have you fucked any other men in the last few months?" Another pause, and then, "This is a little personal, but... when's the last time you menstruated?"

"I do not know?" She joins him looking into the water.

"Before I came to your time? I thought perhaps it disappeared due to that."

"Were you fucking anyone before you came here?"

The image of a tall African man enters her mind. The way he held her; comforted her through her tears. She smiles when she thinks about how gentle he was when he was the one initiating their intercourse.

"Ejiogu," she says quietly.

"Eh-gee-what?" Max asks, looking at her, clearly unfamiliar with the name.

"Eh-gee-oh-goo," she pronounces slowly. "Ejiogu. He came from the Igbo tribe in Africa."

"And you were fucking him?"

Jaclyn's lower lip trembles a little before she can answer. "It was a little more than just fucking. He cared for me, and I him."

"I think you found the father."

She rubs one of her eyes with her knuckle, rubbing away the tear that's starting to form. Jaclyn doesn't really want to let Max see her like this, so she gets up from the bench.

Not facing him, she says, "I need to be alone. We will continue the lesson later."

Then Jaclyn heads north as more memories flood her head.

It's after sunset by the time Jaclyn gets home to Dick's apartment. She's tired, and she would really rather go straight to her room than have to talk to anyone else, so she hopes Dick has gone out with Sue.

The lights are on when she opens the door a fraction,

and she realises her hopes were perhaps a little too high. If she's lucky, he'll be in his room and she won't need to talk to him anyway.

Unfortunately, when she opens the door wider, she instead finds Dick eating dinner at the table with a woman. Though the woman is not facing her, she can tell it's not black-haired Sue. Has Dick found a redhead to date now too? She doesn't really want to interrupt them if it is a date, so she tries to sneak past quietly.

"Jack," the woman's voice says behind her, and she stops in her tracks.

It's a familiar blend of a Scottish and English accent. The woman hardly needs to say anything for her to know exactly who she is. No one else calls her that any more. She turns around slowly, not quite sure what to expect.

Katherine's eyes pierce her heart and take her breath away as Jaclyn stumbles backwards. Dick, who has been watching her, quickly stands and rushes to the rescue, catching her before she falls completely. Her whole body begins to tremble, so Dick helps lower her to the ground, while he remains in a crouch behind her so he can massage her shoulders to help relax her. Jaclyn can barely believe her eyes. It's almost as if she's looking at a ghost.

Though Kitty looks older now—aged more than Jaclyn has in the time since they last saw each other—and her hair has grown, no longer the scruff it was when she was pretending to be a man, Jaclyn can still see exactly what she saw when she fell in love with her. The sad but forgiving smile plastered over her face, telling Jaclyn that Kitty still loves her too.

She doesn't need to know how Kitty found her. She

knows it was Prudence.

"Why did you come?" Jaclyn asks, not wanting to believe Prudence without hearing it from Kitty's own lips.

"I've missed you, Jack." Kitty remains seated at the table, shy and tentative.

Jaclyn replies in the most scathing tone she can manage. "That is no fault of mine."

"Do you wish me gone?" she asks, tapping the fingers of her right hand on the table.

Jaclyn very slowly shakes her head.

"Should I leave you two alone?" Dick asks from beside Jaclyn.

"Please," Kitty says, keeping her eyes on her former lover.

Jaclyn switches to a slow nod, also unable to take her gaze away from Kitty.

"I'll just be in my room if you need me." Dick speaks only to Jaclyn, then gets up from his crouch and heads down the hallway.

Once he's gone, Kitty tilts her head to the side and smiles softly. "I find it intriguing that you settled down with one of my descendants."

Jaclyn looks at her, confused. She turns her head to glance down the hallway at Dick's door, before focusing back on Kitty. "Dick?" Kitty nods her reply, and Jaclyn shakes her head while saying, "I did not know. He informed you of this?"

Nodding again, Kitty adds, "I had a son. Charles." She smiles sadly. "It is really good to know he survived after I had to leave him." Her lip trembles before she breaks down into huge sobs.

Jaclyn has never seen Kitty like this. All the grief she felt inside had always been kept private. Despite the fact that history has shown Jaclyn that Kitty did not want her comfort, she can't help getting up off the floor to tend to her. She wraps an arm around Kitty and simply holds her close, letting Kitty's temple rest against her chest.

After the sobbing dies down, Jaclyn can't help commenting, "I never imagined you lying with a man."

This elicits a smirk, followed by a giggle from Kitty. "Nor I." She smiles at Jaclyn, and holds her tight. "I do not miss him, but I do miss my son."

Finding out about Kitty's baby causes Jaclyn to wonder how she would react to her own news, but she decides to wait for the right time to talk about it. She comes away from Kitty's side and finds her own seat at the dining table.

"Dick told me you wrote a book." Jaclyn hopes changing the subject will take Kitty's mind off her sadness.

"I've written more than one now." A smile slowly forms on Kitty's face again. "It's what I do, back in London. I write books for children." There's a hint of sadness in her eyes again. "I think of stories I would have liked to tell Charles and write those."

"You used my songs," Jaclyn says bluntly.

"Are you upset?" Kitty's eyes dart back and forth, trying to read Jaclyn.

After a moment's silence, Jaclyn shakes her head. "No, not about that. It was nice to know you still thought of me after you left."

"I couldn't prevent it." Kitty's face scrunches up. "Even after learning what you did to Prue, I still loved you."

"Yet you also never stopped loving her," Jaclyn throws

back churlishly.

"I can't help who I love, or how many I love, but I was a lot more upset when I learned what she did to you."

Jaclyn can barely believe how civil Kitty is being in this conversation. She wonders if it's a wisdom that comes with age, remembering Prudence's comment about how long Kitty has been in this century.

"How long has it been for you, since you last saw me? How old are you now?"

"Nine years," Kitty says, not needing time to calculate it. "I am thirty-five."

Jaclyn doesn't know whether she should laugh or cry. "I remember when we were the same age."

"You don't look any older than you were when last I saw you," Kitty says with a crooked smile.

"It has only been about a year for me."

"Oh."

Then it occurs to Jaclyn that she now has a smaller age difference with Nikki. She still can't believe she was rejected because she'd been with a man, and now that Kitty has revealed the same, she is curious to see how she would react.

"Kitty," Jaclyn starts, "I..." The words won't come.

"You want to know why Prue did what she did?"

It's not what she was planning on saying, but now that Kitty mentions it, she can't help saying, "I do not understand why she cared so much about Sir Bromley."

"Do you still have the jewellery you took?"

Jaclyn finds herself wondering if there's anything Prudence didn't tell Kitty about her now. Does she already know about the pregnancy too? She nods slowly in response.

"Have you taken anything from those you've murdered here?"

Her mouth falls agape, hating Prudence for reading so much in her head, telling her about those she's killed, and yet disbelieving that Kitty can remain so calm and straightforward as she asks these questions.

"Why are you asking me these things when clearly you could get your answers from *her*?"

Sighing, Kitty confesses, "I rarely see Prue now. True, she helped me find you, but I asked her to do nothing more. Dick told me about the murders."

"Are you going to tell me it is wrong, too?" Jaclyn stands up and places a fist on the table. Her face scrunches up a little as she tries to hold back her emotion. "Because I have already learned that."

Jaclyn turns around and starts to head toward Dick's room, but she's stopped by Katherine pulling her around again by her shoulder.

"Wait," Kitty says, then pulls Jaclyn in for the most passionate kiss she's had for a long time. It's filled with the years of love that held them together. When Kitty pulls away, she adds, "I don't care that you have already found someone else. I don't care that you are still a pirate at heart. I want you back."

Jaclyn searches Kitty's eyes. "Dick told you about Nikki?" When Kitty nods, Jaclyn reminds her, "You know I cannot be unfaithful."

"Then leave her." Though Kitty is taller than Jaclyn and looking down at her, it amuses her to see how much her eyes can plead.

"It is too late for that."

When Kitty frowns, Jaclyn finds pleasure in having the upper hand, but she hides it. Before long, the truth will come out.

"You married her?" she asks.

Jaclyn shakes her head. "She already left me."

"I do not know why anyone would want to do that."

"*You* left me," Jaclyn says bitterly.

"However, I did not *want* to." Kitty sighs. "My father was dying and I needed to return to him."

Jaclyn can't help feeling sad for her now. "I could have come with you."

"It was something I needed to do alone." Kitty takes Jaclyn by the arm and pulls her down to sit beside her on the hallway floor. Leaning against the wall, she asks, "Why did Nikki leave?"

Supposing this is as good a time as any to bring the subject up, Jaclyn takes a deep breath and informs her, "I am with child."

Kitty looks at her blankly.

"It is Turtle's," she adds, answering Kitty's unasked question. "Did Prudence tell you she took him, too?"

There is silence between them as Kitty shakes her head. Then she tilts it slightly, a questioning look on her face. "That is not good enough. Nikki left simply because she did not want children?"

Jaclyn's breath gets caught in her throat.

"There's more..." Kitty whispers mostly to herself. Raising her voice a little, she tries to comfort Jaclyn. "Tell me, Jack. I will not desert you as she has."

"She... she said she did not approve of my history with

men." Jaclyn closes her eyes and tries to take deep breaths to calm herself. "Kitty, I do not even understand why that should matter. I was never unfaithful to her."

As Jaclyn opens her eyes again, she watches Kitty lean her forehead into her hand. After a pause for thought, Kitty says, "For goodness sake, she's one of *those* lesbians?"

"You have clearly adapted here better than I have, my love, as I do not even know to what you are referring." She hadn't meant to use the term of endearment, but it seems old habits easily return. She hopes Kitty didn't even notice.

Kitty sends her a sad smile. "Oh, Jack," she says, then takes Jaclyn's hand. "There is much I could teach you, but I propose for now we just stay on this. I don't know how much Nikki showed you of her lifestyle, but I will assume you know people like us are more accepted now. They know we exist, and it is discussed." She takes a deep breath, and rubs her palm over the back of Jaclyn's hand. "Some women who are attracted to other women do not like to associate with those who also like men. They think you should choose one or the other, that you cannot possibly love both."

There is silence between them for some time while Jaclyn ponders this. It sounds a little too much like her inability to believe Kitty could love both her and Prudence, but she doesn't want to bring that up again, and besides, that's different. Kitty should still have chosen between them, even if she did have feelings for both. What they're discussing—it's not like Jaclyn wants to be with both of them at the same time. She's someone who is only attracted to the person she's with at any given time... isn't she?

That's not the question she wishes to be asking herself

right now, so she thinks more about the consequences of Nikki's assumptions. Would it not have made sense for her to have outright asked Jaclyn if she had been with men before? Assumptions nowadays are certainly different than they were in the seventeenth century.

"Perhaps this is why such things were never discussed in our time," Jaclyn finally considers. "It was at least assumed we were all attracted to men."

"If it had bothered me, I would not have pursued you after you married Mr Marshall."

Kitty's words put Jaclyn onto a different train of thought. "Did you marry the father of your child?"

Pulling her hands away from Jaclyn's, Kitty shakes her head. Then she bites her thumb, anticipating the next question.

"Who was he?" Jaclyn asks, leaning in closer.

After a moment longer chewing her thumb, Kitty takes a deep breath, and explains, "Charles Bromley. That's why Prue went after you for stealing from his father."

Jaclyn's body arches back, and stiffens. "You were with him immediately after leaving me?"

Grasping Jaclyn's face in her hands to make sure their eyes are locked, Kitty pleads again. "The baby came much later, but you have to understand, I had no one else to turn to in London. He was there and willing. Prue saw what was happening before I did."

Pulling away again, Jaclyn gets up and barges in to Dick's room. He quickly pulls his quilt over his half-naked legs, and stomach. Jaclyn holds back a smirk, realising what she accidentally walked in on.

"I thought you were making up."

"Do you mean you were imagining us in bed together?"

Dick shrugs guiltily.

"Do you think that is appropriate behaviour toward your grandmother of many generations back?"

He starts coughing, choking on saliva that accidentally went down his windpipe as the thought registers in his mind.

When Jaclyn goes over to comfort him, Kitty enters the room, but remains in the doorway. "I can't change the past," she says, "but I think we can have a future together. One in which we can marry now, just as you desired."

Images of an actual wedding with Katherine enter Jaclyn's mind. She smiles, seeing how happy they are; how happy Kitty looks when she sings to her. Dick's there, acting as the man who walks her down the aisle. Then Prudence shows up, naked, stealing the show, and her bride. Jaclyn shakes the thought from her mind.

"I am not ready to discuss this matter. Perhaps you can meet me by the Statue of Liberty ferry tomorrow, at sundown, and we can discuss the matter then?"

Jaclyn has figured out that this is the earliest in the day that Prudence has ever shown her face, and is curious to see if she will again. She needs to know that Kitty no longer desires the mermaid.

"As you wish," Kitty says, bowing her head, then departs the room.

Shortly after, Jaclyn hears the front door close.

The following day, both Jaclyn and Dick wake to the sound of someone banging very loudly on the front door. They enter the hallway at the same time, both wrapping dressing gowns around themselves.

"Kitty?" Jaclyn asks.

"Or the police?" Dick sounds more anxious than Jaclyn.

Dick turns first and heads toward the banging, with Jaclyn creeping behind him. When he reaches the door, he looks through the peep hole rather than answering it immediately.

"Who is it?" Jaclyn whispers, but he doesn't reply.

Instead, Dick greets their visitor, "Sue?"

"I wanted to apologise about yesterday," she says.

Jaclyn has no idea what she's talking about, since she wasn't there. Hiding behind Dick, she realises Sue probably doesn't even know she's there, so she steps aside and gives her a shy smile.

"Oh." Sue looks disappointed. "Have you already moved on from me to her?"

"What?" Dick turns around and takes in Jaclyn's image before turning back to Sue. "Oh, no. You knew she was staying here, didn't you?"

"She's not here half the time, I never know what's up."

"You can stop talking about me like I am not here," Jaclyn interrupts.

"Sorry, Jaclyn." Sue looks at Dick again. "May I come in?"

Dick steps aside to allow her just that, and the three of them head to the couch, Sue in the lead.

After taking their seats, Sue speaks first to Jaclyn. "I was just wanting to talk to Dick, but I suppose having you here, too, might be beneficial." She focuses back on Dick. "I am sorry for eavesdropping; I shouldn't have done that. But... on the other hand," she quickly looks between the two of them, "it helped me know you better."

Dick looks confused. "What do you mean?"

"Dick... I've never been to Langkawi. That mermaid legend I told you about... I learned about it from an actual mermaid when I was eight."

Now Dick is not only confused, but looks like he's been blinded by the headlights of a car that is about to hit him.

"I feel comfortable telling you this because I know you believe in them, and from your conversation I was able to discern that Jaclyn knows, too." Sue looks over at Jaclyn again.

"The one I know is the most vile creature to have ever walked this planet."

Sue bites her lip, then turns to Dick. "Why do you think I wanted to turn that book into a film?"

"What book?" Jaclyn interrupts.

"Oh, it's just an old story Dick asked me to find for him."

"Written by Katherine Grayson?"

It's Sue's turn to look confused. "Yes... how did you know?"

Jaclyn punches Dick's upper arm, hard.

"Ow!" he cries, rubbing the pain. Then with a sigh, he tells Sue, "Katherine is Jaclyn's ex-girlfriend. The one you were eavesdropping on."

"But..."

"I know, the book was published in sixteen sixty-five. Jaclyn's mermaid sent them here from the past."

Sue's eyes are wide with awe. "I suppose that explains the pirate comment." She bites her lip for a moment. "And I guess that also explains why Jaclyn looked a bit like a pirate when I saw her down in Washington..." She trails off, lost in her own thoughts. No one speaks until she comes back to them. "That reminds me! My brother told me that he thought you'd make a good costume designer because of that outfit."

Jaclyn had completely forgotten about that.

"Knowing you have firsthand experience would make you a valuable asset to our team," Sue adds.

"Pardon?" Jaclyn is not really sure what Sue is asking of her.

"I think Sue wants you to help her and her brother turn Kitty's book into a movie."

"Aye," says Sue, smirking at herself.

"I will consider your offer," Jaclyn says, then excuses herself so she can have some privacy with her thoughts in her room.

Jaclyn doesn't know the first thing about movies, or storytelling. The songs from the book are hers, but aside from that, what help could she provide? Additionally, isn't she meant to be stripping away her past to find out who she really is?

After half an hour alone with her thoughts, there's a knock on her door.

"Breakfast?" Dick asks.

Jaclyn picks up the satchel that's sitting in front of her on the bed, then comes out and joins him at the table for scrambled eggs on toast. She doesn't see Sue, so assumes Dick must have sent her home. Picking at her food with a fork, Jaclyn decides she's not really all that hungry.

Instead, she opens her satchel and takes out Bromley's jewellery. Placing it on the table, she says, "I want you to have these, Dick. They belong to you, as I should not have taken them from your family."

"Uhh… thanks?" He doesn't go to grab them, choosing to keep eating instead.

"Will you come with me to meet with Kitty?" Jaclyn asks. "I do not think I can go alone."

She avoids mentioning that part of the reason she wants him there is so she can tell if Prudence is around.

Swallowing his last bite of food, Dick agrees.

Jaclyn and Dick stand at the edge of the water, shivering a little in the chilly November air, as they eat the hot dogs Dick had bought on their way there. The sun is already starting to set, but Kitty is not there yet. Having been in London rather than New York all these years would not have been conducive to her understanding how long it would take to get there, and Jaclyn has no idea how far away Kitty's hotel is.

On the up side, Dick isn't frozen in place, so Jaclyn has someone to talk to while she waits.

"What are you going to tell her?" he asks.

"I do not yet know."

Jaclyn takes a deep breath, then notices Kitty's long red hair blowing in the distance. She admires the way Kitty's coat outlines her curves in a way her doublet intentionally never did, and catches her breath in her mouth.

"Are you okay?" Dick asks.

She quickly nods in an attempt to reassure him.

When Kitty arrives, she greets Jaclyn by pressing her lips against Jaclyn's, reminding her of everything she's missed. Many memories of their stolen moments, hidden away from the other pirates, flash before Jaclyn's closed eyes.

They remain shut and begin to water as Kitty pulls away, and Jaclyn says, "If you desire to know how I feel, then know this." She takes another deep breath and opens her eyes. "I still love you."

She turns to look at Dick, who now looks frozen. Beginning to freak out a little, she punches him on the shoulder, and he shakes out of his trance.

"What was that for?" he asks, sounding frustrated.

"I thought Prudence had you under her spell. You do not hear any strange singing?"

He shakes his head.

"Jack, Prue is no longer going to haunt you," Kitty informs her.

Jaclyn tries to choke back her tears, but then starts blubbering, and falls to the ground. Kitty joins her down there, and Dick distances himself so as he doesn't interfere in this emotional moment.

"What's wrong now?" Kitty asks.

"You do not understand," Jaclyn says, trying to calm down. "It does not matter if she physically avoids me; she will continue to haunt me indefinitely."

"I'm sorry," Kitty says, and bites her thumb while she tries to decide what else to say. "I can do my best to help you through the pain."

Kitty takes Jaclyn's hands and holds them tight, but Jaclyn doesn't reply.

"Come back with me to London," Kitty adds.

"I do not think I can right now." Jaclyn is able to hear her own breath as she pauses to think about what else to say. There is a chance she will say something she will later regret. "All I have ever done is go along with what was expected of me by others, but especially you..."

"That's not true," Kitty interrupts. "You know that's not true, or you would not have come out as yourself to our crew."

"Do you have any examples aside from that one?" Jaclyn asks, a little louder than she had intended.

Jaclyn's question is met with silence, and she pulls her hands away. Dick seems to take this as his cue to start wandering back toward them.

Standing, Jaclyn says, "I think it is time I start figuring out who I really am..."

"No more murders," Dick interrupts.

"No more murders," Kitty agrees, rising.

"I need to strip away everything I know, so yes," Jaclyn smirks, "that means no more murders." She looks solemnly at Kitty. "But it also means I need to be away from your influence. At least until I can find my own place in this world."

"What are you going to do with Turtle's baby?" Kitty asks, sadly.

"That is something else I am going to have to discover in time."

Jaclyn embraces Kitty. She kisses both of Kitty's cheeks, left then right, then pulls away.

"Leave your number with Dick so that when I feel I am ready to talk with you again, I can go to him." Jaclyn hugs Kitty one last time. "Goodbye, my love."

Then Jaclyn starts walking toward Battery Park, leaving Dick and Kitty to do as she requested. *I hope that was the right decision.*

Dick soon finds her sitting on a park bench, looking at

the Hudson. He sits down beside her, matching her silence.

"What do I do now?" Jaclyn finally asks.

He shrugs in response. "Anything you want. Isn't that what you told me the day we met?"

Jaclyn can't help but smirk. "Yes, I suppose it was."

A few more moments of silence come between them, but it is not awkward or uncomfortable. Jaclyn just wants to be able to consider her options. She supposes she could try to get back into singing, but then there is also that invitation from Sue to work with her.

Smiling to herself, thinking it might be a way to help Dick in the relationship department, Jaclyn says, "I believe I may wish to discuss Sue's proposal with her."

ACKNOWLEDGEMENTS

This story would not be possible without the support of
several friends. So much so that I could not publish this
book without crediting their input.

There are three people I can thank specifically for what
generated the spark for this novel. First, my wonderful
husband, Jeremy Malcolm, for buying me some gorgeous
burgundy sleeves for Valentine's Day in 2011. These sleeves
made me think of pirate fashion, and so became the start
of a pirate costume.

From there, as R Kevin Garcia Doyle and I had discussed putting together a short film, he suggested I write
a film about a female pirate.

The screenplay that came from that was written for
Gary Dreslinski's LJ Idol competition. The feedback on that
screenplay led to me developing the idea further.

During the competition, I moved to writing prose about
Jaclyn when working with Sally Bell and Kristen Duvall,
both of whom have shown me much support to continue
developing my characters. I also worked with Jeremiah
Murphy on another companion story. After the competition, Jeremiah became my editor. He's the person I

discussed plot points with before anyone else, and also proofread this novel prior to publication.

Jeremy and Jeremiah deserve a round of applause for how much time they spent with me on every chapter before anyone else saw my story. I don't think I could've kept this project up without them.

A few more names I don't want to forget to thank:

- Tara Calaby for her continued support for over a decade;

- Lisa Emmanuel for her feedback on my cover design;

- Kris Fricke for help with the sailing and boat references;

- Laura Begley for her attention to detail with the whole novel;

- Nana Kwesi for his encouragement and help researching Ejiogu/Turtle's background;

- Kerry Lynne for her feedback on descriptions and pirate and sailing knowledge;

- Rebecca Freeman and Lauren Mitchell for reading the whole novel prior to the final draft; and

- Dion, Nichola, Perrie, Ginamarie, Sophie, Esta, Lisa, Jax, Sharya, and Jem for reading excerpts of the novel and offering feedback on those sections.

Lastly, thank you to all my supporters on my Indiegogo campaign at http://igg.me/at/adrift. Thank you for believing in me!

I just want to quickly plug some of the aforementioned people:

R Kevin Garcia Doyle is an improviser who performs as part of Oil in the Alley and On the Spot in Honolulu, Hawai'i. Check them out on Facebook, YouTube, and iTunes.

Gary Dreslinski's LJ Idol can be found at http://therealljidol.livejournal.com.

Jeremiah Murphy's characters Max Fuentes and Sean McCoy can be found in adventures on his Web site at http://www.jrmhmurphy.com.

Lisa Emmanuel is a graphic designer, and I highly recommend her work. You can find her portfolio at http://be.net/LisaEmmanuel.

Kristen Duvall (http://www.kristenduvall.com) is a writer and the owner of Fey Publishing (http://www.feypublishing.com).

Jax Goss (http://jaxgoss.wordpress.com) is a writer and my partner at Solarwyrm Press (http://www.solarwyrm.com). She published *Fae Fatales: A Fantasy Noir Anthology*, which includes a short story about my mermaid, Prudence.

Music

I do not quote lyrics from actual songs that are still protected under copyright, because I didn't want to have to worry about someone claiming I couldn't. Instead I'd like to encourage anyone who is interested in this referenced music to seek it out and obtain a legal copy of it.

"My Heart Will Go On" is the theme from the movie *Ti-*

tanic, sung by Celine Dion. This song will forever hold a place in my heart, as I associate it with the passing of my mother.

"One Love" is by Bob Marley.

The song Yun sang was "Sweet Home Alabama" by Lyrnard Skynard.

Although not directly referenced, Nikki sang "Just the Way You Are" by Bruno Mars.

"Sure Thing" by Miss Spring is fictional, and was created for this book.

The hip-hop artist Nym-B$$ was created by Jeremiah Murphy in one of his short stories about Max Fuentes.

Supporting the World Literacy Foundation

By purchasing this book, you are supporting the World Literacy Foundation. I decided I wanted to donate 20% of the net profits of this book for them in part because, though Jaclyn is from a time when girls generally were not taught to read or write, her being illiterate is not unique in the 21st century. According to the WLF, nearly two thirds of the world's illiterate adults are women, and one in five adults cannot read or write (source: http://worldliteracyfoundation.org/why-literacy.html). Those are staggering statistics to me.

If you would like to further support their cause, check out their web site at http://www.worldliteracyfoundation.org and click the donate button.

ABOUT THE AUTHOR

Dominica Malcolm was born to American parents in Western Australia in 1983. She has been living in Kuala Lumpur, Malaysia with her husband and two children since 2008.

Finding humour to be an important aspect of life in her teen years, she got into writing and performing stand-up comedy at only 16. After taking a break from performing to focus on university, she then travelled the world for seven months, only to return home to Australia to study screenwriting and filmmaking.

You can find many of her short films, comedy music videos, and some of her stand-up comedy, on her YouTube channel (http://www.youtube.com/DominicaMalcolm).

Her Web site at http://dominica.malcolm.id.au contains further details about her background as a writer, filmmaker, comedian, and travel addict. When she blogs—at the same address—the topics include her travel experiences, diversity in the media, crowdfunding, and other subjects she is passionate about.

Follow Dominica on:

Facebook: http://www.fb.com/DominicaMalcolm

Twitter: http://www.twitter.com/dommalcolm